A Rune's Blood Moon

A Runes Blood Moon

Book ISBN: 979-8-00508-3

Cover Design: K.R. Simons

Editing and Proofreading: K.R. Simons

Publisher: K.R. Simons. Las Vegas, NV.

Author's Notes

Hello, everyone! I just wanted to say thank you for finding what it was that made you pick this book up, I very much hope you enjoy it! I certainly did while writing. To be honest, I can't even believe I had written all this in the timeframe I did. But here it is, and I can't wait for everything else that is to come!

While I can't fully say this is necessarily a dark romance or dark fantasy, there are darker themes associated with both and multiple things that may be triggering throughout the series (and yes, hehe, this will be a series;) , – including, but not limited to: past abuse (molestation, mentions of rape, torture), mentions of mental health (depression, suicide, self-harm, PTSD), explicit sexual acts (BDSM, bondage, degradation, primal play, CNC, knife/blood play, breath play, temperature play, edging), explicit violence/fighting/torture.
If any of these may be too triggering please take care of yourself first.

Thank you!

For the oldest daughters who never ask for help because they can do it themselves

–

I know. . . I secretly want a man to say 'I know you can, but let me help you anyways' too.

Table of Contents

Races/Beings Guide

Primordials: powers that are higher than all others, the creators of all – (gods, goddesses, deities)
Celestials: appear to have god-like powers, considered immortals – (devils, demigods, angels, demons)
Six Beings of Moral:

Witches (considered immortals, five different sub-races each with their own abilities)

Mages (considered non-mortals, thirteen different sub-races that coincide with the thirteen elements)

Fae (considered immortals, five main sub-races each with their own abilities)

Shifters (considered non-mortals, five different sub-races with their own abilities, able to shift their humanoid form into one other form)

Vampyr (considered immortals, need blood to survive, born with one natural power usually a type of elemental ability, able to hone one learned magic they're destined for, able to share magic with someone they bond to)

Humans (considered mortals, typically have no magic, may have "gifts" if an ancestor had magic)

Magic Guide:

Aura – the visible core/spirit of one's magic (when it's seen it's usually visible as wisping tendrils of mostly translucent ribbons around a person, each one "feels" different [signifying how strong or powerful they are] and usually is tinted a color that resembles the person's magic or soul)

Magic – the movement or act a being does showing their abilities
(for example: a water mage using water to blast something is their magic vs their aura being ribbons around them the color blue and it feels like a storm in the middle of the ocean depicting how powerful they are) *Note: some use the word aura and magic (as well as ability and power) interchangeably*

Syngenia University

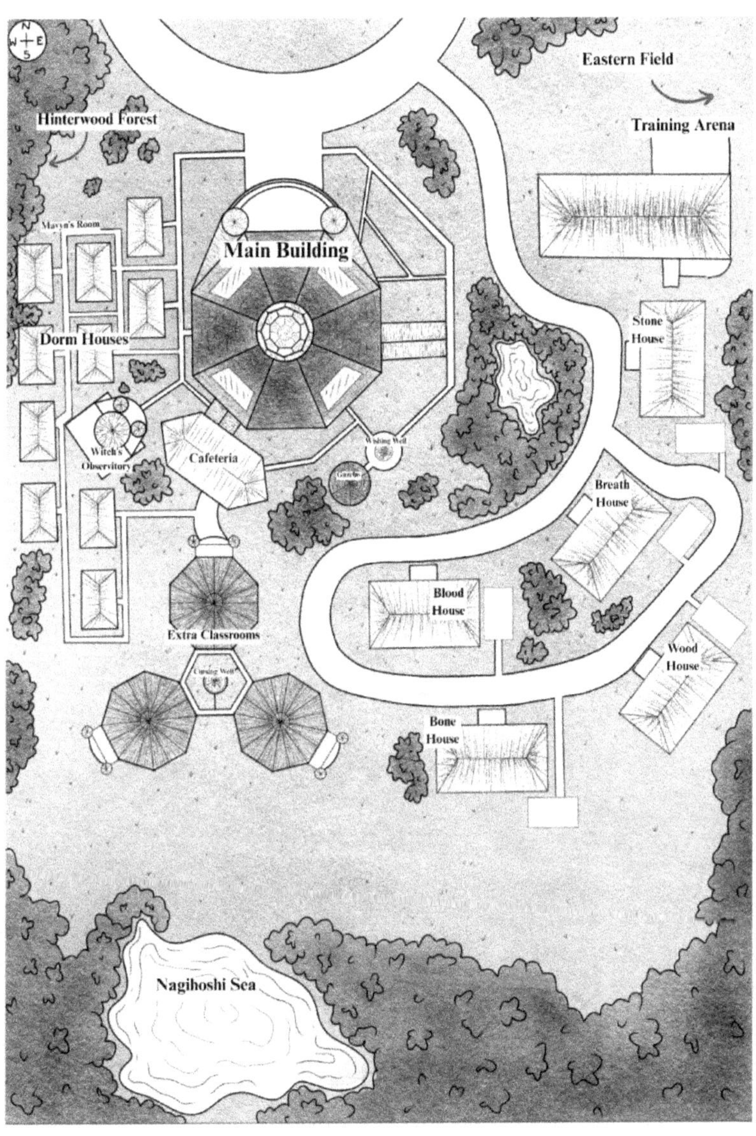

One

Mavyn – August 5

How old are vampires. . . well, let's get one thing straight. There's a difference between vamp*IRES* and vamp*YR*. Vampires are created and vampyr are born. Yes! I said it! The non-aging, bloodsucking, sun-fearing, *Dracula-ish* creatures can be birthed.

I will not go into detail about how that happens because it's the same way humans conceive. If you want a detailed description of *that*, go find Ms. Elaycia. She knows all about – to put it bluntly – sex. I'd be surprised if she didn't since she is a succubus.

As far as my previous question. . . vampires can be any age. Much like the vampyr, once turned their aging slows. It doesn't stop all together because of celestials and tied fates and mortality and all that, but it does slow to a near stop.

The oldest recorded vampire lived over ten thousand years. Though in recent times most die off well before they hit a thousand. Especially in this age and realm.

Vampyr are a bit different. For one, only a vampyr can create a vampire, vampires cannot create more vampires. Next, they technically cannot die naturally, however some do age at different rates. All vampyr are born as humans – and most other beings – are. Babies. Unable to protect themselves and dependent on another.

They're weak, powerless, helpless, useless, insufficient, and ineffective.

At least, that's what most of the Mage Board Councilmen will tell you, and mages as a race. In truth, the baby vampyr are actually more dangerous. Just like scorpions. In addition to most of the stereotypes humans have for regular vampires, vampyr also have inherent magic. Something most of the Mage Board loathes.

And with only just being born and needing to mature, baby vampyr do not have the capacity to regulate their abilities.

All vampyr are born with a natural gift. That's their magic. Usually it's some form of an elemental power. Something of natural origins that you cannot learn.

Then they have the capabilities of an inherent learned magic. Something that is destined for them that they must hone, an ability they only receive after some divine altercation – or something like that.

And lastly, there's a given or tied magic. Something they can receive if they blood bond themselves to someone else.

It's all quite intriguing when you think about it. And that's just the vampyr. You still have mages, shifters, fae, witches, and all the subgroups within them.

It's all facts I was forced to cram into my mind. So many details to remember because without them I would have failed the entrance exam. And I needed to pass that damned exam.

Six hundred and forty-seven questions, two half page responses, and one three page-long essay.

It took me twenty-two hours. A test that not only questions you on the six beings of moral, but also tests your intelligence and academics.

Considering I never went to school you would think I should have failed that part. But the vampire who fed me the blood and injected me with the venom of a vampyr also transferred a bit of knowledge.

Not that I was ever dumb. I spent the majority of my life in libraries. I've taught myself sciences, mathematics, philosophy, literature, arts, politics. But my knowledge held nothing to what was within that test.

I didn't have much of a choice in the matter. It was either take the test and try to pass or die. I was stamped an illegal vampire, and unless you have the paperwork you're dead.

I don't know why the vampire fed me that blood and venom, or which vampyr it belonged to, or why he wanted me to pass this test and attend this university, but here I am.

Before me looms the great Syngenia University. Which I feel like is a playoff of 'syngèneia' which means 'blood' in Greek. Or something along those lines, and I only know that because that's all the vampire would say after he shoved the few drops of blood down my throat.

Why exactly it's called that? I don't really know. What I do know is that Syngenia University does not exist on Earth. It is on a world called Miy that exists in an entirely different universe to Earth.

Students mill around, some of them carrying boxes and bins, others leading as other people do. It's move in day for the accepted. Move in day for me.

According to the professors and graders who were overseeing the test, no vampire has ever completed the test, let alone passed it. And not only did I pass it, but I did so without missing a single question. Which with my status and lack of money, I was granted the only scholarship this school offers.

This is how I gain my so-called 'citizenship'. How I'm stamped a legal vampire. I need to graduate.

Such bullshit.

Gripping my umbrella tighter, I scan the yard again through my tinted sunglasses. There's a slight overcast today, but even that wouldn't protect a normal vampire. So I play along with what the Mage Board believes and start walking towards one of the tables where schedules and tablets are handed out.

There's four tables in total, each one organized by race. There's one for the mages, the shifters, the fae, and the vampyr. Walking towards the vampyr table, I ignore the shifting eyes and not very subtle whispers.

Another differentiating thing about vampires and vampyr, the vampyr *can* go out in the sun. So, technically they're not necessarily *sun-fearing*.

Wearing non-holed jeans, boots that cover my ankles, a long sleeve turtle neck, a hat, plus the umbrella singles me out. Especially because it's warm and not even that bright.

There are three guys and two girls sitting on the other side of the table. Each one of them has a murderous expression as I approach. Designations are listed by everyone's names so I have no doubt they've read *vampire*. Despite the vampyr creating vampires, they hate them.

The unwashed, degenerate copycats of the sophisticated, elegant, ethereal beings. I've got five fucking years if I don't want to risk getting my head detached from my body. This is going to be hell.

The girl sitting in the middle with burgundy hair and cat-like green eyes notches the corner of her lip up. Turning her nose away as if she smells something bad. How unoriginal.

As I finally stop right at the edge of the table, she lets a bit of one of her gleaming fangs show.

Vampyr have retractable fangs, unlike vampires. I slide my tongue over my own but not hard enough to cut. Deciding not to be a major bitch like she is, I refrain from showing off my own.

"Hello," I drawl. "My name is Mavyn Tsuki. I'm a first year student."

One of the guys sitting next to the redhead rolls his eyes over me with a cold gaze. "You know most first year students don't make it to graduation. How tragic would it be if you were one of them."

"It would not be tragic at all," I state. Rolling my eyes I hold out my hand right within the edge of the shadow of my umbrella. "Can I have my schedule now?"

He blinks at me, surprised, as if I wouldn't have a comeback to that. Or maybe it wasn't that I said anything, but *what* I said.

It's not a lie. I highly doubt it would be all that sad for anyone if they ripped my umbrella away and exposed me to the sunlight.

The guy on the other side of the redhead shuffles through some papers with a bored expression and holds up a piece of paper and a kindle-sized tablet.

I take it quickly and then spin on my heels to get out of here. It had gotten significantly quiet as everyone watched the exchange.

They all stay silent as they watch me leave too. Good. I'm exhausted and all I want is my shitty dorm room I know I'm about to get and at least eight hours of no one bothering me.

Classes don't start until Monday which gives me the rest of today, tomorrow, and Sunday. Despite being in another universe on another world, most social structures and things like that are the same as Earth. They don't have Instagram or iPhones, but I'm sure this tablet is something of a similar format.

Following the map in my head I had memorized when the advisor was bringing me here, I head through several courtyards until I get to the west side of the main building where most of the dorm buildings are. It's split into male and female buildings with your grade picking how close to the main building you are or not.

My building, because I'm a first year, is kissing the forest that surrounds the university.

Fine by me.

There's still more people out. Other's moving in and the rest moving back. Most of them stop to stare and then quickly turn away to whisper. After I was stamped an illegal vampire I expected to be killed then and there.

I wasn't closed off to this knowledge that magic existed and whatnot while on Earth, but whoever my parents were either ditched me or are dead.

I was found on the side of a trail by some hikers and brought to the nearest town somewhere in norther New York. From there I was placed in the foster system, quickly adopted by a couple that liked whips instead of belts, went back into the foster system after they both had abrupt heart attacks, ran from those abusive foster homes, came across a strip club – modern name for what is a brothel – run by a succubus and from there I was sort of kept and looked after by the females.

They kept me safe and taught me and in exchange I helped make little medicines and tonics. Despite not being mortal, magical beings still get hangovers and headaches – surprisingly.

I finally come to the last building with a twisting forest literally hugging the back side of it. I sometimes wonder if it would have been better for the Mage Board to just kill me when they found me. They killed the vampire who fed me the blood. But I guess the enforcer must have said something because after being brought into whatever blacklist site they had, I was simply thrown in a cell.

Three days later was when a lower advisor for the Mage Board came and asked me who I was and where I came from. He asked me why the vampire fed me that blood and how I felt because of it. I more or less stated the truth.

I am an orphan who runs along the streets of New York City and helps out with legal medicines to those who ask for it.

I didn't tell him about Ms. Elaycia and her brothel – even if she's kept everything above board and legal regarding the humans who venture in – because the Mage Board hates the lower level fae almost as much as they do the vampyr and vampires. All it would take is one thing to have her shut down and thrown in some sort of torture chamber they call a prison.

So I kept it short. Said I knew a few neighborly fae and shifters, but I have actually never met a vampire or vampyr before. I didn't know why I was fed the blood or venom or what that vampire could have wanted from me.

At the end of my interrogation the advisor lifted his sleeve, took a small thin blade, and cut a two to three inch wound on his arm. Blood immediately began rolling down and dripping onto the floor. The metallic scent filling the room with a reddish-black aura. It wasn't quiet as coppery as humans blood is, but it had been just as red.

I figured he wanted to see what kind of bloodlust I would initiate since all newly turned vampires can't control their hunger for it. I, however, lifted the top corner of my mouth in disgust and rolled my eyes before closing them and leaning my head against the wall.

I had been just as tired then as I am now.

The advisor was obviously shocked and the next day I was brought before the Mage Board and they said with my immense control I could attend Syngenia University if I was able to pass the test. I had heard the name spoken by two people before. The first being Ms. Elaycia who would reminisce on her past, and the second being that vampire as he was shoving blood down my throat. If I bloodlust I would have been immediately killed.

Now here I am. And fuck, Ms. Elaycia is going to kill me. Not literally, but I do wish I could have said goodbye to her.

Entering the nearly crippling building I finally close my umbrella and am greeted by a front desk area. There's a girl with long blonde hair pulled up into a high ponytail on the same tablet I just received. She looks up just as I'm removing my sunglasses and arches a brow.

"And here I thought this was one of those stupid rumors," she says boredly. "I'm assuming you're," she looks down at something on the desk she's sitting behind, "Mavyn Tsuki?"

Approaching the desk I nod. Blondie stands, but it's

only to grab a key and piece of paper behind her. She shoves it at me and then sits back down ignoring me. On the bright side, at least she didn't sneer like the redhead in the courtyard.

"Thanks," I murmur as I look over the sheet. It lists my room number, my roommate, where the shared bathrooms are, and all the information my schedule wouldn't list.

Turning, I start making my way to the stairs I had seen when I first came in. I pass a couple girls but now that I'm inside and there are so many scents and perfumes and incense, and without having my sunglasses on and umbrella blocking the nonexistent sun in here, they can't tell what kind of being I am. Even if I can pick up distinct notes signaling shifters and fae. It smells the same as in the brothel.

Reaching the third floor I follow the sign that reads where three dash twenty-three is. Apparently it's the last door at the end of one of the halls.

It's not as loud as I thought it would be here. And despite the shabby wall paint, the decades old carpet, and the dim lights that look like they're about to go out, it's not that bad. It's how I expected the dorms for a regular college in America to look like.

The door at the end is already cracked open when I get to it so I simply toe it open even more. After being brought before the Mage Board I was immediately sent to the test room where I had to take my exam and then holed up in a cell until I was able to come here for move in day. Meaning I only got to bring the clothes on my back and the few pieces of jewelry I already had on. Honestly, I'm surprised they didn't take those from me as well, considering they took all the rest of my nick nacks I had on me.

Motherfuckers.

Holding my papers, the tablet, my sunglasses, and

umbrella, I stand in the doorway and look in. The ceiling is vaulted with two square windows almost completely covered in ivy. There's two twin beds in each corner with two desks almost touching each other against the wall and under the windows. Then two wardrobes against the wall across from the beds. The one directly to my right has its doors open with someone rummaging inside. There are also boxes and bins and two suitcases covering the left side of the room.

Clearing my throat, I take a step in. There's a bang and a squeak before a head of curly white hair pops out of the open wardrobe.

"Oh my goddesses, you scared me," she heaves, a hand over her heart and wide eyes behind circular framed glasses looking at me. Her surprised expression turns to a wide grin. "Oh! You must be my roommate. Mavyn, right? I'm Jullia."

She steps over and holds her hand out. One of many positives living in the brothel with multiple beings is all the things they teach you. One of the biggest things being learning how to read body language. With the exception of a few outlying situations, no matter what your body will almost never lie. Instinct, intuition, and muscle memory overpower all else even if you are completely in control of your body. Most of the time, anyways.

Jullia, she said her name was. The smile on her face hesitates the longer I let her stand like that. To most it would look like she was willing to get to know me and wants to try being friends since we'll be living together for the next year.

But her body betrayers her.

Her shoulders are tense, her heart is pounding with her blood rushing, I can scent the beading sweat along her hairline and neck, and there's a barely noticeable tremor in her hand.

"You're a mage, right?" I sigh, my shoulders weighing

down with exhaustion. “You don’t have to be nice to me. I know the mages hate vampires and as a precaution it’s listed when I was apparently turned, so if you want to drown me in my sleep I won’t hold it against you.”

Walking into the room I set my things on the desk and then faceplant into my bed. A groan leaves my throat as I sink into the shitty bed. I can feel the springs and the thin blanket is already scratching my face but I actually couldn’t care less.

Something must have snapped the water mage out of her stupor because I hear her shuffling away from me and things getting moved.

“Mavyn,” she calls and I hum in answer. Too tired to do anything else but delirious enough to actually answer. “I don’t hate you. Most vampires don’t have a choice in being turned and judging you before I even know you is unfair.”

My brows furrow as I turn my head so I can see her. Pretty toffee-colored skin, soft doe-eyed lavender eyes, that curly white hair reaching her mid-back. She’s wearing regular jeans and a t-shirt with some sort of band name I’ve never heard of before.

“And I won’t be drowning you,” she says like an afterthought. It makes my lips twitch. “Actually, I’m surprised you could even tell I’m a water mage. Most people can’t tell which element I possess.”

Shc looks nicc. Shc has that girl ncxt door vibc mixcd with nerdy book girl who also reads smut. There was a girl at the brothel just like her and an ache begins to form in my chest. I miss my home.

“Thanks Jullia,” I gurgle out with half my mouth smushed into the scratchy bed. Pushing up to my elbows I look over the room again. Behind me, next to my wardrobe there’s a mini fridge I know has a couple packs of prestored blood. It’s a necessity the school provides for beings who need blood to survive. "If it's any consolation, I've been tested almost every day for a month before coming here to see if I'll go into a blood frenzy. Hasn't happened, it won't be happening, and anyway, I don't like water mage blood. No offense, but it takes like seawater and rotten fish. No offense."

Her shoulders drop the tiniest bit and she chuckles. It makes her curls bounce and her aura gets brighter. Twinkling like fairy lights.

"No offense taken," she says as she smiles at me. "Though I guess this just means that vampires and vampyr are really different. My boyfriend is a vampyr and he would disagree with you."

She winks at me and then stands to finish sorting through her things. Smutty book girl for sure. I go back to laying all the way down and heave out a breath. My entire body relaxes into the shitty mattress and I know I should go shower and change, but the only thing I have is the school uniform provided.

I've had to re-wear this outfit since I passed the test a month ago, one more day won't kill me.

Something dings and Jullia shuffles as sleep is about to take me.

"Oh," she softly gasps, then she clears her throat. "Hey, Mavyn? Are you actually sleeping?"

Yes.

"Not yet," I mumble.

There's silence for a moment.

"I thought vampires didn't sleep. At least, that's what Asher says, I've never met a vampire before. Is this the reason you don't have a bloodlust? You sleep instead, like Nezuko from

Demon Slayer?"

I don't even have the energy to crack an eye open. I grumble instead.

"Well, okay." Her voice is brighter, the fear before I could read from her gone – or at least mostly gone. "There's a first year party tonight though, a swinger type of thing in the ballroom. I know afterwards all the societies throw their own parties, did you want to go with me?"

No.

"Would your boyfriend mind?"

The Mage Board hates vampires above all other races, even more so than they hate the vampyr. And the vampyr hate the vampires just as much. Which makes a mage and vampyr dating interesting, but more importantly I highly doubt Jullia's vampyr boyfriend would want his mage girlfriend near a vampire.

"Only if you swear a blood oath with me," a deep voice resonates.

"Asher," Jullia gasps. You can tell just from her voice she has a big smile on her face. "I thought you weren't coming in till Sunday! Oh, Mavyn, this is my boyfriend Asher. He's a third year same as my older sister."

Letting myself internally scream for a second, I retch my eyes back open and push myself to sit cross-legged on my bed. Ms. Elaycia would scold me for having shoes on the bed but the bed is shit anyway.

The vampyr who appeared is tall. Taller than most humans I've seen on Earth and many other races of being who have come through the brothel. He has olive toned skin, green eyes that are solely focused on me with a hard edge, and black hair short on the side but long and fluffed on top.

He's handsome, but in a sharp, I can kill you before you blink, touch my girlfriend and you're dead kind of way. He does his own inspection of me before staring for a long time directly in my eyes.

"What's a blood oath?" I ask, finally breaking the silence.

He arches a brow and tightens his arm around Jullia. She stays silent, a look of almost guilt passing over her face.

"It's a promise tied with blood and magic. If you break it your body will instantly kill itself."

I've heard of blood oaths before, but I was never taught how to do one. I'd get knocked upside the head if I ever asked, though from reading and watching t.v I'm sure the process isn't much different then what I'm assuming.

"Okay. I assume it's a promise that I won't physically hurt Jullia? How do we do this?"

He arches his brow a notch higher before finally letting go of Jullia and taking a few more steps into the room towards me. "I give you a drop of my blood, you give me a drop of yours, I'll draw a rune on you activating the oath and you specify the promise. Relatively easy, though both parties need to be truly willing for it to cement."

The tiniest bit of fear plucks in my chest. "I thought blood sharing was a. . . personal affair. Can't I just make the oath to Jullia?"

His eyes darken to almost black and a rumble in his chest makes me realize asking that may have been a mistake.

Jullia wraps a slender hand around his bicep and she takes her other to rub circles in his back.

"Asher, please calm down. She didn't mean anything by

it, it's okay."

With her presence he takes a deep breath and briefly closes his eyes. That still doesn't release my own tension and it racks up even more when he shakes his head.

"You make the oath with me or I'll drag you out of this building and into the sun."

Jullia's face drops but she doesn't say anything. Just fucking great.

Internally screaming again, I shift and get off the bed to stand. "Fine," I grunt. Holding it out, I wait for him to do whatever he's going to do.

Bringing his own finger up to his mouth, he opens and slices the pad across his fang. Much less blood beads and then he takes my hand in his other and pulls it up to his mouth while bringing his finger to mine.

That tremble of fear ignites again as I slightly jerk my hand back a bit. "You're just pricking it, right? You're not actually going to bite me?"

He almost sneers before he nods. Taking his thumb between my own and my index finger I wait for him to cut mine. He hesitates for only a second before pricking his fang into the pad of my thumb and licks up the drop. I do the same to his.

Closing my eyes I almost lick his thumb again before he rips it away from my lips. Running my tongue over my teeth I revel for another moment in the flavor. Smooth, earthy rich blood with a crackle of smoke. Delicious.

Finally opening my eyes I'm greeted with now bright green ones staring in shock at me.

"Your blood. . . "

"I know," I nearly sneer, arching one of my brows, "it's

disgusting."

He closes his mouth and squints at me as Jullia stands to the side flicking her eyes between us. Looking down at his thumb, he rubs it on the lapel of his jacket before giving me a knowing look.

"The promise," he urges and I don't even have the energy to roll my eyes.

"I, Mavyn Tsuki, give this oath that I will not intentionally physically harm Jullia Waterstone in any way."

Grabbing my hand again, he slides my sleeve up and pauses for only a moment at the scars he finds before wrapping both hands around my forearm and begins murmuring. The move was so abrupt I couldn't stop him before he saw the scars, but obviously now it's too late.

All there is now is pain.

In the background – barely – I think I hear Jullia gasp but I'm not entirely sure. My vision is white and stars go off like fireworks behind my eyes.

The whole thing takes four seconds before he's finished and lets go. It doesn't help though as pain singes along my nerves, needling through my body.

I take slow deliberate breaths and blink to try and right my vision and get rid of the pain. When I can see again I notice his entire demeanor has changed. He gives me a questioning look, but that sharp edge around him softens and now having my attention he smiles.

"Nice to meet you, Mavyn. Now you can tag along with us to the parties tonight if you want."

I glance at Jullia who's still looking at my arm. Not wanting to talk about it, I shove my sleeve down and turn back to my bed to face plant again.

“Thanks, but unless it’s mandatory I have no other clothes and I really just want to sleep on an actual bed for a minimum of ten hours.”

I face plant. The silence after my words stretches for a moment. Then there’s nothing, and I’m asleep.

Two

Mavyn – August 8

Ten hours turned into twelve, then sixteen, then twenty-four. Eventually I had to get up to drink some water because dehydration was starting to initiate. Jullia kept looking over worriedly throughout the weekend but she didn't say anything about my behavior. She also didn't ask about my scars.

I ended up trying one of those blood bags stored in the mini fridge and gaged so hard I nearly retched all the water I had drank.

Jullia's boyfriend had been there and laughed at me while she fretted and asked if I was okay and needed something else. All students were granted a free breakfast, lunch, and dinner but they were only available when the term started and only during the days there was class. I really just needed regular food. Since I didn't have money either I had to suffer through my hunger because no way was I drinking that nasty blood. Not until I really was starved and absolutely needed it.

Instead of answering I simply glared at Asher and then face planted once again in my bed to sleep the remainder of Sunday away.

All the sleeping should have helped, but only drinking enough water to stay alive and no food makes me feel like a zombie now as I walk behind Jullia and Asher to the main building where the cafeteria is. They've been joined at the hip and he even came up early to walk with Jullia.

It would be sweet if I wasn't hungry, hot, and irritated. The uniform is closer to a slutty maid costume than a pristine universities required apparel. A snug white button up with a navy blue tie, a black blazer with white stitching, a black pleated mini skirt, and what are supposed to be navy knee high socks.

Mine are longer, ending just above mid-thigh to cover my legs from the sun and a pair of ballet flats. The schools summer uniform. My winter one is no different except instead of a blazer we could wear a sweater vest and we were given winter coats and boots.

There's also a red stitched ouroboros. A perfectly circular snake with all the minute details eating its own tail over my left breast on the blazer. It symbolizes what I am. Since there has never been a vampire student and there never intended to be, I get to wear the vampyr symbol.

Asher has one on his blazer in the same spot, though instead of white stitching lining his he gets a silvery color symbolizing his third year status. Jullia has white like me, but instead of a red snake she has blue ripples stitched over the left side of her blazer symbolizing being a water mage.

But despite the summer attire, it's still hot. There are no clouds today and the sun beats even with my umbrella over me. And because of the open sun and not wanting to risk anything, I had to wear gloves.

Jullia glances back to check on me and slows her and Asher so I'm beside her instead of behind. The last couple days he's been nothing but cordial. Aside from laughing at my dislike for the blood that must have been donated from a water mage, he's been relatively nice. Not getting annoyed when Jullia fusses over me – which is an entirely abnormal response.

"So," she hums as we walk through another courtyard making our way towards the largest pair of doors I've ever seen. "Are you ready for your first day? After breakfast we can walk to our first class together. Are you excited?"

Jullia had babbled about nothing throughout the weekend whether I was asleep or not and Asher was there or not. It was kind of nice, even if I didn't care to actually listen to most of it. But I did catch bits and pieces. Her family, her education, her relationship with Asher.

I know *she's* excited to be here.

"I'll feel better once I've eaten something. As long as it's some form of eggs and bacon," I grumble. It's been a while since I had to go days without food. I had gotten used to the pleasures of the brothel.

Jullia makes that puzzled face again as she peers at me. The same one she had when I said I was going to sleep.

"You are a weird vampire," she states. "Can you even eat regular food? Or is it because you're newly turned? You do know that with your systems you can't digest food anymore, right?"

On the other side of her Asher fails at holding in his laugh and snorts. She glares at him before turning back to me.

"In order to study at Syngenia you have to pass an exam so I assume you know about all this. At least, it seemed like you did, but how much really do you know? I know only humans can be turned into vampires so do you know everything or just the basics? If you don't mind me asking!" she finishes. Doe-shaped eyes wide behind her glasses and unconcerned with the stares I'm receiving. Probably made worse by Jullia saying rather loudly that I'm newly turned, but I couldn't care less about that.

I shrug in response. "I knew a bit from before. I was mostly raised by a succubus in New York and she taught me a lot. I was taking a new route through the city when I was ambushed by a vampire. I hadn't met any up until that point, but he grabbed me and shoved a vile of blood down my throat. He stabbed me with something I assume transfers the vampyr venom into my blood and then everything went dark."

It had been my fault. I wasn't paying attention when I walked down that ally. Didn't notice the faint scent of rotting flesh that accompanies vampires unless they cover themselves in perfumes.

Jullia and Asher both went silent beside me so I turn to find them both giving me looks. Jullia looks like she's about to cry and Asher has a calculating expression on. I sigh at both of them.

"It's not that big of a deal," I say, because it's really not. "At least I'm not dead." Well. . . not anymore.

Asher hums, looking forward again. "True. I wonder who's blood and venom it was though. For your eyes to turn pink means it was a vampyr with red eyes. And all red-eyed vampyr are either higher ranking council members or royalty."

I don't say anything to that but Jullia does ask several questions about it. It may be called the Mage Board, but the councilmen who make up the board are each from a different race. Having all except a vampire, a witch, and a human.

I also don't comment on my eyes or the rest of my appearance. Jullia had been kind enough to let me borrow a towel and a pajama set so I could finally shower last night. It had been a dream to wash my hair and actually scrub the grime from my last month and a half.

Jullia says the campus has jobs everywhere, including graveyard shifts so I don't have to work in the sun. It shouldn't have been a problem anyway, but I'm not going to say that. It would be best if I got through these next five years with only Asher knowing about one of my little secrets.

The three of us walk through the double doors that reach at least fifty feet up with the opening a good thirty-ish feet wide. Made out of some sort of stone with different carvings all over it. Once we're inside I drop and close the umbrella. There are windows in here but I'm tired of holding it up and all I have to do is avoid the sun patches.

I don't bother taking off my sunglasses though and simply follow Jullia and Asher. The latter waving and smiling and high fiving people he knows. Thankfully he doesn't stop and chat with them and we weave between the tables and benches that cover the majority of the cafeteria to where a line is already starting.

Threading her arm through mine, Jullia pulls me closer and earns a few people who weren't already whispering to do so. This poor girl, I hope she'll be able to make some friends after this.

Whispering to me, she says, "It's not usually like this, but since it's the first day everyone is required to show up to breakfast. After this it doesn't matter whether you wanna show up to eat or wait till lunch."

We reach the end of the line and wait as Jullia starts scanning the crowd. Her lips curl up even more as she dashes off towards someone and squeals.

I think she most definitely has too much energy.

"Oh you haven't even seen her energy," Asher says. I don't think I said that out loud.

I glance at him before watching Jullia hug another girl. She said she had a sister here too. With their matching curly white hair and smooth skin I assume that's her. Though said sister has a slightly darker brown tone.

"Can you read minds?" I ask, curious.

He grins at me and shakes his head. "Super hearing. You barely breathed those words, but I could still hear them."

Ah, of course. I forgot. Super hearing, super speed, super healing, super basically everything.

"How do you have two elemental magics?"

His brow arches as Jullia starts pulling her sister towards us. I watch the exact moment the sister sees me and realizes what I am. Her reaction is not like Jullia's.

"I don't," he clips. And he gives me the same look I gave him after he tasted my blood.

"Don't want?" a voice asks. A slightly deeper voice than Jullia but same note. Her lavender eyes that look exactly like Jullia's glare at me. "Are you bothering Asher?"

Jullia makes a distressed noise and pulls her sister back. She has the same silver thread through her jacket as Asher and a matching blue water mage symbol to Jullia on her blazer. So she's a third year, and I can almost taste salt in the air from where she must be pulling magic towards the surface.

"Hanna," Jullia grits. "Stop it. Mavyn is my roommate and she's non-threatening."

Jullia's sister – Hanna – scoffs. "Sis we're gonna have to up your instincts if you're telling me a newly turned vampire is non-threatening. She turned barely a month and a half ago. We'll all be lucky if she doesn't suck us all dry in our sleep."

Every eye around is now solely focused on us. Hanna was not quiet and exhaustion begins to weigh again. I really do just want to go home now. Or at least be eating something.

"Hanna," Jullia snaps, making her sister turn towards her. "Mavyn made a blood oath to Asher. She can't hurt me. That's first of all. Second, we've been together all weekend and she barely cared at all not only when she must have been hungry, but when I cut myself she didn't even notice. Stop being overdramatic and causing a seen."

I glance down at Jullia's thigh where there's not even a scar. Asher made sure there wasn't a scar. He also glared at me when Jullia had been cut but I only rolled my eyes at him and rolled over to the wall my bed was against to go back to sleep.

Hanna blinks at her sister and then at me. "You," she jabs a finger at me, "were in the presence of fresh blood not even two months after turning and didn't devour my sister?"

All eyes are turned to us now and the line for the food has stopped. Even the workers are watching us and at the worst moment a waft of eggs and buttery toast comes by making my stomach grumble. Hanna, Jullia, and Asher all look at my stomach with perplexed expressions and I groan.

Pulling the sunglasses off I rub at my face. "The only thing I want to devour right now is a full plate of breakfast foods. I don't even care what's on it at this point. I haven't eaten in three days and I'm fucking hungry. Now is everyone going to continue staring at me or can we move this damned line along?"

Hanna is still staring at me with shock though now suspicion is threading in through there. In the blink of an eye she takes her nails and rips into her palm before shoving it in my face. Salt explodes in my nose as I step back and try to push her hand away.

"You said you were hungry," she urges. "Come on then. Have a *bite*. Let's go, vampire."

Her sister and Asher both try to stop her but before they can she rubs her bloody hand over my mouth. Jullia stares in horror at me with Asher furious and a commotion at the other end of the cafeteria sounds.

"What the fuck is going on," a voice thunders. Cloud cover comes out of nowhere darkening the room and blocking out the sun.

Asher pulls out a piece of cloth from his blazer as he holds Hanna back and gives it to me. Jullie turns towards the owner of that voice and starts stuttering with an explanation trying not to get her sister in trouble but also trying not to get me in trouble either.

Hanna is still glaring at me, though the longer I keep my mouth shut and don't let my tongue lick up her blood her fury starts turning into disbelief.

"Enough," he thunders again. Silencing Jullie as he finally stands before all of us. "Mr. Ruleten, would you tell me why you are holding Ms. Hanna Waterstone and why her hand is bleeding." I can feel – actually *feel* – his eyes shift me and I finally look up. "And why the fuck is Ms. Waterstone's blood on a vampires mouth."

There's people behind the male, but I can't quite focus

on them yet. Before me is a god. At least, that's what Ms. Elaycia would say. She would say that any time a male came through the brothel that even she would serve for free.

He's tall. Not quite as tall as Asher, maybe an inch or two shorter. His hair is wavy and longer, just barely covering his ears. It's dark red, but the kind that would look black in lower lightning. Skin a shade or so lighter than Asher's and red eyes ringed within gold.

I've never seen eyes like that.

Finished with my assessment, I look behind him to four others. Two of them having to be students because they're wearing more or less the same thing as me, and the other two I'm sure are staff – professors or deans or whoever else.

"Mr. Ruleten," the man growls. It makes Asher jerk with Hanna still caged in is arms. I take the moment to look down at the white cloth and use it to wipe my face. Out of the corner of my eye I see Hanna's eyes widen.

Asher clears his throat. "It was an accident – "

"If you're about to tell me," he interrupts and silences Asher, "that this vampire accidently bit Ms. Waterstone I need you to move it along so I know whether or not I need to detain the vampire."

After I have the blood wiped from at least my lips and the rest of my mouth and chin as best I can I huff and look to the ground off on the side. At this point they should just kill me. It would be easier for all of them.

"Do you find this situation an annoyance, Ms. Tsuki?"

His voice is all power, all commanding, all consuming. It forces the listener to bow, to submit, to heed. Especially when he says your name. But it makes me realize now what kind of being he is. I had forgotten that in addition to the six beings of moral – five of them being able to attend the university – the celestials are also able to attend. Them being the demons, the angels, the demigods, and him. The devils.

"Yes," I answer plainly.

He hums and his power pushes into the room like thick fog. Only this, I'm sure if he wanted to, could suffocate you. It feels almost the same as the man who adopted me when I was a child.

"You find this situation – you biting another student who was unwilling, which is grounds not only for expulsion but imprisonment and death – to be an annoyance?"

Straightening my back, I clench the bloody cloth in my hand and look him dead in the eyes.

"I find the fact that you jumped to conclusions before Mr. Ruleten had a chance to finish his statement and immediately want to blame me to be an annoyance."

The room goes dead. The gold in his eyes flare. I'm very sure I'm about to get my head ripped off. Sad. . . I won't be able to say goodbye to Ms. Elaycia and the rest of the house. But maybe then I'll stop feeling so tired.

Instead of my head detaching from my body, the male turns his head towards Asher. Waiting. Asher doesn't hesitate.

"There was an unprovoked altercation. Hanna started it, though I'm sure she didn't mean to take it so far. Mavyn didn't do anything, as well, she proved that she does not have any bloodlust. Not only did she back away from Hanna when she began bleeding but she didn't even drink any of it with it being on her mouth."

How every diplomatic. Stating what happened but not completely throwing Hanna under the bus. I doubt even if he did much would happen to her anyways.

The devil returns his gaze back to me. Red eyes that are no longer blazing with gold flicking to my mouth and then to the cloth still clutched in my fist.

"When was the last time you fed?" he demands.

Perfect fucking timing as my stomach grumbles and surprise lights in his eyes as he glances at my stomach. I clench the cloth tighter and dig the nails of my free hand into my palm.

"I tried to on Saturday. Before that it was probably when the vampyr blood was shoved down my throat."

He raises a brow as more surprise glints in his eyes. "Tried?" he echoes.

Huffing, I drop my shoulders and look over a bit longingly at the breakfast I still haven't eaten. "Yes. Some donated blood from a bag."

He glances at Asher and he nods. "She barely took one sip before almost retching it back up."

I glare at Asher. "You would have too. It was nasty."

"To be fair," Jullia's soft voice interjects, and she flinches when eyes go to her. "That batch was donated from water mages and Mavyn already said she can't stand the taste. But that doesn't diminish that she didn't lick my sisters blood from her lips. That shows immense control."

The devil turns back to me and I return to staring at the food. Eggs, bacon, potatoes. There's also fruits and I think I see steamed vegetables. God I would love nothing more than buttered and lightly salted steamed vegetables.

"It does, Ms. Waterstone," he rumbles and Jullie relaxes a bit. "Ms. Hanna, will there be any more altercations?"

He doesn't look at her. I know because I can still feel his eyes on me.

"No," she states. Strong and proud. "I only wanted to make sure my sister was safe since they will be rooming together."

"Good. And Ms. Tsuki?" I look up at him with dead eyes. My stomach growls again making everyone give me perplexing looks. "Make sure next time you keep your attention on me when we're conversing."

Motherfucker.

Gritting my teeth I barely dip my head to nod. His eyes darken but he says nothing else before turning and leaving. The second his back is to me I take the cloth and fold it up before wiping my face again. I can still scent salty seawater and fucking rotting fish. I wasn't lying to Jullia when I said I did not like water mage blood. I actually hate it.

Taking in my surroundings again, I notice Asher has let Hanna go and Jullia is currently glaring at her. The two staff members with the devil left with him, though the two students haven't. Two males with gold stitching in their blazers, with a gold embroidered dragon on one and a silver embroidered pair of feathered wings on the other as their symbol. I would wonder what race they could be, but I'd have to care for that.

Turning towards the line again I glare at every single person who looks back at me until they start moving. Great first fucking day.

Me, Jullia, Asher, and Hanna all get food and I follow Jullia and Asher as they take a table closest to the door and near where the people Asher had first greeted were. Not that any of them come near us. Hanna disappears further into the cafeteria and everyone else slowly goes back to what they were doing.

The second I sit down I dive in.

Fluffy eggs, crispy bacon, golden potatoes, a cup of

mixed berries, and best of all my steamed vegetables. I can feel both Jullia and Asher's eyes on me but I don't pay them any mind as I start shoving food into my mouth. I get through half of everything and already I feel a million times better.

God it's so good I could almost cry. Nutrients and flavor and my body is already thanking me.

"I don't think I've ever been so happy about regular food before," I hear Asher murmur. "I also think that's the first time I've seen her smile.

"That *is* the first time she's smiled," Jullia whispers back.

With only a couple pieces of potatoes left I finally look up and see their trays are still mostly full. Shoving another fork full of food I blink at them.

"This is actually the most *alive* I've seen her," Jullia sort of croaks. "Does this mean you were starving for three days?"

She looks panicked and Asher is also looking a bit worried for me. Swallowing my bite I take my cup Jullia had kept filling with water and drink the whole thing.

Sighing in content, everything relaxes. "Yeah," I answer on a sigh. My tone light and unbothered. "Though normally it wouldn't be so bad but they had me locked up for a month and they only fed me regular food when I finally annoyed them enough to."

Jullia's eye twitches and she stares at me for a moment before taking her hands and rubbing them down her face.

"I really thought vampires couldn't eat regular food. Or at least, they didn't need it to survive. But you do?" she asks, but she doesn't really ask me. She sort of throws the question out there. "Or do you just get very sluggish and that's why you sleep too? I don't understand."

Asher gives me an amused look I ignore and shove the last bit of food on my tray into my mouth.

"Or is it," she tries, "that you haven't fully turned? Is that why you also don't have any bloodlust? Did the transition not fully complete? I remember reading about that once but it's impossibly rare. Yet you can't go in the sun and still drink blood?"

Asher rubs his hand on her back as he continues eating his breakfast. I let her stew as I take out my tablet from the inner pocket of my blazer and turn it on. It's more or less like an iPhone. There are apps already on here and ones you can download and you can customize the screen.

I hadn't done anything with it until last night after my shower. Jullia helped me fully set it up and showed me how to use it. She also downloaded the social media app everyone uses that is more or less like a mix of *Facebook*, *Instagram*, and *TikTok*. She made an account for me and followed herself and Asher through it. I haven't looked at it since.

Instead of clicking onto the square app showing a circle split in four, each quarter a color relating to one of the main elements, I click on the app that shows my class schedule and the portals for each class. It's a bit like *Canvas* – not that I used it at all since I didn't go to school during the time when schools were using it.

My and Jullia's first class is Magic History which is quite literally the actual name. *Magic* History. Our teacher is Professor Asier who Asher had said good luck to us to. The professor also teaches Intro to Power Compulsion which Jullia explained to me was basically us strengthening our mental state to be able to better understand and control whatever abilities we have.

Because it has more to deal with control over our mind and bodies all first years take that as well, and me and Jullia have that together. Our third and last class for today we'll take after lunch.

There's no work load in the portals yet. I'm assuming we get them after we actually begin classes. Pretty much everything else we need is on the tablet as well. All the text books and even a notes tab you can use to write or type notes.

Since I couldn't bring anything with me and have no real school supplies Jullia also let me borrow one of her stylus pens for the tablet so I can at least take notes. After classes, depending on how much school work I have, I'm going to the advisor building to look for a job. It's not that surprising

No. Even if I have all the school work in the world I'd still head in because it's not even about needing a lot of money, I just need enough for at least some school supplies, hygiene stuff, and maybe a non-school uniform outfit.

Asher stands after finally finishing and kisses Jullia on the head and waves at me before leaving. She stands a second later and I follow as she says we better get to our first class.

Asher winced when we said who our professor was. I really hope he was exaggerating about whoever Professor Asier is.

Jullia links her arm with mine as she navigates the school. Leading us to the building where the class is and following a bunch of other students. The whispers from students gradually get quieter as they enter the classroom.

Asher probably wasn't exaggerating, but with my belly full and body rested there's an almost excited energy. Despite what happened this morning I feel much better and maybe it won't be as bad as I initially thought.

Too bad I walk through the classroom door.

Three

Varian – August 8

I can count on one hand how many people have been able to glare at me and live. I guess I'll now have to say both hands because the little bloodsucker is glaring at me.

Surprisingly, Ms. Jullia Waterstone who has her arm linked with the bloodsucker scolds her and pulls her up the stairs into the lecture hall. She grumbles something back I can't quite pick up but holds her glare as she stares at the floor.

They take two seats on the third row near the middle. Callahan comes through the door next and his eyes zero in right on her. I'm sure Thorne and Darian clued him in on what happened earlier this morning.

Very curious how a newly turned vampire not only didn't attack first in what I could tell was a very aggressive situation, but she didn't even lick a drop of the blood smeared on her face. She actually wiped it off and looked almost repulsed by it.

Callahan makes a beeline to the open chair beside her. Being in the same grade as her, and being a devil like myself, he'll be the perfect person to watch her. Even if the Dean says we should be fine and the Mage Board is forcing the university to take her, a vampire is still a vampire. There's a reason one does not sit on the council and there are none in the school.

Except the bloodsucker. Though she hasn't sucked anyone's blood – yet.

She doesn't give Callahan even a glance and continues to glare at her tablet. There's a stylus in her hand and she's either writing or doodling something on the screen. Her friend whispers to her and I wonder – aside from being roommates – how a mage befriended a vampire. Not only that, but how a vampyr would let his girlfriend be close to one. Especially so freshly turned.

And those pale pink eyes. Whoever's blood she drank must have been someone very powerful. Maybe that's how she was able to subside her bloodlust.

Returning my focus on the chalkboard I begin writing. I've been forced to teach the same four classes at this university for nearly a hundred years now. Each year has been even more excruciatingly boring than the last.

Except now.

When I turn back around the last student has taken their seats, the bell rings, and all eyes are on me. All eyes, except a particularly pale shade of pink. I do believe I told her to make sure she's always looking at me.

Stubbornly, or perhaps stupidly, she keeps her eyes on her desk. Arms crossed and leaning back in her chair.

What a fucking brat.

Callahan beside her grins at me with his meddlesome smirk. Everyone else seems to hold their breaths as they wait for me to speak. Good.

"My name is Professor Asier. I will be your Magic History teacher, and for most of you your Intro to Power Compulsion class." I let my words ring in the room before continuing. "Your syllabus is now available on your tablets and I expect all of you to read everything over on your own time. To start today off, does anyone know the beginning of Syngenia?"

The bloodsucker blinks like she's just remembering something as the pink in her eyes fades to a shade lighter. I had looked into her paperwork and aside from the documents of how she was turned and her exam results, we have nothing else.

Her only name is Mavyn Tsuki though the enforcers who caught her couldn't find documents in the human world of anyone by that name. It's not that surprising since it's listed she is an orphan. It's probably a name she made up.

Her friend raises a hand and I nod to her.

"Syngenia University was established five thousand years ago after the War of Gods finally ended, but if you're referring to Syngenia the first land of magic, that would be the beginning of the first universe the Goddess of Breath created."

The bloodsucker lowers her brows as she glances at her friend. Ms. Waterstone doesn't seem to notice as her eyes stay on me waiting for what I'll say.

"Correct." But as I say that the bloodsucker quirks her lip as if my response is distasteful. "Do you have something to add Ms. Tsuki?"

She freezes in place though her eyes finally slide to me. Looking at me for the first time since she entered, and I can't read a single thing from her. Not only does she not give anything away, but she already has mental shields up. Powerful ones, too.

"Syngenia is also the name of the first vampyr born, named after her mother, the first blood witch. Both of them existed before the university and the first land of magic."

That's impossible.

Callahan is gaping at the girl like I would be if I wasn't frozen in shock as I am.

"And actually it was not the Goddess of Breath who created the first land of magic, it was a joint effort between the first breath and wood witch. Though many did believe the first breath witch was a goddess."

She states it like she knows it's fact.

How the fuck does she know that?

Only humans can be turned into vampires. And no mere human would have access to knowledge like that. I'm not even allowed to fully teach it because of the guards that are on that kind of knowledge. Unless. . . maybe it's not *her* knowledge but the knowledge of whoever's blood she drank that turned her. That has happened before. Memories being transferred. But it makes me wonder who's blood it could have been.

"That," I finally choke out, "is correct. However the answer I was looking for was the one given by Ms. Waterstone. Now."

I turn towards the chalkboard so I don't have to look at

her for a minute. Her bored glare returned the second I said *however*, and fuck I need to calm down. The little brat needs to be taught a lesson.

Writing the list on the board I announce the assignments everyone needs to start and Callahan waits until after I'm finished to knock on my mental shields. He, like me, can communicate through mind links, but unlike me he cannot always get into everyone's heads without permission. He's still young, though.

I like her.

Looking up at him, I glare. His response is to laugh in my head.

Come on now. You're gonna tell me you don't? With all that firecracker and bratty energy? I mean, did you see the way she looked at you?

I fucking know that Armani, I don't need you reiterating it.

He chuckles again, though it's lighter as if he's trying to keep me from hearing it. I try to focus on the paperwork in front of me but my brain will not make sense of it at the moment.

Apologies apologies. I just don't think I've ever seen you so knocked off your axis. I don't blame you. When she mentioned the witches even I couldn't believe it. Weren't those history books locked up by the Board?

They were. Do you think it could be memories from whoever the owner of the blood that turned her? If they were a powerful enough vampyr it could be possible. There aren't many clans with red eyes to begin with.

Want to ask Thorne? He's not doing anything, we could ask now?

Yes. Only because if she has other memories, other knowledge hidden in her mind, it could help. . .

His realization floods my mind and a second later I can feel Thorne Arcturus' mind.

Is this about the girl? I hear through my head. Callahan's giddiness accompanies it. Already having so many minds in mine is giving me a headache.

She knew about Syngenia the Blood Witch and her daughter.

Thorne is quiet for a moment before bits of his surprise weave through my mind. He's gotten better at shielding his emotions even while inside the mind of another.

You think she could possibly just know that, or do you think it's from the blood of who turned her?

The blood, I answer. *She has pink eyes meaning whoever's blood it was had red ones. And her control over her bloodlust, her eating regular food. . . I've never seen a vampire do that before.*

It isn't possible, Thorne agrees. *Even through the vampyr history when the strongest vampyr known turned their own vampires his blood wasn't powerful enough to stop their bloodlust. They were able to get control of it sooner. That being a year verses it normally takes multiple years to fully control it. It shouldn't be possible if she was only turned two months ago.*

So what? Callahan interjects. *You think she's not a vampire? The enforcers said they watched her turn, saw her get burned by the sun, and she drinks blood.*

I don't know. She could have maybe reacted differently to the blood and venom. Maybe she has dormant magic from an ancestor and that's what helped her with her bloodlust. All I know is that she's an anomaly the Mage Board threw in here.

Thorne hums. *You think she's a spy? Maybe she isn't newly turned and that was just an excuse? Or are you thinking maybe she's a blood demon?*

Could be, Callahan chirps. *Maybe she is a spy, but she did eat enough regular food this morning to fill up one of the swim teammates and she looked like she enjoyed it too. Regular vampires can't do that. No matter how many years they've lived. So maybe blood demon. Unless she's actually a vampyr and pretending to hide from the sun? You thinking about taking a sip of her blood, Thorne? Or at least see if the sun actually burns her?*

Thorne hums in either contemplation or agreement. I'm not sure which as he slowly starts slipping from the link getting lost in his own thoughts.

I look up to see the bloodsucker's face smoothed out as she writes on the tiny tablet. Does she not have a regular notebook and pen? Why write on that small thing?

Callahan shrugs his shoulders as he glances at her before poking her with his pen. Her face contorts for a split second into a frown before she evens it out and looks over to him.

Thorne fully leaves our mind link and I focus enough on Callahan so I can hear his physical words as well as his mental.

No paper and pen like the rest of us, firecracker?

She arches a brow at him before looking down at his notebook and then at her tablet. Her friend side-eyes them but focuses on her work. The bloodsucker says something but since I'm in Callahan's mind I can't actually hear it.

She asked why I cared. He tells me while chuckling.

Just curious. I'm Callahan. Callahan Armani. Her best

friend's eyes widen but she doesn't look at the bloodsucker or Callahan. Ms. Waterstone must know that name. I'd be surprised if she didn't. The Armani's have been the Devil Councilmen on the Mage Board since the beginning of it. *I figured someone who knows about blood witches would have proper school supplies.*

She rolls her eyes and goes back to writing on the table. Completely ignoring Callahan and his shock floods my brain.

What a fucking brat.

And I just bet you'd like to teach her a lesson wouldn't you, Asier.

Lust floods my brain and I kick him out of my mind. I can see him silently chuckling but I ignore it as I refocus on my work. It doesn't help though because the lust is lingering in my mind and fucking hell that kid. He didn't need to fucking say that shit to me.

I drag my hand down my face and berate myself about getting back to work. Despite my loathing it I do have a job I need to be relatively good at.

Finally, I'm able to focus and I can get through the rest of class. The bloodsucker doesn't spare me another glance and keeps her face perfectly neutral. Callahan doesn't try talking to her again though I'm sure he wants to. He keeps looking at her like she's something he'd want to eat.

I end the class with listing the work they need to finish before next class. All of which is in their portal. Once that's done the bell in the northern belltower begins ringing and they all start filing out. Callahan stands and begins to turn towards the girl but she and her friend are already halfway through the isle on the opposite side.

Ms. Waterstone is whispering to her, too quietly for me

to hear. But the bloodsucker rolls her eyes at something as they come down the steps. I'm sure they went that way to avoid Callahan but that just means they'll have to pass me.

"I'm being serious, Mavyn" Ms. Waterstone whispers, both of them getting closer to me and allowing me to hear them. "Callahan is the son of the devil councilmen in the Mage Board. Even Asher prefers to stay away from them."

"I said okay, Jullia – "

"Okay is not enough. You looked both him and the freaking professor straight in the eye. You can't do that," she stresses. At least Ms. Waterstone is smart enough to know that. Even if I command all a person's attention when speaking, they look at me but never in my eyes. Let alone glare at me.

The bloodsucker huffs and I'm sure she rolls her eyes again.

"And we're close enough that said devil can hear everything we're whispering about."

Involuntarily I look up and low and behold the bloodsucker is staring directly at me. Her friend makes a noise, but she simply quirks a brow and stares directly into my eyes.

"Plus," she continues to whisper, "in my early childhood I was raised by a devil. The egotistical assholes don't bother me."

They both walk past me and over the top of their heads I catch Callahan with wide eyes watching them before flicking up to me. He must have heard her too. And for all unholy gods who the fuck is this girl?

They exit the class and Callahan begins strolling over to my desk as the last couple students leave too. He waits until they're all out before nodding his head and making the door slam shut. Giving us privacy while also creating a sound barrier around us as an added security.

"Sooo," he drags out. Then he huffs out a breath. "What are we planning to do?"

Releasing a breath as well, I drag my hand over my face and lean against my desk. I have absolutely no idea.

"Because if you're thinking about the rebels and whatever their plans are with the Mage Council, I doubt one little girl is gonna be a problem. Or," he drags the word out like he does so often, "are you thinking about the oracle and the damnation of the burning sun?"

So many thoughts. Too many thoughts. So much stress is going to actually end up killing me. The damn emotion is reducing me to a mere mortal.

"I'm thinking, firstly, that I want to know why the Mage Board allowed a vampire into the campus. See if Darian can contact the enforcers and if they're on anyone's payroll." Rubbing my face for what feels like the millionth time today, I heave. "And just see if we can get as much information on her as possible. Have Thorne ask Asher Ruleten and I want to know why he lets a vampire near his little girlfriend. We'll start with that."

Callahan nods and begins skipping towards the door. Dropping the sound barrier and opening the door, he tips an invisible hat off to me and leaves.

Unholy gods, fucking Mage Board. Even the councilmen on our side are still politicians. I need a damned drink.

Despite myself I look over to where she was sitting. I shouldn't care. What the fuck does it matter to me what she is or why she's here. Unless she is a spy from the Mage Board. And if she is, then at least she can say in the afterlife that she was the first vampire to step foot in Syngenia University.

Four

Mavyn – August 8

I may have sort of lied a teeny, tiny, itty, bitty bit to myself. Technically, I wouldn't burn when sunlight touched my skin. However, when you have a runic curse etched into your skin and shitty luck, bad things that shouldn't happen to you tend to simply just happen.

Case in point.

The sun is hitting my bare face and I can feel the needles of pain pricking as the rays begin burning my skin.

Someone behind me screams and I let myself revel in the warmth for a moment. I haven't been able to have the sun directly on my face for thirteen years. It was my sixth birthday present and just turning nineteen a month and a half ago marked the thirteenth anniversary.

Something gets thrown over me and I'm assuming a body crashes me into the ground. Whoever had been screaming turns to yelling. Words flying out of their mouth and another person interjecting. Jullia and Asher I assume. My head feels a bit dizzy now and for some reason I can't quite make out who is who.

All of a sudden I'm no longer on the ground but pressed against warmth. It has to be a body because I can smell blood. Pressing my nose closer to it I hiss as pain erupts over my face and head but that delicious blood invades my nostrils and I lick my lips.

Mavyn, Mavyn, Mavyn.

It sounds like a chant.

Other words are said I'm sure. I can't make them all out. But I do make out one.

Blood.

Yes, I think. *Smooth, rich blood does sound delicious.*

Just hold on, someone screams – in my head, in the air, in my bones. It echoes as pain prickles specifically in my scalp and I know I had been so close to that delicious blood but now I'm not. My fangs ache in my mouth and I'm hungry.

Please, I beg. I don't typically beg. But sometimes that's all you're able to do and I can tell I'm far too weak right now.

Shhh. It'll be alright.

Lies.

That's what *she* had said. She always said it before he came in.

Everything aches now. I can feel it. Wounds that should have already been healed a long time ago rage. Burning and burning and burning.

Why the fuck is she burning up?

Because the Sun Devil said he would burn me for all eternity.

You'll be fine Mavyn. Just hold on.

They sound like they care. Why do they care? I can't remember right now. Burning and burning and burning. Ms. Elaycia never let me burn. Where did she go?

It hurts.

It always hurts.

. . .

Voices are muddled together, words being mixed and all I can taste is rage. Why does it feel like those videos of the North Sea?

Either my brain or my body or my conscious registers I'm awake now and pain sparks along certain areas of my face. They're accompanied by the worst headache I've ever had. I can feel my heart pounding against my skull.

AND SHE IS A STUDENT SO SHE SHOULD BE JUST AS PROTECTED!

Ms. Waterstone I under –

No you fucking don't you cock sucking fuck!

Jullia Waterstone! He is still –

NO! I don't give a flying fuck who or what he is. Mavyn has been nothing but polite to everyone, Hanna. She has shown nothing but control. And all she gets for it is trying to be killed!

Ah, yes. I had been burned by the sun. Fucking curse.

She spoke! Jullia, that must have been Jullia who squealed. Her voices grows a bit louder as she rushes out a bunch of other words. I still have yet to open my eyes but already I can feel my symptoms subsiding. I hadn't been exposed for too long.

"At least we can deduce that she is, in fact, a vampire," a lazy voice drawls.

"You piece of shit, rich ass, lazy mother – "

"JULLIA!" Hanna interrupts. I can tell that's Hanna now. "Calm down right the fuck now!"

I finally crack my eyes open and see nothing. It takes me a couple times to blink and soon stars start to dance but light floods with them. Lifting my hand I use my index finger and thumb to rub my eyes. The limb feels heavy, but at least I can do that. Even if it makes the headache worse.

"Mavyn!" Jullia rushes out. "How are you? Are you okay? I mean I know of course you're not okay, but you're alive at least. Are you still in a lot of pain? The healers have tried giving you some pain relievers but they don't always work the best."

"Jullia," I grumble. I feel like I could take a nap. "Take a deep breath, please."

I hear her do it and I do one with her before putting my hand down and opening my eyes without difficulty. Jullia is standing on the right side of what looks like a hospital bed. Hanna is behind her with Asher next to her but closer to the foot of the bed.

On the right is someone who looks like they're around my age dressed in a white coat and another dressed in scrubs. They're both clutching a clipboard and staring wide-eyed at me. Neither of them looking like they're gonna say anything.

And lastly at the end are two faces I've recently seen. The first had been the guy who sat next to me in class. He said his name was Callahan something. Aria or Armory or something like that. Jullia had been stressing after the class about how I can't just ignore him cause he's a hotshot and his dad is the devil councilmen for the Mage Board and I told her I couldn't care less.

The one beside him had been one of the guys who was with Professor Asier when he found us in the cafeteria. The one with a gold dragon as his symbol. He's taller than Callahan and Professor Asier. Tanned but not as dark as either of them. Black hair styled on the top of his head and a pair of dark red almond shaped eyes.

He has the same symbol as Callahan, though instead of a red and gold stitched dragon it's only a gold stitched one. So not a devil but maybe similar. Demon, maybe?

Dismissing them, I loll my head to the side and look at Jullia. Her emotions are written all over her face. From her distress to her panic to her anger.

"What exactly happened?"

Just then another person enters our little section. The doctor and nurse step away as a man in a dark suit approaches and behind him is Professor Asier, the second guy from the cafeteria, and an older woman with a white lab coat.

The woman comes up to the left side of the bed and offers me a warm smile. "Hello, there. You suffered a bit of a traumatic event, I'm going to need you to answer some questions for me. Okay?"

My nonanswer seems to be answer enough.

“Alright. Can you tell me your name?”

This is going to be annoying.

“My face is no longer stinging. Could I just get a blood bag, I’ll be fine after that.”

The doctor’s face goes sullen and she squints at me. “Are you unable to tell me your name?”

Blowing out a breath I roll my eyes. My hands goes up to my face but I stop at the last moment realizing I probably should not rub my still healing face.

“Fucking hell,” I mutter under my breath. Louder I answer, “My name is Mavyn Ellora Tsuki. I was born June twenty-first nineteen years ago. No idea who my parents are but that’s because they dipped three months after I was born. I was found somewhere in upstate New York and was later entered into the American foster care system. The day I turned nineteen some vampire shoved vampyr blood and venom into me and due to my control of bloodlust the Mage Board allowed me to take the entrance exam and I was given a full scholarship to Syngenia University which was established five thousand years ago after the War of Gods.” Looking her dead in the eyes I finish with, “Happy? Can I have the blood bag now?”

The room is silent and all eyes are on me before the doctor looks over to the younger doctor and nods her head.

“Not water mage blood, please. Sorry Jullia but it really is disgusting.”

Jullia doesn’t respond but the female doctor does nod at that and the younger one all but runs away. The nurse decides a second after to follow and now I’m left with the rest of everyone.

The man in the suit who walked in first takes a step closer to the bed and seems to bore his eyes into me. He is the Head Dean. I remember him from when I took the exam. He had been there to personally oversee me and make sure I couldn't cheat in any sort of way. He had also seemed like he wanted to beat into, but simply sternly said, 'Don't cause any problems at my school.'

He should have been more concerned with his other students.

"This university takes pride in its safety for its students. However, we can only do so much for those who come forward." Just like with Asher's words to Professor Asier, the Dean is also careful with his. "Would you be able to explain what happened, Ms. Tsuki?"

He's glaring at me but I barely notice as I remember. Me and Jullia had just met up with Asher after Professor Asier's Magic History class. He was going to walk us to our next classes. I had pulled out my umbrella because we were going to be walking through a court yard and right after I stepped into the sun something had ripped my umbrella away.

Then there was warmth. Then a burning.

"What happened," Jullia angerly interjects, "is Thorne Arcturus purposefully tried to kill Mavyn. He was the one to snatch her umbrella away while she was clearly in the sun without warning."

Hanna jerks Jullia back as the Dean's glaring eyes don't leave me and I look past him to who I'm assuming Thorne is. The one standing beside Callahan who I'm wondering if is a demon. If so, I wonder what kind. Like all other races, there are subraces for the demons too.

"I believe," he lazily drawls, "what actually happened was I unfortunately, accidentally bumped into the vampire and she lost her grip on her umbrella herself."

Jullia starts to argue but even Asher is behind Hanna trying to get her to be quiet. The Dean raises a brow at me. "Well? Do you remember, Ms. Tsuki?"

The younger doctor returns with a clear bag full of red liquid with a tube I can use like a straw. I push myself up to a better sitting position in the bed and snatch the bag out of his hand before sucking it down within seconds.

Mmm. . . it tastes sweet. A mixture of stardust, berries, and a hint of floral. Faerie blood. A female faerie too, guys always have an earthier bitterness.

The one bag is nowhere near enough, but I'll eat more at lunch and at least now I can feel the wounds on my face fully healing. There will probably still be some marks left that'll take a day or so to fade, but at least they didn't scar. I wasn't out long enough for them to scar.

Handing the empty bag to the young doctor, he takes it and dips away. Finally placing my focus on the Dean who looks like he's about to burst a blood vessel, I give him the answer he wants.

"Unfortunately, I do tend to be a bit clumsy." The words sound hollower than I intended them to be, but they echo in my mind alongside a memory from a long time ago. It makes me feel almost numb. "I'll try to be more careful next time."

I can see out of the corner of my eye Jullia gaping at me, as well as her sister and Asher staring with shocked eyes. The Dean doesn't hesitate and nods before storming off. Behind him still stands Professor Asier who's peering at me with probing eyes, Callahan and Thorne with matching blank expressions, and the last one I don't have a name for with curiosity in his icy blue gaze.

He's the one who has the silver embroidered wings. And if we're following the theme, he's either going to be a demigod or an angel. Since his symbol is a pair of wings I'm going to guess angel. I wonder if he has actual wings.

Deciding to now ignore them, I turn back towards Jullia who looks like she's frozen in shock. Glancing at Asher, I ask, "So what happened after? And how long was I out?"

"Only ten minutes," an unfortunately familiar sounding voice answers.

Callahan steps around Professor Asier to stand on the left side of the bed. His hands are in his pants pockets and he has a smirk on again.

"Bit impressive, if you ask me. Even Thorne felt a bit surprised with how fast you opened your eyes." He licks his lips as his grin quirks. "As far as what happened? Well Ruleten picked you up to bring you here and you had been begging for his blood. Tell me though, why was it you were begging for *another* taste?"

I don't know if it's anger or suspicion or maybe even jealousy, but he says those last few words differently. His tone got a bit darker and I can sense tendrils of his magic.

Now that my face is more or less fully healed I take my hands and rub at them. The headache also subsided a bit, but the action causes a pulse to make me flinch. That doesn't stop me though because I rub it again and a third time for good measure. I'm still hungry. And now I'm exhausted.

Still. . . I raise an eyebrow at the devil. "I didn't know you were the owner of Asher's blood. As far as I was aware blood sharing was allowed as long as both parties were consenting."

Professor Asier's eyes widen and Thorne 'whatever his

last name was' drops his mouth open before snapping it shut. Callahan, however, goes extremely still as he watches me.

Asher, for some reason being nervous, steps in. "It was most definitely not blood sharing." Agitated and almost afraid. "She made a blood oath to not harm Jullia, that was it."

Exhausted with all of this and wanting my shitty bed, I throw the blanket over my legs off and swing my feet to the right. Jullia has her mouth screwed shut with Hanna, both standing behind Asher and both with their eyes on the floor. Though as I begin to stand up Jullia looks up at me with both hurt and anger.

My vision goes in and out for a second but I stay conscious and simply keep a tight grip on the bed so I don't sway.

"Same difference," I mumble.

"The fuck it is," a drawling voice responds, though it's now threatening instead of lazy.

When my vision clears I look over at the celestials. Callahan looks much more relaxed and has a smirk on his face again. Professor Asier has his stoic scowl back on, the possible angel still looks curious, and the possible demon is glaring at me now.

I rub at my face again. It makes the headache worse but I don't care.

Ten minutes. That's what Callahan said, meaning I have fifteen left to get to my next class. Then lunch is after that. I'll have one more class and depending on how I feel after maybe I'll do a rest day and go look for a job tomorrow.

"Whatever. I don't care." Looking up to Asher I sigh. "I'm sorry for that, I hope I didn't hurt you. It had just been a while since I drank and after getting burned it just heightened the hunger. Not that you have to worry about it anyways, I would have been otherwise fine."

Someone hums but I don't bother turning around.

"I thought I made it clear that when I'm speaking to you, you look at me, Ms. Tsuki."

Oh not this shit again.

Now fully on my feet, I turn to face the professor. Focusing solely on him and waiting for him to say whatever he's going to say.

"How is it you do have such a control over your bloodlust? Especially for being turned not even two months ago?"

He sounds cold and detached. It could be simply curiosity because it is an anomaly. Ms. Elaycia had said it normally takes vampires multiple years to get a handle on it. And even then they still wouldn't turn down blood if it was right in front of their face.

But there's a strain in the professor's body. His words were open for me to answer but his body is demanding that I do so. It's made more apparent by a subtle shift in the air and a tickle in my nose. All of a sudden I have a wish to tell him everything. To blurt it all out.

What a clever devil.

The corner of my lips slightly curl. His nostrils flair at it.

"A devil," I answer. "One I'd say is nearly exactly like you. He taught me *all* about control."

"I've never heard of a devil wanting to adopt a human," Callahan says, though I know what he's trying to ask.

"Oh, his generosity knew no bounds." And that's not a fucking lie. "The nonmortals on Earth are a lot different. His wife was a mage, they were fated, but she couldn't have kids. Nonmortal children are rare and I just so happened to have similar features as her and being a toddler I was the next best thing. Any more questions?"

I point that question to Professor Asier since he so needed to know how I have such control over bloodlust. My answer to that also wasn't technically a lie.

Callahan chuckles and asks another fucking question. I had meant mine to be rhetorical.

"What *are* your natural features, firecracker?"

Not this again with that stupid nickname. I scoff at it but shrug my shoulders. Brushing my hands around my neck I flip my hair. Then I gesture to myself. "Basically this. Black hair, I just dye it blue and pink at the ends, but my eyes used to be brown. Very boring, very original. Can I go now? I have a class to get to."

Callahan shrugs and turns towards the others. Professor Asier spins around and leaves without a second thought and not caring about the other two I grab my blazer that had been draped across a side chair and start making my way out.

Asher pulls Jullia and Hanna along and eventually begins to lead because I don't actually know where I'm going. My internal map of this place began and ended with where my dorm building was, where I needed to go to eat, and where my classes were.

Eventually he leads us down a hall the opens up into another courtyard. Stopping, Asher turns towards me and offers my sunglasses and umbrella. I really fucking hate this umbrella.

Taking them, I slide the glasses on and open the

umbrella, but now that I'm ready no one wants to move. Finally, after thirty-ish seconds, Jullia moves to stand in front of me and looks directly at me.

"Why did you do that?"

This is the first time I'm hearing her speak like this.

Cold and detached and all that does is hide how hurt she is. I can't blame her. She tried to stand up for me and I basically shut her down. The only person in this school who has given me any grace.

God I'm a bitch.

Letting the umbrella fall to my side I remove my sunglasses so I can properly look at her. Her lavender eyes watering behind her glasses and her jaw clenching.

"Thorne, the one who exposed me to the sun, he's a demon, right?" She blinks, registering my words and then barely dips her head. "And Callahan is a devil. The last one in the back, is he an angel?"

She nods again and I'm sure there's some sort of understanding happening in her mind because her lips start to purse and her brows begin to lower.

"So they're all celestials and at least one of them is closely related to someone on the Mage Board. I, a lowly being of moral, who is hated by all the races, would have pleaded my case, won because there were too many witnesses, and then eventually ended up accidentally dead because I decided to mess with people who are in a position of power I am nowhere near."

Jullia squeezes her eyes shut and sighs. A look of dejection but understanding replacing the hurt and anger.

"If I want to be stamped as a legal vampire I need to

graduate this stupid university. If I have to bow my head and beg and grovel and submit a bit before some assholes, so be it. And trust me, Jullia. . . " I wait for her to open her eyes and look back at me. "I've had it a hell of a lot worse. Not in recent years, but still. They now know I burn in the sun, and hopefully my responses answered their questions. Let's just. . . move on."

Jullia sighs again before fisting her hands and stomping her foot. "Okay. Fine. I will. But it's still not fair. Just because Callahan and Thorne's fathers sit on the Mage Board doesn't mean they get to do whatever they want. But I will agree, we can move on."

She nods her head and then gives me a smile. Content with that I put my sunglasses back on and pick up my umbrella. Jullia comes to stand at my side and threads her arm through mine. Looking over at Asher and Hanna I realize I forgot they were there.

"Let's go to class then," Jullia announces, "even though I'm already late."

Neither Hanna nor Asher objects so we exit the hall and walk under the rays of the sun. Jullia tenses beside me but it doesn't affect her walk. Asher moves to stand on the other side of her and while Hanna stays on my side she still keeps space between us.

"It makes you wonder though," Hanna says after we've walked to the next building where my and Jullia's next classes are, "why did Thorne, and it seemed the rest of them too, want to see if you did burn in the sun? Did they think you couldn't? Were they questioning if you were a vampire or something?"

When I turn to Hanna she meets my stare head on and no longer looks like she wants to put a stake through my heart. Jullia hums and Asher looks like he's curious too but he pulls Jullia away saying we'll talk about this after class.

Perfect timing too, because the old sounding bell rings and Hanna dips to her class while I go to walk through the door of mine. Even though I'm early and no one is here yet, I can relax in one of the chairs.

She does have a point though. It wasn't just Thorne either, because Callahan, Professor Asier, and the angel were also there. Were they all questioning whether I was a vampire or not? I could understand my control over bloodlust after so soon from my apparent turning, me being hungry for regular food, and me actually being able to sleep could be curious, but there shouldn't be suspicion unless there's already something else to be worried about.

Maybe it's just a misunderstanding and they simply have too strong of a hatred for vampires and just wanted me dead. That would be a more rational answer, but even I remember someone – I'm pretty sure it was Thorne's voice – saying they could deduct that I am in fact a vampire.

I would be more curious, but I just hope their suspicion is doused and they'll leave me alone. I really hope everyone just leaves me alone for the next five years, actually.

Fuck, and it's only the first day. If I can get through the rest of this week it will be a literal miracle. One can freakin hope.

Five

Thorne – August 8

She smells like blue belladons. It was frustratingly one of the only things I could think about the second I got a wisp of her scent. Even now the scent is still stuck in my nose as if my body doesn't want me to forget what she smells like.

Her scent should have been gone by now and I can't actively scent her from here. The lecture hall has enough seats to sit a hundred and ninety-nine percent of those seats are taken. She sits in the first seat of the second row and I am as far as I can possibly get in here while still being in a desk.

She should be smelling like rotting flesh. That's how all

vampires smell, unless they bathe in perfume and lotions. That's probably what it is. The sweet mixed berry scent with a slight creamy and floral undertone. Just like the sapphire blue bell-shaped flowers that grow in my mother's personal garden at the estate.

Despite it being a perfume, it still makes me want to sink my fangs into her neck. Even though I know all I'll get is a disgusting rotting taste that'll stick in the back of my throat for days. Vampire blood is tainted human blood. It tastes like death.

Still, my fangs begin to ache.

I may be a blood demon and much more powerful than most vampyr, but we still share similar attributes. One of them needing blood to survive and having retractable fangs. Not that I tend to keep them hidden. Though even if I tried to in this moment I wouldn't be able to. They ache, and they want blood.

Her blood.

Or at least the promise that it would taste as sweet as that perfume she smells like.

The professor drones on about whatever lesson he's teaching. The girl paying rapt attention and for some reason is using her tablet and a stylus to take notes. She looks relatively normal. Boring and original, as she had said to Callahan. The only way you would be able to tell she's different is her eyes.

Aside from her scent there's nothing remarkable about her. Even her energy and aura is weak. I won't know for sure until I taste her blood, but thinking about that and who else has tasted it makes adrenaline flooded with rage coarse through my system.

I had been so close to ripping Ruleten's head off when she insinuated they blood shared. Only because of years of control was I able to stay rooted to the spot and let Ruleten get a word in. She had shrugged it off as if blood sharing wasn't a personal, should-be private, intimate thing between those of us who drink blood.

Throughout all the races there's only a few of us. Vampyr and vampires being one, blood demons like myself, and some devils. Blood sharing can also be done with someone who doesn't necessarily drink blood but there isn't an inherent, instinctual reaction from them because of it.

I haven't even practiced in it, though I have drank the blood of many during intimate moments. I refuse to let anyone drink my own blood.

And she shrugged it off as if it meant nothing. Fucking vampire. At their core they're filthy humans, who to them now have a godlike power, never caring about traditions and inherent instincts and the respect for the actions that relate back to our first ancestors.

This is why they're not welcome within the university or within the Mage Board.

Not that I care much about the Mage Board and their political bullshit, but it further proves that humans are worthless. And by association, vampires are as well.

I've proved well enough that she is one, but I'll still taste her blood to be sure. Her anomalies are strange, but it could be just whoever's blood now also courses through her veins or the vampire species as a whole are adapting. Either way, those two reasons are neither my concern.

If we fully prove she's a vampire then her past checks out and while it's still suspicious the Mage Board let her into the school, the likelihood that she's a spy is nearly zero.

At least then as well when I taste her blood I can see most of her memories. I'll be able to confirm then as well.

There's a light feathery knock in the back of my conscious and I let Callahan into my mind. We chose not to say anything even after the girl left the infirmary in case there were wondering ears.

You still gonna bite her?

Just to be sure.

Someone, another mind chuckles. Callahan must have brought Darian with him.

Are you sure it's not because she smells so sweet? Even without fangs I was tempted to sink my teeth into her neck to see if her blood tastes as good as she smells.

Callahan chuckles with him. *Aren't you angels supposed to be all light and innocent? It almost seems like you're more tainted than all of us, Darian.*

If only you knew, devil.

It's a perfume, I answer Darian. *Vampires can't naturally smell like that. I'll be lucky if I can even swallow a mouthful of her rotting blood.*

Darian hums within my mind and I can feel his disagreement.

She burned in the sun, I snap at him. Pushing his disagreement away. *The only being who actually burns in the sun are vampires. Which rules out vampyr and blood demon.*

Callahan hums now. *Were you actually considering she was a blood demon?*

I thought about it since she had a need for regular food. Her stomach had actually growled in the cafeteria, meaning she needed the food. Not even vampyr really need food like that if they have a healthy enough supply of blood.

Both of them contemplate.

After I taste her blood we'll know for sure. They both bring their attention back to me. *The first week parties start tomorrow night and last till Sunday. She'll have to come to at least one, I'll do it then. Then we can be done with her.*

I can feel Darian's emotions and thoughts disagreeing with me on my last statement as well. From what I'm feeling he seems like he's just beginning with her. I pick up a bit of that from Callahan too, but as far as I'm concerned they can do whatever they want to her.

That fury-coated adrenaline does not flush my veins at the thought of my brothers playing with her. Even if we don't share blood by birth, we're as close as true brothers could get.

With a last thought telling Callahan to get out of my mind, he leaves dragging Darian with him. Sitting back in my chair I look over the girl. It doesn't make sense for her to be a vampyr or a blood demon since she burned in the sun. Unless it's possible or her to be a vampyr without the strand of DNA allowing her to walk in the sun. It could explain why her eyes are pink as well, her blood is weak.

With those attributes she could have been mistaken for a newly turned vampire. Especially if a true vampire did try to turn her as well. But that wouldn't explain why she let the enforcers and Mage Board believe that. Unless, of course, Asier was right and she is a spy.

So many questions for the little poison drop. I wonder if she's as deadly as she smells. After all, blue belladons are the one plant deadly to all. They taste divine, like the most holy fruit, but they can kill anything within seconds. If my mother hadn't been there when I was younger with a readied antidote I would have been dead within seconds.

The professor starts to wrap up the class and she looks

so content. Completely unbothered by the fact that she almost died. Even when the sun first hit her face, it almost looked like she was welcoming it. Instead of immediately cowering like any other vampire she basked in the light. She closed her eyes as if she was savoring the warmth before Ruleten threw his jacket over her and tackled her to the ground.

Speaking of, I need to go hunt him down for answers. As the society president for the Stone House and him swearing into the house as a member, he has no choice but to answer to me.

My first question will be what her blood tasted like.

What. The. Fuck.

The bells ring signaling the end of this class and the students begin standing to leave. I do the same, nearly jumping out of the chair and leaving through the back door instead of the main one she goes through. I need to find Ruleten now, and not because I need to know what her blood tastes like.

He should have lunch at this time. It's the same timeframe as his girlfriend has, I remember him gushing about the ordeal and how she'll be starting classes. The same girlfriend who's rooming with the girl and who he made a blood oath with. Of all the people I know, very few of them know how to properly do runic magic. Especially powerful enough runic magic for something as powerful as a blood oath.

I take the long way to the cafeteria so I know I'll miss the girl and cut through all the people like a knife in water. Even if I have to drag Ruleten to Asier so he can influence his empathic magic and make Ruleten tell the truth, I'm getting my answers.

The sneaky little brat didn't seemed fazed by Varian's magic even though she had to be. No one can resist empathic magic.

She said a devil raised her and was just like him, but even then no one compares to Varian's power. Yet she looked at his truth pulling magic and fucking smirked at him. I swear even I could hear his thoughts about wanting to throw her over his knee and spank her ass red.

I find Asher's green eyes right as he sits down on a bench. His girlfriend is right next to him and I don't see her across from him until I'm already beside their table. I can already hear the whispers and feel the glances as I peer down at the little vampire. The anomaly who is currently shoving roasted vegetables into her mouth.

And fucking all that is unholy, her damn perfume invades all my senses.

"You could at least chew," I drawl. I don't even process saying it. My head almost feels cloudy with her sweet scent and a throbbing ache in my fangs.

She whips her head up and focuses glaring pink eyes at me. Her cheeks are slightly puffed, full of food, and she slowly chews only once before swallowing. Undeniable proof Callahan and Asier were both correct about her being a brat. Not that I didn't believe them, but now it's directed at me.

"Wouldn't want you to choke, after all."

I still don't fully process what I'm saying. She really must bathe in that perfume to smell this strongly.

She snorts as she licks her lips and stabs a piece of carrot. I track the movement of her tongue before it slips back into her mouth and she widens her lips to stuff the carrot into her mouth. She chews it a few times before swallowing. Slow and deliberate, though there's a sudden shift in her energy. Despite it being weak, I can sense the subtle roil through it.

Stabbing a piece of broccoli now, she says, "Thanks for

your concern, but you don't have to worry. As I already told the Dean, I'll be more careful to minimize any accidents that could happen."

Despite the force that she stabs her vegetables her tone is almost meek. Completely at odds with her defiance and glaring eyes. Though after a moment her shoulders hitch in and she bends her head down to take her bite but keeps her head there.

I glance over at Ruleten's girlfriend and she also has a submissive form with her eyes glued to her lap. I wonder what must have changed from the infirmary to here to make both of these girls have defiance etched onto their skin bow.

Jullia – that's her name, Jullia Waterstone – had been spewing profanities at me with abandon for what I had done. Yet now she looks like she'd rather hide in a hole.

Good.

Ruleten better keep her in her place because the next time I won't be so lenient.

"House President," Ruleten cautiously murmurs, gaining my focus. "Was there something you needed?"

Peering over at her, I realize she's stopped eating. So much fire and blaze and it's all doused now.

"Yes," I clip. "You. I have house things I need to speak with you about. Now."

I turn and leave, giving Asher Ruleten no choice but to follow. Despite her not having enough power to do so, I do feel her eyes on my back. The little poison drop following me with her gaze.

It takes me ten minutes to get back to the Stone House manor. While there are dormitories for the students of Syngenia, there are also societies who have their own manors. There's Stone House, which I am president of, Blood House, Breath House, Bone House, and Wood House.

Blood and Wood are female run, with Stone, Breath, and Bone male run. My house being one of the strongest both in physical power, but also ability wise and of course, mental wise. Each house plays off of the five different races of witches. They nearly don't exist anymore, but they used to over a thousand years ago.

The War of Gods five thousand years ago was the beginning of their near extinction. One of the six beings of moral, they had been even more influential and powerful than the other five combined. It was even spoken about after the war to group them with the celestials. But that was a long time ago.

Walking into one of the smaller foyers, I wait for Ruleten. He's a decent enough male with powerful earth elemental magic and a type of healing magic you wouldn't assume a vampyr would have. He's never caused problems within the house and has actually helped more than once in the three years he's been here.

His cautious footsteps echo down the hall and I finally take a seat in one of the plush reading chairs before the fireplace. It's still too warm to have one lit, but sometimes the house does what it wants. Enchanted by powerful magic from when Syngenia was first created as a school.

"House President," he greets as he enters.

Then he waits just inside the doorway for me. I wave him in immediately and he goes to take a seat across from me.

"If this is about Jullia I want to – "

I hold up my hand and he shuts his mouth. "I'm sure you'll communicate efficiently what actions would be best for her regarding certain company in the future. This is not about her. It's about her roommate."

A tinge of anger spirals for a second before he hides it. I doubt anyone likes being told to put their woman on a leash, especially when Asher is so down bad for the mage, but I will not tolerate her actions a second time.

"You want to speak about Mavyn?" he asks, covering up that anger.

I nod. "I want you to tell me everything you know about her."

His muscles tense but nothing else.

"I don't know all that much."

"Tell me what you do know, then."

His slight hesitation makes me curious about what he's going to say. What secrets she's divulged to him.

"Well. . . I met her Friday when everyone was moving in. I wasn't supposed to be back until Sunday but Jullia told me her roommate for the year was going to be a newly turned vampire. First looking at her she looked horrible. Like someone who was half-starved and hadn't slept for weeks."

He clears his throat and adjusts his position in the chair.

"I told her I needed her to make a blood oath if she didn't want me dragging her into the sun. She didn't seem to care and agreed immediately. Just from that alone it didn't seem like she would have hurt Jullia even if she was provoked. She just looked exhausted. But we did the oath, I cemented it with the rune, and then she basically slept all weekend."

"What did it taste like?" He gives me a puzzled look so I spell it out for him. "Her blood. When you tasted it, what was it like?"

His face slightly pales and I'm sure he's remembering when the girl compared what happened to blood sharing. As a vampyr, he knows exactly what that means and the significance of it.

"It wasn't as disgusting as I imagined a vampire's blood to taste. It was stale, but not rotting. And I only had a drop of it. That I swear, Thorne."

I fucking knew it. The cunning little liar could never taste like the one thing better than anything else but is also the thing that will kill you.

Waving at him, I urge him to continue. Relaxing a bit more, he does.

"She really did sleep practically all weekend. Sometime during Saturday Jullia said she finally woke up to drink a bunch of water, but after that she fell back asleep for another twelve hours. She would wake up every so often for something. Sunday morning she woke up again to try some of the bagged blood, but she barely took a sip before she was done. Then she drank more water and passed out again. Jullia said she didn't wake up until late Sunday afternoon and even then she didn't say anything much.

"I walked them both this morning from their room to the cafeteria where everything had happened. Everything else I know is what she had stated in the infirmary. Oh, and when I was placing the rune on her to cement the blood oath I rolled her sleeves up and there had been scars covering her forearm. Most of them looked like burn scars, but there were a couple that could have been from knives and there was a scared bite mark too. A fanged bite mark. Aside from that it sounded like she's spent her whole life in New York City and in her later childhood years and up until she was turned she stayed with a succubus. And Jullia said she sometimes has nightmares."

I seem to keep a good enough handle on my composure

because Asher doesn't seem to register the fact that my blood is boiling. It shouldn't be, and yet the fact that she has someone else's fangs scarred into her flesh makes me want to rip the head off of whoever that mark belongs to.

Once again, the irrational feeling of wanting me, and only me or my brothers, to have a claim over her surfaces. I have to blame that damn perfume she wears. There's no other reason I should be feeling this possessive over a dirty tainted brat.

Standing, I nod to Ruleten. "Make sure she shows up to one of Stone House's parties this week."

I don't wait for him to acknowledge or agree, I simply leave. I need to go take a very long, very cold shower or go hit something. I should have training later, but I can't wait for that. Darian should be in the arena by now, I'll have him spare with me.

She's worked her way into my senses and imbedded claws into my mind. I'll need to drink her blood to also help right my mind. Proof that she does not taste as good as she smells. Then I'll have to make sure she never wears that damn perfume again.

I'll be back within my right of mind by the end of the week. For now I'll view this as a show of control and will power. Soon enough the little poison drop will mean nothing.

Six

Mavyn – August 12

"Come on," Jullia whines. "It'll be fine, I promise!"

This is the third night in a row, the millionth time today. One week down, a billion more to go. That's a sort of positive at least. That and the fact that nothing else has happened to me this week. It's been radio silent from the celestials and Professor Asier has more or less avoided me.

The only non-positive is all week Jullia has tried to get me to go to at least one party with her. The start of some sort of party binge or spirit week or whatever they want to call it started Tuesday night. Since we have a sort of block schedule Tuesday was the official end to day one of school. That means everyone celebrates.

It's also the start of initiations month. For the next thirty-four days, until the full moon next month, students will be sought out by the five *Houses*. Societies that are more or less like sororities and fraternities. Though it's dipping closer to cult than a girl or boyhood.

Scrolling through the advisory careers tab, I come to the bottom with no new openings. Sighing in defeat, I toss the thing onto my pillow and roll to my back to stare at the bland ceiling. Apparently no one is hiring. Which means no job, which means no money, which means I have nothing.

"You're forgetting," I finally answer Jullia, "I have nothing to wear, no means to buy food after all the drinking I know you're going to want to do, and no means to buy food tomorrow or Sunday to replenish all the nutrients I lost from drinking and puking all night."

She harrumphs and climbs onto her bed to pout. My excuse tonight is even more sound because the cafeteria only serves food during days we have classes. Meaning weekends I'll be left to dry. Not the worst predicament since I'm no longer receiving water mage blood bags, but blood only sustains me so much.

There's a soft knock on the door before it's opened and Asher walks in. He's dressed in dark jeans and a polo with sunglasses on even though the sun is about to set. He's also been encouraging about getting me to go.

"Asher!" Jullia jumps up from her bed and practically tackles him. "Help me convince Mavyn to go out with us. Didn't you say tonight is the start of all the real parties. The ones the societies will be throwing and those are legendary. Please tell my boring, introverted roommate that she should at least live a little and can borrow my clothes since she doesn't have to cover up with there being no sun?"

True, I don't have to cover up since the sun will already be set, but there's another problem with that situation anyway.

Dragging myself into a seated position, Jullia grins at me. Giving Asher a dry look, I say, "Close the door and turn around."

His eyes slightly widen as he doesn't hesitate to do so and Jullia squeals as I start unbuttoning my shirt. I'm still in my school issued white button up since I haven't changed into the pajama set Jullia has let me borrow yet and I have nothing else to wear.

Since it's a pair of pants and long sleeve, and I always change and shower when no one can see me, she hasn't seen my body.

Unbuttoning the last button I pull the shirt off me and watch in almost slow motion as Jullia's excited eyes dim and her whole demeanor shifts. Asher, with his back still to me but beside Jullia to see her expression, tenses his shoulders.

They saw only a piece of it a week ago when Asher had to put the rune on my arm.

All up and down my arms, my shoulders, across my chest, my stomach, and covering my back are scars. There's a flower, a dark blue bell-shaped flower that can kill every creature nearly immediately. It's a poison you need the antidote immediately after ingesting in order to survive. Though if done correctly you can ingrain it into weapons to weaken nonmortals and leave permanent scars.

I've been told I sometimes smell like that flower. Like a deadly poison. It's because remnants are trapped within my scar tissue. If diluted an insane amount it won't kill you, but that's another reason I get so easily tired. Poison lines the majority of my body, flowing through my veins, sucking my energy dry.

Jullia finally makes a move but it's to cover her mouth as a choked sob escapes her throat. Shit.

"Okay," Asher rushes out, "I'm sorry Mavyn but Jullia is staring at you like – "

His words don't even make it out as he had been grabbing for Jullia and already halfway turned. Olive green eyes track up my arms, over my chest, across my stomach. Modesty was a luxury I never got to learn, but at least I still have my bra on. And I know Asher's gaze isn't lust filled.

No. His eyes match Jullia's, minus the tears. Though his had shown more horror. Snaping his eyes away, Asher pulls Jullia into him but she refuses to look away from me.

"Oh Mavyn," she sobs. Grabbing for the long sleeve sleep shirt, I pull it on to cover the scars. "I saw the ones on your arm," she hiccups, "but I just thought. . . oh my goddesses I'm so sorry."

It may only have been a week, but Jullia feels like more than just a roommate. She reminds me of Cordellia and maybe it's just because I miss my home at the brothel, but I've let Jullia take me in just as the girls in New York did. She feels like a close friend I'd want to stay close with even after we graduate. She feels like how a best friend should feel like.

Sitting in the middle of my bed I pull my knees up and rest my chin on top of them.

"It happened a long time ago," I try to console. "It really isn't – "

"Those are torture scars," she hiccups harder. "Don't say it isn't bad or try to downplay it. Those were burns, and scars that had to be from other weapons. And those were bite marks,

Mavyn. Scared *bite marks* with fang imprints, at least a dozen of them. Don't try to say it doesn't matter."

She pushes out of Asher's hold and stomps over to me. Crawling onto my bed she sits right beside me and wraps her arms around me. Warmth envelopes but it doesn't burn and a solid pressure of comfort wraps around me.

Asher watches us with an expression of disbelief, though I'm sure that's more because of my scars.

"It happened a long time ago," I repeat. Quieter and more detached. I can feel Jullia silently sobbing. Even as she holds me tighter. "I don't even remember most of it. Except sometimes. . . "

"The nightmares," Asher murmurs in understanding. I was positive Jullia had told him. Especially after the third time when I had woken her up because of them.

Yes. Those damn nightmares. They didn't start until after the devil and mage who first adopted me had already died. Another remanent making it impossible for me to forget about those seven years in hell.

I blink and Asher somehow disappears from the room. Jullia continues to hold me with tears I can feel dampening the sleep shirt. I wonder how someone could have so much love in their heart, could be such an empath that their heart hurts for someone they've just met.

I blink again and we end up laying on my bed. Even though she's slightly taller than me and definitely has a few more pounds of muscle, her head is tucked underneath my chin with her arms still wrapped around my middle.

There's a reason I don't like showing anyone my scars. Initial expressions are usually horror or disgust. Then pity and sorrow tend to work their way through. Ms. Elaycia had nearly had a heart attack the first time she saw them. Cordellia did too.

Then they cried like Jullia is doing. I didn't know succubi could cry, but Ms. Elaycia did and then she took me under her wing and the last five years she's been more like a mother than any of the other woman who've taken me in before.

God, I miss her. I miss her and Cordellia and Nana in the kitchen and Rosemary with her big sister vibes and Ana who never leaves the attic. I miss our Sunday brunches when the club is closed all day and the night markets we used to go to and family dinner.

That's what the club was. Even if it does hide a brothel behind legal affairs it felt more like a home than anywhere else I've ever been. Ms. Elaycia would make some of the other girls hug me a lot too. She said physical contact was essential, not just as a sexual need but as a humane one.

Both the six beings of moral and the celestials need physical contact. It's ingrained in our biology, whether certain races want to admit it or not.

I wrap my arms around Jullia as she continues to cry. I don't know who's comforting who at this point, but either way it feels nice. I wasn't lying to Jullia when I said all this happened a long time ago. But even Ms. Elaycia would brush that off. She would tell me some scars linger even after they've healed and faded.

These scars, my scars, will never fade. Even the bite marks. That's another cursed thing that damn devil did to me. In addition to powdered blue belladon that was imbedded into the weapons he used, he was able to somehow add them into his fangs.

I can't die from the wounds since they were never fatal, but with the poison they'll never fade either. They ache sometimes too. I wish I was back in my room where I had my herbs and tonics and creams. Nana would always help me make a salve to ease the ache of my scars. Help neutralize the poison for a time.

I really do miss them. I hope Ms. Elaycia is okay.

Eventually, Jullia falls asleep. Asher doesn't come back to the room and I curl her body closer to mine. Using our body heat to keep each other warm and soon enough my eyes are drooping. I know I have homework to finish, I still need to look for a job, but it feels so much like home does. So I pretend, and I sleep.

. . .

I hadn't felt when Jullia got out of bed or heard when Asher came in. Since Jullia had helped me hang up a blackout curtain over my window the only light is from Jullia's window on her side of the room or her lamps.

When I woke up it had been dark, but I'm sure I hadn't slept for all night and day. Until the door opens and in walks my roommate and her sister.

"Oh! You're up, I'm sorry did we wake you?"

Stretching out my body I groan at the feeling and then roll over to sit at the edge of the bed. I'm still wearing my school skirt and stockings.

"Why is it so dark?" I ask. My voice groggy and still heavy with sleep. My eyes start to get used to the dark until Jullia turns on one of her warm toned lamps. It illuminates the room enough as Hanna inches in. On the ceiling over Jullia's window is a twin sheet blocking out the light. "What time is it?"

Jullia turns on another lamp that has me blinking and rubbing my eyes to adjust to the light as she throws a bunch of bags onto her bed. Hanna also has a couple bags and sets them down beside the foot of Jullia's bed.

"About two in the afternoon, are you hungry?" Jullia asks.

Rubbing my eyes, I stand up and tense every muscle to keep from swaying. I need some water. Water and food and a shower. Jullia pulls out boxes and walks over to me. It looks like some kind of ToGo container and when she opens it the aroma of miso, chicken, rice, and vegetables fills the room.

My stomach actually growls. Sat in their little compartments is a bowl of soup with noodles and chicken, a section of fried rice, and a whole section of steamed vegetables.

Jullia also holds up a spoon and fork in her other hand and gives me a sheepish smile. "You always ask for extra veggies so I figured I'd get you some, but you also need carbs and protein, and you had said earlier you loved noodles so here."

My stomach grumbles again and I catch Hanna giving me a perplexing look.

"You really do need normal food. . . "

Jullia glances back at her sister but doesn't say anything as she places the steaming food on my desk.

"Eat," she orders. "I know you need it and then I need you to have a bag of blood because you haven't drank any since Monday. Then we're going to set up a projector and watch romcoms and eat trash all night."

Hanna pulls out a little camcorder looking device and sets it on Jullia's desk. I'm still standing by my bed watching the both of them. Jullia ends up giving me a stern look and gestures towards the food cooling on my desk.

Despite the fact that I'm sure Jullia paid for this with

her own money, and I can't pay her back right now, I sit and eat. Nana would give me the same look and stern talking to. Reminding me that while a lot of people are manipulative and selfish, there are still a lot who do kindnesses out of the goodness of their heart.

I pull out my chair and sit. Grabbing the spoon to stir the noodle soup that smells amazing. I doubt Jullia will make me pay her back for the meal, but I'll do it anyways. Or I'll repay her back with something else.

Jullia watches me take the first bite before she turns to start fussing with her movie night props. It doesn't sound like a bad plan, though I wonder how comfortable Hanna would be here. She's gotten more relaxed around me, though she still seems very wary.

Shrugging it off I start downing the rest of the food. The soup is perfectly flavored and the chicken is juicy. Plus, the rice, broccoli, carrots, cauliflower – I've always had a love for vegetables.

When I'm finished I pack it all up and set it at the corner of my desk to throw away later. Jullia and Hanna already have our movie night set up. A projector positioned in the blank space over the door with microwave popcorn and other snacks ready. They've also set up drinks and few wine bottles without any labels.

"Oh, that's Hanna's friends special blend," Jullia explains. "He makes all kinds of spirits, though these ones are sweeter and he uses the faeries method so you don't taste the alcohol."

Hanna makes a face at her sisters. "Way to just blurt that all out, Jules."

"Oh please, half the staff goes to him too. You said so yourself."

The sisters roll their eyes at each other but there's no malicious intent with their actions. I'm guessing it's just a sibling thing.

Hanna turns to me with a hesitant expression. "I'm sorry. . . about my actions before. Jullia is a lot more welcoming than I am, but we've been told our whole lives that you can't trust vampires. We're not exactly taught a lot about them except that they were once human and even after finding control they always have a bloodlust."

That is very mature of her. Most people would have just pretended like it never happened and moved on.

I nod. "Growing up I wasn't taught much about them either. There is a woman at the brothel who did tell me a bit about them though. We all called her Nana, she basically said the same thing, so I don't fault you for it. Though if I did have bloodlust I would say shoving your bloody hand in my face was stupid. Newly turned vampires are faster and stronger than even old vampyr, so Asher wouldn't have been able to stop me before I ripped out your neck."

Her face goes slightly pale and I wave it off.

"That's just some other facts. But I don't have bloodlust and would need to be drained of a lot of blood or starved for a very long time to initiate it."

Jullia hums and then asks, "So then why do you not have bloodlust? Why also can you eat food and sleep? That still confuses me."

I shrug. I could tell them the truth. I can't say I necessarily trust either of them, not that it matters that much anyways, but I'm sure if word got out the Mage Board would spin it to make it seem like I played them to get a free education. Syngenia is not cheap.

Even if they didn't listen to me about my case and shut down everything before I could get a word out. But it would probably be best not to risk that.

"The Mage Board was just as confused, but it saved me from being burned alive. I just need both regular food and blood to survive."

They both give me curious gazes. Their minds working on trying to figure out why I'm different to other vampires. Hopefully it'll just be that I'm different, not that I'm not a vampire. Or any other reasons.

Jullia throws a thick blanket on the floor between our beds. Then she lays down a few more blankets and pillows. Hanna unfolds her own blankets she must have brought. I'm honestly a little surprised she's not out partying.

"No parties tonight?" I ask. Jullia winces and Hanna side eyes her.

"Yes," Hanna almost grits. A bit softer she says to me, "Last night was the first night all the society houses threw their parties. The society houses are big here. Practically everyone wants a chance to join one of the houses and being in one of the houses is golden."

"Are you in a house?" I ask. I think Jullia mentioned Asher was in one but I wasn't fully paying attention. I remember him calling the demon house president though.

Hanna shakes her head. "I was in Wood House my first and second year, but I left this year because the president was going to start making us do blood oaths. You made a simple one to Asher, but most people can't make them because they don't have the power or runic magic for it, and they're special. It's not like blood sharing, Thorne had been right when he told you that in the infirmary, but you do still share blood and that in itself is a special thing."

She quirks a brow at me and even Jullia is glancing at me as she fluffs a pillow that's already been fluffed.

"What's with the frown?" Hanna asks me. I right my face to neutral and shrug. "Don't try to dismiss it, blood sharing in any form is like a sacred right it's – "

"Not that important," I interrupt.

"Yes it – "

"No," I snap. Silencing Hanna and making Jullia freeze. I close my eyes and try to take a breath. I also pull my nails out of my palms, not realizing I had been slowly embedding them. "It's not that important," I slowly repeat. Much quieter though more strained.

When I open my eyes I catch Jullia staring at my arms. She looks sad again and stands up straight to look me in the face.

"Mavyn. . . "

I release a breath through my nose and let my shoulders drop. Trying to release all the strain in my body.

"It's just something I don't like talking about. Okay?"

Both of them nod. And before either of them can say something someone knocks on the door. Hanna goes over to unlock and open the door. Jullia gives me a sympathetic look, one I appreciate but one I wish she didn't have to give me.

We both turn to see who's at the door and it feels like a slow motion movie as Hanna opens the door all the way and Asher comes stumbling in. Stumbling, because his face looks like it was bashed in, there are cuts along his jaw and neck, he has an arm wrapped around his middle, and his other one looks odd. Like his shoulder and elbow are not right.

Jullia screams and Asher winces as Hanna grabs his side to help him. I stay rooted to where I am because his blood is flooding the room with that earthy and electric scent. I'm not close to a bloodlust and even if I was I would still have some semblance of control, but it's not just his blood.

Jullia seems to snap out of it because she rushes to his other side and helps him to her bed where he falls and groans. So much blood, too much blood. His and another's mixed in.

"What happened?" Jullia sobs. Her cries echoing in the small space as her hands skim over his body. "Who did this to you!?"

Hanna glances as me as I slowly approach. She worries her bottom lip between her teeth as I come to stand behind Jullia. Asher is still groaning in between trying to console his girlfriend. I doubt he's accomplishing what he thinks he is.

Pulling the longer of my four necklaces out of the collar of my shirt I finger the chain until I find the charm I'm looking for. Unscrewing the bottom from the main chain, I pull the small vial containing a bit of powder.

Bending down so I'm eye level with Jullia I grab her chin and face her to me. Her face is just as red and blotchy as it was when she saw my scars. Tears running tracks down her cheeks as her hands stay gripping to Asher's.

"He's going to be fine, Jullia."

I enunciate each word so she will clearly understand them but she frowns anyway.

"How can you say that when he looks – "

"Because," I interrupt. "I'm going to help him. At the brothel I was more or less an apothecary. I can speed up his healing."

She sniffs and backs away to let me have better access to him. So trusting with her eyes begging me to help him. Even though he'll probably be fine, though it may take days longer for him to heal when it should only take moments.

Scooting closer to the bed I wait till Asher's eyes are on me.

"Who's blood is mixed in?" He shakes his head but I scoff at the action. "I don't care who hit you, I'm sure Jullia will make you tell her later. I need to know because whoever's blood that is is slowing your body's healing rate."

He cracks his lips open and croaks, "I'll be fine."

Jullia gasps behind me but I wave my hand at her to be quiet. Fine. I don't actually need to know who's blood it is. I'm mainly curious as to who's it could be. To be able to use it to control an aspect of someone else. Plus, it smells like divinity. I wish I could taste it.

Raising up on my knees I hold out the small vile. "This is rucksile." His eyes widen at that and I understand why. "If you drink this with my blood it'll neutralize whoever's blood is in your system and help regulate your body's normal healing." Glancing over at Jullia I ask, "Can he drink some of my blood? I won't drink any of his. Or would you prefer he drink from you? He still needs at least a mouthful of mine but then – "

"It's fine," Jullia rushes out. Flinging her hands at me. "Just help him, please. He should have already been healed by now and he looks like he's still bleeding."

Turning back to Asher, I ask, "Are you okay with drinking from me?"

He makes a gurgled sound and I wonder if part of his jaw is broken or if it's the cuts on his throat. Either way, I take that as confirmation and bring my wrist up to my mouth. Pulling my sleeve back I feel eyes on the scars peeking out but I don't pay that any mind as I drag my wrist under one of my fangs.

The prick barely registers and the scent of my blood mixes with Asher's and whoever else's is there. Lifting the vile over Asher's mouth he opens and I pour the powder in. His face twists but I hold my wrist over and let the trail of blood fall into his mouth.

He groans in the back of his throat as I watch him swallow. Then he swallows again, and again, until the trail turns into a light drip and Asher is able to move his arms. Faster than a blink of an eye his hands wrap around my wrist and his fangs are embedded half in my wrist, half in my palm.

The first pull he takes is strong. I can feel every drop of blood flying through my veins and into his mouth. My heart stays steady as I stay calm. He hasn't released any venom from his fangs into me and I appreciate that. Most beings who have fangs and drink blood have a poison within them. It acts as both an aphrodisiac and a way to kill their prey. It's why blood sharing tends to be so personal.

But I'm surprised Asher has enough control himself to be able to control it. When they're younger, those with fangs can't control the production of their venom and often times it'll leak out of their teeth. As you get older you learn to gain control of it, but even then there are sometimes when you can't. Like when you're extremely wounded or on the verge of bloodlust.

The three of us watch as his wounds start stitching themselves up. The bones of his right arm – the one that hadn't looked right – shift and crack. It must have been broken in some way. And lighter, we hear them throughout his ribs too.

Turning to look at Jullia her face is nearly white. Eyes wide as she watches Asher's body right itself.

He takes another pull and then releases my arm. There's still blood over his face, but at least all the wounds are closed. With both of my hands free I re-screw the vial back onto my chain. There are a few more, all differently shaped holding other little powders and tonics.

Sitting up, Asher doesn't groan this time and flexes and stretches out his arms.

"Thank you." His voice rough and coarse.

Jullia steps back up and points a finger in his face. "Who the fuck did that to you, Asher Rowsan Ruleten? I swear to the goddesses I will strangle you right here right now if you do not give me a name and a reason for why the fuck you look like this."

He winces and looks away from her. Though his eyes do glance at me before snapping away.

Standing up, I back away from him and try to distance myself from the blood still on his face. An irrational urge to lick it off his face crosses my mind but I am not a dog and I am not going to hit that kind of low.

"There are only three ways for someone to control someone else through their blood," I announce. Asher winces again as Jullia and Hanna look at me. "The first way is if you're a blood witch. That was one of their specialties. The second is if a being has that particular blood art. With that, only the high fae, vampyr, some devils, and blood demons are able to be born with that kind of magic. The last is if a blood tie is cemented between someone who can already use that particular blood art."

Jullia whips her head back to Asher. "Thorne's a blood demon. He wanted to talk to you Monday. You said it was house stuff, but you also had a meeting with him this morning."

Asher sighs and then gives me a pained look. Hunching his back he lets his face fall into his hands and rests his elbows onto his knees.

"I'm so sorry, Mavyn," he sighs.

For some reason I felt like after everything that had happened Monday this week was going by too smoothly. Still, I had wished.

Seven

Mavyn – August 12

Lifting his head back up the look Asher gives me is almost pitiful.

"Truly, Mavyn, I'm so, so sorry," he nearly. . . pleads? Begs? Though I wouldn't know what he's begging for. Maybe for me to forgive him? "I'm bound in Stone House and Thorne is president of it. Unless I go through the full process of leaving whatever Thorne says goes."

A slip of panic works its way through my system. Combined with the lack of blood in my veins it's not a very good combination.

"What did he say?" I murmur.

Wiping his hand down his face, he looks at the floor. "Monday when he called me he said he just wanted to know about you. He wanted me to tell him everything I knew."

My heartbeat spikes but I don't move from my position and wait. I need to wait.

"I didn't have a choice," he pleas. "I told him everything I knew about you, which wasn't a lot to begin with. Most of it was what you had already outed in the infirmary. I told him how you slept all last weekend and about the blood oath. He had asked what your blood tasted like and I swear Mavyn, I told him it wasn't good."

Both Jullia and Hanna stay quiet, though the former looks cataclysmic and the latter is bouncing her eyes back and forth between me and Asher with curiosity and slight suspicion.

"I had to tell him the truth for everything else, but that was one thing I didn't tell him about. I said it didn't taste as bad as I thought a vampire's would, but it was still stale."

Hanna's eyes slightly widen as she stares at me and Jullia shakes her head with frustration.

"Okay," she huffs. "First of all, why does Thorne care so much? With that you also need to tell us what happened today. And second, why would you lie about what Mavyn's blood tastes like? Why does it matter?"

Did I not just agree with myself about trying to keep my secrets secret? What a fucking bitch of a situation. Maybe the universe hates me.

But. . . at least my anxiety goes down. The panic that was reverberating in my chest subsides and I let out a long breath I didn't realize I had been holding.

"She's not a vampire," Asher answers. To which I give the best performance of my life by giving him my most confused look accompanied by a 'huh'.

Asher blinks at me as he sits up and stares at me. Surprised and confused at my reaction.

"What? No!" God this better be convincing. "The devil who scarred me used weapons with blue belladon. That's why I still have clear scars even now. The poison is embedded in the scar tissue and over the years has slowly seeped into my blood. I'm immune to the one thing that will kill anything."

Turning my face to the ceiling I close my eyes and sigh. All that I'm saying is all technically not a lie. That is the reason my blood tastes good and I smell like the flower. Even if I could be turned into a vampire I would never have that rotting scent or taste.

"I'm more immune to blue belladon than what should be possible. And because the flower has been said to taste like the best thing you could ever taste, I don't want others who drink blood to go seeking it."

Asher's confusion evens out as he nods. "That's why it helped neutralize Thorne's blood and help heal me. If you mix a small enough concentrate with rucksile it becomes like a super healing tonic."

I nod. "The deadliest poison known to all, and yet you can make a lot of healing remedies with it if you know what you're doing."

Jullia holds out her hands as she shakes her head. "Okay, okay, okay. That explains that, but why did Thorne want to know about it and why did he beat you to within an inch of your life, Asher?"

He rubs his face again. "The last thing he told me

Monday was to get Mavyn to go to at least one of the parties. I don't know why or what he wants but since last night was the first party he threw I guess he expected you to be there." He looks up at me. "When we didn't show he held a meeting today to which he asked me why you weren't there. I told him I didn't think you would be attending and suggested he just leave you alone. This is the aftermath of that."

Jullia's face falls as she goes to sit on the bed with him. He wraps his arms around her as her shoulders start shaking.

Staring off into an empty space, I cross my arms and think. I'm guessing he still doesn't believe I'm a vampire. With all the proof he and the other celestials have been trying to seek, plus my unusual behavior – and I'm sure being a blood demon Thorne can scent my blood and the sweetness to it – it makes sense. What doesn't make sense is why they care. Aside from Thorne wanting to drink my blood, it shouldn't matter.

"Thank you, Asher." I tilt my head at him. "I would prefer if no one knew about my blood. Not just because people would want to drink it, but because I don't care to tell them how I happened to become this way."

He nods and then Hanna steps in.

"Is that why you need to sleep and eat, even for being a vampire? Did the poison change your biology, even after you were turned?"

Good. I wasn't sure if this excuse would work, but it seems being the only known person alive with the one thing that does kill all in her veins I guess I can make my own stuff up. Even if I'm not technically lying.

"I'm assuming. Even before I tended to need a lot of sleep and I would eat a lot of food. My guess is that it takes a lot of energy from my body to keep the poison from eating me alive. It's why I eat a lot of nutrient rich foods."

They also taste good, but I don't specify that.

"It hasn't been so extensive the last couple years, either I've been able to manage it better or my body has adapted to it. That's the only anomaly I could think of that would make a newly turned vampire need food and sleep and not have a bloodlust."

Hanna squints at me. "Makes sense, but you're saying you've *never* had a bloodlust? Even right after turning?"

If I was going to be honest I would say I've only once gone into a bloodlust, but that was long before I had supposedly turned into a vampire. Which means I can't say that.

"I was hungry afterward, but not in a bloodlust hungry. Actually," I add, "they had put me in a cell for a couple days before an advisor for the Mage Board came out to see me. He cut his wrist and even then, after not having any blood and not being given regular food, I didn't so much as twitch at the scent."

Both Hanna and Asher give me perplexing expressions. I'm sure Jullia would be too but her face is still buried in Asher's chest.

"But anyways," I stare straight at Asher, "thank you for keeping that secret from Thorne. And I'm sorry he beat you up because of it."

He shrugs it off and finally Jullia straightens out of his hold.

"But," she interjects, "what do we do now?"

All four of us stay silent. True. With Thorne still having a suspicion and with his beating to Asher I doubt he'll just drop it. I wonder if I threaten him with Nana he'll stop. She's not much when you first look at her, and she's had over a thousand years to control and hide her magical energy and aura. And as a bone witch she has power greater than most beings.

Actually, that might not be a bad plan.

"What?" Jullia blurts. I look at her looking straight at me. "What are you thinking?"

A slow grin curls on my lips as I continue thinking about it. Not that I would have any way to pull through with my threat, but maybe announcing it is enough. Especially if I use her blood I have stored in one of my vials.

"I think we should go to his party tonight." All three of them look at me like I've grown three heads. "What's a blood demon most afraid of?"

Now all three of them look like I'm crazy. It only makes me smile more.

"Uhh, something that can kill them?" Hanna tries.

I shrug. "More or less, yeah sure. I guess I should have said who. My point though, a blood demon is only as powerful as their blood and body is. Take away one of those and they're crippled. What is the one race known for controlling bodies?"

Asher laughs in disbelief. "You're insane. How are we going to find a bone witch willing to help us? Witches are more or less extinct now." At least I didn't have to spell that out. I guess Nana was right about that being a universal truth after all.

Taking off another charm from my necklace – this one a long thin vile – I unscrew the lid and let the scent waft into the air. Nana had said it was a precaution, just in case I needed an additional threat I could back it up.

Asher's eyes widen at that and Jullia stares at it with questions. Of course she would, not all races can scent things the way others can.

"This is the blood of a bone witch. Nana, she works in

the kitchen at the brothel." I screw the lid back on and chain it back to my necklace. "So, we go to the party and if Thorne tries anything again I threaten to sick who has always been like a grandmother to me on him."

The three of them continue watching me like I'm not real.

"What kind of fucking place were you living at before you came here?"

I just laugh at Hanna. "I told you. A brothel. Well, actually it's a strip club in New York, but behind closed doors it's a brothel. It's home."

I miss it. But no time for reminiscing. Jullia agrees with my plan and Hanna goes along with it because she says she was going to be hanging out with us anyway. Asher looks nervous about it but doesn't go against it.

Jullia kicks Asher out for now as the three of us get ready. Jullia pulls dresses and tops from her wardrobe for the three of us to wear as Hanna gets out Jullia's makeup kit.

"Pants and a long sleeve," I state. Jullia doesn't question it as she hands me a pair of skinny jeans and a tight fitting ribbed turtleneck. I've reasoned with myself that I don't have to feel guilty for borrowing Jullia's clothes tonight because I'm hopefully getting Thorne off my back as well as Asher's. I don't need anyone else getting hurt because of me.

I lay the pants and shirt on my bed as I start stripping. There's a tiny gasp behind me and as I turn I just now remember that Hanna is still in the room and she hadn't seen any of my scars before.

She's standing in the middle of the room holding what looks like a sparkly lilac dress but it almost slips through her fingers as she stares at me.

Fuck.

Is it bad I hope she's not like Jullia?

"You kept talking about scars. . . "

Her words trail off as her eyes continue to trace over my body. I watch them eye the teeth marks and the ones from knives. Since my back is facing her she'll be able to see the ones from whips and other things I can't always remember. That devil had been cleaver with his punishments. And his little mage fated never cared enough to stop his atrocities.

Pulling Jullia's shirt over my head I begin pulling down my skirt and stockings. "There's more on my legs," I call out. "Just to give you a heads up."

Neither of them say anything as I straighten in just the shirt and underwear and lay my skirt and stockings on the bed. Then I grab the pants and shove a leg in. They're not quite as tight as I'm sure they would be on Jullia. She has slightly bigger muscles than I do.

At least I can wear my heeled biker boots with this outfit. They had been what I was wearing when I had been "turned". I wish I had the rest of my clothes and shoes. Jullia had mentioned a family's day, I wonder if Ms. Elaycia would be able to come visit. Or if I could visit them?

Sitting on my bed to put on my shoes, I finally face the two girls and both of them are awkwardly quiet. Hanna is already changed and pulling out makeup with Jullia still rummaging through her closet.

Sighing, I rub my eyes with my thumb and fingers. "Okay," I announce, getting both of their attentions. "I know it's a touchy subject, I know it might be difficult or you feel weird about it, but they're just scars."

Jullia's face wobbles and Hanna looks guilty.

"It's awkward, I know, the girls at the brothel had the same reactions. It was a really bad point in my life. But the devil is dead and not even a witch was able to get rid of the scars. You can ask questions if you want, you won't hurt my feelings and I will tell you if I don't want to answer something so you won't push boundaries. I don't talk about the bite marks, and don't touch me unless there's a barrier of clothing or something between us. I would also prefer if you didn't tell anyone either."

Jullia throws a piece of clothing onto her bed and comes towards me. Sitting down beside me, she wraps her arms around me like she did last night.

"I'm sorry. About what happened to you and about being awkward about it." She pulls back and gives me a watery smile, though no tears spill over her cheeks this time. "Thank you for telling me."

I give her a small smile as Hanna asks, "When did you get them?"

Jullia makes a noise and growls at her sister. "You cannot just ask that Hanna!"

"She said we can ask questions," she argues. Jullia scoffs and shakes her head. It makes me feel better.

"It's fine." I wave Jullia off and she winces before going to her side to change. "I was found on the side of a trail when I was about three months old in upstate New York on Earth. The devil and mage adopted me when I was three. He didn't start beating me till I was almost five. I remember because the day I turned five was the first time he left a wound that would scar."

Jullia turns to face the wall but I had seen her face paling. Hanna also hunches in on herself but tries to keep a neutral face.

"I lived with them for seven years, and a week before I

turned ten they both died. They both had heart attacks was what I heard, though I didn't know devils could have heart attacks. After that I went into the foster system and honestly that was its own hell. I ran away when I was thirteen and met Ms. Elaycia the day I turned fourteen. And despite her being a succubus and living in a brothel, it was home, and they are my family."

Jullia smiles at that and Hanna nods, accepting the answer. Turning back to her makeup, Hanna begins with whatever she's starting on. Jullia skips over now with a smile and urges me over.

"Come on, this is the best part."

"You sound like Cordellia," I mumble. Jullia quirks a brow but I pull my chair over and sit next to Hanna.

Me and Jullia watch as Hanna carefully uses brushes and spungs to sweep and glide the products onto her skin. Not that she really needs it, but the girls at the brothel always got onto me about rolling my eyes at makeup.

They always said they needed a controlled base for everything else. Sometimes they would practice on me or dress me up for fun when it was a slower work day. I didn't hate it, it often felt calming when they would brush over my face. Like when they would play with my hair.

That was the best part about having older girls acting like big sisters. We were always dressing up and having tea parties.

Hanna doesn't do much, not like the girls at the house, but she still looks more. . . more. She and Jullia have that natural dye-eyed beauty, but she just looks even more gorgeous. With her curly hair she's left loose and framing her face. She has it shorter than Jullia's, the curls ending right on top of her shoulders.

Jullia begins on her makeup and I inch back as Hanna looks at me. She smiles at me and I inch back more because it looks entirely too malicious for my liking.

"Your turn."

It sounds like a threat.

"Actually – "

"Nope," Hanna interrupts, popping the p in the word. "I am glamorizing you because that outfit really isn't doing much. At least we get to see your waist, which I am jealous of, but this will be my repentance for being a bitch you."

I. . . oh fucking hell.

Sighing in defeat, I scoot my chair closer and it earns a triumphant smile from both of them.

Pulling out more product, Hanna turns her chair so she can face me and takes my chin in her hand.

"What was it like living in a brothel?" she asks me.

"Just like this," I answer dryly, though truthfully. But it makes me smile, and then Hanna scolds me saying not to move too much. "Yeah, just like this. Ms. Elaycia said I could work under Nana in the kitchen. On the outside it is a strip club, but upstairs and behind the stage and private rooms are more exclusive rooms hidden by a barrier.

"Not all the girls who were there are for hire like that. Most of the regular strippers are human and don't even know about it. Only the for hire girls live in the apartments behind and above the club. Ms. Elaycia owns the whole building. And we're all basically one big family."

Hanna finishes brushing product around my face and starts focusing on specific places. She doesn't tell me to stop talking so I don't. I like talking about home.

"Ms. Elaycia is like the mom, Nana is like an old grandmother who pretends to hate everyone but would kill for any of us, and Rosemary has been there the longest and acts like a big sister to everyone. She's actually a goblin and attended Syngenia with Ms. Elaycia. She showed me her true form once and for all the humans would know they'd have thought she was some elven princess."

I purse my lips to keep from smiling wide at that. Despite what humans think goblins are not short little green monsters who are mean and cruel. Those are gremlins. Goblins, while some have different colored skin and they do have long sharply pointed ears, look almost ethereal. Like war gods and goddesses.

Defined and sculpted muscles and bodies but celestial features. I can see why most wear enchanted amulets or apparel to make them look more humanly, even here at Syngenia.

Hanna hums as she blends some more and then begins working on my eyelids.

"Then there's Ana who stays in the attic. She's like me, an orphan Ms. Elaycia took in. She's a panther shifter and doesn't do well around other people, especially males, so Ms. Elaycia let her turn the attic into her own private tower. I would spend a lot of lazy afternoons up there with her reading or painting. She loves concocting new flavors for things – cakes, teas, syrups. I always got first try.

"Cordellia would get second. Jullia reminds me a lot of her. Cordellia is a half-waterway shifter. She can shift her legs into a tail and webbing attaches from her arms to her sides so when her arms are extended she almost looks like a manta ray, but her chest, back, and face stay the same. She told me before that instead of waterway shifters her and her ancestors used to be called Le'af's. It was the name of the overall race for sirens, mermaids, and most waterway shifters, but she said no one really knows about that name."

Jullia hums and asks, "Is that why you have so much information about things that aren't common? I had meant to ask before after our first Magic History class. You knew that Syngenia was first used as a name for the first blood witch and her daughter."

Hanna stills the brush dusting over my eyelid. "That's old knowledge," she hesitantly adds. "Not even the professors are able to openly teach that unless a student explicitly asks. Most things before the War of Gods aren't commonly known and I think the Mage Board does that on purpose. There's a reason there aren't any humans or vampires on the council, and why there isn't a witch seat anymore."

Jullia hums again. "Yeah, even Professor Asier was surprised you knew that, Mavyn. Did your bone witch teach you that?"

I slightly shake my head and Hanna grumbles at me.

"No, Nana has taught me a lot and she is older than this university, but she didn't tell me that. That fact. . . " I hesitate for a moment as I remember it.

Sometimes if a vampyr is powerful enough and the human they're turning has a strong enough mind, some memories from the vampyr can transfer over. It's not common, but it does happen and it's rare enough that not too many people know about it. I guess I could also blame the poison if anything.

"I think the vampire who shoved the blood and venom into me wanted me to attend this school." Hanna fully pulls the brush away and I open my eyes to look at them. "He kept repeating the word *syngenia* as he did everything and afterward I started knowing things. The Mage Board didn't think I would pass the exam, and I shouldn't have been able to."

They both stare at me and for a moment I worry I shouldn't be telling them this. I'm not outing my secret, and I still have that knowledge so the Mage Board can't really do anything about it, but there is always a chance they could just say I cheated.

Dropping my shoulders, I decide I don't care if either of them want to report me. I doubt they will, but I won't be surprised if they do.

"I'm far from dumb, but my knowledge doesn't really extend to linear algebra or astrophysics. A day or so after I ingested the blood I also seemed to have gained, whoever the vampyr is, his or her text book knowledge. I don't know who they are or have received any memories from them, but I have their education. Syngenia being the name of the first blood witch and her daughter was one of them."

I shrug and discretely pick at my fingers.

"All the rest of the knowledge seemed common enough for the school so I figured that answer would have been obvious."

Both sisters make the exact same face at the exact same time. Slightly tilting their heads while peering at me as I know their minds are working.

"You are quite the paradox," Jullia hums. Hanna's face says she agrees but she doesn't say anything as she lifts her brush back up and I close my eyes letting her finish.

It takes Hanna about thirty minutes to finish with my face and when she's done it feels just as heavy as it always does when I have makeup on. Like there's a skin tight mask over my face.

She looks happy enough though as she marvels at her work. "Those boys are going to die when they see you like this and you threaten to sick your bone witch grandmother on them."

Jullia marvels at my face too and smirks at Hanna's words.

"Oh, this is going to be so much fun."

Eight

Castiel – August 12

Of all the forms I can shift into, it's always the smaller ones that annoy me the most. Only because it takes immensely more concentration and power to transform my body.

Larger animals and creatures – no problem. But the second I need to shift into something smaller than a wolf expect a five minute delay and my grouchy ass.

Varian will be getting the brunt of it. This was his favor asked, and I am even more annoyed because it was the first thing he said to me after being gone for a decade.

I was expecting a banquet, frilly flowers, food and wine,

my favorite devil, and catching up on all the same bullshit of the last ten years. Instead, I find my friend of over two centuries grumbling and snapping about the Mage Board and bloodsuckers and there's not even a hug before he asks me to go spy on someone.

Slithering around the corner of the dorm house, I pause beneath overgrown grass and watch as four people make their way out. Three females and a male. Two water mages, a vampyr, and what is supposed to be a vampire.

There's no way this is her.

The vampire the Mage Board allowed into the school after passing an exam not even I can pass one hundred percent. Who is able to somehow eat regular food and needs sleep but doesn't have bloodlust despite being turned into a vampire two months ago.

I can scent each of the students. Vampires smell like rot. Like decay, as something that was dead should be, but her. . . she smells like an impossibility.

Maybe Varian is right and she's a spy. She could be a vampyr or a blood demon, since she needs blood just as much as regular food. Though Varian did say when she was exposed to sunlight she did burn.

I wonder if Thorne has already tried her blood. I haven't been able to speak to him or Darian yet as I came here right after seeing Varian, but I will need to. Because she does not smell like a vampire.

Following after them, I stick to the taller patches of grass along the walkway and shift my scales to blend in better. I'm sure they're headed to one of many parties being thrown. It's a Syngenia tradition. It's been happening for as long as I can remember, both as a former professor and former student.

Not that she specifically looks like she's going to a party. Her friends do. The water mages dressed in short dresses and the vampyr in relaxed clothing. Even with it still being warm, she's wearing pants and a turtle necked long sleeve.

I wasn't able to see her face when she walked out, but the attire does not scream party. At least not for Syngenia's standards. But I have been gone for a decade, maybe something has changed.

All of a sudden, she stops. Her long hair that reaches her hips dyed with highlights of dark blue and soft pink swaying with the motion. I stop too, waiting along the edge of the walkway and coiling my body together to keep from being seen.

It must not help because she turns around and looks directly at me. And fucking gods, Varian did not tell me how pretty she is.

No. Pretty isn't even a good enough description. She's. . . otherworldly. Captivating, ethereal, magnetic.

Pale pink eyes lock on my golden serpentine ones. Since I had been on the edge of the walkway I had changed my body to a grayish white color to match the stones with ripples of faded green to mimic the shadows from the grass blades.

I wonder how she was able to tell I was here. I don't give off any energy or aura when I'm shifted as a regular animal, and I'm too small for instincts to feel a threat lurking by.

Her lips part as she kneels down and peers at me. Those pink eyes are framed by black eyeliner and long lashes. There's a rosy hue over the bridge of her nose and cheeks with a light dusting of freckles. Those lips that had parted are painted a cool toned red and they shift into a soft smile.

"Well, hello there," her coos. She extends her hand out slowly and cocks her head.

Her friends are looking at her like she's crazy.

"Uh, Mavyn," the one with longer curly white hair calls. Varian did tell me that was her name. Mavyn Tsuki. "I don't know if you know this but snakes in Syngenia tend to be venomous. It would probably be best to leave it alone."

She hums but doesn't pull her hand back. Inching forward, I watch each micro expression she makes.

"You forget, Jullia," she calls softly, "I have literal poison running in my veins. A little venom won't hurt me."

Her friend looks like she doesn't believe her, but intrigue and curiosity peak as I slither up to her. Stopping right before her hand, I lift my head up and rest in a position cobras tend to be in right before they strike.

I wonder what she means by that. Poison running through her veins. Does she mean the vampire's venom? If so she would have said venom, not poison, and even then she also said my venom wouldn't hurt her anyways.

She relaxes more as I nudge my nose to her fingers. Flicking my tongue out, I taste her skin and blue belladon explodes in my senses. A flower that can kill even the highest celestials.

Arching over her hand, I begin curling up around her arm. My body gliding easily over the material of her shirt, though I would prefer to have skin on skin contact. I want more of that taste, of that poison that kills all but tastes like magic.

Once the entirety of my foot long body is around her wrist and forearm, she cradles me and stands. Turning back to her friends – all of whom are watching her like she's crazy – she chuckles at them.

"Like when an extract of blue belladon is mixed with rucksile to act as a super healing tonic, extracts of straight blue belladon act as taming and calming aromas for some reptiles and arachnids. I had a pet viper at the brothel."

A brothel?

Had she been working there before she was turned? If she had been turned? I still don't understand how she can smell this good and be a vampire.

The vampyr nods. "I remember reading that in my text books when we were learning about poisons and venoms last year. Though it would still be best to put it down and leave it here. Just because blue belladon can calm snakes doesn't mean they won't bite. And Jullia's right, this isn't Earth. Snake's here have stronger venoms."

She takes her other hand and strokes a finger over my head. Her friend who spoke first speaks again.

"There are also snake shifters, Mavyn. For all we know that could be a. . . yuh know. . ." She makes bug eyes at Mavyn and does a gesture with her hands. ". . . Thorne's lacky."

She chuckles again as she raises her arm so my face is level with hers. Her pinky eyes look a little bit more vivid now.

"The smallest any shifter can shift to is a regular house cat," she states. "Unless it's a child, any adult who tries to will either break their body or mutilate it so badly that they can't shift back. Ana told me that once, and Nana backed it up. It's not possible for shifters to shift this small."

She pulls her arm back down and starts walking.

"And what if it's not a shifter?" her friend asks. "There is someone I've heard of who can shift into animals as small as bugs."

The other water mage scoffs. "Please, Jullia. Castiel D'etre hasn't been seen in like. . . ten years. Why would he come back just to spy on Mavyn? I highly doubt Thorne or even the Mage Board cares enough about Mavyn's poisoned blood and all her anomalies to get him to come spy on her."

The girl, Jullia, grunts. "I'm just saying it's a possibility. Thorne is already acting like a psychopath about all of this."

"Actually," the vampyr interjects, "Darian would be more like the psychopath. Thorne is cold and calculated, but he's not as apathic as Darian."

"That's the angel?" Mavyn asks. She's still stroking my head and her warmth has me curling tighter around her.

"Yes," the vampyr answer. "He's also the Breath House president, but he'll be at Stone House tonight. I haven't seen or spoken to any of them since this morning but both Darian and Callahan were at Stone House last night so I assume they'll be there again. Hopefully nothing actually happens."

"You think your bone witch's blood will be enough?" the water mage asks. And shock vibrates through me at that. There's only five witches I know of who still exist on Miy, and I know there's a couple on Earth, but for a vampire who's only recently been turned to know one. . . ?

"It should be. Nana said blood demons would run from bone witches, even if they were on the same side. It's an instinctual fear passed down for thousands of years." She shrugs. "If he doesn't care then I'll threaten his morality. Instinct can be overruled, but you can't go against your spirit and soul."

The vampyr hums. "I forgot about that. Blood demons can't drink the blood of anyone who says no and can't coerce them after either."

"Yup. Though that doesn't stop the other celestials from trying or simply taking my blood and offering it to Thorne before I can say no, so hopefully Nana's blood will do the trick."

How very curious. She doesn't sound like a spy, but she definitely does have secrets.

"Well," Jullia says a bit more cheerily, "then I guess let's hope for the best. And Mavyn, you are not bringing that snake back into the dorm room. It may not bite you, but I'm not going to risk it not biting me."

Mavyn sighs and peers down at me with a sad expression. "Just for tonight then. I don't have any means of getting you food either. Maybe if you feel up to it you can bite Thorne for me."

Someone snickers but she only curls those red lips at me and what I would give to not be in this form but still wrapped around her.

"We're here," the vampyr calls. And then her scent shifts. It gets a shade stronger.

A shade more deadly.

Nine

Darian – August 12

My father had warned me a vampire would be attending Syngenia this year, though I wouldn't know why he cared to. Neither of us care about vampires and he isn't a councilmen. The only reason he does know is because his best friend and old schoolmate is.

It's the only reason we all know Callahan despite him being younger than me and Thorne. And it's perfect that this is his first year at Syngenia with the vampire. Though I thought vampires were meant to smell like death. She smells too sweet for death, though I can't pick up exact scents.

I do, however, pick up exactly when she walks into Stone House.

Weaving between people, I sip my drink and exit the kitchen being used as a bar to enter the hall that leads to the grand foyer where the main party is and the front door. Keeping to the shadows of the hall, I walk down and peer around the corner where the front is.

Here comes trouble. All five foot five of herself. Too bad I don't have fangs, or they'd be sunk deep in her neck right now.

Despite her not showing a bit of skin, her shirt is pulled tight showing every little dip and curve. Perky little tits, a waist I'd be able to wrap my hands fully around, an ass that would perfectly cup my –

"Don't."

I don't take my eyes off her as I grin at Callahan. The little pup has grown fond of her. We all know it.

"And what is it I should not be doing, Armani?" I taunt.

I can feel his heated glare on the side of my head. Despite being two inches taller than the devil, Callahan ranks a decimal point higher in power than me. And I've seen his training with Varian. He's not as brutal as Thorne or I am, but he is just as calculated.

"Leave her alone until Thorne is done with her," he mutters, though not meekly.

"Thorne isn't the boss of me, devil."

I can feel his frustration but he doesn't say anything to that. He's technically a decimal point higher than Thorne too. Being a devil has its perks, even as a young one.

"D'etre is on her somewhere. I can feel him"

I hum and scan her backside as her and her friends walk deeper into the house. He's probably shifted as some sort of small animal wrapped around her. Lucky bastard. I didn't even know he was back.

Leaving Callahan, I follow after her. Entering the throng of drunk people where the majority of the party is. Flashing lasers and strobe lights the only illumination. For most races the dark isn't that much of a problem, but most of the races here are smashed. As the little troublemaker will be soon enough. Thorne wanted me to make sure of that.

I track her as she weaves in with her friends. They're the same three who were with her in the infirmary. The two mages and the vampyr. Though that vampyr should still be bedridden. I had watched Thorne beat him into near oblivion this morning. He infected him with his blood which should have made it so it would have taken weeks for him to fully recover.

Yet here he is, not a scratch on him.

Thorne won't be pleased with that. I grin at that. The blood demon likes to play boss.

Though I guess it doesn't much matter now since she's here. Right into the pit of vipers.

They push through the crowd towards where the serving hatch is that is currently acting as a bar. There's a line but the vampyr pushes through. As a member of Stone House he gets first pick over everyone else.

He greets one of the bartenders for the night and gets served four drinks. The other three he hands to the girls and I watch as little miss trouble takes a sip. While her friend who had been screaming at Thorne earlier this week winces and coughs, the girl simply raises a brow at her while slowly sipping.

I know damn well Thorne told the guys not to be stingy

with the drinks, so the mage's reaction is valid. Even her sister makes a face, but trouble drinks it like ninety percent of it shouldn't be burning down your throat.

I sip my own drink and revel in the burn. If she didn't react to the drink then that would lead one to assume she's drank strong stuff before. Meaning getting her traditionally drunk could pose as a problem. I took precautions anyway.

They start heading towards another room that isn't as hectic as the first. The lights are still dimmed though more people are sitting and conversing or straight up making out. I wouldn't mind joining, maybe with a certain rosy eyed troublemaker.

My dick jumps as I imagine her kneeled before me. Rosy eyes watering, cheeks flushed, red lips stretched over –

"Don't get distracted."

Holy fuck, can a guy not just finish one damn –

"Darian," Thorn snaps. Interrupting my thought again. I think I'm about to pummel my best friend. "I can't have her saying no to me, I need to taste her blood."

I growl at him. "Don't get your fucking panties in a twist. I'm watching her, I got it."

"Really?" He raises a brow at me before glancing down. "Because it looks to me like you're getting distracted."

I roll my eyes. "If it makes you happy I'll get her drunk enough before I fuck her. To make it easier you can just be in the room and bite here when my dick is shoved down her throat. She won't be able to say no then."

He doesn't say anything for a moment and turns to watch her. I watch the moment he locks his eyes on Ruleten and I grin as his eyes narrow at him. I'm sure he was expecting the vampyr to be bedridden for at least a week. No one can withstand the power of a blood demons blood.

"I don't care how you do it, just do it."

Then he walks away and I start moving towards them. Ruleten sees me first and nudges his girlfriend. Her back is to me and instead of being discreet or cautious she whips around and levels a glare I'm sure most people wouldn't want thrown their way.

The scent of salt needles my nose, but the closer I get to them the more of that sweet scent from Trouble I get. Despite having to see when her friend whipped around, little miss trouble keeps her back to me. Her hips sway slightly to the bass as she sips her drink. The colors in her hair glinting every so often under the lights.

"Vampire," I purr when I'm right behind her. The mage and vampyr don't do anything but glare at me. I catch a flash of light gray scales and golden serpent eyes peak out of her hair. So Castiel is on her, but she has to know about it.

Without glancing at me, she states, "Angel." Then takes a sip of her drink. Most of it is already gone.

Castiel slides along her head and over her ear. Dipping down to arch under her jaw. She raises her hand and strokes a finger down his belly side.

"You do know that's a ghost viper, *Trouble*. Their venom paralyzes its victims and causes nerve damage at best, and with your size you'd be lucky to just die immediately." She continues stroking Castiel and I bet the fucking demigod is just basking in the attention. Taking a step closer so I'm now just a hairs breath away, I lean down to murmur in her ear, "And that would just be a – "

She cocks her head before I can finish my statement,

turns making her shoulder brush my chest before placing her palm over my heart, and then she shoves me. And she shoves me fucking hard.

I skid back several feet. Those that weren't shoving their tongues down someone else's throat stop what they're doing to stare. Most of them gawking, but I can't focus on that because this little five foot nothing actually pushed me away. And she did it with a move that seemed like it had no power.

Thorne said she barely had any power to her. Her energy barely a flicker and her aura was even less than.

"Don't fucking touch me."

Her words low and cold. Eyes tracing over me and hardening. There's a shift in her and her eyes flicker for a moment before she turns back around and sips her drink. No one moves. No one speaks. No one even breathes.

Before she can finish swallowing her drink I have my hand wrapped around the back of her neck and another fanning over her stomach, pinning her back to my chest and twisting her head so her face is in front of mine.

"Don't tell me what I can and can't fucking touch, trouble." My lips murmuring the words over the top of hers. A ghost of a touch and fuck that sweetness explodes in my senses. Sweet and a hint of floral. My hands tighten around her. It tastes like a drug I know I'll never get over. "Fucking trouble."

Her eyes flare with an expression I'm all too familiar with and it would make me excited but instead of fighting she freezes. The panic and fear that had been consuming those rosy eyes turns dull as her entire body stills. She doesn't necessarily tense, but her body does brace.

"Sun devil," she mutters, barely a breath.

I drop her and step back. Her body crumbles to the floor

for not even a second before she jumps up and backs away from me. Dead eyes flaring back to life as she looks at me like I'm something she's about to eviscerate.

Normally I would be turned on by it, that flash of fear right before I fuck them past their limit, but there's something different about hers. And calling me a devil when she knows I'm an angel rubs me wrong. I could have been born a devil since my father is one, but I took after my mother's genetics and I won't let someone scorn them.

"That's a bullshit nickname, trouble," I grumble. The cup she had been drinking from is now on the floor and both her hands are fisted. I wonder if she would try to kill me. She apparently has the strength to try. I forgot newly turned vampires are faster and stronger than they appear. But that is usually accompanied by bloodlust – which she has proven she doesn't have.

"You touch me again and I'll rip your throat out." Violent, dangerous, *deadly*. She sounds like she means it.

I can feel him before he even steps into the room. His aura is stronger now, I'm sure everyone can feel it.

"I'd be careful who you threaten," Thorne's cold voice drawls. "And in who's house you do it in."

The music has stopped and more people crowd in the doorways to watch the spectacle. They don't fully enter, not wanting to be in the crossfires, but no one can resist a good show.

Rosy eyes snap behind me. "Keep a leash on your winged bitch then."

If there was someone still breathing before, they certainly aren't now. Little troublemaker is about to be in an unholy amount of even more trouble.

I smirk as Thorne slowly stalks towards her. He's still in his school uniform, though his blazer is gone and the sleeves of his white shirt are rolled up with the top few buttons undone. So much controlled fury roiling with his aura as his red eyes stay locked with rosy ones.

Thorne stops about three feet from her and slips his hands into his pants pockets. I cross my own arms and lean against the back of a couch as I watch the show with everyone else.

"As far as I'm concerned," Thorne rumbles, "the only one needing a leash is you. Probably a muzzle too."

Rolling out her shoulders she simply crosses her arms and smirks at him. The girl's got balls at least. Standing up to a blood demon, and she had done the same to Varian too. . . so it makes me wonder why she froze with me.

"You come near me with a muzzle and I'll peel the skin off your bones."

She says it the same way when she threatened me. Like she could actually pull through with her threat.

Thorne tisks. "Did I not just say where and who you threaten?" In a blink Thorne is before her with a hand wrapped around her neck. In another blink he has her back against a wall and his fangs an inch from her neck.

Then something I wouldn't have thought would happen does. A small blade soars through the air slicing Thorne's shoulder and nicking the top of the girl's.

Thorne's head whips towards who threw it, and who knew, the little water mage has balls too. And clearly a death wish. Then Thorne lets go of Trouble and pulls the knife that embedded itself into the wall. There's a sweet aura around the knife, the scent almost exactly like Trouble's.

"Where the *fuck* did you get a weapon made from blue belladon?" he growls. Blood staining his white shirt and the temperature in the room drops as Thorne says that name. The name of the one thing that can kill all no matter what you are.

The water mage disregards Thorne as she peers down at Trouble.

"Are you okay, Mavyn?" she calls. Staying near her vampyr boyfriend who's wrapped protectively behind her. He looks like he's about to faint.

Trouble coughs and rubs at her throat but pushes off the wall to stand up. Thorne turns down to Trouble and grips her shirt to look closer at the small wound. Though that doesn't matter, if the knife was made with blue belladon they're both dead.

"You realized you just killed us both," he snarls, pointing the end of the blade at the water mage. "You will be put to death for this."

Trouble scoffs as she shoves Thorne's hand away. "Don't be so dramatic, demon. We'll live."

She grabs one of the necklaces I've seen her wear before. It's a thicker chain with charms around it. Most of them looking like little vials or compartments. She unclips one of them as Thorne looks like he's mixed between panicking and reveling. He's said before that to experience blue belladon is like nothing else. Its taste will make you crave nothing else but it for the rest of your life.

She unscrews the tiny lid and a waft of aura so powerful we all scent it. Blood that has magic exceeding far beyond what I could ever do.

She feigns surprise as she smirks at Thorne. "Whoops. Wrong one, wouldn't want to waste Nana's precious bone witch blood." Thorne goes so pale as he stares at her. She keeps eye contact as she screws the cap back on and hooks it back. Then she grabs another vile and unhooks that. "Here we go. The antidote to blue belladon."

Tilting her head, she watches Thorne carefully as she takes a step towards him. He looks like he's about to pass out. I know the poison acts fast, faster than what should be possible.

Extending her hand, she says, "Here. Don't choke."

His hands shake as he takes the vile and straightens his face. Replacing his bored expression even as his body trembles.

"This isn't enough for both of us," he grits.

She shrugs and he waits another second before emptying the antidote into his mouth. I watch as her eyes track his throat when he swallows. Her pupils just barely expand but she blinks a few times before extending her hand again.

Thorne hands the vile back and she screws and locks it back onto her necklace. I wonder what the other little containers hold. More antidotes for things, or maybe poisons?

But that doesn't matter because she's about to be dead from that poison. The knife did cut her, I can see her blood bleeding onto the shoulder of her shirt.

"You don't seem to care that you're about to die," Thorne drawls. Back to his regular composed self. Just as the poison acts quickly, the antidote does as well.

She shrugs again and gives him a dry look. "Why do you care? Don't you believe your life would be better if I, a little ol' vampire – who by the way couldn't care less about you and only wants to finish these five years so she can go back home to her regular life – was dead?"

The seconds tick by and even I hold my breath waiting

for the moment she'll just drop dead. A bit of a shame. Thorne doesn't respond to her and seems to be waiting too. She arches a brow at him, glancing at me for a second, before spinning away towards her friends.

"Asher, is there any food in this house? I'm starving now."

Her roommate relaxes a bit before taking a step towards her but before the vampyr can answer Thorne is behind her with his hand wrapped around the back of her neck. Pulling her towards him, he points the knife still in his hand at the mage.

"How are you not dead?" She groans in frustration be he just yanks her head back. It makes my dick jump. "No one is immune to blue belladon. I can smell the poison coursing through your veins. You should be dead by now."

His fangs elongate as he dips his head closer to her still bleeding shoulder. She makes a small noise and elbows him while grabbing his extended arm and spinning him to face her. With how strong I know Thorne is the move shouldn't have actually moved him, but her technique and power somehow does.

"I do not consent to you drinking my blood," she states, the words making a breath of a ripple in the air. They hit Thorne like the shove she gave me did and something in the air rumbles. "Clearly your instincts are shit, are your morals?"

Thorne clenches his jaw as he straightens to his full height and looks down at her.

"Why aren't you dead right now?" he asks in a deadly calm.

She groans again and rolls her eyes. *Fuck.* The little troublemaker needs to stop doing that. Callahan glances at me as I discreetly adjust myself. While I'd love to take her to one of the empty rooms and see what other little noise she can make, I am more interested in figuring out why she isn't dead right now.

Taking both of her hands she rubs at her face and then glares at Thorne. It would be fucking sexy if I also wasn't concerned about what it means that she isn't dead yet.

"Maybe I'm just stronger – "

"Answer the fucking question, Mavyn."

She jolts when he says her name. He says it like a possession and I wonder if she could hear that. Her eyes shift around the room and for the first time I realize that it's been cleared out but for us and Trouble's friends.

Callahan leans against a wall and has a sound barrier up around us. His eyes are glued to Trouble and the white threaded through his gold color are lit.

"This is so over-fucking-dramatic," she mumbles under her breath. Louder, she says, "The blue belladon in that blade is a weak, diluted powder. I was exposed to it when I was younger so small diluted doses like that don't have much of an effect on me. Though now I will be needing a lot of blood to help dilute the poison further until it's out of my system."

Thorne's eyes flick down to her arm. "Roll up your sleeves."

She makes a confused expression but when Thorne steps towards her she jumps back. Concern mixed with fear replaces the confusion and she crosses her arms as if that could stop a blood demon.

"Roll up your fucking sleeves – "

"I don't fucking have – " she interrupts.

"*Mavyn –* "

"*Thorne*," she snaps back and Thorne lets out a frustrated breath.

"Do you always have to be so fucking stubborn? How were you exposed to such small concentrates of blue belladon that you didn't die right away being so young?" She scoffs and turns her head away. "Unholy gods can – "

"What do you fucking want from me?" she shouts. "What? Just say it point blank. You want me dead? Get in fucking line. You want to know if I'm actually a vampire? What more proof do you need! God you paranoid motherfuckers. Yes! I have scars on my forearms made from weapons embedded with blue belladon. I had a bitch of a life. That's how I'm not dead right now. What else? What fucking else do you want from me?"

She heaves and the pink in her eyes has deepened to almost a shade of red. I think this is the best fucking show of my life. All that's missing is for another heated spat before they're clawing all over each other. Maybe then Thorne could taste her blood and I'd lick up the mess.

Glancing over at Callahan I almost pity the devil. He's too soft for his little crush. His muscles strained like he's holding back from going over there and comforting the vampire.

Hmm. I could see it.

Thorne with his fangs in her neck and her head thrown back. Callahan would be behind her holding her up. He'd skim his own fangs over the other side of her neck as his hands were soft and gentle, tracing every line of her body. And I'd be on my knees before her. One of her legs draped over my shoulder as I finally figured out if she tastes as sweet as she smells.

Callahan chokes and all eyes glance at him as he looks up with wide eyes at me. I smirk at him as I fill that image of all of us with my lust and he glares at me.

If you don't want to see it stop looking.

Put up some damned shields then, he snickers, but I can feel his lust too. The devil would like that scenario very much if it ever happened.

I wonder if Varian and Castiel would like that too.

They would.

And I full on grin as I look back to Trouble. She looks exhausted as she glares at us.

"I'm going to need blood or I'm going to pass out in a little bit," she grumbles. "I'd appreciate you telling me what else you want from me so I can answer and then leave."

Thorne cocks his head and then turns to her friends. "Leave."

Her roommate mage straightens and looks like she's about to argue when Thorne releases a wave of raw magic. The vampyr grabs the mage and pushes her behind him as he faces Thorne, readying his own magic as the room charges with power.

"I do not appreciate your defiance, Ruleten. Leave so I can speak with the vampire myself. On my soul I will not drink her blood and she will be returned to you. . . alive and well."

The vampyr looks over at Trouble but she looks like she really is about to pass out.

"Fucking hell," she mutters. "Fine. It's fine, just get me some blood."

Her roommate makes a noise but the other mage pulls her as the vampyr dips his head and they exit the room and sound barrier. All that's left are the vampire, Castiel still wrapped in his serpent body around her, Thorne, Callahan, and myself.

"Blood," she demands, though weakly. She sways slightly and rubs at her forehead.

"Callahan," Thorne orders without looking away from her. Callahan heeds and strolls up to them. "Here's your blood."

She looks confused as her eyes move to Callahan. Though they shift slowly and now her eyes are a paler shade of pink, lighter than they were before.

"I'm not drinking a devils blood," she breathes. "Get me a bag, I'm sure you have some."

She sways again and Callahan takes a step towards her. When Thorne doesn't hold him back he grabs Trouble's arm and she sways into him. He wraps his arms around her right before her legs give out.

Sweat starts to line her forehead and I wonder if maybe she was wrong and maybe she is dying. What a waste that would be.

Callahan puts an arm around her back and slips his other behind her knees before lifting her up bridal style. She doesn't fight and my interest in this show is now waning. It's getting boring now.

"You said you need blood," Thorne lowly drawls. "Callahan consents, it'll be better than whatever you would drink from a bag."

Her head lolls to the crook of Callahan's neck as her hand opens the collar of his shirt more to expose his neck and shoulder. We all watch as her tongue peaks out and drags along Callahan's collarbone.

Nevermind. This is interesting.

Callahan visibly stiffens though his face doesn't crack. I'm sure he's all kinds of turned on by his little crush licking him. Too bad he's too much of a lover boy to do anything about it in this moment.

Cocking my head I track the movement of her little pink tongue licking the devil again. I'm almost jealous. Then her jaw clenches and she huffs.

"Devil," she slurs. "No."

Thorne huffs under his breath and then turns to me. "Then drink Darian's. He's not a devil."

There's a whimpered sound that comes from the back of her throat and for some reason it makes me fist my hands. She curls smaller into Callahan's arms and barely shakes her head.

"Sun devil." She makes that whimpering sound again. "Don't wanna burn."

"I am not a fucking devil," I growl. She had called me that before too when she was frozen in terror. I like them scared, but not when it prevents them from running. And she braced, she didn't fucking run.

She whines and I shove off the couch. This is boring now. She won't drink my blood, she won't drink Callahan's, I'm out of here. The night's still young and I need a good hard fuck after the troublemaker has basically given me blue balls.

Thankfully the party is still thrumming with life. No way am I wasting it.

Ten

Thorne – August 12

What a fucking brat. I'm half tempted to just tell Callahan to drop her and leave her here for the night. But even as I think about trying to do that, my body won't let me. Something about the situation keeps nagging me.

Maybe it's just because she saved my life. She could have easily taken the antidote instead of giving it to me. Even if she doesn't die from it, this isn't much better. With how she looks she's closer to going into a bloodlust and most would rather just die.

Callahan is glaring at me as I watch her. She's panting

now, her fangs gleaming in the low lighting and sweat drips down her brow. D'etre slithers into view as he slides down Callahan's leg and begins to shift. In this state I doubt the vampire will notice. Her eyes are squeezed shut anyway.

It takes him a couple minutes before a naked demigod stands between us. He runs a hand through his golden-brown hair and blows out a breath.

Uncaring that he's naked, he turns to me. "No way is she a spy. She's got secrets, that's for sure, but she wasn't sent from the Mage Board."

Castiel D'etre. The original spymaster himself. Over two hundred years old, a full shifter demigod – making him the only shifter who can shift into any animal, creature, or beast – and now professor at Syngenia University.

"Thorne," Callahan growls. "She's going to go into bloodlust soon."

Fuck.

Looking at D'etre I nod to the vampire. "She's not sticking her rotten fangs anywhere in me."

He rolls his eyes before turning around to face Callahan. An artwork of intricate symbols and runes cover his entire back. All painted in gold, depicting him as a demigod. Proving his holy blood.

Callahan shifts untrusting eyes to D'etre. Of all of us he's the only one who hasn't met D'etre. For the last decade he's been off wherever doing whatever. I had barely gotten to know him before he left, but Asier has told me stories about them.

"The only bloodsucker who's ever bitten me was Varian," he muses. Then walking towards them he says, "Don't worry devil boy, I'm just lending my blood to the little vampire so she doesn't go into bloodlust and kill us all."

"So over-fucking-dramatic," she mumbles. D'etre chuckles at it but Callahan continues glaring at him.

"At least put some fucking pants on. Vampires can't turn anyone but they still have venom in their fangs."

Glancing back at me, D'etre raises a brow but I only stare at them. Shaking his head the demigod disappears leaving only a few light wisps of smoke before reappearing with a pair of slacks on.

"Happy, devil boy?" Callahan almost snarls but the vampire whimpers again and he has no choice but to yield.

D'etre takes her quickly and then heads to the couch. Her hands are already latching onto his neck as her nose traces up his chest.

"Gods," she mumbles.

D'etre chuckles as he sits in one of the reading chairs and positions her with her knees on either side of his hips. "Not quite, poison flower." She hums as her tongue replaces her nose and D'etre's hands tighten on her hips. "Fucking gods."

She hums as she digs her nails into his shoulders and opens her mouth wider to reveal her fangs. But before she pricks D'etre's skin she tenses. Her body vibrating with tension as she pulls back and lays her forehead in the crook of his neck.

She whimpers again and I swear to all that is holy if she does it again I'm snapping her neck.

"You – you don't h-have to," she stutters out. Her voice cracking as her body continues to shake.

D'etre widens his eyes as he looks over at me. Out of the corner of my eye I see Callahan with the same expression pointed at her. That should be impossible. She's too newly turned and too close to a bloodlust to still stop when the points of her fangs were a hairs breath from a *demigods* blood.

Taking one of his hands, D'etre runs his fingers through the hair at the nape of her neck and pulls her head back. Tilting her head, he positions her back as she was with her fangs nearly touching his neck.

"I consent, poison flower," he murmurs. "I give my blood freely."

She hesitates for a second longer before slowly sinking her pearly fangs into the crook where his neck meets his shoulder. For some reason I hold my breath as I watch her take her first pull of his blood. And then her body relaxes into him and she groans.

Callahan doesn't hesitate as he storms out of the room and down a hall. D'etre removes his hand from her head and places it back on her hip as he gets more comfortable in the chair. I can see the exact moment her venom begins to affect him but he keeps her sat above his dick and keeps his hands firmly on her hips.

"You gonna babysit me all night?" he calls. His pupils have swallowed up the entirety of his eye making the color a true black. Despite being a holy demigod, his eyes are a shade lighter than true darkness.

"I'm going to make sure she doesn't suck you dry," I state, to which he chuckles.

"If you're so jealous about it why didn't you offer up your blood?"

The corner of my lip pulls up as I round the couch and sit adjacent to them. "I am not jealous, and no one ever drinks my blood."

He clicks his tongue as she shifts in the chair. "I forgot. Blood demons with their morals and souls and blood sharing.

You know it's not the same. You wouldn't be drinking her blood. . . " His eyes spark as he trails off. If only he'd be discreet about it. "Ah, but you want to."

"I do not."

He chuckles again. "I don't blame you. I've also tasted blue belladon before, and she's dripping in it. I'm almost envious you have fangs and I don't. I wonder if her blood would taste as sweet."

Ripping her mouth away from him, two trails of blood drip down her chin. There's a sneer on her face as she glares at him.

"Try to lick even a drop of my blood and I'll rip your heart out before shoving it down your throat," she threatens, and it sounds like she means it.

Pushing at his chest, she shoves off him and stumbles before righting herself on her own two feet. Using the back of her hand she wipes her mouth, smearing her lipstick, and backs away from both of us. She doesn't look as bad as she did before, but she still looks unsteady.

Shaking her head, her body tightens and she straights her back to glare at us.

"I said a fucking blood bag," she grits.

"And I gave you one."

She growls. Actually fucking growls. "For someone who's all high and mighty about blood sharing you sure don't give a shit about anyone else's morals on it."

"To be fair," D'etre interjects, "I – "

"Was not speaking to you," she snaps. Silencing the demigod but I can feel his blood rushing south. "Now tell me, high and mighty demon, what else do you want from me?"

Her pink colored eyes stare hard at me. Her smeared lipstick makes me want to storm over to her, shove her down to her knees, and smear it all up and down on something else. But that thought has to just be a remanent from when Callahan had said he'd let her drink from him and Darian's lust was still floating in Callahan's mind.

She rolls her eyes when I don't answer five seconds after she asked her question. "If you're still so fucking conflicted about who and what I am then by all means drag me outside when the sun comes up. I am too fucking tired for this shit. Just when things were going so fucking good fate wants to be a bitch. God, can I not just get a damn break?"

She rubs at her face and now her makeup is blotchy and smeared everywhere. Mascara running down her cheeks and smokey shadow rubbed all over her lids and under eyes. She looks a bit unhinged as she rants.

"I know," she huffs, "I'm sure everyone gives the same fucking excuse but it's not like I chose this! If I could be in New York away from all of you I fucking would. I never wanted to go to this damn school, I never wanted to meet any of you, I did not want any of this! Okay!? So just pretend I don't exist and I promise I'll stay as far as I possibly can from you."

D'etre is glancing between us but with a stone expression and she is burning with a begging. It looks wrong on her. Begging. After everything that has happened. . . her maneuvering me, her confidence, her fire.

It's like when she had been all head-on stares, rolling eyes, smirks in the infirmary and then hunched shoulders and submissive in a weak way in the cafeteria early this week. Like when I watched her brace in front of Darian when she had handled him fine enough a second before.

Once again, having no patience, she drops her shoulders and sighs. "Please." And hearing that word makes me want to rip out her tongue so she's unable to ever say it again. "Just pretend I don't exist."

Wrong.

That's all my mind is telling me about this situation. Why is she so willing to beg? I'm sure she could figure out a way to demand it of me. My instincts are not shit and that scent of bone witch blood did still me. I have no doubt she can pull through with whatever threats she makes, so if she were to do so again I would relent.

So why isn't she?

Why is she begging?

It's grating on my nerves.

"You didn't drink enough blood to be satisfied."

She gives me a blank stare. "No," she huffs, exhausted. Maybe she's too tired to fight. "I drank just enough so I won't pass out while walking back to my dorm. I have blood bags there that will help a bit more and then I'll probably sleep all weekend."

"Why wouldn't you drink from Callahan or Darian?"

"I won't drink from devils."

D'etre frowns as she peers at her. I cross a leg over my knee. "Darian isn't a devil."

"Well he looks like one," she tries to snap but there's no power behind her words.

"Why don't you drink from devils?"

I don't know why I'm prolonging the conversation. D'etre said she's not a spy, she can't be anything other than a vampire, and now I know why her scent is so sweet. I should be done with her. Let her scram back to her dorm and do as she says, pretend she doesn't exist.

She sighs and pulls the edge of her sleeve up an inch. The point of a scar from some sort of blade peaks through and right next to it is a scarred bite mark. It makes my blood rush and I can feel D'etre's blood boiling. Obviously neither of us like the fact that she's marked, though we don't show it and I don't know why I care. I have no claim over her.

She lifts her arm up as if I can't already clearly see it. "The devil who adopted me had a thing for my wrists. So much so that it left a clear scar, and because he was able to embed blue belladon into his fangs like they do to weapons, the poison is trapped in the scar tissue. He would try to make me drink his blood."

She pulls her sleeve back down and gives me a deadened expression. She doesn't seem to notice I'm about to punch a hole in the wall. Maybe it's a good thing Callahan left because I'm sure he wouldn't be able to hold it together as well as I am. Not even D'etre is fully holding it together because his demigod aura is fuming.

"Am I freaking done now?"

Taking a slow, deep breath, I ask my last question for now. "Did that devil give you the other scars?"

She glances down at her forearms and grows even more somber. "They were my distraction when he would feed. He always kept a small knife embedded with blue belladon on his waist. I was too small and could never stab him so I did the next best thing."

Her heart stays steady, her scent doesn't spike, there's no indication she's lied to me. She hasn't *lied* at all. Meaning a devil has marked her and the untouchable poison for all flows through her veins. A diluted enough concentrate that someone could drink from her, taste that poison, and not die.

I'm glad Callahan cleared everyone out when he did. No one needs to know about her blood or they'll be after her for the taste. And *fuck*, she's invoked my morals so unless she takes them back I'll never taste her.

"You can leave now," I announce and she doesn't miss a beat shooting straight for the door.

She does pause before the hallway entrance to glance back. Pale pink eyes looking at D'etre with something similar to guilt or regret.

"Thank you," she murmurs. "For letting me feed from you. Even though I would have been fine, I. . . owe you."

D'etre nods stiffly at her and then she's gone. Apparently she has a moral code of her own. No wonder she didn't want to feed from anyone.

Without a word D'etre gets up and leaves too. I'm sure he'll be heading over to Asier to inform him on everything if Callahan hasn't already. At least we're finished with all that. Asier can relax knowing the Mage Board isn't yet retaliating on him and by extension us.

The night has just begun and it already feels too long. I think I'll just skip the parading, I have too much shit to do tomorrow anyway.

Eleven

Mavyn – August 15

I did what I told Thorne I would do. I walked in a daze back to my dorm room where Jullia, Asher, and Hanna were waiting. I drank every blood bag in my storage, gave a rundown – I think – to everyone, then passed out.

I didn't wake up till later Sunday night to Jullia reading in her bed. She had left a cup of water on my desk that I guzzled down. Then she told me the showers were empty and I nodded as I grabbed the towel she was letting me borrow and made my way over.

It felt good to wash the grime off from the night. I had

told Jullia I'd wash her clothes before giving them back, but she said she never wears the pants and the shirt was ripped so I could just keep them. I felt guilty about it but I promised myself I'd find a job this week and pay her back for everything.

I'll have to pay the demigod shapeshifter back too. Turns out Jullia was right and Asher is still going on about it as the three of us head towards the cafeteria for breakfast. Keeping to the routine we had last week. Asher picks us up and we go to breakfast before me and Jullia walk to our first class.

I wish he had just been a regular snake. I miss my own viper. I miss home.

Nothing happens this Monday as we make our way to the line. People still sometimes stare and whisper, but no one approaches me and I'm more or less left alone.

Jullia nudges me and I blink sleepy eyes at her. Food is a must now since I've gotten enough sleep. After eating I'll be back to normal. Then I have to figure out an excuse for why I don't have a finished Syngenia origins paper that is supposed to be due today.

"I know you don't look at it," she whispers, holding out her tablet to a paused video. "But you kind of went viral. Someone had recorded you shoving Darian away and calling him Thorne's winged bitch. Just an fyi in case anyone says anything about it."

She presses play and there we are. Asher keeping hold of Jullia to the side with me in the center and the angel behind me. His hands are caging me in and then I shove him. It didn't look all the powerful, but it pushes him back a couple feet. The side of his face caught on camera with a shocked expression.

Yeah, bitch, I bet you didn't know I could do that. There's actually a lot I can do, but I don't have a training class on my schedule. You can't start taking those until second year.

Which Jullia thinks is bullshit since she does train, but apparently the school isn't designed to create only warriors.

Still, it could be some sort of extracurricular or like an elective. Not that I was able to pick my classes anyway, but still. I wonder if students are able to use the training arena and gym after classes. I'll have to ask Asher later since he is taking a training class.

The video comes to Thorne telling me not to threaten people and that's when I call Darian a winged bitch. It makes me smile because I look badass with my makeup and crossed arms. I have a bad habit of not standing up for myself – or so Ms. Elaycia says – but there are times when I can do it. And I did it then beautifully.

The video ends right as Thorne appears in front of me and then Jullia scrolls to where all the views, likes, and comments are.

The first comment I see is 'from now on my bet's on the vampire'. When I look up to Jullia she's wincing and I give her a look.

"Did you read the other comments?" she asks hesitantly.

Looking back down at the screen I take my finger and scroll down more. There's a few more comments about how badass the 'vampire' is, but then I see why Jullia is being so cautious.

"I'd be her bitch as long as she kept those long legs open," I read. Turning a few heads that I ignore as I laugh. Despite being so energy-less, it's kind of amusing. I wave Jullia off. "Don't even worry about that. I lived in a brothel for five years, comments like that don't faze me."

She expels a breath and clicks out of the social media

app. "Oh my goddesses. Good. . . that you don't care about them I mean. It's still shitty, guys being disgusting like that, but I'm glad you're not, like, triggered."

Shrugging I grab a tray and slide it along the edge to start piling food on. "It doesn't matter where you go males are still all the same. Animals." Turning and giving Asher a sweet smile, I say, "Except you, Asher. One of the good ones."

He wraps a hand around Jullia and kisses the top of her head. I drop my smile and roll my eyes at them. Damn lovesick fools.

After we've got our food we sit in the same area we sat all last week. The surrounding tables are mostly Asher's friends or house-mates but they never join us. I told Jullia and Asher they don't have to always sit with me, but they both shrugged that off. Even though I know Jullia has started to make some friends in her other classes.

If they're not bothered then I will force myself not to be bothered as well. Asher fills me in on his weekend at the house. He hasn't seen any sign of Thorne or the rest of the celestials and apparently neither has anyone else in his house.

Not that I give a single shit. I hadn't wanted to reveal the fact that there's poison in my veins but at least hopefully it'll stop any more questions about my race. And from what Hanna and Jullia have said everyone was cleared out right before Jullia threw the dagger at Thorne. Meaning no one else knows we were poisoned.

I haven't asked about the dagger or why Jullia has it, and I don't think I'm going to. I don't really want to know. I just want to finish this school and then go home.

Jullia drones on about the school work and I listen only barely. I should have spent all weekend doing said work, but now I have a shit ton of papers to write and equations to solve and I need to profusely thank Nana and Ms. Elaycia for not putting me into an ordered school system. At least next year I can pick the majority of my classes.

Jullia nudges my hand and I focus on her face. She gives me a look. "You ate everything, are you okay?"

I look down at my empty tray. My belly is full and I have more energy than I did all weekend, but I still feel like shit.

"You think I'll get kicked out if I fail Magic History?"

Jullia blanches but it's Asher who nonchalantly says, "Most definitely. Of all the classes that is the one you don't want to fail." Jullia smacks his shoulder as he chuckles. "Don't worry about it, Mavyn. You still have the rest of the year, one bad grade on an assignment won't fail you."

I'm still not fully convinced but Jullia announces we better go so we put our trays away and start heading out. It's over cast today but the clouds aren't thick enough for me to go without the umbrella. At least Jullia hides underneath it with me. She did the same thing last week too, saying I was lucky because at least I had a shield against the heat.

Asher parts ways as we make our way down the rest of the hall. Other students are meandering in, and I catch a glimpse of dirty blond hair ducking in. Crossing my fingers, I hope nothing happens. Callahan wasn't explicitly involved in anything. All the drama happened between me, Thorne, and a bit of Darian – not including Castiel D'etre in the end.

All I remember of the devil was him leaning against the wall and then picking me up before offering me his blood. I'd rather rip my own neck out than drink the blood of a devil ever again. No offense to him or anything, he's more or less left me alone out of all of the celestials, but trauma is a bitch.

Professor Asier isn't here when we enter, and instead of

taking the stairs closest to the door to our row, I pull Jullia to the other side so I don't have to scoot past Callahan. I can feel his eyes tracking us as we move, and Jullia says nothing about. I'm sure she also wants to stay out of their sights after threatening and almost killing Thorne.

Nothing is said as I get to my seat and sit in it. I set my tablet and Jullia's stylus on the desk and keep my eyes forward. Clearly luck isn't on my side because Callahan crosses his arms as he leans back and fully turns his head towards me.

"Why don't you have a notebook?"

He's only loud enough for me, and possibly Jullia to hear. Jullia had offered to get me a notebook and some pens but that I fully shut down. I can't exactly say no to toiletries or clothes because that's a need, but taking notes on the tablet hasn't been bad enough for me to ask for something else.

Clicking onto my notes tap, I open my Magic History folder and open a blank page. "Because I am a nobody vampire who was snatched by enforcers and given no notice or funds when I was shipped off to this school wearing only the clothes on my back."

I write the date in the upper left hand corner and then click out of the page to open what should have been my finished essay. Instead I'm short three pages, a cited sources page, my intro paragraph, and it should be printed out.

Jullia pulls out her finished, printed essay from her backpack and sets it on top of her notebook. Then she glances at me and winces right as the door to the class shuts and we all face forward.

Professor Asier is late. . . only it isn't Professor Asier it's the motherfucking demigod.

And he's staring straight at me with a goddamn smirk.

Jullia makes a noise in the back of her throat as he approaches the desk and places a briefcase on top of it. Then he proceeds to take off his jacket and roll the sleeves of his white button up. I swear every girl in here but for me and Jullia sigh at the action.

Callahan softly clears his throat but I don't bother looking at him as the demigod slips his hands into his pants pockets and faces the class.

"Good morning, class." Why the fuck is he talking like that. All deep and rumbling and like he's trying to get us off. I mean, he sounded like that Saturday night but I thought. . . actually I don't even know what I thought. I was too exhausted and hungry. "I'm sure you're expecting Varian, but unfortunately he was called away for the day so I will be taking over his classes. My name is Castiel D'etre."

Murmurs go up and I catch bits and pieces of "demigod" and "spymaster" and "sexiest male alive". I'd roll my eyes if he wasn't staring directly at me.

A girl in the front row lifts her hand and the demigod glances at her before nodding. She rests her arms on the desk in a move that shoves her breasts up. I don't know why she does it since our uniform doesn't allow for her cleavage to show, but who am I to judge a lady trying to get some.

"Professor D'etre," she purrs and now I do roll my eyes. Nevermind, I do and will judge. "Does this mean you will be teaching at Syngenia? And will Professor. . . Varian be coming back tomorrow?"

The demigod leans against the desk as he crosses his arms. Large, powerful, stupid arms that are covered in gold markings and symbols. Some of them almost look familiar and unconsciously I lean forward to get a better look at them. I'm pretty sure he had them covering his chest too when he let me feed from him, but I can't fully remember.

The most that I remember from that night was him saying I'm not a spy and his golden blood filling my mouth. I've never had demigod blood before, and I wish I never did because I want more.

He smirks at the girl. "Professor *Asier* will be back tomorrow, and yes, I will be a professor here at the university. I'll be taking over Professor Mackly's Race Insight and Theology class after this one, as well as Race Anatomy, and I will be helping Professor Asier with the training and External Controlling classes. Though those two are for year two and up."

No. Fucking. Way.

I clench my teeth together because I have Professor Mackly's Race Insight and Theology class after this one. I was supposed to be done with these meddling celestials.

The demigod returns his eyes to me and I look off to the side so I don't have to look at him. He is the only teacher I will be looking at all freaking day since Professor Asier is also my professor to Intro to Power Compulsion at the end of the day.

"Now," he begins. "Professor Asier did leave notes for today. You all have been learning about the history of Syngenia and how it was first created. He also said you all should have an essay to turn in about it. Go ahead and pass them down the rows to the right and then to the front."

Everyone starts shuffling papers and I sigh in defeat. Jullia gives me a sympathetic look as she hands me her stack of papers and those from down the row. I take them and hold them out to Callahan without looking at him.

After a couple seconds and they haven't been taken I turn my head and he's watching me with a brow raised.

"What?" I grit.

He takes the papers. "Where's yours?"

"I was comatose all weekend thanks to your ass of a house president and your buddy-buddy professor. I didn't get to finish."

Leaning back into my chair I cross my arms and stare at the tablet on my desk. I never actually went to school, but I always completed every task ever given to me at its deadline. All my chores were finished when they needed to be, every side project I was given was completed when needed, any homework I got from Ms. Elaycia or Nana was done and handed in for them to inspect.

Not being able to finish this essay grates on my nerves because it's not that I didn't know how to finish it or I didn't have enough time to do so, I simply was passed out. I wasn't able to eat anything all Saturday and Sunday and after being poisoned and only having a limited amount of blood my body was completely diminished and resorted to going unconscious to try and preserve any energy left.

And it's Thorne's fucking fault. Him and all the rest of them and their paranoia and not getting me a fucking blood bag. That still wouldn't have been enough, I needed a feast of regular food and then a solid eight hours of rest.

Instead I got demigod blood that although was good did not come from a bag and I had no means to buy myself any food anyways.

Fuck you, you motherfucking vampire bitch for shoving that vampyr blood into me and the enforcers for not listening when I said I wasn't turned and the Mage Board for shucking me off to this fucking school without any supplies. And fuck this school for discriminating against vampires because everyone has hiring flyers and posters and portals open but none of them want a vampire.

I'm going to die here, and it's not even going to be because of another student or staff.

With the demigod shuffling papers on the desk I lean closer to Jullia. She tilts her head towards me as I whisper, “For family day can we go see our families or do they come here? And what if they’re on Earth?”

She leans back as she thinks about it. “You’re asking because of Ms. Elaycia?” When I nod she tilts her head to think more about it. “If they were granted access to leave Earth and enter Miy then yes. You’d also have to get access if you were to leave for the day and visit them.”

Well that’s not gonna happen. At least for me getting access. And I don’t even know if they know where I am. I didn’t tell the enforcers or Mage Board where I had been staying before. I didn’t want to risk Ms. Elaycia getting in some sort of trouble.

“Do they know you’re here?”

I pull the shortest of the four necklaces I always wear. It’s a thinner silver chain attached to a small circle of blood stone with silver detailing wrapped around it. Nana has a matching blood stone but hers is a slightly larger circle she wears as a ring.

“If I smear my blood on this stone Nana will know something’s wrong and I need her help.” I whisper back. “I don’t know if it tracks me too, I’ve never had to use it before. Do you know anything about blood stones?”

She shakes her head as the demigod clears his throat and everyone silences as we all face him. I turn my head straight but I return my eyes back to my tablet on the desk. He tells us to open our textbooks to page thirty-two and as most of everyone pull out physical textbooks to open, I click on the digital version.

The rest of class is boring as Professor D’etre teaches us about the evolution of Syngenia University. For some reason he doesn't mention the witches. Professor Asier didn't either, and while I know their populations started to decrease after the War of Gods, there seems like there are a lot of holes in the history.

Starting off with the fact that it was not a mage who built up the structure of the university, but a goddamn vampire. I can imagine Nana going off on all of them for their shitty history. But after last week when I said Syngenia was first noted as the name of the first blood witch and her vampyr daughter, and how everyone reacted, I thought it would be best to not comment on anything.

Not even Hanna or Asher knew that was when the name was first used. So from now on I'm going to be keeping my mouth shut.

Professor D'etre ends the hour and a half long class by saying our assignments are on the portal and then the bells ring. Turning off my tablet, I stand and me and Jullia walk in the opposite direction as Callahan.

Pushing Jullia ahead of me when we get off the stairs I say, "I need to ask the professor a question."

She nods and waves as she hurries out. My next class – with said professor – is in thirty minutes but Jullia's next one is in ten.

I use my umbrella like a cane as I force myself towards the professor. He's sitting at the desk looking over whatever papers are on there. He doesn't look up at me until the class is empty. Well, empty except for Callahan, who waits by the door.

"Yes, Ms. Tsuki," the demigod drawls as he smirks without looking at me.

The top button of his shirt is undone, but it isn't open enough for me to see if there's still a scar at the crook of his neck. Anytime the devil would force my fangs into his skin the marks would take weeks to heal even though they should have done so within maximum a day.

"Would you like to see it?" he hums. I snap my eyes from his shoulder to nearly black eyes holding amusement.

"See what?"

"Your mark."

And my umbrella creaks as I grip it tighter. I'm about to snap at him that no, I do not want to see it but his fingers are already undoing the next couple buttons and he's sliding his collar over. Right there in the spot where his neck meets his shoulder are two small puncture marks. There's the tiniest bit of berry and floral scent and I grit my teeth.

He always loved when my marks didn't fade for a long time. Always making me bite in visible places. Showing them off when he was around and taunting me with them.

You are mine, he would growl in my ear. *This is proof of that.*

You wanna know why I won't ever go into a bloodlust? This is why. I refuse to mark anyone. I never wanted to mark anyone ever again. And for nearly nine years I kept that promise to myself.

And then I fucked it up. I can't even blame him or Thorne. It was my choice. I could have shut my brain down and knocked myself out. I could have disregarded his consent and walked away. Even when I drank from the girls at the brothel when they let me, they always opened their own skin up and let me drink. My fangs never pierced their skin.

My fangs haven't pierced anyone's skin in nine fucking years.

"I'll make a balm for you that will heal that within hours," I say. I sound like a robot with how monotone my voice is. All the anger, all the energy, all the fight going out like a flame doused. "It doesn't look like it's healing like it should."

Something flashes across his face and he rights his shirt and covers the mark. A fucking mark with *my* fang imprints. It would be better if he skinned that part of himself to get rid of it.

"I did give my consent, Mavyn," he murmurs softly. "You don't need to owe me anything."

Except I do. Nothing is ever given for free. There's always a price. Always something that comes back to bite you in the ass. It's not even about morals, it's about fate and karma. I have to keep a balance because the universe already hates me. The one Earth is in and apparently this one too.

"Mavyn," he says, a bit louder and with more force. It makes me focus on him and not the thoughts in my head. I must have spaced out or something. I was trying to figure out where I could get more rucksile. "You. Don't. Owe. Me."

Each word is its own statement. He enunciates each in case I couldn't understand the meaning of those four words together.

"I'm not that devil," he says a bit softer. How did he know I was thinking about that? It makes me frown and I take a step back from the desk.

"I know," I snap. To which he drops his shoulders and relaxes his body into the chair. Not sitting straight up and making himself slightly shorter. As if he's. . . "*Don't*. Don't do that just because you pity me for my past."

He keeps his face neutral, though I can see his muscles jump as he clenches his jaw. Tension thrums through his body and his breaths get just a hair shallower. The body doesn't lie.

"I wanted to know if your Intro to Power Compulsion class was going to be in here or in Mr. Mackly's classroom."

Hisdo eyes don't waver from mine for long seconds. What I would give for some sort of memory potion. Better yet, give me a time machine so I can go back to Saturday night. That's all I would ask. So then I could crawl into a ball instead of sinking my fangs into his neck. So he wouldn't have a mark made by me on him.

"It'll be in Mr. Mackly's," he finally answers.

And with that I turn and make my way towards the door. Callahan waits there watching us. I don't want to wonder if Thorne ran his mouth to the rest of the celestials but I can't help it. Does Callahan also know about the devil feeding from me? Did Thorne tell him that I said the devil used to try feeding his blood to me?

Saying the word 'try' doesn't technically make it a lie. There were times I would refuse and the devil would grip the back of my head and shove my fangs into him. There were a couple times when I was able to not swallow it. I let it run down my chin and be wasted.

Those days the beatings would last even after I would wake up from being unconscious. The longest one was when I had gone unconscious and woken up six times before he stopped. He liked those times because then I would beg for his blood to help heal the wounds. Help take the pain away.

Callahan doesn't stop me or even follow me as I leave the room. I head down the hall and round a corner to an empty alcove before slamming my back against the wall and heaving. I release my hold on my blood and let it rush through my veins. Let my heart pound in my chest.

So much control, so much concentration, so much contained emotion. All the fucking time.

I let it all out. I let it rip through my chest with a fire and some sort of pitiful sound escapes from my throat. Sliding down the wall I push my spine into it and hug my knees. Wrapping my arms around, I dig my nails into my thighs and squeeze my eyes shut.

It feels too close to burning but I don't stop it. There's a type of control in self-destruction. A power in it because it's your choice. And when you've lived a life where so many of your choices are taken from you, you do what you can to gain some of it back.

You can't be destroyed if you've already done it yourself.

Opening my eyes I let myself burn for another moment longer before focusing on a chip in the stone wall and shoving it all back in. All the burning and fire and emotion gets locked up as I force my blood to slow and my heartrate to drop. All that energy and aura that had been flaming curls back into me reducing to an almost nothingness.

Releasing my hold around my legs, I straighten my back and push off my knees to stand. Taking in as much air through my nose as possible I softly close my eyes to hold. My limbs get floaty as I focus on my steady heartbeat and warmth floods my body. Sixty-three seconds before I release all the air in my lungs and then I suck in another deep breath to hold it again.

This time I wait till seventy-seven seconds before releasing. It would be better if I was barefoot and toeing some grass, but the grounding breathing helps, nonetheless. Maybe tonight I'll slip out to lay next to the forest by the dorm building. Maybe it'll help reset the flow of my body.

Speaking of. . . a sharp pain slices through my lower abdomen. Fucking hell, this next week is about to be a bitch.

Twelve

Mavyn – August 17

Honestly, he's giving Landon vibes. . . is the first thing I hear when Jullia approaches me. I'm leaning against the doorway to the training arena. The massive room looks like three warehouses connected with a loft styled upstairs holding every piece of gym machinery you could need.

Downstairs are padded sections for one on one combat and so many other things I can't fully concentrate on because Asher is facing off against Thorne and both look pissed.

Jullia blocks my view and in the back of my mind I remember her approaching me and saying something. She said a name. . . Landon?

"Who's Landon?" I ask. Tilting my head to peer over her shoulder to watch as Asher lunges first. Neither of them have weapons and the fight is supposed to be purely self-defense, but Thorne delivers a solid left hook and I'm surprised Jullia is being so calm about this.

She slaps my shoulder and it was hard enough to sting. Giving her my full attention, I glare. She glares right back.

"Your boyfriend is getting pummeled and you don't seem bothered," I say dryly.

She tenses a bit before taking a deep breath and dismissing my comment. "They're not allowed to use any abilities so he'll be fine. Now, how did the interview go?"

Right. The whole reason I'm here.

"Fine. They said I can start tonight after this session is finished." Done paying attention to the fight I fully survey the arena.

There was a position for the cleaning crew for the school and while there are no students on it with only staff, the advisor seemed like she was tired of seeing my face every other day and said I could work on probation for this first week to see how it goes. The head of the cleaning crew didn't seem to care that I was a vampire, but he did say since I was new I was on gym duty.

"That's awesome," Jullia gushes. She turns around and steps back so she's beside me now as her smile tightens watching the fight. "And Thorne is Landon. Landon King."

"Huh?"

She smirks and then sobers. "I'll lend you my book, *God of Ruin*. Landon is the main male character and Thorne gives his vibes. Though Thorne isn't so much a narcissist and psycho. I could also see Kai Mori vibes too." She hums. "I have to remember to reread that series when October hits."

My eye twitches as I side-eye her. "I would prefer not to read a sex book where Thorne is more or less the main character, thank you."

Someone chokes and we both turn to both Asher and Thorne staring at us. Well that's just fucking great.

The former gives a cocky smirk to his girlfriend who's face is bright red. The latter burns dark red eyes at me while taking his hand and wiping the corners of his mouth. His abs and biceps flex with the movement and I flex my own abs hidden under my shirt to keep from moving.

Slowly turning away from me he starts making his way to the edge of the mat where bottles of water are. The muscles in his back ripple as he bends down to pick a bottle up to chug.

"Well," Jullia whispers, "I wouldn't judge – "

Before she can finish whatever it is she was going to say I push off the wall and circle her to exit through the hall. There's a staff common room at the end of the hall with lockers for those that work in this area of the university. There should be a coverall jumpsuit for me in one of them and the training class should be about done by now.

Jullia's light chuckle echoes after me but she doesn't follow. Entering the code to the room that the head of the cleaning crew gave me, I enter to find it empty. Good. I need to change out of my uniform and there isn't a bathroom in here.

I don't have anything to wear under the coverall unless I want to wear my uniform, but I'm just going to have to deal with it until I can get paid. Going to my locker – number four – I twist the notch on the lock to the numbers the head of the cleaning crew also gave me and open it on the first try. Inside the locker is a dingy brown long sleeve jumpsuit that looks similar to what mechanics wear.

On the floor of the locker is a pair of black boots that should be my size and a cap sitting on top of them. With a backwards glance at the door, I begin undressing. Hanging my blazer on the only other hook in the locker, I toe off my flats and then slip the thigh high socks off.

My skin pebbles being exposed to the cool air and I'm sure if there was hair on my legs every strand would be raised. Cordellia had said on multiple occasions I was lucky I didn't have to shave or use creams to get rid of the hair on my body – since I don't have any. Most of the time I'd just dismiss her comment but every once in a while I would remind her that I may not have hair on my body, but that's due to the poison in my blood and I still have scars covering every other inch.

I didn't tend to remind her because she usually forgot about them as a whole. She – and most of the girls at the brothel – didn't pay any mind to them. Even when they were exposed, when I would wear my little dresses or a t-shirt and shorts, it was as if I didn't have them. I never had to cover up around them.

Yet another reason I miss home. Clothing rubbing over the scars always feels like they're getting irritated. Even though they've long been healed. It's fine in the winter because they don't ache as much in the cold, but especially when it's warm or I get sweaty they sting.

Taking one of the socks off, I replace it with a leg of the jumpsuit so my skin it's exposed for longer than it needs to. The last thing I need is someone walking in and seeing the scars.

When I have both legs in I button the jumpsuit up to my hips and then undo my skirt to pull over my head. Half-way done. Undoing the buttons of my shirt, I keep my back towards the door and pull the jumpsuit up over my shoulders before shimmying out of my school shirt and pulling it out from its trapped position between my back and the jumpsuit.

Once that's done I shove my hands through the sleeves of the jumpsuit and finish buttoning the rest of the buttons. The top one stops right beneath where my collarbones are. Barefoot, I walk over to the full length mirror beside the lockers and stare at myself.

My hair is already tied up in a messy low bun so I just need my shoes and cap and then I'll be done. The only problem is that one of the bitemarks is very clearly visible just over the neckline of the jumpsuit.

Motherfucker.

I need this job. I can't not work and it's required to wear the jumpsuit. I could wear my school shirt but. . .

Grabbing the boots and hat, I slap the locker shut and shove my feet into the shoes. I cringe at not wearing socks, but I only have the thigh high ones and I'm not wearing those. After lacing them up I click the lock in place, pull the hat over my head, and go over to the chart on the wall to sign my name. It'll let whoever comes in here know I'm out with a cart full of all the cleaning supplies I'll need.

Wheeling it out I exit the room and pull the neckline up with one hand while I steer the cart with another. Hopefully – I've been saying that too much recently – but hopefully no one wants to stay after to keep practicing.

Jullia is still near the doorway and she jumps as I stop beside her with the cart.

"Holy goddesses! Don't sneak up on a girl."

Rolling my eyes, Asher skips over to us without a scratch or bruise on him. He cocks his head at me and his eyes glance down to where my hand is clutching the neckline.

"I see you got the job. . . you gonna be good?"

I don't see Thorne or anyone else behind him so I drop my hand for a moment and rub at my face. I can feel Jullia stiffen next to me but she just hums quietly to herself.

"I'll be fine. I used to clean all the time in all sorts of unpleasant places. Is there anyone going to be staying after?"

I grip and pull the neckline back up as I look past Asher again. There's still a few guys working out upstairs but that doesn't bother me. Most of them look like they have earbuds or headphones on. Hopefully – there I go with that damn word again – it's like the gyms in America and people don't give two shits about who's next to them.

"No, there's more parties tonight so everyone's cutting their after training workouts. The place should be empty in about thirty more minutes."

I nod. Good. I'll start in the back where there's nobody and work my way here. I'll do upstairs last in case there's any stragglers left.

"Well," I announce in a burst of energy, "you guys have fun tonight."

Jullia smiles at me and then holds up her hands. She has them cupped together so I'm assuming there's something in them and I really hope she isn't going to give me something.

"Don't look at me like that," she grumbles. Opening her hand she reveals wired earbuds and what looks like a small mp3 player. "So you can at least listen to something while you work. I downloaded the songs you've saved on your tablet to it so you can listen to your music and I downloaded that list of songs you wrote down too. The one of all the songs from Earth. I have a universal converter which allows me to download songs, shows, and movies from Earth so I can play them here."

Warmth from both gratitude and guilt invade my chest. She's told me that before. It's how she's able to watch all her anime shows and read all her e-books. Jullia thrusts the device into my chest and gives me no choice but to take it.

"Don't even think about giving it back. It's an old thing I don't use anymore so you might as well put it to use."

Unwrapping the wire I click on the screen and it's more or less like an mp3 player. The screen lights up with a playlist titled *Mavyn's Essentials*.

Needles prick at my nose and my eyes burn as I mumble out, "Thank you."

Jullia waves it off but gives me a hug before she and Asher leave. I put the earbuds in and press play on the playlist. Buffalo Traffic Jam's *Fool's Gold* starts playing and I have to close my eyes for a moment to stop myself from allowing any tears to spill over.

People take music for granted. The power of melodies and lyrics and beats. There's magic in music. It can heal the spirit and soul. It can give hope to those in despair and shield the mind when there's nothing to shield your body.

I lied to Thorne when I said I used to harm myself to distract from the devil. A good enough coverup to explain the scars. What I really did was hum melodies. I'd trap my conscious in my mind and surround it with songs.

Then afterward when the nightmares would take over I'd play music to help keep them away. Ms. Elaycia gave me a music box that would repeat over and over and a majority of the time it would stop the nightmares.

Music has saved me more times than I can count.

The song ends and I finally open my eyes. *You Again* by Jonah Kagen starts playing, and despite it being a sad song I smile. I can't relate to it but I can feel the movement of it anyway.

Slipping the device into my pocket, I release my hold of the neckline and begin wheeling the cart into the room. And since no one is around who could hear me, I start humming to the music. In addition to listening to the music, I would occasionally sing too. Ms. Elaycia loved having me sing at night when she wanted a more sultry vibe for the back end of the club. Despite it being for getting men even more so in the mood, I still loved it.

The piano version of Jade LeMac's *Constellations* starts up and I start mumbling the words to it. I had written over a hundred songs on that list Jullia had been talking about. Knowing her she probably added every single one on here.

I'll have to do something extraordinary to say thank you. This. . . giving me music. . . there's no greater gift.

Pulling out the bucket and mop, I start cleaning this first section. With my music time moves differently. Faster, or maybe I finish the tasks faster. I never minded cleaning – as long as I had good music. And with *my* music, nothing could much bother me right now.

Section after section, area after area, equipment after equipment. I don't miss a single inch of anything. This room is about to be cleaner than it has ever been before.

". . . long tan legs and her cowboy boots," I hum with a smile, "sippin on shine in her daisy dukes, take me for a ride on the way you move, drivin' my blues away. . . "

You can't not bop your head to Joseph David-Jones. Even though I've only listened to two of his songs, no matter what mood I'm in they always hit.

"Let's yippee-ki-yay in my black Chev-aay, Z seventy-one on a bale of hay, damn, you look good on my tailgate. . . drivin' my blues away."

I finish mopping this mat and wipe my forehead. Who needs a workout when you can just clean a gym? My arms slightly tremble as I lift the mop and stick it back in the bucket of dirty water. Flo Rida is currently blaring in my ears with *Good Feeling* and I take a mini break to nod my head to the beat as I shimmy my shoulders.

"I get a feeling. . . that I never, never, never, never had before, oh no, I get a good feeling. . . " The laser feeling base drop hits and I do a little spin while nodding my head to each bump of the base. "Let's get it, let's *FUCK!*" I rip the ear buds out and clutch my chest as I veer back. There's a slight smirk on his face before he neutralizes it. "What the fuck are you doing here!"

My heart is pounding in my chest and threatening to come out through my throat. Thorne is standing about ten feet away doing nothing but watching me. At least he has a shirt on now.

But. . . how long was here there? He couldn't have been there for long. Why is he here? Doesn't he have president society things to do? Aren't there parties he should be at?

More thoughts and questions ping pong in my head as I take long, deep breaths. Normally I'm more aware of my surroundings, especially when I have both earbuds in. I'm usually able to sense when I'm being watched. That just means he couldn't have been here for long. Unless I was too absorbed with the music to notice?

"Can I help you with something?" I ask cautiously. Before today I hadn't seen him since Saturday night. I haven't seen Darian either and Callahan hasn't tried speaking to me since Monday when he asked about my paper.

I had finished it Monday night and went to Professor Asier's classroom Tuesday morning before breakfast to see if I could hand it in. He wasn't there so I had just left it on his desk with a note stating I was incapacitated because of circumstances that were out of my control. I don't know if Thorne or Castiel told him about what happened, but he didn't say anything today about it and my grade on the portal had been updated to a ninety-four percent out of a hundred.

There weren't any notes for why I wasn't given a hundred percent, but I'll just assume the six points were docked because it was technically late.

Whatever.

"What were you singing?" he asks lowly, which for some reason is one thing I didn't think would come out of his mouth.

My heart returns to its normal pace, but it feels like its beats are stronger. Thumping hard against my ribs as I shift my weight and lick my lips. His eyes dart down before looking back up with an expectant expression.

Lady Gaga's *Applause* can be heard from the earbuds and I didn't realize how loudly I had the music.

"Uh. . . a song?" I shift again. I don't know if he knows about the things from Earth. "*Good Feeling* – from Flo Rida. . . ?"

He cocks his head and glances down to my hand still tangled with the wire. His body it nearly entirely rock solid. I can't make out what he's thinking or read anything from his body language. Jullia didn't make it seem like listening to human songs would be illegal or anything. Maybe he's just curious?

"Do you sing often?"

His tone also isn't telling me anything. Mild curiosity – maybe. Or maybe I'm too nervous to read anything from it. Nana says I can be oblivious sometimes even though I'm an excellent observer and can notice things others don't.

"Yes. . . ?"

Something lightens in his expression by a decimal point. "Are you asking or telling me?"

I give him a dry look. "I did on Earth."

He hums and slides his hands into the pockets of his shorts. They're the same ones he was wearing when he was training with Asher. I've been here for at least two hours so does that mean he hasn't gone back to his room to change?

"What's your favorite song to sing?"

My shoulders tense and it must be a visible reaction because his eyes drop to them.

"Why are you here?" My voice sounds more solid now. More blunt, less hesitant.

His face goes back to a cold mask as she shrugs. "I heard someone singing and was wondering why there was someone still in here." His eyes rove down me and lock somewhere around my neck and chest where my necklaces are. His dark red eyes start to slightly glow. I blink and he's now standing directly in front of me. It makes my heart jump again and when I try to step back his hands grip my arms and hold me in place.

"*What. The. Fu –* "

"Who is he," he growls. His voice so low and gravely I almost couldn't make out the words. I'm about to go off on him when he growls again, "Who is he. Who put a mark on this body."

He doesn't ask it, he *demands* it. So much power rolls off him it reaches every corner of the room instantly. His aura is so deep and thick I can almost see it. The red wisps weaving in and out of visible sight.

A cold sweat breaks out over my skin that causes my scars to itch. I forgot about that scar still visible. He can see it clear as day.

His hands tighten and I squeeze my eyes shut against the rumbling power of his magic. It feels almost suffocating. So much death.

"He's dead," I choke out. Keeping my eyes firmly shut and head slightly turned away. His aura is more than the devil's ever could be. "The devil, he's already dead."

Long been dead, too bad I'm still haunted by him.

So much, too much, too all-consuming his magic is. More than I have ever felt before. Emotions can heavily influence the power of your magic but his anger is unwarranted.

Clearly my words don't satisfy him because his aura is still visible when I crack my eyes open. One of his hands leaves my upper arm to grip the collar of my shirt and it snaps me out of my frozen state. I take both of my hands and grip his wrist to stop him from pulling my shirt even further down. If it gets pulled down another inch the top of one of my other scars will be seen and if this is how he's acting from just seeing one of the bite marks I don't want to imagine how he'll react seeing the other scars.

Not that he has any reason to act in any sort of way towards them. He has no reason to be angry or demanding or anything else he could be feeling in this moment.

So why the fuck is he making a big deal about it?

"You said he bit your wrist," he growls. "Where the

fuck else did he bite you?"

He tries to tug my collar but I plant my feet, tighten my core, and hold his arm in place. His eyes flash in rage but I cement myself where I am and don't budge. My body has waned since I haven't trained in the last two months, but that doesn't mean that I'm weak.

"Take your hands off of me. Now."

Slow, deliberate words. There's no power or aura to back my words up but my tone holds an air of deadly energy anyway. It's enough to make Thorne pause and actually look at me. Dark red eyes shining with an inner light behind them focus straight on mine. His pupils are blown making his glowing iris's look like thin rings of red light.

A breath passes before he takes a measured step back and releases me. Immediately I take several steps away from him as I pull the neckline of the jumpsuit up. His eyes don't leave mine as I do it and I wonder what is about to happen next because why does he freakin care.

He *should* care less about me. I am no one to him. I am *no. One*. And that's the truth of it. So insignificant am I that a lone fucking scar shouldn't matter. Even if I were to strip to nothing right now it shouldn't matter. The scars that cover my body. They. Don't. Matter.

You don't matter.

Your worth is designated by what I say it is.

Curling my nails into the collar, I squeeze my eyes shut and block out the words. His voice fracturing within my mind the same as if he was right here in front of me speaking aloud. An echo etched into my skull, his voice a sound I've never been able to forget. His deep timber, the rumble that comes from his chest, the instinctual knowing I always got when is tone darkened signaling he was about to sink his fangs into my flesh.

It's trapped in my head. The voice, the words, that same instinctual knowing.

"You can't bite me," I whisper out loud. Because I know in this physical space I am not six years old in that manor standing before *him*. I am nineteen, stronger than I was before, standing within the grounds of Syngenia University on Miy before Thorne. Before a blood demon who cannot bit me, cannot mark me, cannot drink my blood or force me to drink and mark him.

I open my eyes to gold. White threads of light flicker through with a ring of black around golden iris's. They look like twin suns.

People forget the power of a sun. We need them for life. For warmth and growth and stability. But get too close and you burn.

Everyone forgets that message of Icarus. People like to romanticize the story. They say he may have fallen, but to fall is to know what it was to fly. That doesn't help a dead man. That doesn't save you as the wax melts and the wings break.

Thirteen

Callahan – August 17

I was supposed to be meeting Thorne for a training session. He didn't care to attend any of the parties tonight and I haven't cared to attend any after last weekend.

It should have been my blood she was drinking. My neck her fangs sank into. My body she left a mark on. Not the demigod with his divinity and righteousness and golden blood and *fucking* thoughts about her scent and body and red lips.

He didn't even shield his mind. He let his thoughts wonder free and his want and *need* of her flooded my mind. His fucking pride at her choosing him.

I needed to beat someone and there wasn't a chance I wouldn't try to kill Castiel if he and I got into a ring. So I asked Thorne instead and I expected to find him warming up on one of the training arena's mats. I did not expect to find him standing in front of Mavyn with his aura filling every corner of the room. With her looking like she was about to run from terror.

For the first time I had heard her thoughts. Varian had agreed when I told him I couldn't read her thoughts and there was a powerful shield around her mind. He said he couldn't read her either, and unless he wanted to force his way into her mind he didn't think he would be able to.

But I heard them then.

The scars that cover my body. They. Don't. Matter.

You don't matter.

Your worth is designated by what I say it is.

Then she told Thorne he couldn't bite her but it sounded like she wasn't entirely speaking to him. She whispered the words with a power as if they were a mantra she was already repeating.

That's when I stepped in. When I appeared in front of her and wanted to wrap my arms around her. I wanted to protect her, wanted to hold her, wanted her to know she was safe here with me. But I kept my arms at my side as I waited for her eyes to open. I didn't want to scare her.

Now that they are open, those soft pink iris's on me, I might just have to kill Thorne too. Why is she looking at me like she's waiting for me to burn her? Like she's waiting for me to reduce her to nothing.

No one should have that kind of power over her.

"Firecracker," I murmur in a soft tone. Her eyes don't

waver or flash or give any indication that she heard me. It makes my chest ache. "Mavyn," I try.

Her hands curl tighter around the collar of her shirt. Her knuckles white from how hard she's holding on. Did Thorne try to do something to her? I've always known him to be an asshole, but I never thought he would be *that* kind of asshole.

Ramming into all of his shields I roar into his mind, *DID YOU TRY TO TOUCH HER?*

His aura still fuming in the room flinches. Thorne's shields are the strongest I've ever encountered and even Varian has trouble getting through when we're training our mental shields, but emotions can influence the strength of someone's aura and right now I'd say I'd be able to get into even Varian's mind.

Not like that. His voice is quiet in my mind. Lethal. *She has a scarred bitemark on her chest from the devil who had adopted her when she was younger.*

Castiel's one saving grace was that he did not bite Mavyn back. He did not leave a mark on her. Because for someone else to have already done it. . .

In the hierarchy of power, the gods are above all. Demigods and devils are right below them with angels and demons right below us. So when the aura of my magic fans out in a tidal wave of pure wrath, exceeding the bounds of Thorne's magic, it doesn't come as a surprise.

For a moment I'm worried it will terrify Mavyn even more, but instead of terror she looks at me with a sort of awe. Her mask of stone finally cracking and she takes a full, deep breath before relaxing her body. She drops her arms and the collar of her cleaners uniform drops a couple inches to reveal the mark Thorne said would be there.

A pale white scar with fang imprints. Seeing it makes my magic pulse.

"You are not the Sun Devil," she states. "I remember the feel of his aura that was always wrapped so tightly around him. His power was barely mediocre. You feel closer to a god than he ever did."

Taking a step back, she reaches into her pocket and pulls out a small device. It looks like a music player and she presses a button before pulling the wire connected to it up. She stuffs it and the wire back into her pocket and then heaves a sigh as she looks around.

"You can stop expelling your magic. I'm fine now."

She wraps an arm around herself to scratch the forearm of her other one.

She has scars on her forearms she gave to herself because the devil would bite and drink from her. There's a bitemark on her wrist and I assumed that was the only one. The devil was able to embed blue belladon into his fangs and that's why they're still potent scars on her and why she smells like the flower.

So much for trying to calm down. Mavyn squints at me as another wave of power rolls through the room. She looks like she's almost chastising me. As if I didn't just learn she has another scarred bite mark on her skin from someone who used to abuse her.

I remember she had said the devil who adopted her was generous. Did she mean it as a snide remark? That he wasn't generous with his charity but generous with his punishments?

She said Varian was nearly just like him. Is that how she views us?

"Callahan." That's the first time she's said my name. It

makes my heart trip. "The room had already felt suffocating with Thorne pushing his aura into every corner of the room, can you both just chill? I don't understand why you're making such a big deal about this."

She's got to be kidding.

"You have a scarred bite mark – "

"That doesn't matter," she snaps at me. "It's a stupid scar I get to live with for the rest of my life. I don't need you or anyone else pointing out what is very clearly fucking obvious to me. It means a shitty devil used me as a blood bag for a few years and *nothing* else."

So she does know about the significance of scarred bitemarks. The type of claiming they are and the primal nature of them for those of us who have fangs. She knows *exactly* what it means. . . and she's shoving it away as if it means nothing because she wasn't given a choice in being marked.

Is that why she was so upset when Castiel flaunted her bitemark on him?

I'm going to beat his fucking ass.

The devil tried to feed her his blood as well, Thorne adds. Our minds still linked meaning he can hear every thought. *And because of the blue belladon that was within the fangs and the knife she used on herself, she not only smells like the flower but her body is continuously acting to survive against it. That's why she needs regular food as well as blood, and why she apparently sleeps too.*

That would make sense. That would also explain why she didn't die long after she should have when she had been cut with Thorne.

After Castiel took her I couldn't stand to watch her feed from him. To feel his pride and lust. For some reason it's different feeling it from Darian and Thorne – even from Varian too – but I don't like the demigod. So I had left, and I had not wanted to hear about whatever else had happened that night. It must have been afterward when Thorne learned all of this.

"Are you alright?" I ask cautiously.

She flashes irritated light pink eyes at me before giving us her back and surveying the arena. "Is there a reason you both are here? I have a job I need to finish."

I almost forgot the whole reason I was supposed to be here in the first place. There's a cart beside her I hadn't noticed before. Cleaning supplies, buckets, rags all are piled on it and I fully comprehend that she's wearing the same jumpsuit the cleaners around the school wear.

"You got a job?"

Her shoulder stiffen. "So?"

Unable to stand still, I shove my hands into my shorts pockets and shift my weight from foot to foot. "It won't be a lot with school and all the assignments?"

Her hand grips the stick of the mop as she huffs. "Not all of us are blessed with access to our mommy and daddy's money," she snaps. "If I want to be able to finally afford basic necessities, not to mention actual food over the weekends, I need money. I can't ask my family because they don't even know I'm here so I don't really have a choice, Callahan. Now is there a reason you both are still here or will you be leaving?"

Back to all her fire and sass. It makes me wonder where it had went before. Why it comes and goes.

"We're training," Thorne finally answers. "You can clean later."

A beat passes, and instead of snapping back her

shoulders drop an inch and she turns to face us. A solid wall of nothing greets me and I'm so close to trying to push past her shields to figure out what she's thinking.

"Will you be using the machines upstairs?" she asks cordially. "I can clean up there until you're done?"

I test her walls. Run invisible fingers around her mind to see if there are any cracks or fractures I could slip between. For most people there's always something. A weak link, an area they can't fully shield. Especially when their emotions are raging, most people can't deal with their emotions while holding a strong enough shield to prevent a devil from going in.

Not all devils can infiltrate minds, but most can.

And yet. . .

A small, barely registered pulse ripples from her. Vampire's don't have a lot of magic as is, aside from their gained strength and occasionally they can pick up bits of magic from whoever's blood they drank that turned them if it's strong enough. It's why she feels like she doesn't have any magical energy and barely any aura around her.

However, that single, small pulse was pure wrathful power.

Slowly, she turns and pale pink eyes lock on mine with so much darkness. So much violence and I have no doubt she'd be able to pull through with the threats she had spoken to Thorne and Darian last weekend. Her controlled fury rivals even Thorne's.

"I said you weren't like the Sun Devil," she murmurs softly. "Did I speak too soon?"

Such quiet words spoken, but they pierce my chest with so much force. The Sun Devil was the one who abused her. The one who fed and scarred her. He –

Was a devil, I hear Thorne murmur in the back of my mind. *The likelihood he was able to get into her mind is high.*

And I just fucked up.

Her body fully faces me now and I glance at the bite mark on her chest. I refuse to believe he did it like a claiming mark. The only reason it's scarred as it is is because of the blue belladon.

"If you ever," she rumbles with a deadly sort of quiet, "try to get into my mind again. . . I *will* make you beg for death."

Oh fuck I've messed up. I messed up monumentally.

"Mavyn, I'm – "

Her hand snaps up, silencing me before she turns those death laced eyes on Thorne. "Can I continue my job upstairs and finish down here when you're done?"

Thorne must nod or acknowledge her because she turns back around and puts her mop and bucket back on the cart before rolling it away. No second glance back, no last words, no care that I am wanting to fuck myself up because I hurt her.

I shouldn't be this attached to someone after only just meeting them. I *know* that. Love at first sight doesn't really exist. Lust at first sight does, enraptured at first sight does, but not love. I wouldn't call what I feel for her necessarily love, but it is more than just lust or enrapturement.

I want her. I want her more than I should given the circumstances. And I just blew it by doing the exact thing the monster who abused her for years did to her. On top of that, I *am* what they are.

Devils and demons have always gotten criticism because of stereotypes humans have made up. Despite the fact that we're not on Earth, devils and demons are associated with

Hell, Nihel, damnation, curses, evil, darkness. . . we're not white shining holiness.

I had been enamored when she didn't seem to care what I was. When she rolled her eyes at Varian and acted as if a devil was just like everyone else. She didn't care despite having every right to be afraid of our race. And then I fucked it up.

I. Messed. It. Up.

Like with everything else. I fucking ruined it.

A hand claps on my shoulder but I'm rooted to the floor. I can't move, can't process, can't think of anything other than the hatred in her eyes at what I did.

"*Breathe*," a rough voice growls. A familiar voice. A voice that has been there time and time again. "You need to fucking breathe, Callahan. Your blood is rushing too fast."

He's right. I know he's right. I cannot have a fucking panic attack right now. I cannot pass out right now.

I *know* that.

But my brain won't slow with thoughts and comments and berating me again and again and again.

"*Callahan*," Thorne growls again. Two red orbs glowing against black, two red eyes making a light within the nothingness. A type of grounding. "Good. Now breathe."

I breathe.

Sucking in a lungful of air before slowly releasing it. His hands that were gripping the sides of my head hold steady until my heart is no longer pounding and my blood is no longer rushing. He stays, eyes locked on me, until the voices dissipate and I'm back in the present physical world.

He takes a step back and observes me. "Do I need to

call your mother?"

My mother, a devil herself, has only ever been the serene against the raging storm that I and my father am at times. She knows exactly how to calm us from both anger and episodes like this. But she thinks my anxiety and self-hatred has been getting better.

"No," I gruff. "She'll just argue that I should come home. I don't need to worry her."

He watches me with a stone solid expression. Powerful red eyes probing.

"Do you still want to train, or do you need to take a break?"

Quiet humming sounds and we both turn our head to face the machinery upstairs. She probably thinks we can't hear her with how soft it is, but she's right by the railing that overlooks part of the area. There's bits of words I can hear her sing.

Her voice sounds faint but gentle. And then her words register.

". . . got a paper and pen and a page with no space. . . filled the hole in my head. . . forgot how to cry, who am I to complain. . . "

It's a sad song. It's something I would listen to.

Thorne's presence draws closer to me. "Go take some time," he says, though is sounds more like a demand, "I don't think it's good for you to be near her right now."

Except everything within me is telling me the opposite. I should be with her. I should be doing everything in my power to make her forget about that devil who hurt her. I should be able to take all her pain away.

But that's the problem. . . because I am also a devil who hurt her.

Fourteen

Mavyn – August 21

Females should be more worshiped than they are. They should be bowed to like gods. Revered because we are divinity, we are the definition of holy, we are – "

"Delirious," Jullia interrupts and I roll over to smush my face into my pillow and groan. "Are you sure you're okay, Mavyn? You've been grumbling like this all weekend. I know you haven't really eaten any regular food, but you said you'd be fine with enough blood and water. . . "

Another cramp seizes my uterus. They're always the worst right when my period comes and right when it ends.

Which wouldn't be a problem, only vampires once turned no longer get periods.

Curling up into a fetal position, I don't answer. No one has really questioned the amount of times I've had to go to the bathroom. I don't bleed outright. . . or at least I can make it so I don't bleed outright but I can only keep the blood contained for so long which means I need to use the bathroom at least once an hour.

That's the only reason no one has been able to scent my blood on me. If anything I probably just smell a bit sweeter than normal.

I wish I had my things. I have a balm I rub on my abdomen that helps with the cramps and a tonic I add to teas to help with all the other side effects. It's not monumental, I can still go to class and do my job – which I have been doing these past four days, but it's still a bitch.

"I'm dying," I groan. The words muffled by my pillow practically shoved into my mouth.

Jullia makes a distressed noise and I can hear her getting off her bed.

"Do you need more blood? Or is this a side effect from the poison?" Her anxiety is like a ball hovering right over her. "Want me to see if they can give me some pain relievers at the clinic?"

If only they would work.

Rolling back onto my back, I take a deep breath and blank out the pain. It's not too bad, not like it can get. Pain-wise it's definitely an eight out of ten, but my management of it is like a three. It hurts, but it's a pain I can handle because I'm used to it.

Doesn't mean I want to though.

Turning my head to the side I see Jullia standing in the middle of the room looking stressed. This poor girl, I doubt this is how she thought her university life would go.

"I will live," I sigh. "And this just. . . happens. . . occasionally."

Like once a month.

She relaxes and nods her head. "Is it a human thing? With all your anomalies I wouldn't be surprised." I hum. Technically, humans have menstrual cycles too. All females except goddesses and vampires. At least in some format or another. "Ah, okay. Did you need anything?"

I wave her off. She goes back to her bed to finish whatever homework she has. I made sure to do everything I needed to yesterday before I had to work. I have it off tonight and tomorrow night, but I'll be back Tuesday after classes. That'll be the start of my official pay period. The head manager loved my work in the arena.

Turning back towards the ceiling, I try not to think about that first day I had to clean it. Key word is try.

Stupid fucking demons and devils. Stupid fucking morals too because I highly doubt Thorne would have cared so much about the mark the devil left on me if it wasn't because Thorne is a blood demon and they have "feelings" on stuff like that. Claiming's and blood sharing and ownership and fated shit.

Deep in the resets of my brain I know it's important. But also it's all bullshit. None of it matters. Just because someone bites you doesn't mean you actually *marked* them. And a true claiming mark won't fade.

Except, of course, when the fangs are embedded with blue belladon and then they just can't fade.

Motherfucker.

I've already concluded I'll be alone for the rest of my life. To be honest, I'm surprised I'm still a virgin after everything with the devil. Looking at it realistically, I'm sure he was waiting till I was a bit older. Which is a shitty, disgusting, abominable reality, but it's truth.

Then all the abuse in the foster homes and the sleazebag males who I could physically feel the lust from. You would think a strip club and brothel was the furthest place I would be, but Ms. Elaycia puts our safety and needs above everything else. And she's never pressured me to go anywhere near those secret rooms or the stage.

Even the male workers Ms. Elaycia employs and the few she houses are only ever respectful. One of them, Caleb, I actually miss him too. Rosemary is like all of ours big sister and Caleb is like our big brother. The damn mage – of all things – is the perfect boy next door vibes.

And sure, he'll flirt and play around but it's only ever platonic. I can *feel* that from him. He never pushed past my limits. He also let me drink his blood. And mhm, light mage blood tastes like freedom.

He would be able to do this thing where he created this ball of light and could make it warm giving the impression of the sun. It never burned.

What I would give for that warmth right now. What I would give to go roll in the grass on a warm, sunny day.

"Jullia?" I call. She hums in response. "Do you know anything about runes or runic curses?"

I can tell she stops what she's doing and turns to look at me. "Where did that question come from? I don't really know much except what is talked about. Runic magic is technically a learned magic anyone can do, but the mental aspects of it are why not every does do it. It's more than just knowing numbers and symbols and having intent."

"Does Asher know more about it? He knew how to make a blood oath."

She hums again. "Maybe. . . his ancestors used to be one of the main experts in runic magic, but after the War of Gods a lot of the knowledge wasn't passed down. He only knows how to create the rune for the blood oath and how to draw a protection circle. Maybe a few other ones too, but that's it."

I wonder if the library would have more information. Nana said she wasn't an expert in runic magic – though she seemed like one with how easily she could do them – and she said she couldn't break mine. She said I'd have to find someone who is an expert in runic magic and explicitly knows runic curses.

"Why. . . ?" Jullia asks again.

I blow out a puff of air. "Just curious, I guess. I've seen runes around the school. Do you know anyone who would be an expert in them? One of the professors maybe?"

I slide my eyes over to her and watch her ponder. Her lips form a thin line as she glances at me, and when she notices me watching her she winces.

"Don't tell me it's Thorne."

I want nothing more to do with that fucking demon.

Her expression softens a bit. "No, but. . . " Why does there have to be a "but"? ". . . the only professor I know of who might know about runes is Professor Asier. Asher's first year he said Professor Asier subbed for his astronomy with relative astrophysics class and there was a chapter about how runes correspond with astrophysics. Asher said it was one of his favorite classes and chapters even to this day."

Ahh, so not the demon but one of the devils. He hasn't talked to me or interacted with me since the first day. Even when he came back for the next class after the demigod subbed he didn't even look at me.

Not that I've given him a reason either. I've made sure everything has been turned in on time, if not before then. Same with the demigod too, now that he's my race insight and theology professor. My only days I'm free of them are Tuesdays and Thursdays when I have philosophy and physics and astronomy with relative astrophysics. And even then, Callahan is in my astronomy class but at least he sits a few rows behind me so he's not next to me.

"Are you going to ask him?" she asks me.

"I don't know."

Someone knocks on the door and that must mean it's about six o'clock because Asher always comes over to bring dinner for him and Jullia. The last two Sunday's I've been passed out so his look of surprise mixed with guilt as Jullia opens the door and lets him in is no surprise.

There's a plastic bag with takeout in his hand.

"I thought you'd be a sleep," he says as he crosses the room to set the food on Jullia's desk. It smells like chow mien. "If I had known I would have gotten you something."

He shrugs out of his jacket and drapes it over the back of Jullia's desk chair. I wave him off and look back at the ceiling.

"I'm not hungry."

Which is a lie because I didn't eat any food yesterday and haven't eaten anything today. Asher scoffs lightly under his breath. Yeah, even I wouldn't believe that.

"Want me to go grab you something?" he asks, even

though he already has his shoes off by the door and is crawling onto Jullia's bed. She snickers at him as she moves all her notebooks and textbooks. Part of me thinks it's weird no one has laptops since they have other modern twenty-first century technology.

I wave at him again. "I might go out anyway." Not that I have any money to buy food, but maybe I will see if Professor Asier is in his classroom or office.

"The sun doesn't set for another almost two hours," Asher supplies, even though I already know that. That'll be the one plus to fall, the sun setting sooner. "Where are you gonna go?"

"She might visit Professor Asier to ask about runes," Jullia whispers not so discreetly.

"What do you want to know about runes?" Asher asks me, which is followed by a slapping sound. "What?"

"You and Hanna are the most un-discreet people I have ever met," she grumbles.

They make me smile. "I was curious about runic magic and runic curses. I wanted to know if anyone knew about them. Or maybe the library has some books on them. . . ?"

There's some shuffling and then the smell of orange chicken enters the room and I don't know how but my stomach doesn't growl.

"You won't find much in the library," Asher answers. "They stopped teaching runic magic years ago. Professor Asier would be the only one who knows about it. His graduating class was the last one to learn about it, I think. Him or Professor D'etre. Either of them should know about it."

I can hear him shoving something into his mouth and chewing. A sharp pain slashes through my abdomen and it makes me realize the majority of the pain from my cramps has mostly stopped. I should be finished menstruating today, but now I'm just hungry.

"He doesn't have hours posted on the portal, does he?" I ask. Going out to ask him will also give me an excuse to get away from that good smelling food.

"Mhmm. Unless he took them off, but you can always go see if he's there if you really want to. He is a good professor."

I'd roll my eyes but I'm too distracted by the food. Groaning, I heave myself up and turn to sit on the edge of the bed. Asher is cozy on Jullia's bed as he shoves food into his mouth while peering over at Jullia's notes.

She looks over at me with wide questioning eyes. "You going? Want us to come with?"

Asher makes a face that I do roll my eyes at. "Nah, I'll be fine. Eat your food, I shouldn't be long."

Pulling over my heeled boots, I slip them on and then stand. Over the last week Jullia has been leaving clothes in my wardrobe that apparently she "can't wear" or are "too small" or some other excuse she throws around. So now I have three pairs of jeans, five shirts, two sets of pajama's, a new pack of underwear – because Jullia "accidently bought them and doesn't need them" – seven pairs of socks, two baseball caps, and a pair of tennis shoes.

So today I'm in one of her long sleeve, white ribbed turtleneck tops. I have it tucked into dark washed jeans that would drag on the floor but because of my heels they hit an inch above it. Since it's going to be dark soon I don't bother taking my gloves or glasses and just grab my tablet and umbrella.

With a half wave, I leave the love sick fools to their dinner and exit the room. My tablet pings immediately with a message from Jullia.

Ice Princess: *If you need anything just let us know! Also I'll be tracking you*

She ends the message with a winky face and I roll my eyes but smile at the message. Such a stalker.

Turning off the tablet, I start heading out. There are noises coming out from behind closed doors. Music, shows or videos playing, voices, fucking. The dorms are separated by gender with the first year dorms being furthest from the main building, but there are no rules about anyone going into other dorms.

You would think with how prestigious it is that there would be more rules and regulations. But, of course, this isn't America – or Earth for that matter. And while English is a widely spoken language here, it is not native and had been brought over with how many people kept traveling back and forth from Miy to Earth.

It's something Ms. Elaycia and Rosemary had told me. They also mentioned various landmarks and would draw out maps for me before. I never thought I would actually be attending, so I never paid much attention to them. But I remember the gist – even before the map was downloaded to my tablet.

The main building is shaped like an octagon, where the wisteria looking Willow of Lore rests. It was a symbol that was created after a war between gods and right before the university was built. Stories and songs are whispered about it and its spirits who come out once a year to hum their melody.

The main building was built around that tree, with the

center of the building hollowed out and a dome of glass above to let in natural sunlight as well as moon and starlight. The rooms and stories that make up the perimeter hold most of our classes, with the cafeteria on the south most side of the main building – opposite of where the main front doors are.

Other buildings that make up the rest of the lecture halls and classrooms surround the southwest side of the main building. With the dorms to the west, and the society houses curving around the east and southeast side.

On the east side there is also the training arena and gym for those that have certain classes, as well as the east field which is past the society houses and extends acres. An expansive space that eventually leads to a cliff overlooking a sea with forests and woods surrounding it.

It's a beautiful place if you think about it.

If only I was here because I wanted to attend and not because it was either be here or be dead.

I glide down the stairs and pass the girl who gave me my key by the front desk. She gives me a mock salute when she sees me before going back to her tablet. Jullia had told me her name's Ricka and she's a lightning mage in Asher's class.

We haven't had many interactions but Asher and Jullia said she thinks I'm a bad bitch and votes for me against the celestials. Even though Ricka herself has a RBF and 'don't come near me or I'll fuck you up' energy, she seems cool enough.

Better than that red-headed vampyr bitch on my first day. Thankfully I haven't seen her since then.

I open my umbrella right before I push open the doors and to be honest, I could probably go without. If I had worn one of the baseball caps Jullia gave me I'd be good because the back of the dorms face west and the sun is mostly behind the trees now.

Keeping the umbrella open anyway, I rest the pole on my shoulder and slightly twirl it as I walk towards the path that leads to the main building. There's not many people out. A few on blankets having a little picnic, others out for simple strolls. With no parties on Sunday nights the campus is really calm. It almost feels eerie. Especially with all the gothic architecture and stone statues and overgrown foliage in certain areas.

This is how I imagined it would feel like to study at Oxford. Ana would tell me she always wished she could live that dark academia university life. She loved reading R.F. Kuang's books and all the intellectual and philosophical writing.

I'm personally a fan of her debut series. . . sometimes I wish I was more like Rin. So much rage. So much burning.

I adjust the angle of my umbrella as I enter an unshaded part of the path. My shadow elongates up the stone walkway. Glancing up, I survey the area before reaching my hand out of the safety of my umbrella's shadow.

Warmth seeps into my hand and fingers before it starts stinging. It's not exactly an instant thing. The sun gives off pointed rays that are stronger than just the overall light. Those pointed rays and where they touch are what start burning first.

Needles prick my skin as individual burns begin forming. I pull my hand back before they can develop into blisters and start smoking. Less than ten seconds was my hand under the sun. Random red marks are left around the top of my hand and fingers. Pain shoots through my arm as my body begins slowly healing them.

Usually it'll take about twenty to thirty seconds before blisters start forming and I begin to become incapacitated. Right after that my skin starts smoking and around a minute is when flames start forming and licking over my skin.

Not a long time, but I don't burst into flames right when the full force of the sun hits me. It still takes time, and seconds can feel like an eternity in certain circumstances.

When my hand is back to its normal skin color I contemplate doing it again, but I come to the hall that leads into the main building. I'd rather see if Professor Asier is available so I can ask my question and then leave. Maybe I can stop by the clinic and get some more blood bags so I don't feel like complete shit in the morning.

Hopefully he's in a good mood. It would probably be easier for me to just ask him tomorrow when I see him in class, but at least this way I get out of the dorms, maybe get some more blood, and I'll still possibly get some answers.

I do wonder though, why they don't teach about runic magic anymore. Of all the learned magics runic magic is probably the strongest. There's been records of the weakest of all races using just a single rune to decimate whole lands.

Entering one of the corridors, I take it down until I reach the southern tower and follow the lone hallway across from the tower entrance to one of the courtyards. Scones lining the walls are lit as shadows start growing from the setting sun.

We're nearing the end of August, meaning next month will be Hextillus – which is the month that was added making there thirteen months instead of twelve. Three hundred and sixty-four days. Thirteen months, each month having twenty-eight days. On the first it's always a new moon, and on the fifteenth it's always a full moon.

April, or Aprilis on Miy, starts the new year off. Aprilis first being the spring equinox and the first day of spring here. June twenty-first is the summer solstice, Septmust or September first is the autumn equinox, and Novam or November twenty-first is the winter solstice. Following the phases of the moon and the solstices and equinoxes following which days or nights are longest and shortest.

Much, much simpler than Earth's traditional calendar around most of the world. Not that it bothers me since I grew up with it and Nana taught me this calendar too. Most of the girls at the brothel follow this calendar anyway since it syncs up with their inner auras.

I come to the short corridor where Professor Aseir's class is, but when I try the door it's locked. I think he had said his office was somewhere around here. I step back from the door, looking side to side, about to take another step back when I feel it.

When I feel *him*.

"What are you doing here, Trouble?" he drawls.

The fucking angel.

Fifteen

Mavyn – August 21

Trauma being retained in muscle is the bane of any survivors existence. Because no matter how much you think you've moved on, no matter how much you force your mind to continue forwards, no matter what you tell yourself. . . your body never lies.

I *know* he's not a devil. He's not *him*. But he *feels* like one. I hadn't lied when I told Thorne that.

His aura is so similar. And my body remembers.

It starts with my muscles tensing. Waiting for that inevitable blow – whether it be from a physical weapon, his teeth sinking into my skin, or forcing my fangs into his. And while I force my blood to stay steadily flowing, force my heart not to pound, I can still feel the adrenaline flushing my system.

"Cat got your tongue, Trouble?"

Ice and frost. I focus on that because he is not burning and heat and rage.

Twisting my head I'm greeted by icy blue almond shaped eyes. So, *so* similar to *his*. But his hair is white threaded with silver. The devil's had been solid black.

He cocks his head at me and his lip twitches. As if he wants to sneer but doesn't quiet do it yet.

"Why'd you burn your hand?"

My heartbeat trips. "Were you following me?"

He smirks now. "Not until I saw you expose your hand. So tell me, why'd you burn yourself?"

Fuck. I hadn't felt his eyes on me before. I wasn't even distracted either. Normally I'm good at knowing when I'm being watched. An instinctual thing that's been engrained into me from that damned devil and his fated mage.

"I wanted to ask Professor Asier a question," I say instead. Answering his first question. I'd ask him if he knew where the professors office is, but I don't want to risk him asking for something in return for the answer. I already have to figure out how I'm going to pay the demigod back. Even though he hasn't flaunted my mark or asked for anything – yet.

Darian hums as he slides his hands into his pockets. My body relaxes the slightest bit and his eyes rove over me probably seeing it. Though I roll my eyes at myself because just because his hands aren't out doesn't mean he still can't use some form or magic to hurt me. I don't even know what his specialty is.

He's an angel so I know he has wings, but angels have all sorts of magic.

Huffing, he turns and begins walking. After a couple strides he stops and turns back. "You coming? Asier's office isn't over here."

Steeling myself, I raise a brow at him. "And what is it you want in return?"

Nothing is given for free.

"Tell me why you let yourself burn."

Rolling out my shoulders, I shrug and begin following him. "I miss feeling the sun. It's not that deep. As long as I'm not exposed for more than a few seconds I'll heal fine enough. I miss the warmth."

I almost say I miss the warmth without the burning. He probably wouldn't think much of it since I can burn, but the runic curse that was placed on me is more than just me burning in the sun.

He doesn't say anything as he starts leading the way. The last time I felt warmth without the burning was when Caleb made his ball of warmful light that mimicked the sun. It had been the first time since I was six I had felt warmth like that. The kind you can feel in your bones. In your soul.

God I miss him. I miss all of them and home. It's only been two months but I more than anyone know how long time can feel in short periods. A whole eternity can pass within seconds.

"What's a sun devil?"

His question makes me almost jump. I didn't think he'd ask any more questions, and I especially didn't think he'd ask that question.

He doesn't look at me when I glance at him. His strides are long but I've kept up fine enough, though I've stayed about half a step behind from directly beside him.

I shrug, even though he can't see it. "It was what the devil who adopted me when I was younger called himself."

I can see his shoulders stiffen and his neck strain. A chill fans off him making me shiver. His aura roiling and anger accompanies it. Not surprising since he probably knows the devil abused me and I called him the same thing.

"Why did you call me that?"

His voice is quiet and calm, but in the same way the calm is before a storm. Or rather, in the eye of the storm.

Facing forward, I don't look at him anymore.

"You look like him," I state. "And your aura feels similar to his, though I can see it's stronger. I have no doubt you would be more powerful than him even as an angel."

He stops abruptly and turns towards me. I jerk back so I'm a step away from him and not almost brushing his shoulder with mine.

"You can see my aura?"

Oh fucking hell.

I keep my body still and my expression neutral. Nana taught me enough about each of the races including vampires, but she never mentioned if they're able to see auras. Most people can feel them. Aura is how you can tell the magnitude and essentially vibe of someone's power, where magic is the action of it. Aura is the spirit and soul where magic is the body and movement.

Jullia's aura tends to be cold but soothing. Gentle waves in the middle of the sea. Her magic is controlling and manipulating water – among other things.

Nana's aura is power and death. A pyre of bones cracking beneath roaring flames. Her magic is controlling and manipulating the body – whether that be one still alive or already dead. As long as it still has bones.

But I can also see that Jullia's aura is ribbons of white light threaded with strings of the darkest blue. Nana's is a coil of slithering threads usually always wrapped around her body in pitch black. Though at the very center of herself I have seen a ball of dim white.

I never told Nana I could actually *see* auras at times. Is that not normal? Darian is looking at me like it's not normal.

He takes a step closer to me and I take one back. His expression turns guarded as he surveys me again.

"You said you can see my aura," he states. I neither confirm nor deny. "Who's fucking blood turned you?"

I don't answer that either because it didn't seem like he was actually asking me. More like he was thinking out loud.

Stepping back, he spins on his heel and continues walking. I follow after a beat and he says nothing else until we come to a section of the school I haven't been to before. There's a closed door at the end of a hallway Darian bangs on before leaving without a second glance.

The thick, dark wooden door cracks open and gold ringed red eyes peak out. They look at Darian's retreading back first, then they snap to me and dark brows lower.

"Ms. Tsuki," he rumbles as he opens the door a bit more. It allows me to see his white button up he usually wears, though it's a bit rumped, the top few buttons are undone, and his sleeves are rolled up. "Is there something I can help you with?"

I try to look past him into his office, but his broad freakin shoulders block the view. Stupid tall ass men.

Clearing my throat and straightening my back, I ask, "I wanted to ask if you knew about runic magic? I had some questions about them, but I can't find any books about it and I was told you had taught a chapter about them in the past."

His brows raise a fraction as his eyes barely widen. His posture relaxes too and it causes his hold on the edge of the door to widen.

"Yes, I did a couple years ago," he confirms. "But runic magic isn't taught at Syngenia. That's why there are no books about it. What exactly do you want to know about runic magic?"

I frown at him. "But isn't runic magic the oldest learned magic? It dates back to the first blood witch and born vampyr. Weren't you able to learn it when you were a student? Why would they stop teaching it?"

Surprise flickers again in his eyes as he releases his hold on the door and crosses his arms.

"I graduated from Syngenia almost two hundred and fifty years ago, Ms. Tsuki. Many things have changed since then."

Two hund – damn. *God*damn. Growing up in both worlds of mortal and nonmortal I forget about things like that. Like how for most beings they don't fully mature until they're twenty-five and then that's when they're aging starts to slow.

And devils. . . well devils can live for centuries. Two hundred and fifty. . . ? So in human years he's probably somewhere between late twenties to late thirties.

Not that he looks it.

"Well," I drawl, trying not to think about his age, "is it

banned? Speaking or learning about runes? If not, could you answer some questions for me?"

Or are you too old to remember?

His eyes flicker with something as his expression darkens a shade. Opening his door wider, he says, "I am not too old to remember, Ms. Tsuki."

Oof.

I wince and double check all of my mental shields. Normally I have them completely closed and guarded, even while sleeping, so a being would have to force their way in if I didn't allow them access to my mind. That thought, however, must have slipped between the cracks. Every once in a while it will happen for thoughts I don't have to explicitly keep locked up. But I catch a bit of a smirk before he turns around and moves deeper into his office.

I take that as my invitation and clear my throat as I contemplate closing the door or not.

"Close the door, please," he rumbles as he wonders over to a wall solely made of shelves and full of books.

Clicking the door shut, I stand awkwardly as he peruses the shelves and I take a moment to observe the office. It's not small. The wall to the right is also completely covered in shelves with books and other things filling it. His desk is set before that facing the room and the other wall full of books where he's still looking through.

The far wall is covered in maps and paintings, with a longue area in the left corner and a bar cart against the wall. There's also a fireplace large enough that I'd be able to stand in without hitting my head and lay down in while still having room to stretch out.

Overall, it's nice. Moody but could be cozy with enough

space that he could hold a small class in here if he wanted. Everything neat and organized and clean.

Returning my gaze to Professor Asier, he takes a few books off the shelves before turning back to me. So much commanding power in those eyes. I try to forget that by never looking him in the eye unless he explicitly speaks to me. Which hasn't been since our first class.

"You can come in."

Of course it sounds more like a demand instead of a suggestion. But since he seems like he's willing to answer me I follow him over to his large desk where he sets the books down. This desk isn't like the one in his classroom, the top is completely level.

There's a lamp turned on in the corner and a few papers fanned out. A couple of them have grades on them.

"If you were busy," I say, "I can just ask tomorrow after class."

I feel weird now. Of course I could have waited till tomorrow, this was just my excuse to get out of the dorm. And thinking of that makes my stomach grumble. Which of course the professor hears.

He quirks a brow at me, eyes dipping to my stomach as I cross my arms over my chest.

"Castiel told me about the blue belladon trapped within scar tissue." I freeze. Oh fuck my life. "That's why you need to eat regular food and sleep whereas other vampires don't need either."

It might make him mad, but I slide my gaze away from him and shrug a shoulder. Of course they would have told him. I don't know what their relationship is with one another, but they're all buddy-buddy. It's annoying.

"And. . . ?"

He huffs under his breath. "Why do you want to know about runes?"

Looking over at the books they just look like regular leather bound hardcovers. There's no title on them and they're not as thick as I was thinking they would be.

Straightening my back, I meet his eye again. For some reason his heart beats a fraction harder when I do. "Do you know about runic curses?" And now his heart trips.

His eyes darken as he repeats, "Runic. . . *curses*?" I nod once and a look of hesitancy with suspicion shadows his face. "Runic magic is neither good nor evil, only the user can condone morals, however using runes to influence curses goes against its nature. All magic should follow the balances of the universes."

I nod at all that and wave a hand as I turn away to think.

"I know all that," I grumble. Staring at a point I let my mind wonder into the past. "But runic curses are the hardest to break because of that. I'm not asking because I want to cast one, I'm asking because. . . "

I had been young when he did it. I don't remember the symbols he carved into me or the process of how it all went down. He had done it in the middle of the night when I had been half asleep and after that all I felt was burning.

That's all I felt the next four years.

Shutting my eyes, I rub them and then exhale before looking back up at the devil. He's watching me with a curiosity and I shift in place at it.

"Do you know anything else about runic curses?" I ask. "Or do you know someone else I can ask?"

Crossing his arms – I involuntarily glance down at them

– he leans against his desk and gives me a pointed look.

"Why do you want to know about runic curses, Mavyn?"

Something, somewhere south, flutters when he says my name like that. I don't think he's called me by my first name at all and hearing it in his deep tenor voice makes me clench.

What. The. Fuck.

The gold ring in his eyes flare a bit and I immediately look away as I shift again.

"Curiosity."

He hums but he doesn't sound convinced. I don't blame him.

Turning back around, he opens one of the books and murmurs deeply, "Come."

My blood rushes before I can calm it and I involuntarily clench around nothing again. If I'm not careful I'm about to be smelling much sweeter with that berry and floral scent and it won't be because I'm bleeding.

Which also reminds me, I'll have to go to the bathroom soon.

Worst fucking timing. Worst of all is it's not just my ovulation phase when I'm. . . hormonal. Always towards the end of my menstruation entering my follicular phase for a couple days I swear I'm ovulating more than my actual ovulation phase.

And he has the fucking nerve to say that fucking word with his fucking voice.

Taking a deep, quiet breath, I regulate my blood flow and heartbeat and walk over. He's already leaning over a book with the chapter header labeled 'Mortem'.

"How comforting," I murmur under my breath but Professor Asier huffs a laugh at that.

"Runic curses are forbidden," he explains. "The only thing that will be mentioned in any book about them is that they taint the soul and lead you to your death."

Pointing at something, I lean closer in to read it. Only I can't because the rest of the text is in Latin, but I do see a few words I do understand.

Cursed. Death. Blood. Runes.

Nothing that could help me understand the context, but he helps with that.

"Runic curses are a type of magic one learns themselves. They draw regular runes but twist them by imbuing them with dark contexts and negative aura. It's not necessarily something that can be taught by another."

He turns the page and I take another step so I'm now right beside him and I'm able to better look at the page. He stiffens next to me but I focus everything onto the page and the runes drawn out on it. Words I can't understand scribbled with diagrams and arrows.

"Because of that there isn't an exact way to break them. Depending on what the curse is someone who is an expert and has explicitly studied runes could possibly counter the effects, but it's unlikely that the curse would be fully broken."

Turning the page, I study the runes drawn here and read the words associated with them in my head despite not knowing what they really mean. I shift my weight and place a hand on his desk as I turn the page again.

"Would it be possible to counter a runic curse with

another? Two negatives making it neutral?"

Something shifts and without looking at him I focus on his aura. His feels a lot like Nana's with all its power and death. But his is stone still. Same with his body, though a heady scent trails around him and his blood is rushing. I can almost hear the beat of his heart pounding against his chest.

Following his blood from his heart it trails down until. . .

I tense my own body. He had stiffened while speaking but I had only asked if runic curses could be countered with another curse. So why is his blood rushing? Why is his blood rushing like *that*? Is he. . . is he turned on by runes? Is *that* why they don't teach this kind of magic anymore? People get off because of it?

Oh my fucking god.

I didn't think they were sexual in any way, but then again what the fuck do I know?

Snapping up, I scoot a few steps away from him. Clearing my throat I gesture towards the book.

"So – uh. . . " Fuck. Way to make it awkward, Mavyn. I shake my head. I always told myself I would not kink shame and I do not judge sexual preferences, but just. . .okay. I shake my head again. "Sorry. Uhm. . . countering. Is that possible, or would someone who's an expert just need to know the curse and see the runes and then possibly counter that way?"

I shift in place and refuse to look at him. That had been Ms. Elaycia's only request when she took me in. Everyone has preferences and different things that get them off and unless it's nonconsensual and harmful without any sexual gratification for any party we shouldn't judge.

And I'm not judging him! If he gets off from talking

about runes or practicing runic magic or anything of the sort I will not judge. It's just. . . surprising. He's a professor, and while he's hot, it's one of those things you shouldn't know about your teacher.

Cordellia liked those kinds of romances books. I'm sure Jullia would too, but I would prefer no part of that.

He's watching me. I can feel his eyes on me despite me looking anywhere but at him.

"That I'm not sure about."

Sixteen

Varian – August 21

It has been almost two weeks since the last time I spoke to the bloodsucker. And in those two weeks she hasn't looked at me once after the infirmary. I haven't been much better, but she is purposefully keeping her attention away from me.

And right now all I want is for her attention to solely be on me.

An irrational thought. A remanent of the lust Castiel tries his best to hide from me for her. But I made it worse when I told her to come. Her scent was slightly sweeter when I had opened the door to what it normally is. A scent I now know is because a devil had marked her when she was younger and his fangs were embedded with blue belladon.

It's extraordinary how she's semi-immune to it. Thorne had also reiterated what Castiel had said about that night when she and him were cut with a blade embedded with the poison that kills all. Castiel discreetly flaunted her bitemark on him all weekend. He explained in full detail how her venom felt flowing through his blood.

Then his mood sobered after subbing for my class on Monday and Callahan had seemed more irritable than normal. Neither have told me what happened – if something did happen.

Thorne also let me know there's a second bitemark near her collarbone. She didn't say there was another last weekend to Thorne and Castiel, so it makes me wonder if there are more.

"It would just depend on the curse," I continue. Trying my best to ignore her scent. "I would have to know what it is in order to know if I could counter it or not."

Her scent changes. It dips more floral and I wonder if she knows most races can scent when someone is aroused.

It shouldn't make me as prideful as it does because I shouldn't be feeling anything towards her at all. I believe I've kept my own scent hidden well enough. I had to concentrate hard when I opened my door to sweet berry and florals. Darian had already been halfway down the hall and I almost gave myself away when I looked at her.

I haven't seen her in anything other than her uniform, and even that has made me take more cold showers than I have ever needed to before. But at least the blazer they all wear hides whatever shape she has. Right now in her fitted long sleeve and tight jeans I can see every curve.

But she shouldn't scent me at all, so I wonder what

made her jump back. And why is she asking about runic magic and curses. How does she even have any of this information?

"What curse are you trying to break?"

There's no shift in her posture, expression, energy. It's as if I simply asked what time it was instead of what is probably one of many secrets she's keeping. From what I know she had been staying in a brothel in New York City of America with a bone witch of all races.

She shrugs a shoulder and still refuses to look at me.

"Mavyn."

Her light pink eyes snap to me and her scent deepens like it did when I told her to come. I didn't consciously intend for it to have a double meaning, but I'm also not entirely ashamed of it either.

I should be. And yet I can't seem to care because her pupils expand and I can see her thighs clenching together.

Fuck I need to get my head on straight.

Expanding the shadows of my mind I find Castiel in his office next door.

Come here and make an excuse that you need me, I practically growl. Because her scent is consuming my office and my fangs are starting to ache wondering if she could taste as sweet as she smells and she looks –

Why, Castiel drawls with a deep chuckle in my mind, *do you feel so sexually frustrated?*

Now. Cas –

There's a knock on the door that makes her jump. Breaking eye contact with me she turns towards the door and subconsciously takes another step towards it.

He chuckles again in my mind as I march over and nearly wretch the door off its hinges. With the full force of scenting her now though, his eyes widen a fraction and his pupils blow wide.

Oh.

"What can I help you with, Professor D'etre?" I ask cordially. My words completely at odds with my actions and my energy that's about to spill over.

He glances behind me and clears his throat. Parting his mouth a crack, he switches to breathing through it instead of his nose. It doesn't help much, but it's better than nothing.

What the fuck were you doing? he says in my mind, his voice edging a bit darker than before, before saying calmly out loud, "I need some help finishing some paper work for the new trainees in our external controlling class. It needs to be finished by tonight. . . if you aren't busy."

"He's not," the bloodsucker announces. Her voice clipped and neutral. "My question was answered, I'll be leaving now."

I glance back at her and she looks as composed as she did when I opened my door. Her pupils no longer dilated, her body relaxed, her face expressionless. The only outlier is her scent which has somehow gotten even sweeter.

"I actually need to leave anyway, I have a paper I need to finish," she adds. Taking a step towards the door and looking at me expectantly.

Why is her scent now stronger?

"You didn't answer my question."

Her jaw clenches and I can feel Castiel staring at me.

What question? he asks within my mind. *I thought you*

wanted an excuse to leave.

"It was a hypothetical," she answers dryly. "There are runes all over the school and I was curious. I know they're powerful, and I thought maybe there was a way to reverse my curse."

I can feel Castiel's shock along with mine. She's cursed?

She raises a brow. "You know. . . isn't being turned into a vampire a curse?"

Oh.

Oh.

"I thought maybe there was a rune that could undo this. Maybe then the Mage Board would let me just leave since I'm not a vampire and would solve everyone's problems."

Castiel leans against the doorframe and crosses his arms. He's more or less in the same outfit as me, though his skin is lined with his golden markings.

"Unfortunately, turning into a vampire isn't a runic curse," he adds. To which she makes a face at him but doesn't say anything. She made the same face when her roommate said the first mentions of *Syngenia* was the first land of magic. And again when I was teaching who had first created the university.

It's her tell when she disagrees with you. And since she stated that Syngenia was first known as the name of the first blood witch, I'm going to assume she not only disagrees with you, but knows for a fact you're wrong.

She shrugs and then shifts on her feet. "Well, either way I have my answer. I need to go now."

She takes another step though neither myself nor Castiel move. Her light colored eyes flick between us and breathing through my mouth is no longer helping because I can almost taste that sweet berry and floral scent.

"Why do you smell so sweet, poison flower," Castiel murmurs and her eyes widen a fraction at it. I can feel his lust and hear his whispering thoughts about what he wants to do to her.

"I need to go," she repeats. Teeth gritted and now her hands are fisted where they're crossed over her abdomen.

Castiel hums. "So you would taste as sweet as you smell. Tell me, poison flower, where are you bleeding from?"

Like a piece clicking into place, my mind makes the connection.

She has poison trapped within the scar tissue but it's not stuck there. That's why she needs food and sleep and why she's semi-immune. The poison has been seeping into her blood so like with any other being, when their blood is exposed it heightens their scent.

Which means this entire time she's been bleeding.

My muscles tighten as I glare at her. "Where the fuck are you bleeding from?"

Was it Darian? Did he do something to her? Or did someone else try to do something before she got here?

She glares right back at us. "May I go?" she growls. Like a little kitten.

"No," Castiel says the same time as I do. Repeating what he said, Castiel asks, "Where are you bleeding from?"

Her hands tighten around her middle area and Castiel jerks back at hearing my thought. A thought that couldn't possibly be plausible, but I can feel his agreement anyway. Only it's impossible. Vampires can't menstruate.

Letting out a frustrated groan, she hunches an inch over as she winces. "Holy shit, unless you want a bunch of blood all over your fucking hard wood let. Me. Go." Wincing again she breaths out, "Fucking cramps."

Cementing what I thought.

Only it's not possible.

Castiel shifts and says, "There's a bathroom in my office." Causing her to clench her jaw and straighten before marching straight towards the door. Sliding past me, uncaring that her entire front brushes along my side, and out the door.

I hear a heavy door open and then shut as I turn to face Castiel with a look of disbelief.

"How is that – "

Not out loud, I interrupt.

He nods and then blows out a breath. *It can't be possible, right? I mean, we both know how vampires are turned and what changes are made to their human bodies. The only reason they need to drink blood is because they're dead and drinking blood is how their own cycles through their veins.*

I know.

Could it be because of the poison? Or is the new generation of vampires evolving? She needs blood, that isn't an act. And she burns in the sun.

I shake my head and drag my hand down my face. None of this makes sense.

Extending the shadows of my mind further I reach for Thorne. It takes a few seconds before he opens his mind to me.

I'm on call with my father, As –

She's menstruating, Castiel blurts. I'd laugh at the bluntness but Thorne processes the words and his shock splinters through.

Inaudible whispers come from Thorne before he fully has a presence in my mind.

That's impossible, he states. Like a fact. Because it is a fact and yet here she is.

Well clearly not, Castiel huffs. *Varian opens the door and from her scent you would think something was happening but instead I realize she had to have been bleeding. Afterall, the poison is in her blood as well as her scars. It could have only been that strong if she was bleeding.*

Castiel gives me a pointed look.

Though I'm sure other things influenced it.

I did not fuck her, I grumble as I glare at him.

But you thought about it.

And I roll my eyes at him as his office door opens again. The bloodsucker emerges and jolts when she sees us where we've been the whole time. A guarded expression contorts her face and her scent is now just barely sweeter than it normally is. Just a hint of berries and floral.

"Would you mind – "

"No," she snaps, interrupting Castiel as she straightens her back and gives us both a deadened expression. "I realize how much coming here was a mistake, so let me just make this clear. I am not a spy and I don't give a single shit about why you thought I was one. I am only here because it's either this or death and unfortunately I do want to live a bit longer. So I will keep any and all interactions strictly about classes. You *will* do the same. I won't go near your business, and you don't go near mine."

So much power in her words yet not a single thread of power around her. She speaks as if she's a celestial with power higher than all of us. As if she isn't a vampire who was formerly a human.

"Do I make myself clear?"

Her voice shifts. The power in her words darkening. For some reason it sounds like a threat. Saying without saying all the things she could do if we don't agree.

Who raised her after that devil to have given her so much confidence?

Castiel and Thorne both stay quiet, though I didn't directly ask them that question. But I can feel Thorne thinking and I'm about to ask her when her energy shifts. Her soft pink eyes deepen a shade and for the first time I can feel a whisp of her aura.

And all I get from it is blackened rage.

Only a moment. A split millisecond I feel it before she goes back to feeling like nothing. Though her body relaxes with a predators calm as her eyes bore into mine.

Almost.

I *almost* submit before catching myself and I can feel Castiel and Thorne's astonishment at that. Only one person has ever been able to make me submit, has ever had the power to be more dominant than me, and they've been dead for nearly a hundred years. Yet this little bloodsucker nearly did it with almost no aura and the smallest amount of magic a non-mortal could have.

Frustration flickers through my body as I shove Castiel and Thorne out of my mind. She's a complexity I can't figure out and secret after secret continues to reveal itself. I want to know every crevice of her mind and thoughts and past while also wanting to bend her over my –

No.

No. Fucking. Way.

Gritting my teeth, I glare like the devil the humans believe in. Yet she doesn't back down and meets my eye without hesitation.

"We'll keep our interaction limited."

I spin to go back into my office and slam the door shut when her voice physically stills me.

"And stay out of my business."

Like someone who knows they've already gotten what they want. Her tone oozes dark satisfaction and primal confidence. The fucking *brat*.

"Yes," I growl, before promptly slamming my door shut to her.

Seventeen

Mavyn – Septmust 1

I let my heart pound steadily as I round the bend of the path and come back to the tree line. I can see the side of my dorm building as I slow my pace and keep my breathing deep and even. *Rumors* by NEFFEX is blasting through my ears and I smile when the techno bass hits.

After the encounter with the professors about a month and a half ago I needed a release. So I started running again. Endurance and stamina can save you more times than you'd think. It's also a good way to reintroduce my body into working out.

Asher says we can't use the gym since we're first years, but who needs that when you have calisthenics and the outdoors.

Rolling out my shoulders, I start stretching my arms and neck as I pause at the edge of the forest. It's still dark and will be for another hour. Today's the autumn equinox meaning there will be exactly twelve hours of sunlight and twelve hours of darkness. From six am to six pm. Then there will be no more long sunlit days.

Keeping my legs straight, I bend over and fold my hand to the ground. My hamstrings stretch so good and I hold the pose for longer than needed. The first weekend I kept up with my little workout routine was brutal because I didn't have actual food, but since I've been getting paid I've been fine every other weekend.

In the mornings I get up around four to drink a premade smoothie before I start stretching and doing body weight workouts. Then I come out here and run for a good hour through the forest. Then I stretch, shower before the bathroom gets full, and spend the rest of my morning in the room drinking blood until I can go out and get breakfast.

Jullia and Hanna started joining me too, though last night Jullia had stayed in Asher's room at Stone House. She does that every so often and tends to sleep in for as long as possible before joining me for breakfast during the week. And Hanna won't come out so early. I wouldn't either if I didn't care about hiding my scars in the bathroom.

I survey the area as I twist my middle and stretch out my sides. My music is still thumping in my ears as *Power* by Kanye West begins playing. Over the month with my proper nutrients and working out again I've started gaining strength back into my muscles. All I need now is a few training sessions to make sure I keep my power.

Nana had suggested it the second she saw me. She said

I needed to learn how to channel all my energy through my body. I needed to not be weak.

It had been the best thing – on top of all the amazing things – Ms. Elaycia had given me.

Self-defense, martial arts, weapons training. Five years is nothing compared to the training I need to be good enough, but at least I started young so the movements could be ingrained into my body and instinct.

I'm best with distance fighting. Using weapons like a staff, longer daggers and throwing knives, or my whip dart. It should have been the most difficult, but even Nana and Ms. Elaycia said of course I would be a natural at that weapon. A long whip with a blade on either end.

Walking away from the tree line I follow the wall of my dorm building to the front. Ricka looks up from her tablet at me and lazily salutes me before going back to whatever she was watching. She works as front desk and security for our dorm. From six pm till six am, Sunday till Thursday she sits at that desk.

It makes me wonder when she actually sleeps along with all her classes. Despite seeming to always be here Asher is always busy. With classes, training, and his responsibilities for his house.

I enter my room and grab a quick change of clothes for after my shower. There's a communal bathroom on each floor that everyone keeps relatively clean. There are also individual stalls for the showers, but the only privacy is a shower curtain that can be easily whipped open.

Turning on just the sink lights, I blow out a breath thankful that it's empty. It usually is, but there's always the off chance someone is an early bird or just coming back from whatever party or fuck buddy's place.

I pick the last stall in the back, opening the other ones so people know they're open. Then I place my little shower caddy on the built in hook and set my towel and clothes on the bench just outside. The water sputters out for a moment after I turn the handle and it's nothing short of freezing. In the mornings it's always cold, though it will quickly heat up if you give it a minute or so. Best part of magic is having almost instant hot water.

I, however, keep the handle over the cold setting and strip. Once naked I step under the spray and puff out a breath from the cold. Goosebumps cover the entirety of my body as I turn and tip my head under the spray as well. It feels like icicles, but it's better than it being warm.

The cold eases the ache in my scars. Numbs them, I guess. Doesn't matter that I'm frozen after. Usually I'll dry myself off and wrap up in a thick, warm blanket for at least an hour afterward. For some reason the warmth from water feels closer to needles on my scars.

Sighing, I grab my shampoo and begin washing my hair. It's been a long time since I've acted out because of the unfairness. Unable to do things, forcing myself to be content with what I have, not thinking about how much my life could have been different.

The last time it happened I was sixteen. Not that I let anyone know about it. Ms. Elaycia was closing the brothel part of the club down for a week and was taking everyone to her beach front house in Florida. They said they could take me, but I declined. There was no point anyway. I would be stuck in the house during the day like I always am.

The day after they left I filled one of the bathtubs up with water as hot as any normal person could stand it and then let myself practically drown. It felt like the same kind of burning as the devil. Even if the water was warm it would have been the same.

Burning and burning and burning.

But of course at the last moment I flung myself out. Unable to kill myself then and the burning feeling lasted for weeks. I had wanted to scream. I had wanted to find a way to bring that devil back so I could do all that he had tortured me with and more.

It wasn't fair.

But it's never fair.

And it never will be.

So I made myself stop complaining. I readjusted my life to work with my curses. *Not that it always works*. But unless I want to risk the chance he isn't able to help and tell Professor Asier what exactly my curse is, I'm stuck like this.

It's not all bad. Who needs skin on skin contact or the sun.

I let my body relax into the cold spray of the water as I rinse off. The scent blocking soaps I got right after I got my first paycheck help mute the poison. Jullia says she almost can't scent a specific scent on me at all. And it helped mute the scent of my blood from a week ago. Thankfully Professor Asier and the demigod both have not asked or hinted or even looked at me.

I don't know if it's because of the soap or because I've stayed away from them and had went to the bathroom practically every half hour, but I'm safe enough for the next two weeks.

I'm about to turn off the water when the door to the bathroom opens and in comes giggling. My body freezes involuntarily before I force myself to relax.

"Oh!" she gasps in a breathless voice. "Someone's in

here, Cal – "

"Shhh," he whispers. A male with whoever the girl is, both absolute shit at being quiet. "Let's see if you can be quieter than you were earlier."

She giggles and I roll my eyes. I have no idea who either of them are, and I don't care. Once they enter one of the shower stalls I'm out of here. Instead of turning the shower off right away, I peak out of the curtain to grab my towel from the bench sitting right outside.

Kissing sounds and rustling start up but it sounds no different to the brothel so I really don't care. Whoever he is though has his back to me as I snatch my towel and stand as far away from the spray to dry off. No way am I turning off the water until they are in a stall so I'll do what I can to get dressed here. At least with no hot water there's no steam or humidity.

Breathless gasps and mumbling and slurping sounds accompany the water raining down in my stall. I peek out again, using the curtain to cover up as much as I can to grab my clothes now. But this time the guy has the girl on top of the counter by the sinks with her legs wrapped around his waist.

And now that they're in clear light I can see dirty blond hair and golden eyes. Eyes that immediately lock on mine through the mirror.

The girl, someone with long black hair and fair skin, has her lips on the side of his neck. She hasn't noticed me as his eyes widen and I flinch back into my stall. And stupid me because I didn't grab my clothes and all I have here is a towel not large enough to cover the entirety of my body.

There's more rustling and then, "Get out."

Deep, dark, demanding. The girl squeaks but for some reason doesn't say anything and a moment later the door opens and closes.

Now the only sound is the shower and fucking hell my luck must only last in increments because how is this even possible.

"Mavyn. . . " he drawls. His tone neutral so I have no idea what he's feeling but he sounds closer to my stall now. "Are you going to turn off the shower and come out?"

Almost six weeks and I haven't even looked at him. He hasn't spoken a word to me since the gym incident. Neither has Thorne and stupidly I thought I would be able to get through the rest of this year easily. I thought I would be able to finish at least this fucking year quietly.

Invisible.

Ordinary.

Forgotten.

"Mavyn – "

"My clothes are out there and you're standing right in front of my stall," I interrupt. Hopefully he is more of a gentleman and will leave.

"Then grab them and change in the stall. I need to say something to you and I want to do it face to face."

A shiver rolls up my spine. In order to do that I'd have to stick my hand out and there's enough light to easily see the scars on my arm. It's not that big of deal, I hadn't cared before about people seeing them or not. But it's how they treat me afterward. The looks, the pity, the remorse. They see the scars and think I'm fragile.

I had to yell at Rosemary once to stop treating me like that. She wouldn't let me do anything for months when she found out about them.

God damnit. Today has started off so good too and now wariness is creeping in. Everything had been going so good. I've kept up with my classes, I've been working, I've been feeding myself properly, I've started working out again.

"You'll see my arm if you keep staring at the stall," I sigh. I don't know why I care so much about it all anyway. I doubt people would care if the so called vampire had scars at all. It's not like I don't already get stares and whispers and whatnot.

"I already know you have scars on your arm, Mavyn. But I'm not leaving, I need to speak to you."

"You can't just wait outside?" I try. To which I'm greeted by silence. I don't have the energy for this shit.

Wrapping the towel around myself tighter, I turn the water off and grab the shower curtain before cracking it open and reaching one of my arms out. I have to stretch the whole thing out to get where my clothes are on the bench and faster than I was prepared for burning wraps around my forearm and my back is pressed against a wall.

Golden eyes lit up with threads of white are all I see as they stare at the arm gripped in their hand.

"Thorne said – " he doesn't finish as his eyes follow my arm up to my shoulder and then the part of my chest the towel can't cover. The arm he's holding onto feels like it's consumed with fire as I ram the back of my head into the wall and pinch my eyes shut.

Pain.

The kind of burning I haven't felt since the devil last placed his hands on my bare skin.

I don't cover my body just because of the sun. I also cover it because if anyone touches my scars bare of any barrier

– whether that be material or magic – it burns worse than the sun.

It almost feels like I'm about to black out. I forgot how much it hurt. The nightmares don't even come close. I'm not used to it anymore. It's not accompanied by the sexual warmth of his venom flooding my system from his bite or the twisted euphoria from the poisons the mage would give me before she would start with me.

It's only pain.

I can't even speak. I can't even mouth the word stop. I can't. . .

Let go.

I can barely think it and worse is that I wasn't able to properly open my mental shields up enough to just tell him that. My walls get flung open as he immediately lets my arm go and I slide down the wall. It takes too many seconds to snap my shields back up and lock my mind from prying eyes.

Too many seconds too late because I felt him seeing what was exposed. I felt him watching. Even if he didn't enter my mind, he still saw.

The pain lingers for long minutes. It's quiet but for my pants. When I'm finally able to open my eyes I find Callahan still in front of me, though now he's kneeling so my eyes are level with his. And his are pitch black.

No differentiating between his iris and pupil. A primordial stillness has his body stuck in place and I can't sense his aura at all. It's never been possible for someone to completely hide their magic from me. There's always some sort of fluctuation even if they try concealing it to everyone else.

Ribbons of pain still shoot through my left arm as I pull my knees in tighter to my chest and slowly hunch my shoulders.

Any tinge of movement feels like saws ripping at my skin and bone. But he looks. . .

"Callahan."

Barely a breath. Barely anything because if I'm not careful he could eviscerate me. He looks like he's so close to shifting into that *thing* all devils have within themselves. A type of thing – not monster, not beast, not creature, it's a thing – and I know the type of death they can instill. Their *true form.*

"You said he was generous."

Monotone and cold. His voice sounds dead to any sort of emotion. Like someone without a soul.

"Who?" I breathe. I will not speak louder than that in case he does attack. He wouldn't even need to blink in order to decimate me.

The black in his eyes ripple as a sliver of color around what would be his pupil lights.

"The devil." And a bit of understanding leaks through.

I can't believe he remembered that. My description of the devil while I had been in the infirmary. I had said he was generous – though I had meant with his punishments. He was more than generous with those.

He speaks before I can respond. "This is torture." The gold in his eyes consume more of the black in his iris. "He tortured you, didn't he. It wasn't you who cut your arms. It was always him."

Breaking my eye contact, he looks at every scar, every bitemark. I should be lucky he can only see what's on my arms and legs.

"How did you survive this?" he breathes, his voice finally cracking. "You said they adopted you when you were a toddler. Toddlers are between two to four years old."

The black in his iris retreats back to just the outline of his iris and his aura flickers back to life around him. It makes me internally relax as I shift to push myself further into the wall. The pain in my arm is still lingering but not enough to prevent me from getting dressed and leaving. I wish I could take today off and just sleep. I want to sleep after this encounter.

"Mavyn," he says quietly, softly, carefully. "I'm not going to hurt you."

"I know," I snap. At least, I know right now he's not going to. Not with that inner self that is the true form of a devil now locked back inside him. Pushing off the wall, I ignore the lingering pain and cinch the towel tighter around myself. "Now can you turn around so I can get dressed? Or better yet, get out and forget you saw anything."

He stands up with me and his eyes linger on my scars.

"I can't forget that – "

"Then try." I snap again. "Now get out."

His jaw clenches and because he's already seen this much I don't have the energy to care enough. I drop the towel and his eyes flare as I use it to wrap my hair up before pulling on my clothes. Just a loose long sleeve and pajama pants to cover me so I can get back to my room and then I can get ready.

When I look back up at him I'm not surprised by the state of shock or anguish. Scars from objects linger nearly every part of my body, and that devil's bitemark accompany them.

He hasn't moved or said anything, so I huff and start heading towards the door. Grabbing my caddy and dirty clothes while keeping the towel wrapped around my hair. He still doesn't move or speak even after I leave the bathroom. Not until I get back to my room and am about to close the door does a hand stop it.

I glance behind me to see Callahan out of his shocked state. A hard edge lining his features that I can't fully tell if it's pointed at me or not.

"I'm sorry," he blurts. Sounding calm but I can feel his blood rushing. It's rushing so hard I can see the slight movement from his vein in his neck. "Can you just. . . can I just come in? I wanted – I needed to talk to you. I've been needing to for weeks."

I raise a brow and peak behind him as if I'm looking for something. "You sure you have time? You kicked your friend out but I'm sure she's waiting for you."

Yeah. . . waiting to shove her tongue down your throat.

He glowers as I let him hear that thought and only that thought. Blocking him from my head so I can't hear anything he tries to tell me through my mind.

He drags a hand down his face as he shakes his head. "I couldn't care less about her. Now that you're here though, I do need to talk to you. Please."

He says that word like he means it. Like a plea he needs me to answer.

And I know I shouldn't. I have a feeling if I shut him out he would stay out. But for some reason I hesitate. And then for some other unknown reason I open the door just a crack more so he can slip in.

He closes the door right behind him and I leave him where he is as I go to my side of the room and open my wardrobe. My uniform hangs neatly inside with the few clothes I've managed to procure. I haven't been able to get a lot since most of my minimal wage goes to food, but it's enough. I'm now saving up bit by bit so I can start getting proper school supplies.

Bending forward, I unwrap my hair and use the towel to scrunch out as much water as possible. Then I flip it over and throw the towel to my bed. Catching sight of Callahan, he hasn't moved from his place by the door and is now looking over my room.

"Well?" I ask. I'm waiting for him to say whatever it is he wants to tell me.

He doesn't look at me though. "Where's all your stuff?"

Using my fingers to comb through my hair, I turn around and look at the room. The blackout shades still cover the windows so the only light is from the lamp on Jullia's side that I had turned on before I went to the showers. It illuminates enough though.

There are rugs and throw pillows and blankets all on Jullia's side. Lamps and her desk is decorated with cute looking supplies and stacks of her romance books. She's also hung up posters and pictures and fake ivy over her walls. So much personality.

Then you look at my side and it looks as if there isn't anyone rooming with Jullia.

The bed has the same flat pillow, dingy sheet, and scratchy blanket it did when I got here. My desk is empty except for my tablet, music player, and necklaces. Other than that I just have my flats for my uniform by my bed and the few clothes I have are hung and folded away in my wardrobe.

I shrug. "I don't get paid all that much and most of the money goes towards food for the weekends. It's not like I need anything anyways. I was spoiled at the brothel, but it's not like I had anything before that."

He finally looks at me but I turn towards my wardrobe

to grab my uniform so I can get dressed. Since he's already seen everything I pull my top off and throw it over to my bed. Out of the corner of my eye I catch him whipping his head away.

"You didn't tell Thorne about the rest of your scars and. . . marks. Made it seem like you didn't want anyone to see your body."

"So?"

I can hear him shift his weight. "So, why are you so open about it now?"

He doesn't sound anything but curious. I'm sure anyone would be, but it's not my body I care about.

"Modesty was never a luxury I ever had," I start.

"Modesty isn't a luxury, it's a – "

"Luxury," I interrupt while almost glowering at him. "Maybe not to you because you were born with wealth, power, and privileges no one else has, but for the real world it is a luxury. And it was one I never had."

Buttoning only one of the buttons on my shirt, I then slide off the pajama pants and slide on my skirt. I'll put my thigh high socks on when I actually have to leave. It hasn't gotten cold enough outside for the suffocating fabric to not make my scars ache.

"And," I continue, pulling all my hair back and twisting it around into a low bun, "it was never about my body. Not being allowed to have modesty meant my body never mattered, I just didn't want anyone to see my scars. And not even because of any shame or embarrassment or anything else you're thinking. I could care less about them, I've been learning to live with them since I was five, but it's everyone else who always makes a big deal about them. I mean, look at how you just reacted, plus what happened when you saw the bitemark."

Using a wooden hair stick, I secure my hair and grab my socks before closing my wardrobe. Then I open my mini fridge and pull out a premade breakfast shake. Tossing my socks to the bed, I open the bottle and go over to pull my chair out from my desk so he can sit.

Then I climb onto my bed and sit crisscross apple sauce.

"I also can't have people touching them, so wearing clothes that just covers them is easier."

He's staring at me but he's stone still and there's been no fluctuations in his blood flow or his heartbeat. I have no idea what he's thinking, but at least he walks over to sit in the chair. It's directly across from me and his eyes only leave mine for a moment to look at my legs.

"You said can't," he finally says. "Not that you don't want them to, but people can't touch them. Why? I have never felt pain like that, Mavyn."

He relaxes into the chair as his eyes come back to meet mine. I've always found it interesting how some people will look you straight in the eyes and some people won't. So many scientific and psychological studies. Then you have the magical aspects, about finding your fated and souls being bound to others. The closest a person can see another person's soul is through their eyes.

"Did Professor Asier tell you about me coming to him a month ago? Did he say anything at all about the interaction?"

I will not tell him about my menstruating if he doesn't already know about it, and I shouldn't be telling him about this but. . .

He shakes his head and I release a breath I had held in for a second longer than normal. Setting my drink between my legs, I lean back and put weight on my hands behind me before look off to the side.

"Well I went to his office to ask if he knew anything about runic magic and curses. I had asked him if he knew how to break a runic curse."

I should not be telling him this. This guy who I don't even actually know except for what the basics are and what Jullia has told me. This guy who is so close with the celestials who have nothing more than hatred towards me.

But I want to. Because at the end of the day all anyone ever wants is to be seen. To be known. Acknowledgement is a necessity people forget about. To be forgotten is a fate worse than death, so of course everyone wants to be remembered.

"I lied to Professor Asier and D'etre. I said I was cursed because I had been turned into a vampire, but the truth is that the devil had placed an actual runic curse on me a long time ago. A type of curse where it feels like I'm burning whenever there's skin on skin contact with my scars. Which," I look down at my legs, "is everywhere except my feet, hands, and neck."

I was always surprised when the devil never bit my neck. And either Callahan has learned, or it still hasn't fully processed with him because he still doesn't move.

"Feet, hands, and neck," he repeats slowly. "But what about your face?"

Tension thrums through the room with an electricity to it that sparks like tender touches.

He must be paying better attention to my words then. Understanding that like some of the fae, I speak certain words or leave out select information. As much as possible, I try to not – *technically* – lie. What people assume or gather or infer is their fault. Instead of paying attention to my words they try to read between the lines to what I'm trying to mean.

I shrug a shoulder and glance away as I try to remember that night. It's been a long time and so much has happened since then. Bits and pieces and sometimes I don't even think it's real.

"The devil placed the rune on my face when he cursed me." At least one of the runes. The most important one that cemented the curse.

Callahan's voice is just as calm as it has been. He's either in complete control right now, or he doesn't care.

"What about the skin between your scars? Have you ever tried finding a spell or enchantment to make it so no one does touch your scars? If it was possible to place small, individual barriers just over them, that way someone could touch you without touching your scars?"

Keeping my body relaxed and my tone neutral, I answer, "I've never tried it. There was never a reason I needed to before."

That tension thickens in the room and I have to actually try to keep my heart steady and my blood flow even. Yet his stays the same as before. A constant, solid beat from his heart.

Leaning in, he rests his forearms on his knees as his eyes glance down at my legs again. The white scars and bite marks looking exceptionally stark right now.

"Would you want to?" he asks, quieter than he's spoken before. It makes me shiver and I dig my fingertips into the bed to try and keep myself grounded. It doesn't do much.

Why?" I whisper.

And when he looks back up at me the full force of his aura hits me. Like there was a shield over it containing what it was. So clear that I can see it perfectly just as much as I can now feel it. Ribbons of transparent black with threads of white and gold lit through them. Wisping threads of stark black flutter around him too, but they're as thin as actual thread.

So much contradiction, yet so much beauty. And there's no war with it. The darkness is not trying to devour the light, just as the light isn't trying to dimmish the dark. They balance each other perfectly, an equal of harmony.

"Because I want to touch you without harming you."

My mind empties out. For a moment everything is silent.

He says it like it's the most obvious thing in the world. Like I should have already known that. Like. . .

I'm saved from responding because the sound of footsteps echo right outside the door before there's a click and the door opens. Jullia and Asher come in, both of them with worried and conflicted expressions but Jullia smiles at me. That is, of course, before she realizes Callahan is sitting before me.

Both of them freeze as they stare at us. Jullia's eyes zipping from my face, to Callahan, to my legs. Legs which are covered in scars and bitemarks and all visible for everyone to see. Panic replaces all other emotions but I wave her off.

"It's alright, we're fine," I say. Pushing away all the tension and his words and that still electric zipping feeling.

Asher wraps his hands around Jullia's waist as he keeps his eyes locked on the devil. I'm sure he can feel Callahan's aura still filling every corner of this room. Not that Callahan spares them a single glance, his eyes are locked on me. Pulling her flush to his chest, Asher's earthy scent begins to trickle stronger into the room.

Jullia puts on a smile as she shrugs to try and play it off. Leaving Asher's arms to head towards her wardrobe. "As long as everything is okay. . . "

"Yup," I respond, popping my lips to accentuate the *P* sound. "And actually, Callahan was just leaving."

I turn a pointed look at Callahan. I'm sure he won't want to, but he'll have to leave anyway because Jullia will be needing to get dressed and ready, and no way will Asher allow another man to stay in the room with her. He would go up against a devil – and with emotion backing up his magic he'd probably win.

"And if any word gets out about what you've seen and now know," I start, darkening my voice like I have before. Like when I had threatened the other celestials. "I will report you to the Mage Board."

His eyes narrow a bit at that, but otherwise he doesn't do anything. I bet he didn't know I knew that. It's not something widely known as is because not everyone really knows about true forms unless you're a devil or an angel, but if a devil or angel releases their true inner self in any way they're immediately sentenced to death.

True forms are. . . they can surpass gods.

With that threat, I sit up and slide off the bed to stand. I set my drink on my desk to finish later. Rolling my neck out, I clasp my hands behind me and arch my back to stretch it out. Callahan still doesn't move even as Asher's aura continues to slowly fill the room. More threatening now with a demanding energy. Callahan needs to leave now.

A protective instinct to keep Jullia safe from Callahan who is the largest predator in the room at the moment. The same instinct he had when he first met me and demanded I make a blood oath with him. A type of promise that bounds even celestials.

So very curious about a mage and a vampyr. I wonder when they'll fully realize what they are to each other.

In every lifetime.

You are mine in every lifetime.

You. Are. Mine.

Every. Lifetime.

The next beat of my heart thumps in my mind. I squeeze my eyes against it for a moment and when I open them I'm no longer in the presence of contradicting aura that balances itself. Instead the world is tinted in cool tones. Some sort of flake is hovering throughout the air. Snow or. . . ash.

I'm surrounded by a forest. Trunks bleeding black blood with darkness covering their branches instead of leaves or flowers or fruits.

There are whispers behind me. I should turn around to see what it is. Only I already know what I'll find.

A puff of air clouds before my mouth as I exhale. You would think the temperature would be freezing because of that. I know better. I know that freezing is the exact opposite of how the temperature is.

It has been a very long time since I've been here. Since my mind has locked me in the past and afterlife. Since I've been trapped in a nightmare while awake.

I know this only ends one way. I've tried before to not turn around. Spent weeks as my body screamed at me to move even an inch somehow. But the only way I can move is by turning. There is no forward, no back, no escape. There is only turning and facing it.

Fluttering my eyes closed for a moment, the first thing I see within is gold. Light and dark balancing with an aura so powerful it rivals that sun devils. It rivals the bone witch I call Nana.

It rivals the Forgotten God of Blood Moon's.

When I open my eyes a color that is not cool toned wraps around the tree before me. Black blood still dripping from its bark and at its base is a single blue belladon. But despite the black blood, despite the aura that fills this nightmare cage, a color I've never seen here blooms.

Red spider lily looking flowers are attached to a reddish-black vine covering the tree.

They say that blue belladon is the one thing that can kill all – no matter the creature. However, it is also said that the gods cannot be killed. They are the one thing blue belladon cannot kill. If only history was written correctly.

Roi sanguin'divin is the full name. Roi sanivin for short, and it is known as the godskiller. A true thing that can kill all – including the gods.

It is the symbol of the Forgotten God of Blood Moon's. A way to make him remembered. . . and a way to ensure his downfall stays that way.

I finally turn to face my nightmare. Black ribbons with light threaded through and gold accompany me with solace. I will not die here.

I will not die here.

I will not die here.

. . .

Pain.

Eighteen

Callahan – Septmust 1

My aura flinches and everyone in the room feels it. Jullia behind me chokes and I can feel Asher tensing the entirety of his body as he freezes in place.

Both of them were looking directly at her, just as I was. I *know* their eyes were on her, just as mine were. She had just stood up and rolled out her neck and shoulders. Her little skirt showing off her long legs covered in scars and fucking bitemarks.

She had been thinking about something. I could hear her mind working even though I couldn't hear her thoughts. Then something happened. She had thought something and then she turned to ash.

Pieces are floating where her body had just been standing.

No fire, no explosion, no aura, no remnants of a spell or curse. She had been standing here, fine, trying to ignore me, being a brat, and then. . . nothing.

"Where. . . " A choked sob escapes Jullia. "She – I. . . where?"

None of us move as we stay frozen watching ash continue to float. Logical thoughts aren't processing because she was here. She was fine. The sun isn't even fucking up yet so there's no way. . . there's no. . .

SHE'S GONE!

I ram in every shield and barrier and wall of Varian's mind. I don't make it all the way, but it's enough that me roaring those two words through he's able to still hear them.

His thoughts are moving as he opens up the last of this shields to let me in. I'm greeted by his confusion, though it's muted.

Callahan I can't –

She's gone. I now whisper. A breath of a thought barely tangible. *I had been looking straight at her, I didn't even blink, and now there's only ashes. Varian.* I croak. Something inside me is cracking. That *thing* is peering through the fractures of myself. *She's gone.*

My senses are trapped within. I can't process what is happening around me. What the water mage and vampyr say or do. I only see ashes. There's not even a scent. Her berry and floral scent had been muted in the bathroom and even when we were sitting across from each other. But it was still there. I could still scent her.

Now there's nothing. Not even the ash gives off a smell.

For weeks I had been memorizing her. Strengthening my magic and senses and abilities. Sharpening them to the point where I could *feel* when she entered a room without looking. I could *smell* her blood and the poison within even when she was across the room.

I knew when she wanted to counter an answer given in class by the way her eyes fluttered and her top lip twitched. Or when she wanted to roll her eyes at something, she would cast them to the side and they would fluctuate to a darker shade of pink.

I know she eats steamed vegetables with every meal and she doesn't like black beans or tomatoes or mushrooms. She always keeps her back straight when she walks and will only slouch when she's sitting. She always has her school work finished before the deadline and she almost always has her wired earbuds in even when she isn't listening to music. A song called *You Again* is the one she listens to the most out of the hundreds of songs she has.

She'll take her time walking to classes to pet the stray cats around campus and she will let long legged spiders rest on the top of her head throughout the day. Creatures always seeming to follow her and she grants them all a kindness, soft and gentle, no matter how ugly or dangerous or inconsequential they are. It's a kindness she gives with abandon to Jullia and Asher and Hanna.

She is *everything*.

An obsession I can't cure no matter how much I work out, how much I train and spar, how much I fuck every other girl willing. Not that I will fuck them all. Only the ones with dark hair and soft skin. Only the ones that have some sort of semblance to *her*. Because even then she consumes every thought, every action.

And she is *gone*.

Something – a presence – weighs on my shoulders. A strong energy surrounds me and it makes the ashes flutter.

No.

They scatter in the air. Floating over to her bed and on top of her shoes.

She can't be gone.

There's another crack.

No one has ever been able to contain my true devil like she had. My mother had been able to do it the fastest. Then Thorne was able to push it back and keep me sane. But *her*. . . she didn't even do anything. She only said my name and that thing wanted to submit. It *wanted* her.

Then she had snapped at me as if she had already known it wouldn't hurt her.

It wants her now. It won't accept that she's gone. It won't accept that she could be. . .

Another crack.

Callahan.

But it doesn't sound like her. My memory cannot capture her exact voice, her exact tone, her exact pitch. It's a second rate copycat and that *thing* does not accept it.

It needs her.

I need her.

I need her. I need her.

I need. . .

I. . .

Mavyn. It whispers. It has never spoken before. *Mavyn*.

Nineteen

Varian – Septmust 1

The Mage Board has thoroughly instilled that any devil or angel who allows their true inner self – their true form – to consume them they are to immediately be put to death. The magnitude of power that thing inside of ourselves has been said to rival gods.

Morals don't exist for them. Thoughts, feelings – they don't have them. No one knows what purpose they serve, only that they are a type of damnation and shall bring the end of worlds.

And yet. . . when Callahan broke through nearly every shield of my mind and screamed two words into it that nearly fractured my consciousness, I knew one thing. Those things in us. . . they have thoughts. Because it was not Callahan who said those words to me.

It was his true devil.

The thing that is now slowly consuming himself. The black ring around his iris covering all gold and white. His iris and pupil indistinguishable from each other.

With Thorne behind him, his hands firmly griping Callahan's shoulders, I say his name again.

"Callahan." A demand. Thorne was always better with trying to get him back than I was but nothing Thorne said got through. "Let Callahan back."

His body seems like it's made of stone with how rigid and hard he is. His face not even twitching, and his breathing doesn't even move his chest. Black eyes darker than the nothingness between stars continue watching ashes drift.

My brain can't focus on that though, because if Callahan fully unleashes his devil we're all fucked. And most importantly, he's dead.

"Callahan," I try again. If this doesn't work I'm going to have to call his mother. Without fail she has always been able to bring him back.

"She's gone." His mouth moves and it's Callahan's voice but not. It should not be possible for it to speak. "Mine, and she's gone."

I don't dare let my eyes stray from his, even as he continues watching the ash. I don't know how it's possible, what happened or why Mavyn is gone and there are only ashes left, but his true devil is somehow fixated on her.

"We need Callahan back," I say quietly. Cautiously. It

still doesn't look at me.

"She is mine," it says again. "She cannot be gone."

No, she can't.

But I can't even begin to process what has happened or how it's possible. Right now my only priority needs to be to get Callahan back.

"Bring Callahan back and we will find her."

It sounds like a promise, but I don't know how I can keep it. I don't even know what happened.

Finally, solid black eyes inch towards me. There's an unfathomable depth to them that makes you want to look away. Staring at the eyes of a thing beyond parallels. Something too twisted to be a god and yet with power surpassing them. It's like looking at endlessness.

"We'll find her together," I continue, praying to the damned gods above Callahan will come back. "But I need Callahan. I need him back to find her."

There's a ripple in the endlessness of its eyes. Then right around the edge of its pupil red lights up. A sliver of Callahan back.

"I need Callahan back to help me find her."

A shudder works through his body as the black in his iris retreats. Returning back to the edges of his iris and golden eyes are now looking at me. Golden, tortured eyes.

"Varian," he croaks. This time it sounds like him. And then he crumbles.

Thorne is there to catch him as I grip under his arms. A broken sob rips out of his throat as his fingers curl into my white button up. Already rumpled from staying up way too late last night and then sleeping for a couple hours in it.

I hold Callahan and for the first time since coming here look around the room. Ms. Waterstone is hidden within Mr. Ruleten's arms as her body shakes. Sobs heave out of her as Mr. Ruleten stares in shock at the ashes still slowly drifting down behind me.

Swallowing the lump in my throat, I clear my throat and try to get the vampyr's attention. "Mr. Ruleten." He doesn't even budge. Enforcing more power into my voice, I demand, "Mr. Ruleten!"

He eyes too slowly slide over to mine. Caught in a daze as he stares at me but I'm not sure if he's actually seeing me.

Callahan is still sobbing in my arms and Thorne looks nearly distressed. I need to know what happened. I need to see it for myself. And with the true devil still lurking near his surface, I can't go looking through Callahan's mind.

"I need your permission to enter your mind so I can see what happened," I say slowly and with more power influencing my voice. Just barely he dips his head and I don't waste a second in case he changes his mind.

He lets his few walls down so I can walk right in. Strong, well-built walls, but nothing compared to *hers*.

His shock splinters into absolute petrification and I realize he's been hiding his emotions as well. Whatever happened must have been unthinkable.

Passing his emotions, I weave through the library of his mind to the memory of what just happened. Beginning it with him standing behind Ms. Waterstone as she opens the door to her dorm.

The first thing he notices is Callahan. He's sitting on a wooden chair facing one of the beds. The side of the room always so bare, always so sad. It shouldn't be fair that she should have to live like this when it was never her choice to come here. No one should be forced into. . .

I shove past every minute thought and emotion he has. I'm not here for his opinions of the bloodsucker, I need to know what happened.

Looking from Callahan, he finally looks to her. And I almost fracture his mind as she comes into view. As I see her, sitting crisscrossed on her shit-looking bed, arms behind her as she rests on them, with her bare legs exposed.

Bare legs absolutely covered in scars and bite-fucking-marks.

. . . six, seven eight – nine fucking bitemarks just from what I can see. With scars you can tell were made from multiple objects.

It takes every ounce – all the practice I've had these past two hundred and fifty years – to keep from shattering the vampyr's mind. To keep that thing inside me at bay.

Distantly, outside of this mind I'm currently in, someone asks, "Are you okay?"

I nod my physical body because if I were to speak or move in any other way more than an inch that true devil would be unleashed. The type of rage – the wrath that wants to be unleashed. There's barely a couple inches between each scar from one another.

Continuing the memory, I continue flowing through it. Hearing her speak and confirming that the vampyr and mage knew about her scars. She threatens Callahan to keep his mouth shut about them. And then she stands. Her shoulders rolling as she stretches her neck side to side.

And then poof.

There's no flash, to flicker, no explosion. No whisper of a spell or crack of a curse. The sun isn't even up yet so it's not as if she could have burned away faster than half a fraction of time. And now she's gone.

Exiting Mr. Ruleten's head I come back into my own mind and body. Thorne is staring at me as he continues to grip Callahan's shoulders. The latter who's still slumped into me and drenching my shirt with his tears.

He should not be having this severe of a reaction.

But then again, I nearly let go of my control over my true devil when I saw her. Illogically I would say it was with good reason. Those scars, the markings, they couldn't have just happened from accident. And they couldn't have just been from her trying to distract herself from the devil. Those were torture marks.

But I must think logically.

Gripping Callahan's sides, I pull him away from me and up. Easily lifting him so his face is level with mine even though his legs have given out. I'd almost say he looks pathetic, but I can't even think that with everything else that has happened. He needs me and knowing Callahan he does not need any weaknesses pointed out at the moment.

Tears continue to stream down his face in rapid succession. Red already rims his eyes and snot has started to drip down his nose. He looks worse than distraught. He looks as if someone has just ripped out his. . .

I look past Callahan to Thorne and his eyes widen just as the thought enters my mind.

But. . . that *can't be possible.*

Except I look back to Callahan's eyes, the splintered rawness within, and somehow I know.

"She's your fated," I breathe, barely more than an exhale of breath. But it's as if I shouted it with the way everyone else jerks back.

And I see it. I can see it all within his eyes. The only way to physically *see*, to look upon the soul of another. Callahan pauses his turmoil as I watch the embodiment of his soul. A soul that is torturing him because the one who links with him is not here. That is why it was possible for his true devil to be able to communicate with me. Why it wants her.

So much is seen through his gold eyes. So many answers I'm given.

Staring into the eyes of a true devil or angel is like staring at endlessness. It's the nothingness between stars. But looking upon a soul through the eyes of another is like the universe giving you every answer to everything and nothing.

A true form is more than just what we are on the inside. A true form, the reason its power can surpass gods, is because it's an embodiment of fate. And Callahan's fate is death.

"She can't be gone, Varian," he mumbles, his voice choked with emotional torture. "She can't – "

Another sob escapes him and I bring him into my chest for a proper hug. A proper grip on him as his tears continue rolling down his cheeks and onto my shoulder. I'm sure what he's feeling right now is nearly unbearable.

Catching Thorne's eye, I barely manage to get the words I need to say out.

"Get Castiel, now."

I need someone else knowledgeable in these things. Someone who has traveled farther than I ever have. Who knows things I would never be able to learn.

Thorne doesn't hesitate as he lets Callahan go and disappears like a crack of lightning. A lingering scent of copper and ozone accompanies twisting shadows from where he was just standing.

Finding your fated, it's like a piece finally clicking into place with your soul. It's feeling at peace even though you didn't know you weren't already there. And losing your fated. . . that's having your soul ripped apart.

Looking up at the mage and vampyr, I know they're both clueless about what to do next, but unfortunately I'm with them. I try searching the shelves of my memory about anything that could help us figure out what happened. Unless she was able to somehow teleport or fold or shadow twist. But none of the techniques from those forms of transportation would leave ashes behind.

The only way I know for a being to be replaced by ashes is if a vampire is exposed to sunlight for a certain period of time. Eventually they are reduced to ashes. But there was no sunlight exposed. There wasn't even any warmth hinting at a sun summoning spell or a golden runic casting.

There is no explanation I can find for what has happened.

There isn't –

She can't be gone.

Beings can't disappear just straight out of thin air. There is always a remanent of magic or aura or energy or –

Unless she is dead.

But even then there would be some sort of lasting feel of something. No one can completely hide their aura without some sort of fluctuation. It's impossible.

I was given so many answers, all but the ones I need. For twice in my life I don't have the answers. I don't know what to do. I don't –

"What the fuck is going on?"

Something – *something* within. . . or maybe between or after. . . it skips. A fracture line, a hiccup, a choke, a misstep, a single ripple. . . it. . . *changes* something.

I'm greeted by pale pink eyes fanned by long lashes and a single dark brow arched high. Something within rumbles as I trace every feature on her face and then down. Her uniform shirt is only held by one button, exposing slivers of skin from her chest and stomach. And that thing within roils with a force that begins to make itself known to more than just me.

There are more scars and bitemarks on her. More than just on her legs. Legs which I can see because she's only in her skirt and not her tights which normally cover them.

Callahan pushes out of my arms only to immediately crumble to the floor. He crawls – actually *crawls* – to her and wraps the edges of her shirt around her middle before burying his head into her stomach. His arms circle her hips as he sits back onto his heels and pulls her with him.

She makes a tiny gasp as she plops down. Her hands going to his shoulders to steady herself as her thighs spread and her knees land on either side of his waist.

Pale pink eyes snap to mine with alarm as she ping pongs her gaze between the other two who are still here. I had forgotten about Mr. Ruleten and Ms. Waterstone. The former who's shocked state hasn't wobbled and the latter who slides to her knees as she stares open-mouthed at her roommate.

"What the hell is happening right now?" she whispers with trepidation. Wide eyes sliding back to Callahan as he squeezes her as if he's never going to let her go.

"D-don't e-ev-ever leave," Callahan sobs.

Slowly, some sort of realization dawns on her because a mask slips over her face and body as she hesitantly turns her gaze to her bed. To where pieces of ash still drift. She hadn't reappeared where she last was, which was closer to the foot of her bed. Instead, she appeared right in front of her desk.

Taking a step towards her, her eyes snap to me and a flutter of fear flashes in her eyes.

So, *so* many secrets.

"What happened, Mavyn?"

My tone is darker than I intended it to be. My voice lowered and power still thrumming through it. I can physically see her walls building as she neutralizes her face. Then she pushes away from Callahan and he whimpers as the contact between them is lost.

I glance down at all her scars and she stomps over to her wardrobe. Pulling out a long, thick robe, she puts it on before leveling me with one of her signature glares.

"You tell anybody what you saw on my body and I will report you to the Mage Board."

So much threat in her words, and yet it's for nothing.

"I have not done – "

"I saw your true devil," she grits. The color in her eyes fluctuating for a split moment. And damn me but my body flinches. She takes a step back and straightens at it. "You say, think, breathe, out in any way or form nothing to no one or thing."

Rage burns at the command but also at the *wanting* to

submit. The speck of wanting to bow my head for her.

I decimate it. Instead, gritting my teeth and hiss out an 'I understand'. Because it would not take much to convince the Mage Board of her truth. Even if I was able to rebuttal it, any devil able to enter minds would be able to see the truth. For both me and Callahan.

Though, I wonder how it was possible she saw it. My true devil only made a flicker of its presence known when I had first seen the scars on her legs. I kept it locked up after that. I kept my control.

Unless she just played me. She took a wild guess and I confirmed it for her.

The fucking brat.

Just then the scent of copper and ozone sparks and Thorne returns with Castiel. Both looking distraught and now confused as their eyes zip between me, Callahan still on the floor looking mourningly at the bloodsucker, and her.

She puffs out a breath and glares at all of us. "Why exactly are you all in my room?"

She's got to be fucking kidding me.

Twenty

Mavyn – Septmust 1

My bones ache. My muscles, joints, skin – my *blood* aches as it steadily flows through my veins. My heart even with its beats as I force myself to stay relaxed. It had gone on for longer this time. The nightmare lasting for more than just feeling like an eternity.

I wonder if that flower had anything to do with it being different. Roi sanivin doesn't exist anymore, so I wonder why it appeared in my nightmare cage.

That, however, will need to be a thought I think about later. Right now I need to focus on the four celestials crowding my room. Two of which have seen my scars, and all of them I'm sure are wondering what exactly has happened.

Normally it doesn't last this long. From the looks of it I couldn't have been gone for *that* long in that realm. Jullia and Asher are still here, same as Callahan. Though now Professor Asier is here too. Him and Thorne and Professor D'etre. The former who's looking at me like he wants to rip every secret out of my head. I don't think I have to worry about him telling everyone else about my scars because of my threat. The Mage Board is strict about those kinds of things.

However, my secret of what just happened is something I can't just pretend didn't happen. At least the celestials won't let me.

Placing my hands on my hips, I arch a brow and squint at the celestials standing. Callahan is still on his knees where he had been hugging me. There's a tug I feel wanting to pull me towards him. I don't understand what it is or why it wants me to go to him, but I also wish he would stop crying because for some reason I don't want to see him in pain.

What. The. Fuck.

Shaking that thought away, I point my stare to the ones standing. "Why are you in my dorm room?"

Professor D'etre and Thorne are staring at me like I have a second head while Professor Asier is still glaring at me. Thorne is the first to mask his face as he quickly glances behind me where I'm sure ashes are still drifting.

I thought they would have disappeared by now, but maybe they're lingering because of how long I was kept.

Capturing our attention, Thorne states, "You owe us an explanation."

States – like a goddamn demand.

"I owe you?" I question, my voice dropping with a predators viciousness.

The entirety of my body, mind, spirit, and soul ache. I have just been subjected to a type of torture that mars your astral body. Scars shouldn't be able to appear on one's spirit or soul, but apparently I'm just different.

"I. Owe. You. *Nothing.*" Each word punctuated with forced fury. I am too tired to spar in any sense but I will also not allow these men to control me. They will not demand anything of me. I will not –

"You owe me," a quiet voice murmurs.

Dark eyes focused on me and those three words hit with a force they shouldn't have. The truth of them ring out into the room and I drop my hands from my hips to curl them into fists. To dig my nails into my palms.

Professor D'etre swallows and relaxes his stance. "You said you owe me. A price for allowing you to drink my blood."

Oh how I wish I could turn back time. How I wish I could have just starved or passed out or literally anything other than plunging my fangs into his neck.

"Tell us what happened," he continues, "and then we'll be even."

What a twisted fucking price.

Still. . . of all the things he could have asked for. Of all the things I could have given him instead. It makes the corner of my lip curl up before I can stop it.

Blowing out a breath, I release my fists and drop my shoulders. Turning to look behind me, I watch the last of the ashes float before eventually disappearing like smoke.

"Well. . . " I begin. Turning back to them I wonder if

they'll even actually believe me. "Have you ever heard of the sun death realm?"

Callahan stands and wipes his face. Finally he stopped crying. Shifting towards me but not making a move to touch me again. He had moved my clothes so his head and arms in his short sleeve shirt didn't touch me. I wonder if he knows a way to make it so he can touch my skin without harming me.

He waits patiently for me to continue, brow furrowed in confusion and unknowing about the realm. Thorne's face morphs into a similar expression though it's tinged with suspicion. Professor Asier is still glaring at me, though his eyes flicker with questions and curiosity.

Only one person in the room hesitates with their expression. A second too late showing their confusion or curiosity or unknowingness.

I lock eyes with darkness. Golden-brown hair mussed, probably from sleep, with olive skin and gold streaking through the color. I have no idea if they are his actual veins or scars or tattoos, but they're striking. A fitting aesthetic for a demigod. A demigod who can shapeshift into any creature or beast, a demigod who is a spy and has traveled to other universes, worlds, and realms.

The body doesn't lie.

His nearly black eyes don't waver as I continue staring at him. He doesn't waver. Fine.

"It's. . . for lack of better words, a nightmare realm." Turning to the others, I wave my hand behind me. "Just as there are some who can make their dreams reality, sometimes nightmares become it instead. Although, instead of this plane becoming the reality, you are moved to the reality where the nightmare is. This being the sun death realm. That's where I was."

Silence greets me.

"Why?" Callahan's voice is scratchy. Probably from all the crying. "Why does it happen? Why do you go there?"

Technically I could say this wasn't part of the deal. I answered the question. I said what happened, I was in the sun death realm. The how and why weren't part of the question.

But. . .

Golden eyes tug at something and I *want* to answer him. I want to ease him – not that the answer will do that for him. Sometimes it's better to stay ignorant. At times I wish I still was.

Shifting my weight from foot to foot, I look anywhere but at them. This new feeling of something towards Callahan, I'm pretty sure it had something to do with the fact that his eyes and aura were the last thing I had seen before all I knew was pain. It still lingers in fantom ripples through my body.

Not that you'll see a scar or mark or anything letting you know it. Afterall, it may have been another realm but it is still just a nightmare. A twisted psychological game because it's technically all in your head and yet your physical body and spirit and soul are still there experiencing everything.

Sighing, I roll out my neck again and hold in my groan. Today is going to be a long day.

Shrugging, I gesture to nothing. "I don't know." You can hear the exhaustion in my voice. "It's probably a rem – "

I abruptly stop as I snap my eyes up to Professor Asier, D'etre, and Thorne before over to Callahan. My heart trips a beat and I force it to be steady instead of racing like it wants to. I almost just said it's probably a remanent of my curse, but I had only told Callahan about that.

"I don't know," I repeat, giving Callahan a look that

says he will understand. My tone clipped and my words final.

Thorne's face twists into a look of distain as he slides his hands into his pockets. Then there's a nearly audible crack and the room fills with the scent of metallic blood and ozone before he straight up disappears.

It shocks me for a moment. I've seen Rosemary and Nana fold before – a type of portaling where they open an invisible door into what's called the fold, a place in between existence and time and space, and then they open another door within that leads to their destination. I've also seen Cordellia create elemental portals from water – though they can be created from any of the elements.

But *that.*

The smallest wisping of opaque black and gray twist for a moment before disappearing too. It all happened too fast. I've never seen someone shadow twist before.

A type of portaling that aligns with whatever your magic is and flows with your aura. The scent that's left behind is like a calling card of sorts. It's the scent of your aura. And his smells like blood and thunder.

Blood and thunder.

It smells a lot like freedom and peace.

But I shake that random, bullshit thought from my mind and look over to the professors. One who's holding onto his feigned confusion and curiosity, though now bordering on suspicion. And the other who's now just blatantly glaring.

He shifts and pulls his arms up to cross in front of his chest. They stretch out the white button up he's currently wearing and I most certainly do not look at the way his muscles bulge. Because that would be inappropriate, and he gets off on runes, and he's not my type anyway.

What a fucking load of shit, the damned man could be anyone's type.

But that's not the point.

I mirror his stance, not wavering or breaking eye contact because I'm sure he's going to say something and when speaking directly to me I make sure to look at him. Per his demand, of course.

Pompous asshole.

He arches a brow and rumbles out, "Want to try saying that out loud?"

I tighten every hold of my shields within. Like trying to wrap a blanket around yourself, grabbing every corner and edge still you're cocooned in a ball.

That's how you know I'm really tired. My shields start teetering and minute thoughts slip out.

"Say what?" I test. He glowers harder. I roll my eyes, then I face Professor D'etre. "I answered your question. We're even now. Everyone is fine, we all have to get to our classes soon, you can leave."

He looks over to the devil I'm clearly ignoring and then hesitantly nods towards me before shifting towards the door. Professor Asier is still glaring at me – his gold ringed red eyes feeling like a furnace on the side of my head. But eventually, after the world's longest minute, he concedes and stomps over to the door.

Both professors leave and I exhale a breath I had been holding.

I take a blind step back and then crash down onto my bed. Three separate bodies move towards me but I hold my hand up.

"I'm so, so sorry," I start, my voice sounding a bit far away. It took so much strength, more than I should have used, to stay upright and strong. Even holding my hand up shakes with strain. I drop it immediately. "It's never happened before when I was awake. I didn't think. . . "

God, I'm so tired.

How was I able to stand for so long? How was I able to sound so confident and self-assured?

I can feel pressure on my physical body, but it's like my mind is under water. Voices speak but I can't hear the words. I just need sleep, I think. I need to rest after all the shit that happened. Marks are never left, but my body remembers anyway.

Sleep, my body tells me. My mind, my conscious, my spirit. *You have been through enough.*

Ahh, and yet it's never enough.

Someone says my name. A voice that makes it past the barrier of water that's clouding the other sounds. It almost sounds like a prayer on their lips, a begging to be believed. *My name*. A wishing to be remembered.

Oh, you poor ancient right of divinity. How far you have fallen from your throne of righteousness.

As long as something has one of the five pillars of structure they can be killed. Bone which symbolizes the body – Breath – which symbolizes the spirit and/or soul – Stone – which symbolizes the mind – Wood – which symbolizes the balances of nature – and Blood – which was the first physical sign of life created.

Which means it was always possible to kill the gods. You just had to know how to do it. Not that they'd let you remember. There's a reason history gets twisted even with beings who can live for thousands of years.

He says it again. My name.

Then I sleep.

Twenty-One

Jullia – Septmust 1

New moons are always notorious for beginnings. Especially when it's an equinox. We should all be thankful none of the solstices fall on any new or full moons. The energy – magic, aura, vibe, luck, karma – would be indescribable.

That has to be the reason for everything that has happened today. All the. . . impossible things that have happened.

First, the Willow of Lore flooded the grounds with flickers of blue aura. The spirits of the Willow of Lore zipping through the area readying it. The ceremony isn't even supposed to happen for another two and a half months – on the Winter Solstice.

Second, a single bolt of black lightning struck somewhere deep into the Hinterwood Forest. Anything to do with the Hinterwood is never a good sign – but black lightning? Asher said black lightning hasn't been seen since the first years of Syngenia.

And now this.

Too many thoughts are racing in my head as I watch Callahan-*fucking*-Armani hold Mavyn. His father is the devil chairholder of the Mage Board. He's higher than royalty and he is in my dorm room – holding my friend – crying.

And he had seen her scars too.

The last thirty minutes have been. . . impossible. That's really the only way to describe it. How else could you explain all these things happening that have never happened before and shouldn't happen.

Mavyn disappeared into ashes. As if she had been hit by the sun and disintegrated.

Asher had pulled me off the floor before, but I feel like I could slide right back down. She's lying unconscious on her bed with Callahan – her fucking fated! That's what Professor Asier had said, I can't believe I forgot about that.

A new wave of panic and adrenaline and anxiety hits me and my legs wobble. Asher grips my waist and pushes me over to the bed. I'm sure he's probably prickling with every thought about how befriending Mavyn was going to be a shitshow. He had been fine after the blood oath, but I know deep down he wished I was never roommates with her.

Except I like Mavyn. She feels different to all the other bratty girls from my tutoring classes and schooling before coming here. The ones who would talk about me behind their backs and whisper about me and make snarky comments to me. All they ever cared about was wealth and power, and my family is far from the elites, but at least I was able to enroll in the University and they weren't.

But none of them matter because Mavyn doesn't care about that. She doesn't care about how poor my family is or how low on the hierarchy scale they are. She doesn't care about status or what other people think.

And I'm sure there are a hundred other girls like her. I'm not delusional enough to think she's the only one. I've made lots of friends here so far, but there's something *real* about Mavyn. Something gravitational.

I shut my eyes and take a deep, calming breath. I feel every droplet of water through my body and in the air and outside in the dark clouds. Then I release and it causes the temperature to drop. Prints of frost form over my skin as I open my eyes.

"It's going to be fine," I state, calmly and clearly.

I have no idea if it is going to be fine or not, but I'm channeling my inner Mavyn. She always seems calm, always seems to have a plan, always seems to know everything is going to work out.

Callahan looks over to me like he doesn't believe me. His eyes are rimmed red and tears wet his face again. I can feel that water too. It's twisted with salt. . . like the ocean.

I nod to him and try to persuade him with my eyes. "She will be fine, Callahan. She did this before when she first got here and was exhausted. Her body needs the rest, and then she'll probably need to eat a lot of food."

At least I hope that's just the case. I have no idea what

the sun death realm is or how long she was there or why she was taken. She said it was more or less like a nightmare realm. Meaning it has to do with her nightmares, and those are especially torturous sometimes. I had to have Asher draw a sound barrier shield around our room after the first time it happened. She screamed as if her body was being torn apart.

"She just needs sleep," I say again. I force myself to believe it. She was fine when she came back, so she'll be fine when she wakes up.

He sniffles and stands. Hovering over her, he takes his hand and skims the back of his fingers across her cheek. His crying stops at the contact, but after a moment he flinches back. A look of distress passes over Mavyn's face before it smooths out.

A rumble of Callahan's devil aura drops in the room as he whispers, "Hands, feet, neck." And then he fists his hands and takes a step back.

I have no idea what he's talking about or what happened, but he turns towards us and softens his features. Asher still pulls me closer to him and tightens his hold, but Callahan doesn't seem to mind.

"I'll be staying here until she wakes up, but I'm going to get her some food for when she wakes up. Do you know where her key is? Not all of us should miss class."

It takes me a moment to process what he said. After everything my brain is going too fast and yet lagging too badly.

Jerking out of Asher's hold, I step over to her desk and open her drawer. Inside is the dorm key, not that she ever uses it. Asher also created a spell around the room that allows me and Mavyn through without having to lock and unlock the door. It's something most second year and older students have around their rooms. It's something we'll be learning next year. For everyone else they either need the key or need us to open the door for them.

I hand him the cold metal and he nods before leaving.

Fated.

That's. . . a dream. Finding someone your soul is tied to, finding someone who is your perfect partner. It's not exactly rare, but it's also depicted like a fairytale. Some people never find their fated while others have more than one.

I glance at Asher and his olive green eyes are staring directly at me. He softens his features too as he walks over and wraps me in a hug.

"It'll be alright, Le Le," he whispers into my hair. I choke back a sob and one of his hands start soothingly rubbing my back. Even though this isn't why I was looking at him, I'm glad for the comfort. The physical contact. I don't know how people live their lives without it. "Oh princess, it'll all be okay."

I hope so.

I hope all the omens are not telling of something horrible to happen.

Twenty-Two

Mavyn – Septmust 1

I think that was the best sleep of my life. It was pure uninterrupted black abyss. No dreams, no nightmares, no visions, no thoughts, nothing. Both my body and my mind were actually sleeping. Proper rest.

Too bad I can't stay here forever.

My mind starts registering my body and what had happened before sleep. I had passed out. Thankfully falling onto my bed, but Callahan, Jullia, and Asher had still been in the room. After that everything had been black, and I have no idea how long I've been out.

The longest before was six days, but I have a feeling it hasn't been that long.

Peeling my eyes open I'm greeted by my blank, boring ceiling. Off to the left is my window covered by a blackout sheet. That must mean I'm laying properly on my bed. Meaning someone must have moved me.

Callahan.

In addition to my body no longer feeling as fatigued and aching, there is still that slight tug within. Like an instinctual pull drawing me towards something.

My first thought is the one who said my name before. But I don't think so.

Next thing I register is that there's a soft glow coming from Jullia's side and I am not alone in my room. And it is not Jullia or Asher in here with me.

Turning my head to the side, I'm greeted by gold. Gold eyes with black ringing the iris and white threading through. They're watching me with a predatory stillness, though his true devil is nowhere near the surface. Good.

"Callahan," I whisper, my voice scratchy with how dry it is.

He blinks and leans further in. Something delicious wafts behind him and smells a lot like tortilla soup. My stomach grumbles loudly at it. I can't remember the last time I ate something.

His golden eyes fly to my stomach and then his stone still state drops. His shoulders relax and he smirks at me. A slightly dangerous look on his face but I don't feel like I'm in danger at the moment.

Leaning back, he pulls a paper bag across my desk and

that scent of soup gets stronger. It smells divine.

"Can you sit up?" he asks quietly. Keeping the bag right at the edge of my desk. If I were to lift my arm I would probably be able to grab it. He leans towards me with his own arms raised. "Let me help you."

And then he proceeds to slip a hand under my head and his other under my back before lifting me up. He replaces the blanket that had been on me – a blanket that is not mine and I know for a fact is not Jullia's. It smells like cackling embers and cedar. Like a comforting fire surrounded by a serene forest. It's like I weigh nothing with how easy he lifted me. The act itself jars my mind even more and I clear my throat.

"You didn't have to. . . "

What am I supposed to say? Stay? Bring me food? Lift me up like I weigh nothing?

He starts opening the bags and the scent of warm, hearty, soul-blessing food thickens in the air. His body relaxed and his movements sure as he sets up the containers on the edge of the desk. And just as I smelled, one of the round bowls holds some sort of tortilla soup. Little chunks of avocado on top.

Dipping one of the spoons into the soup, he bring the whole thing close to my lips and then gold eyes meet mine again. That tug pulls with a sharp jerk and his eyes flash as if he felt something similar.

"It's hot," he murmurs, "so blow."

Tension tightens between us as some sort of electric spark sputters through the air. Part of me wants to ignore him and tell him to go away. He's friends with the other celestials – who although have mostly left me alone, are a constant present of fuming hatred. At least, Thorne and Darian feel that way. The professors have basically ignored me.

But Callahan had been relatively kind to me. Aside from trying to enter my mind, he hasn't done anything to me. And that instinctual tug wants me to listen.

I blow softly on the spoon before me and then open my mouth to take the bite. Callahan doesn't break eye contact with me and I watch as his pupils blow out. Another sharp tug being pulled from deep within.

I'm going to rip my fucking soul from my body.

He doesn't act on any impulses, just scoops up more soup and waits for me to blow. I have to dig my nails into my palms to keep from making a noise of satisfaction. It's the best tortilla soup I've ever had. Not even Mama Deja's soups can compete. And she's known nationally for her famous soups. It probably helps that she's a faerie and they're known for their magical cooking hands.

He feeds me until the soup is gone and I'm slightly fuller than I was before. The warmth heating my stomach and I lean my head back with a sigh. I'm still starving, but there's still more food and at least I don't feel so weak. I could get up and move if I needed to. I could feed myself.

Callahan doesn't ask or say anything as he grabs another container. Opening it the scent of rice and beans float over. I peak between slitted eyes to see a container holding Mexican styled rice and brown beans with two cheesy quesadillas stuffed with what looks like shredded chicken.

Picking up a slice of quesadilla, he leans back over and holds the thing up to my mouth. His fingers are spread out on the underside to keep it from lopping over. If I were to take a normal sized bite my mouth would touch the tips of his finger.

Keeping in a groan, I push myself further up and then take the food out from his hand. Bending my legs I bring my knees and blanket up to my chest and take a bite while looking away from him.

"You don't have to stay," I say between bites. *Hmhhh.* Cheesy, melted goodness. I think I love cheese almost as much as I love my steamed vegetables.

I eat the whole thing faster than I probably should have, but when I shift to take another slice the container is moved away. Callahan is still holding it and when I look up at him to glare he's already glaring at me.

"What?"

He turns to the side and glares at the wall instead. My stomach – *stomach* – pinches and pulls. It's probably because I ate to fast. Or I haven't eaten enough. Actually I think it's because I need blood.

Taking his hand he rubs his eyes and leans back in the chair with a sigh. I hadn't realized before but he had pulled the chair as close as he could to the bed. His legs are spread wide with his knees pressed into the thin mattress.

"Mavyn. . . " He sounds almost exasperated. It makes me want to roll my eyes. "Why would I leave you?"

I cross my arms over my chest as he looks back at me, but this time I turn my head away. My *stomach* pulls again and I grit my teeth as I dig my nails into my palms.

Why would I leave you?

Why did he say it as if it was obvious. As if him staying was the only option. A promise in his words that he will be staying for longer than just this moment too. A promise he shouldn't make – even if it is only said between the lines.

I will never leave you.

Forever, in every lifetime.

The memory hits me like a blinding light behind my eyes and I sink my nails deeper into my palms instead of flinching. A rush of pain echoes in my body that I don't let show. I keep my hold on how fast my heart beats and blood flows. I keep my energy even and my aura nonexistent. I let nothing fluctuate until the memory fizzles away.

"Because," I grit, my eyes still burning a hole through the wall. "Why would you *stay*?"

I can't look at him. I refuse to look at him. I. *Refuse*.

I will not be trapped again. I will not be locked in a cage within my own body again. I will not be bound.

Already I'm a slave to the sun. I'm a slave in my own skin, unable to have the contact needed for life. I'm a slave to my mind and the nightmares and a monster who should have stopped having an impact in my life the moment his heart stopped.

I will find a way to rip my soul from my body. If Callahan wants it so badly, if fate has been written and our souls are connected, then he can have it. I have no need for it if that is the case.

The scent of embers and cedar fill the room until it smells like I'm sitting before a fire in the middle of a forest. Warm and comforting and calm. Despite all the burning I have always loved fire. I have never been afraid of fire and flame scorching me. Flames of red and orange and blue in the center marking the hottest part. So hot the lines of burning and freezing blur. That burning never felt the same.

"Mavyn." His voice is quiet and his breath whispers along my jaw. So close that I'm sure if I turned too quickly I'd smack my head with his. "Look at me."

It pulls stronger than before. As if someone took their

hand, curled their fingers around my soul, and jerked to towards him. So much need to heed to his words. To *want* to turn my head and lock my eyes with his.

His breath whispers along my jaw again with his exhale. "*Please*."

Berry and floral burst through the embers and cedar. The scents twining together as my nails puncture past the barrier of my skin.

Power pulses from him and I'd grin but for a moment it jars me. For a moment it feels too consuming. But instead of allowing my mind to make me cower, I slowly shift my head and burn raging eyes at gentle gold ones.

It makes me flinch.

A half of a breath gasped into my lungs as my expression drops. He is close, close enough that I can see the individual threads of white through his eyes. Close enough that if I even breathe there will be some form of contact. Not that I could move anyway.

I was expecting him to be glaring at me. His eyes slitted, brows lowered, gold eyes darkened. Instead, he's watching me with a sort of softness I've never experienced before. The kind Asher has for Jullia, and Caleb has for Ana, and unfortunately. . . that sun devil for his mage.

It had been the only time he had looked humane. When he didn't look like a monster. Staring down at his fated with their twisted souls and mangled love for each other.

Something flickers. Past the color, behind his eyes, at the heart of himself. . . I see it.

His soul.

So much like his aura. Black and white. Light and dark.

A contradiction and yet balanced.

Without meaning to I trace his jaw with my fingertips. On the surface, his pupils expand. Swallowing up his color as I skim over his cheek to the corner of his eye.

There's another presence within too. The window showing past his physical body to within allowing me to see everything. A thing – shadow, monster, beast, *true devil* – shrunk so small but wrapped tightly around the same thing pulling within me. A single flickering flame the color of a midnight sky.

The line between burning and freezing.

Warmth floods over my heart in the shape of a hand. His lips ghosting words over my own.

"Your heart has never beat this fast before."

He's right. I lost my grip on my blood. It's now rushing through my veins, heating me from the inside with a need. My body battling with my mind about pressing closer to him. That electricity in the air that twined with tension draws taunt. A single line that is about to snap at any moment.

It feels *right*.

And that's the problem.

He must see it. He *has* to see it. This *thing* will not be lasting.

Pulling back, the window in his eyes shutters close and gentleness turns to sadness. Sitting back in his chair he also removes his hand from over my heart and stares longingly at me.

"I couldn't see your soul, Mavyn."

I know.

Turning away again, this time it feels somber and there's a heavy weight on me now. He won't ever be able to see my soul. No one ever will.

He sighs and I understand his disappointment. If our roles were reversed I'd probably feel the same.

"Are you still hungry?"

My stomach doesn't make a sound but it does roil. He doesn't sound disappointed or angry. I turn my head to look at him and he's just sitting there, waiting for me to answer with a neutral expression.

"You're not angry?"

His brows flicker down. "Why would I be angry?"

I blink at him. Did I imagine it? Did everything that just happen happen in my head?

"I'm not. . . *yours*."

I say that word slowly. Hesitant and unsure because I can't say the other word. Saying that word out loud would mean it's real. Would cement the fact that we are. . . connected. I can't even *think* the word because if I want any hope in un-connecting us I can't believe it. I can't allow it to have any belief or faith because then it will be real.

People forgot the power of belief.

Belief can make whole universes exist. Just as not believing – just as forgetting – can make them disappear.

So I can't believe it.

I expect his true devil to rise to the surface and demand I take it back. The force of his power slamming into me with a need that I believe. It's always the primal part of ourselves that overrule our conscious and morals. And you can't get any more primal than a true form.

But Callahan softens his features and brings one of the containers back over. Setting it in my lap and then letting go so I can feed myself.

"What would you do if I was angry?" he asks quietly.

Fear, pain, regret, fangs. I look at the food in my lap instead of him so he can't see the memories. Cages and chains, beatings, whips, starving, burning, burning, burning.

"Brace," I whisper.

I had done it in the training arena when Thorne grabbed me before Callahan came in. Then again before at the party when Darian grabbed the back of my neck and at the angle – despite there being minor differences and them having different colored hair – I had seen the sun devil.

Psychology says there's two options when faced with a threat. Fight or flight. But in truth there's actually four, the other two people tend to forget about. Fight, flight, freeze, and fawn.

I was never able to defend myself or run away before. And freezing never helps when the threat is pummeling your face into the ground, nor does trying to appease it when it craves violence. When the threat gets off on your pain and blood.

Ms. Elaycia had paid for my weapons training and martial arts classes and self-defense. Nana had practiced with me and honed my skills and technique. Rosemary had sparred with me to strength my body. I am anything but weak.

And yet. . .

Even then. With all the training in the world, all the new muscle memory, all the weapons. . . my mind is my greatest weakness. I could fight a whole army in broad daylight and win, but mention that devil and I'd be open from every angle.

I will always brace.

"I am not angry, Mavyn." Calm and clear words. "You were hurt. All I want to do right now is take care of you."

I pick at the container still on my lap. I feel like I'm fourteen again when Ms. Elaycia was taking me in and showing me how the brothel worked. She said she takes care of those living here. She said she would take care of me.

It had been the first time. . . well, it had been the first time it was said to me without any malicious or derogatory intent behind it. And Ms. Elaycia kept her promise. For five years she took care of me.

I sigh. My emotions are conflicting with themselves. My. . . *stomach* is wanting one thing and my mind is waring with itself and my body is being tugged in too many different directions. I want to go back into that black abyss of sleep. I don't want to think about all of this.

"Come to the Willow of Lore ceremony with me," he says randomly. It makes me look up at him with my brows twitching down. "It's a tradition here. . . the Willow of Lore is a symbol by the gods and each year its spirits perform a ceremony around it. Everyone comes out to watch it."

Willow of Lore. . .

The tree that stands in the center of the university. The school built around that symbol. I haven't had a chance to see it yet. Jullia usually walks by it with Asher when they're coming back from Stone House. It's easier than walking all the way around the school.

"But I thought the ceremony happens on the Winter Solstice?"

It's supposed to. Even though we haven't learned about the tree in Professor Asier's class, I know that. Though, I wonder why we haven't had a chapter on the tree yet. It should have been taught when we were learning about the creation of Syngenia University.

He leans back in the chair and scratches the back of his neck. It causes his short sleeve shirt to inch up and I immediately look away before it has a chance to show any skin.

"It's supposed to. . . "

I look back, directly – only – at his face and raise a brow. "But?"

He huffs as he smirks at me. "*But* for some reason the spirits of the willow came out early and have started preparations for the ceremony. Asher said he and Jullia saw them this morning, and they also saw black lightning strike in the Hinterwood Forest."

Black lightning?

I wonder. . .

Opening the container I finally start eating. My stomach immediately thanks me as I shove a huge bite of still warm, cheesy goodness into my mouth. I close my eyes to savor it and to procrastinate on saying anything else.

So many thoughts and so many questions.

"I would like to see the ceremony," I finally say. I think it will be interesting to actually see how it all works.

"Really?!" I look at him because he sounds both surprised and excited. His eyes are wide and there's a huge grin on his face. He tones it down a bit to ask, "Are you sure you're alright to go through? The ceremony will be happening in two hours and you just woke up from being asleep all day."

His excitement ripples through the room like a young golden retriever would. Floppy ears, too big paws, radiant energy, joy.

It makes me so happy and warm inside.

I look down at my half eaten food and glare. *Fucking hell.*

“I’ll be fine,” I grumble as I take the plastic fork that had been speared in the rice and start eating it. Then I scoop some of the brown beans and eat that too. Normally Mexican food is served with black beans but I hate them, so I’m glad something must be different here. They’re almost like refried beans.

He begins to contain his excitement, but I can see out of the corner of my eye he’s still smiling. He crosses his arms and leans back in my chair as I finish eating the beans and rice and pick up another slice of quesadilla.

Side-eyeing him, I ask, “Are you going to watch me eat the whole time?”

I’m sure he smirks. “I’ve got nothing else to do.”

“What about school?”

Speaking of, I missed a whole day of classes. And attendance is mandatory. Just fucking great.

“Watching you sleep was more important.”

Watching me. . .

I whip my head to gawk at him. “You watched me sleep! All fucking day?!”

And just as I suspected. . . he’s smirking. I think my eye twitches, but I can’t do much else except shake my head at him. Whatever. So he’s a creepy sleep watcher, what do I care.

Finishing my quesadilla, he then slides over another

container and opens it before me. My stomach tugs again as pure happiness bleeds through my veins. So influential that I can't help but smile as I take the large container stuffed with still steaming vegetables.

I inhale probably half of it before I sigh in content. Sliding down the wall I'm still leaning against and popping a perfectly buttery, salty piece of cauliflower into my mouth.

Heaven.

This is blissful heaven.

Opening my eyes I come face to face with gold. Callahan had leaned closer. Resting his forearms on his knees as he peers at me with curious eyes.

I slide down an inch more and pull my vegetables closer to my chest. Finishing chewing, I swallow my bite and contemplate what I should do next. Him watching me so closely like this makes me feel self-conscious. Not even Caleb ever observed me so closely.

Gold fractures and dark blond brows lower.

"Who's Caleb?"

I shrink another inch and a little squeak escapes my throat. I recheck all my mental shields before narrowing my eyes at him. I can't really be mad at him because those with mind magic who can hear other people's thoughts tend to keep that part of their mind open. Always listening, so I have to make sure to keep a tighter hold on my shields.

"No one," I murmur. Looking down at my vegetables and scooping up a piece of carrot to shove in my mouth. "A friend from home."

He hums and when I glance up at him the white threads in his eyes are glowing. Mild curiosity and a look that says 'want to try answering that again' appear on his face. I narrow my eyes and snap my eyes back to my food. I do not owe him any explanation.

He hums again but doesn't push anything. He doesn't say anything as I finish with my steamed vegetables. And this time he does leave, giving me privacy as I get up to change and get ready.

Willow of Lore. . . black lightning. . .

It's starting to sound like these five years are not just going to go by quietly.

Whoever's betting against my life. . . they better be making enough bank to be worth it. This is going to be exhausting.

Twenty-Three

Callahan – Septmust 1

Most, if not everyone, in the school comes to watch the Willow of Lore ceremony. It's a tradition every year, and rumored to be bad luck if you miss it. Though, normally it happens on the winter solstice, not the autumn equinox.

Mavyn had known that. My firecracker knew about it even though the teachers aren't allowed to explicitly teach it. Varian said there are a lot of gaps in the history books. Knowledge the Mage Board doesn't want us learning.

But she knows about it. My firecracker – who's currently twirling the end of a piece of hair around her finger.

This strand mostly blue, with the rest of it hanging in loose curls down her back. It had been curled like that when she came back from her nightmare realm instead of in the bun she had put it in before.

I haven't asked more about it because I haven't wanted to overstep. Already I've gone too far, pushing too many of her boundaries. I don't need her to shut me out more than she already does.

There's also another long legged spider on top of her head. This one with a larger body and bright orange. Its legs scrawny but covered in orange and white striped fur. I'm pretty sure it's a pumpkin cat, which are pest eaters and good for the environment but they're also very venomous.

I wonder where she found it since they prefer deep, dark corners and don't like people.

We walk side by side down one of the last corridors that lead into the first level of the building. The Willow of Lore sits in the very middle of the school. The reason most classrooms and lecture halls are upstairs is because the majority of the first level is taken up by the grounds.

People are already gathered as we turn down the last hall. Hundreds of students and staff stand around as tiny blue lights zip to and from.

Holding out my hand, I wait for Mavyn to take it. She doesn't hesitate and I pull her through the crowd so we can get a better look. Even from here you can see the slightly glowing purple flowers of the tree.

It looks almost exactly like a wisteria tree, though the flowers hang like a weeping willow. And the bark is white, with a deep purple rune right in the middle of it. The symbol of the Willow of Lore.

There's another symbol someone is able to make with their hands. No one does it though because to do it without proper knowledge and intent is to scorn the spirits. And doing that is a death sentence.

There are balconies surrounding above several levels too for the rest of the students. The presidents of the societies and their councils get first pick of wherever they want to stand first, then everyone else files in. Usually they take their seats on one of their benches.

Five benches, each for one of the houses, surround the tree. Long ago it had been for the five sub-races of the witches the houses are named after.

Thorne sits on Stone House's bench in his perfectly tailored uniform. A foot resting over his knee and a stony expression.

Castiel lounges beside him with a book split between his fingers and his signature rumpled white button up. The first several buttons undone to show off his golden markings. Varian stands behind them, gold ringed red eyes roving over the courtyard.

I tap on his mental shields and his eyes fly straight towards me. His nostrils flare as he looks at Mavyn, and I glance back at her to see if she sees him. But she's staring straight at the tree. Pale pink eyes wide with an awe and almost. . . reverence.

Slowing our pace, I tug her till we're slightly behind but in between the Blood and Wood House benches. Vivian and Claudia both sit on their benches chatting with their first year interns. Jada, Vivian's second on her council, glances at me and where we're standing. She raises a brow but doesn't tell us to leave even though we shouldn't be this close to their section.

I may not officially have joined a house, but with my

father on the Mage Board and being close with two of the House Presidents I still get perks.

I loosen my hold on her hand in case she doesn't want to hold it anymore, and immediately she lets go. I try not to let my hurt show, but my devil does pout at the loss of contact. However, she does lean closer to me and shifts her head before whispering, "Have you ever seen the ceremony before?"

Her eyes don't leave the tree and the blue glowing spirits of the willow zip around us. Tiny, fairy looking creatures with a soft blue aura around them, stop before Mavyn. She smiles at them and tilts her head as one of them flies up towards her head. Towards the pumpkin cat still resting on her.

"Hello," she murmurs to them, and eyes around the courtyard start looking at her.

"I've been to one before," I answer her quietly. "My father brought me a couple years ago when Thorne and Darian were attending for their first year."

She hums and lifts her finger up to the spirits. I can tell multiple people around us hold in their breath as one of the spirits float over. This close I can see actual individual features. Their face, body, and even tinier white lights surrounding them and their blue aura.

The softest hum eminates from them and I watch almost transfixed as Mavyn – my firecracker, my *fated* – softly harmonizes with them.

Faster than a blink, the small spirit zips towards Mavyn's extended finger, hugs it, and then zips away. The other spirits that had been sitting on her head with the spider and toying with the ends of her hair follow.

Jada, Vivian, and Claudia are all staring at us with their mouths hung open. As well as the other House Presidents, older year students, and Varian and Castiel. Varian tries entering my mind through our link but I lock it off. I don't want to speak to him right now. Even though he helped me earlier, I only want to enjoy this moment with *her*. With my fated. My apology for all the hurt I've caused her, because attending the ceremony with someone in this fashion is either to cement their relationship, or to start anew.

Mavyn finally notices all the eyes on her and she shifts the tiniest bit closer to me.

"Why is everyone staring at me?" she whispers.

She had looked at the Willow of Lore with awe when we came in, but the true wonder here is her.

"Because the spirits have never approached anyone before and they have never sung for anything but the willow."

Pale pink eyes look at me with curiosity. They're a deeper shade of pink right now and around her iris it almost looks like it's sparkling. A silvery hue ringing her pink eyes that are boarding on red. They look so beautiful right now.

Too soon she looks away and back to the tree. Spirits still roaming around the ground and through the flowers readying it. Soft light beginning to emanate from the purple flowers and a scent of berries weaves through the air.

"That's weird," I murmur. Mavyn hums at me and I take in a lungful of that scent. "Normally it should smell like creamy vanilla, but it's sweeter."

She takes a sniff and looks up to the top of the tree. High above it is a clear glass dome exposing the night sky. The faint outline of the new moon is halfway into the top, middle plane of glass. Normally its phase is first quarter, but since the ceremony for some reason is happening today, it's a new moon instead.

Either way, when the moon is fully within that circular plane of glass, that's when the ceremony will begin.

"It starts with a song," I explain, which gains her attention though she keeps her eyes on the tree. I spot Asher and Jullia across from us behind Thorne's bench. Him, Castiel, and Varian are all still staring at Mavyn. Darian, who's sitting on his Breath House bench is peering at Mavyn too.

Softly clearing my throat, I ignore them and finish explaining. Since Mavyn was born and raised on Earth, and it's not taught about, she doesn't know the process of the ceremony.

"The Willow of Lore was created a long time ago by the first witches as a symbol after the first war between gods. The grounds extending over the roots of the tree a neutral ground for all, including primordials. It symbolizes renewal, growth, friendship, family, and home after tragedy. And the reason the flowers are purple is because while that's the color of royalty, it's also a color not associated with any house or right of power."

The spirits finish weaving around the grounds. Blue light is left drifting like wisping shadows throughout the area and that creamy sweet scent hits closer to berry.

"Once the spirits of the Willow of Lore have finished preparing the ground with their aura," I continue, "they start humming the melody of their song of old. Because spirits can't speak, the words have been lost over time but even if it was known it's not to be sung just as their symbol is not to be made."

"Why?" she whispers, and a hush goes through the space as the moon nearly enters the space it's supposed to. While it is a new moon, a ring of light illuminates its outline making it so we can clearly see it.

"Because," I breathe even quieter, "to sing the words and make the symbol without the proper knowledge of what the Willow of Lore encompasses and without the intent of the magic it's considered a smite to the spirits. Now, it should be starting any moment."

She leans slightly into me and I take a chance and slide my hand around the small of her back. While she tenses, she doesn't move away or say anything.

It feels right to touch her – even if it isn't skin on skin. My hand wrapping around her side and resting there. I'd rest my chin on her head, but I won't be risking the pumpkin cat biting me. So I stay where I am with her shoulder and side pressed into me as her fingers still play with the end of her hair.

There's a hitch in the air right as the moon fully centers in the middle plane of glass. The lights from the scones around the walls douse and the only illumination is from the aura the spirits cast around. The blue light seeming to glow brighter and the deep purple rune in the middle of the tree begins to glow.

A soft hum echoes around the space with individual voices humming along with it. The voices of the spirits – even though they can't sing they can still expel music. And then a beat of divine aura pulses from the tree. Raw power and peace filling every corner of the area and even past it.

There had been one year when I was younger I had even felt the power all the way back at my parents' estate.

The hum rises and different strings of song weave through the melodies. I glance down at Mavyn to gage her reaction and I'm struck as I look at her. As I *feel* her *aura*.

A transparent light of blood red evenly flows around her. It stays close to the outline of her body, but I can *see* it. I can see her aura. Which should be impossible. People can't *see* auras. They can feel them, sense them, know how powerful they are from them and get an idea about their soul through them.

I hadn't been able to see her soul before. The eyes are

the one way to see into someone else and view their soul. It doesn't happen often for people looking into other people's eyes, but for fated it's instinctual. To see that part of ourselves connected to our fated is primal. It's a need greater than much else.

She had seen my soul. I know she had seen it. But when I looked at her eyes, when I tried looking into them – past them – there was nothing. I couldn't see past pale pink.

And vampires as a whole don't have a lot of magic and in turn aura. Most of their aura they get from whoever's blood they drank, but Mavyn had no aura that any of us could read. She wasn't mortal anymore because she was turned so she has a level of power, but to have so little aura that a devil can't feel it means they have no magic.

I had thought maybe that was why I wasn't able to see her soul. Aura's reflect the soul of a person as well as their magic. But now. . .

The melody shifts and her aura grows as tendrils of darker red and sapphire blue weave through her overall energy. It feels like an old type of power. It feels like there shouldn't be a way for her hide it. With how much it is it should be impossible to contain.

Just this bit that I can feel – can *see* – and with what I had felt before when we were in the gym a few weeks ago. . .

Music rises and ribbons of aura-filled light weave through the overall blue. Much like Mavyn's tendrils of red and blue do through her overall aura.

Something zips past the corner of my eyesight and I look up to the spirits of the willow flaring out around their tree. The ones closest to me I can see lift their hands before them and make their Willow of Lore symbol.

Beside me I feel Mavyn shift. She takes a step to the side, out of my hold, and lifts her face to the moon above. Eyes that had been a pale pink are now blood red. A color no vampire should have unless the vampyr who turned them had eyes the color black.

But it doesn't matter because her face looks so serene. So relaxed in peace and another energy starts lightly weaving around her as she lifts her hands before her. My mind – my soul and *blood* studder as her fingers bend and straighten.

I would stop her but that other energy lightens to blue as her hands form the Willow of Lore symbol. An etherealness wraps her as her eyes close and her lips part.

The melody of the spirits drops into a lower beat with power pulsing from the tree. The end of the song coming and the ceremony coming to a close, but instead of all eyes on the rune in the bark they're all watching her.

The notes rise from that lower beat as Mavyn takes in a breath and then her voice joins the hum of the spirits.

Words I've never heard before pour from her lips in a lyrical tone perfectly harmonizing with the spirits. And that blue aura that isn't hers darkens as spirits watch her with a recognition. Their small blue glowing forms drifting towards Mavyn and drawing blue aura around her as they dance.

She adds more strength to her song with a smile and the spirits welcome it. Pulling ribbons of blue around her and her aura that I can still see flares brighter. That sweeter berry scent from the tree strengthening with a floral undertone as Mavyn sings.

Red lines begin glowing beneath the skin of her hands and neck as the song starts to come to a close. They look similar to the gold ones on Castiel, but hers flow to her face as well. The lines of red forming different symbols and markings. One of them glows in the center of her forehead and I realize it's the same symbol – the same rune – as the one on the Willow of Lore.

I realize it just as there's a curl waving through the space of power more harmonious than before and the aura of the spirits begins shifting to a warmer tone. Blue lights dip to the opposite scale and auras of translucent red replace the blue.

Impossible.

The Willow of Lore spirits – which have done this ceremony for over a thousand years, who have not allowed anyone to make their symbol without consequences since the first years of Syngenia, who have not had their lyrical song sung in over a thousand years – *change* their aura.

Beings that are as mysterious as the gods, with power exceeding most celestials, who never let anyone interrupt their ceremony, and who are known for their signature aura color. . . they change it. They change it to match Mavyn's.

A type of blessing that. . . well I don't even know what that means.

Her voice rises with the ending of the song. Cutting off her breath to finish the last words.

Red light – *aura* – floods the grounds with spirits glowing the same as they end their melodies. A last pulse of magic from the tree ending the ceremony and with that final beat the light from the rune on the tree dies. The spirits begin to wink out one by one after.

Opening her eyes, the last of the spirits float before her. Their tiny hands forming their symbol and they do something reserved only for their goddesses.

They bow.

And then we're plunged into darkness. Left with only a faint scent of berries and floral and power older than the first celestials and witches.

Twenty-Four

Mavyn – Septmust 1

The scones on the walls light and every single person here is staring at me. Eyes of all kinds of colors and shades pointed right at me. It makes me want to hide. I wish I knew how to shadow twist right about now.

The first pair of eyes I notice are glaring at me. Dark red, almond shaped eyes across the grounds. So much suspicion and disgust and hatred. It's boiling with his blood moving so evenly through his veins. His heart beating so steadily. You would think it would be rushing with his emotions, but it's a calm sort of loathing.

Abomination.

Monstrous.

Cursed.

After everything – the nightmare and pain, then the gentleness from Callahan, and then the peace from the ceremony – it just makes me want to curl in on myself and pretend to not exist.

The spirits of the Willow of Lore had let me sing with them and for the first time since Caleb and his ball imitating the sun, I felt the kind of warmth you can only get from the sun and its rays without burning. Warmth without the burning.

So much warmth and peace and serene and beauty. Music can heal the soul in a way no god or goddess can. Lyrics and melodies and harmonies, they are a type of magic all on their own.

And that feeling of acceptance and home and a soul that is not scarred or fractured or *cursed* extinguishes.

Like the lights of the spirits going out, plunging the rest of us into darkness.

I don't know what I was thinking.

I don't bother looking over to the rest of the celestials. I don't care to see their hatred or disgust or everything else they feel about me. I should have kept my hands at my side and my mouth shut. I should have stayed pretending to be invisible.

But the spirits had already approached me and it has been so long since I let my control rest and I just wanted. . .

I shake my head and turn away from them. From the tree that now feels no different to any other. Callahan still stands there but I don't want to look at him either. I don't want to look at his golden eyes and chance seeing his soul again.

His hand reaches for me, but I side step him and

continue through the crowd of people. No one has moved or said a single thing, all their eyes still focused on me. But my own are on the ground and once I'm past those that were in the back I make a run for it.

I hadn't worn my heeled boots tonight and I'm thanking my past self for it.

For some reason needles prick at my nose and between my eyes as I fly through the corridors and halls. My arms and legs pumping, I push them harder than I had this morning. Even though I should I don't keep a hold on my heartbeat and blood flow. The organ in my chest thumps at a hazardous pace and my breath feels like razors in my lungs.

Music was always my escape. It was the one thing that fucking sun devil couldn't take away. A passion and worship and honor. Music can unite and the melodies and lyrics don't even matter because it's what you *feel*. Music is the truest form of magic, and yet *he* ruined it.

Sneering at me as if I was a disgustful parasite that ruined the ceremony. As if the spirits didn't accompany me with their song and bow to me afterward.

I round the banister that starts where the path to the dorms are, but I don't take it and instead keep running. There's still too much energy burning within me. My hold on my aura and magic nonexistent right now and after so long with always keeping it controlled it wants to unleash. It wants to roar.

My vision blurs and I nearly trip and it takes me entirely too long to realize tears are muddling my vision.

WHAT DID I DO TO YOU?

I want to scream. I want to rage.

It's not fair.

IT'S NOT FAIR.

IT'S NOT FAIR.

AND I KNOW IT NEVER HAS BEEN AND I KNOW IT NEVER WILL BE.

But that's not fair either.

It's not. . .

I force my body to stop but my momentum keeps taking me forward. Protecting my head, I curl into my body as my shoulder hits the ground first.

I roll into it to prevent from breaking anything because of the impact, but it won't help stop the bruises. With the force I'm sure I'll have scratches and bruises that'll take a bit before they fully heal. At least I hit grass and not the stone pathway.

I roll a couple times before I come to a stop and gasp out a breath. I open my eyes and twinkling lights blink at me. I landed on my back and as I uncurl my body I find nothing broken. Scrapes and bruises for sure, and everything aches, but no broken bones.

The stars above me go blurry before tears roll over the outer corners of my eyes. I don't remember the last time I cried. The devil loved when I would cry for him, but the mage always hated it. That's the only time when she would beat me herself.

Heaving a breath, I furiously wipe my eyes and sit up. Thunder from further away rumbles low and menacing as I survey where I had run to. Towards my right is a house I remember from my first week here. The same house Asher had led us to.

Stone House.

Thorne's house.

I stand up and shove every ache and pain into the recesses of my mind. Instead of the self-hatred and shame and regret I focus on the rage. So, so much rage I've collected over the years. I've harbored like coins of treasure, hidden within the deepest part of myself.

Memories of the sun devil and his fated mage and their beatings and markings I let flood my mind. The times when I was forced to drink the devils religious blood and his fated's rotting water mage blood. When they wanted me to mark them as the devil marked me.

I let my mind fill with the memories of after them too. The lust filled foster men who would try sneaking into my room at night. Or the ones who would beat me until I couldn't move and then try to use me. Or the foster woman who let their jealousy fuel them and wanted to burn and scar my *beautiful* face. Wanted to beat the carnal attributes right out of me.

So much rage. So much fury.

So much *wrath.*

Music and song was my escape from all of it. I was safe. And at least when I would sing it would distract them from wanting to beat me more. There had been a whole month the devil left me alone so long as I sang to them. I couldn't even hate it because music was mine and I have only ever sung for myself.

So why does he have power over me.

Why did he sneer as though I didn't have the right to sing.

Why did he hate me more because of it.

My blood flickers with a life I haven't used since I was ten. A type of burning from flames igniting my bones as I start walking towards the house.

My foot lands on the first step and the doors are thrown open. It lands on the second and the structure of the house groans. I step onto the porch and the foundation trembles.

No one stops me as I enter. The closest creature with enough blood in their body to concern me is still deep within the walls of the main building of the university. I don't waste time letting my aura flood the space. A mist of red roving through the halls, seeking what I wish.

There's a flutter near my left ear and I lift my hand to allow the spider to climb on. The bright orange and white pumpkin cat peers at me with six black eyes as I softly stroke the top of his head. He's been lurking around the window of my room and tonight he seemed like he wanted an adventure. I'm glad he survived my tumble.

When I figure out where Thorne's room is I let my little friend climb back onto the top of my head and then I make my way up. Of course Thorne, House President and son to the demon chairholder of the Mage Board, has an entire suite to himself.

His double doors get thrown open like the front ones did the second I face them. I'm first greeted by an open foyer with a whole wall made of glass exposing the large balcony. Thorne's blood and thunder scent drenches the area. His aura is so strong that threads of it are still lingering about.

I curl my hands into fists as I survey it all. To the right is where his bedroom is. The left some sort of office. The door to it opens and allows me to see a wall of books.

I shouldn't. Knowledge holds power, but the grief has shifted and all I want is for him to feel what I felt. I want him to know what it is to be shown unfairness. I want him to know what it is to burn.

Internally, there's a click. A key finally twisting in a

lock it's been kept in forever.

I uncurl my hands and stare at the space with deadened eyes. Glancing back I lock eyes with red. Pure, damning, wrathful. I tilt my head up at myself through the mirror and then allow that door inside me to open.

I have never been afraid of fire. Not even when the devil tried burning me with flames instead of the sun. That kind of burning. . . it felt like comfort instead of pain. It was the only time I never scarred.

Flames dance as they consume the room. Worls of different shades of blue curl around my hands as I watch the destruction. Keeping it contained to this suite and all the things within. Letting my fire burn Thorne's life here to ash. Just like he tried to do to me the first day we met.

A reaping for what he tried to do, and for hurting Asher. No action is without consequence, and I will deliver his detriment.

Heat engulfs me right as the whole wall made of windows explodes out. Shards piercing the air with the power of my flames and I revel in the destruction. Already most of the space is ashes. The rest of the house safe as I pour every ounce of my anger into my blue flame.

Blood movement catches my attention but they're still outside. Walking through the flames, I make for the balcony and into the cool night air. The dark sky glittering with stars you can only see because there is no light from the moon.

I tilt my head back as sounds of cracking and crumbling echo into the night just as thunder does. It sounds closer than it did before, and towards the main building of the university the sky is completely dark. Though, within that darkness streaks of light flash. Lightning the color of my eyes right now fracturing the sky.

They come closer, devouring the visible stars, and bringing the scent of rain.

A roar splinters the air and I grin at it. Shadows begin curling around the edges of the balcony and I watch, almost transfixed, as forms solidify within them. A single white marking is etched on what I assume is their brow.

Nana did tell me about this kind of magic art. Demon runic magic influenced by shadow magic.

Detaching my flames from my aura, I wrap my aura back up within. Cinching it so tightly within, stuffing it back into the confinements of my veins, until you can't feel a single thing. Until that door is sealed shut and the lock turned. Until there is no fluctuation that could possibly be made because I fade my aura into my blood and let the poison mask it. Hidden from senses while also being in plain sight.

The shadow monsters inch closer. Twisting their heads in odd directions no regular being should be able to. My flames still consume and my grin doesn't fall even as the shadows jerk closer to me. Right before the closest one can sink its claws into me I close my eyes and reach an inner part of myself into the ether.

Thunder rumbles and in a fraction of a second lightning strikes directly where I'm standing. Burning, all-consuming, blood-red lightning latching onto my body and then letting go. It didn't even feel like my feet left the ground.

I open my eyes and I'm facing familiar tree trucks and foliage. Glancing to my left is crumbling bricks and an ivy covered wall.

Turning around, thunder cracks right before silence and then like a clap rain begins pouring. From here I can't see any flames or smoke, but I can still feel it. I can also feel the exact moment they're all doused. Not that it does anything because everything is already gone. There's nothing left in those rooms except ashes.

I skip towards the front of the dorm and for once Ricka isn't sitting in her chair behind the desk. I'm sure she's probably still at the ceremony. All that is something I'll have to deal with tomorrow. Maybe I'll get lucky and no one will ask about how I knew the Willow of Lore's symbol and the spirits song of old. It's not like the teachers are allowed to teach it anyway.

I hum as I take the stairs up. Remnants of the spirits song still stuck in my head. It's the same melody my music box played that Ms. Elaycia gave me. The song and the lyrics to go with it the same one I would hum to myself when I was with the sun devil.

A song said to be needed to be passed down in order to know it. But no one ever says if it needs to be passed down from another physical, alive, familiar person. Afterall, there are other realms between the past and the after.

Opening my door, I'm greeted by darkness and I help the pumpkin cat onto the latch of the window. Then I toe off my shoes and don't bother changing before face planting into my head. For some reason it's softer against my cheek and smells like embers and wood.

That's when I remember Callahan and everything that happened before the ceremony. I still need to find a way to rip my soul out. But that can wait till tomorrow.

Curling around the blanket, I wrap myself up in cackling embers and cedar and drift my eyes shut. That night I'm glad for Asher creating a sound barrier around our room and for Jullia spending the night in his rooms. The comforting and calm from the scent of a warm fire surrounded by serene woods does not help this time.

For the first time neither does the hum of music.

. . .

Burning.

It never matters how differently the story begins, it always ends the same.

Sometimes I am a watcher in my own nightmares. I view it through a screen as it happens to me. Other times there is no screen and I experience it as I have before. And on occasion, from the ground between episodes of pain, I will look up and see blood-red eyes instead of icy blue ones. I'll see long dark hair ending in blue and pink instead of cropped black hair.

Those times the pain feels worse and lasts a lot longer even after I wake up.

It's like that now. Though I don't burst up with heaving breaths and wet cheeks. I open my eyes slowly to a blank ceiling. A point of light cuts through it and I slide my eyes along it to where part of my blackout sheet over my window is smoking.

A bullet sized hole was burned through the material allowing the small slice of light in. The rest of the room is dark and Jullia's scent is fainter. She hasn't been in here for at least a day.

Sitting up in my bed, my bones creak. My blood feels stale in my veins and it feels like ash coats my throat. Thankfully, as I survey the room, it doesn't look like anything was destroyed. Nothing. . . except my bed.

Most of my mattress is burned away to nothing along with my sheets, pillow, and Callahan's blanket. Just. . . great.

Gritting my teeth, I slide my legs over and off the edge of what's left of my mattress and let bare feet touch wood. I had taken my shoes off but I had climbed into bed with my clothes and socks on. Looking down, I'm as bare as the day I was born.

Well. . . almost. I doubt I had a body covered in scars, but same principle. My clothes had burned away to ashes as well.

Standing, my vision goes in and out and I don't even have the strength to tense my body. It feels like falling for a moment before there's a thump and my body hits the floor. This time I allow myself to groan because that *hurt*. Even though fantom pain from my nightmare still lingers.

Flipping onto my back, I wait for my vision to return and then stare at my window. In the corner I catch a bit of movement. My little guy peaks out for a moment and I watch him begin weaving a white colored web.

I'm so tired.

Groaning again, I sit up and take it slower getting up to stand. My vision still blurs for a minute but I'm at least able to make it to my mini fridge and grab a blood bag. Pulling all twelve of them out, I crash back to the floor and suck them all dry.

Mhmm.

Faerie, wolf shifter, goblin, another wolf shifter, elf, some sort of feline shifter, more faerie. It feels like it barely does anything, but regular food will help along with proper rest. The latter will have to wait though, because I don't know what day or time it is and I've already missed one day of school.

Standing – this time there's no faintness – I tap my tablet on and read the date. O'seven o'three – Septmust third, and it's six ten. Meaning I have a little less than an hour and a half until my first class. The dreaded Magic History with a professor I don't want to see.

All day, actually, I will be seeing people I won't want to see and –

My notifications pop up and my first one is a message from my section leader for the cleaning crew.

Fuck.

Today is Wednesday meaning I not only missed yesterday as well as Monday for school but I also missed work last night.

Rubbing my hands over my face, I almost feel like raking my nails down my arms. Digging deep enough to leave bloody trails to help both ground me and punish me.

I click on the message and section leader sent that after classes I need to meet with him immediately. Excuses fly through my mind for why I couldn't come in but I doubt any of them will be sufficient enough. I'm not on probation but I'm sure they've been watching for any misstep to fire me. And there's no way I'd get another job anywhere after this.

Turning off my tablet, I turn away from it and head for my wardrobe. It's something I'll have to deal with later – among other things. Right now, however, I need to get ready for class. And that needs to start with a shower.

Just as I finish tugging a thin long sleeve and pajama pants set there's a commotion I can hear down the hall and then my door gets thrown open.

"YOU CAN'T JUST WALK IN YOU SHIT-EATING – "

"MS. WATERSTONE IF YOU DO NOT – "

"SHE COULD HAVE BEEN CHANGING YOU BAST – "

"JULLIA!"

There's another commotion then frost freezes the doorway and spears out along the floor. Ice begins eating the floor and walls where the door is causing the temperature to nosedive as someone rushes into my room. Jullia's lavender eyes are wide and her hair is actually frizzy as she runs her eyes over me. There's a sigh of release that leaves her lips but it is quickly replaced by fury.

Turning towards the door she screams out, "SHE IS RIGHT HERE YOU FUCKWADS, I TOLD YOU."

"MS. WATERSTONE," a familiar voice shouts back. A voice infused with a power that rumbles through this space and is accompanied by the light disappearing through my little hole above.

Nerves rack up my spine, but I keep control of my heart and blood and the adrenaline that flushes my system quickly disperses. Guards storm into my room and two of them each grab one of Jullia's arms before pulling her back away from me. She doesn't fight this time, but her eyes plead with me for a reason I can't read.

Then a tall devil enters my room with wavy hair that looks black right now. His gold ringed red eyes narrow on me and go up and down before shifting further into my room.

Behind him the Dean enters with his dark suit and scolding eyes, along with two other men.

"Ms. Tsuki," the Dean sneers. "We need you to come with us."

I snap my eyes between the four men crowding my room with anxiety curling around my spine. Surely they won't kick me out for missing two days of school. . . ? Because the two men who entered with the Dean are the same two out of eight people who sentenced me to this school.

I swallow thickly as I nod. The two councilmen watch me with blank expressions and exit first. The Dean gestures for me to next and then he and Professor Asier take places behind me. Along the walls of the hallway are even more guards. All of them pulsing with powerful aura and strapped from head to toe with weapons. Several, I see, are actual guns.

Who needs guns when magic is the deadliest weapon out there?

They lead me down the hall and stairs. Most of the guards strapped in tactile gear exit through the open doors of the dorm building and I follow. My bare foot is about to cross the doorway onto the stone path that'll lead to the main building when I'm jerked back.

Fingers curled into the back of my pajama shirt grip tightly and pull, causing me to crash into a warm wall. The two councilmen who are right outside the door – both of whom are right under the blaring sun – turn to see what the commotion was. I had almost just followed them outside – right into the rays of the sun.

Fingers that were curled into my shirt shift and wrap around my neck from behind. Flaring red eyes glare right at me.

"Are you trying to kill yourself?" he growls. Actually growls – like a fucking beast. His fingers squeeze the tiniest bit harder around my neck but my heart doesn't double. It stays the same, even beat as I stare Professor Asier directly into the eyes.

His flare a bit wider before he shoves me away – *not* towards the sun lit doorway. Rubbing the back of my neck, I glance at the Dean and one of the guards behind him comes forward with my umbrella. I open it before exiting the building and everyone resumes walking.

Students around us watch and whisper. Jullia hasn't come down from the room so I'm assuming they're keeping her there.

They're gonna kill me.

It's finally come.

That's all I can think about as my bare feet step over the pathway burning. My pajama pants are long enough that if I were standing still I could cover my feet with them, but walking as I am my skin flashes free.

There's a slight hiss every once in a while from where the sun's rays hit more than once and I'm unable to heal the slight burn fast enough.

One of the councilmen – this one slightly shorter than the two, with light brown hair and burnt golden eyes – glances back with lowered brows. I'd say he looks concerned, but his eyes meet mine and at my blank expression he turns back around without saying a word.

They could have at least let me get dressed or put some shoes on. Though, of course, if I'm about to be killed then it doesn't really matter. It would be easier if they just let me burn here and now, though. I wonder why they don't. Maybe they suspect me for burning Thorne's rooms down and want to question me before hand? Not that they'd have proof of anything.

They lead me through halls and courtyards I've been through before. Students milling about before their classes gawking at the spectacle. But at a certain point, they start leading me down a way I've never been to before.

Rounding another corner, we're greeted by a large expansion of space that leads to a set of double doors made of gleaming marble. They're pulled open faster than what I would have been able to given how heavy I'm sure they are, and we all pause as dark wrath glows within golden eyes.

"What the fuck are you doing with my fated?" Something within me jerks towards him as he takes careful steps towards us. His voice had been dark and cruel but not consumed by his true devil. "Father. . . ?"

And my eyes snap to the man who had glanced back at me. His hair and eyes are darker, but now focusing on even just his side profile I can see the resemblance.

Shock ripples through the air as the devil councilman takes a step towards his son. The other one whips his head towards me and red eyes with a ring of darker red right through his iris glare at me. The expression seems so familiar. The point of his brows, the twist of his lips, the power and aura and. . .

"Let the councilmen deal with this," a lazy voice drawls. It's accompanied by slow footsteps and then hard red eyes look over to me.

Thorne's face is neutral as his father whips his head to him before righting his expression. He pulls on the lapels of his suit and clears his throat.

"Thorne. Callahan. What exactly do you mean – "

"Why," Callahan interrupts the demon chairholder of the Mage Board, his voice a deadly viciousness as his aura explodes through the space, "is my fated wearing sleep clothes and barefoot? And why do I smell burning flesh?"

I curl my toes into the floor as I grip the handle of my umbrella tighter. I hadn't closed it even after we came inside. I didn't want to risk someone taking it since I didn't technically need it anymore. It would be my only physical weapon.

Pain strikes through my feet up to my legs from where blisters have formed on my feet. It's a feeling I don't make a face to, however I do clench my jaw against the heat. Callahan's fuming eyes that have not left my face slit at it.

I force my shoulders to relax and twist my neck to look at the Dean behind me. I don't bother looking at Professor Asier. For a split second I contemplate fighting my way out. I'd be able to do it, but my bones still ache. My body is just barely alive after the nightmare and the fury from Monday night.

Turning back around I give Callahan a resigned look.

"It's fine," I call. Ignoring his magic seeming like it wants to rip through the walls. "It doesn't hurt."

Which is the biggest lie I could ever tell. It always hurts. *I* always hurt. Pain coincides with existing and for so long I've unfortunately wanted to continue on existing. Except now my time has come.

"Can someone please tell me what is happening?"

Callahan takes another step forward with all his raging power but his father steps up to him and blocks his view of me. "She's being questioned for the destruction of Stone House, son." His voice is gentle and comforting. "Varian is just going to ask her some questions, we'll get some answers, and then all will be fine. If she has nothing to hide she has nothing to worry about."

Silence greets him and off to the side I can see Thorne's brows twitching before he's glaring at Callahan. They must be speaking within their minds.

Two presences approach closer to my back and a hand grips my shoulder. I blink and instead of directly seeing the back of Callahan's father's head I'm now staring at a black t-shirt over a wide chest connected to a head with dirty blond hair and golden eyes.

My nose is practically touching said chest, and if I were to take a full breath my nipples would scrap against it too. That tug coils tightly within and the idea of dragging my chest down his makes my thighs clench.

A wisp of floral hinted berry sweetness wafts up and the chest before me vibrates.

"*Take. Your. Hand. Off. Her. Now.*"

The hand that had been resting on my shoulder disappears and for some reason hearing those words being snarled out heats a fire in my core.

Squeezing my eyes shut, I try to take a breath to calm myself but my nipples, which had sharped to points graze the chest in front of me. I dig my nails into my palms to center myself from the feeling but that fire in my core blazes hotter.

The body in front of me tenses and I clench my jaw and hold my breath to keep from moving.

"Get out."

"Mr. Armani – "

"I will not repeat myself."

There's silence for a moment before, "Callahan. . . "

Then more silence, and then all the presences I had felt suffocating me disappear. All I'm left with is a warm fire and serene woods. Comfort and warmth. I'd breath in the scent but I can't risk any more of my nerve endings being sparked.

The last presence here takes a step back from me. His voice much calmer and much softer than he had been speaking to the others.

"You can open your eyes now, firecracker." He sounds like he's smirking.

Twenty-Five

Callahan – Septmust 3

Pale pink eyes are exposed and I wonder why they're no longer red like they were two days ago. Jullia had told me yesterday morning when I tried to see Mavyn that she was sleeping. One of her nightmares had taken over and there was no way to wake her from them.

So she had stayed with Asher again last night because of her screaming and I wanted nothing more than to wrap my arms around her. Thorne had said we were needing to meet with our fathers before we could do anything today so I was going to go to Mavyn's dorm after.

Instead, I feel her right outside the room where our meeting is supposed to be held and I come out here to see this.

She doesn't look any different. Doesn't look manhandled – which is good for the guards since they'll be allowed to stay living. But she is in pajamas and I can see clear blisters on her feet.

The thing inside me wants to crawl to the surface and make them all pay. No matter that my father is among them, it wants out.

Pink eyes slit at me and soft, plush lips part to speak words I can't focus on. My blood is still rushing and my soul continues trying to jerk us closer. I inhale her sweet scent into my nostrils and resist the urge to moan at it.

I don't know what caused her to react the way that she did, but what I would give to learn how to get this reaction from her again. I can practically taste her sweet scent, dipping to a berries and cream sweetness with her heady floral cut. Being aroused brings her earthier scent out more.

I at least wished I didn't step away because her chest is heaving and her shirt is too thin. Her nipples would have continued scraping against my chest and the second I felt them I was as hard as stone. Even now, I don't think I've ever been this hard in my life.

Her hands go to her hips as she glares at me. "You better keep a lock on that devil of yours, Callahan."

The way her lips roll over my name, I can't help it as a moan slips out. Her pupils explode hearing it and for a moment I can see us against the wall. Her wrists in my hand above her head, her legs wrapped around my waist, my lips on her neck. I'd leave my own temporary marks until she allowed me to mark her true.

My gorgeous, gorgeous girl panting as I rubbed against her center and her berry and floral scent coiled into every corner of the room. Then I'd be on my knees for her. Peeling her pants off, and then her panties which I'd stuff into my pocket for safe keeping. She'd be dripping already.

I bet she's dripping now.

With the way her pupils are swallowing up all the color but for a thin ring of soft pink. Her thighs have been clenched together and her nipples are cutting through her shirt like razor points. Oh, how I would love to flick my tongue over them. Again and again and again, and then I'd suck until dark marks were left over them.

A low rumbling growl comes from her as I focus on her eyes and expression. She's still glaring at me and I can't help my smirk. She looks too cute.

"Stop looking at me like that," she huffs. Then she turns away and crosses her arms.

Guilt prickles through the lust and I suck in a deep breath to try and cool myself. I have to remind myself she's hurt, even though she said she isn't in pain. I'm sure that's a lie. But I have to take it slow. Already I know I'm not good enough for her, but I have to try. And she doesn't need my lust filled brain leading with my dick.

Rolling a hand over my face, I blow out a breath and remember why we're here.

"Do you want a change of clothes?" I ask her. She looks down at herself and extends her leg out to look at her foot. "I can also get some healing balms for your feet."

She shrugs and looks up and away again. "I just want to get whatever it is over with. Your. . . father, he said I needed to be questioned about the destruction of Stone House?"

She turns to me and I refuse to believe it. After the ceremony of the Willow of Lore someone had torched Thorne's rooms at the house. Luckily they didn't spread to the rest of the house, but they weren't ordinary flames. Thorne said they were blue, and he said his shadows felt a presence of raw, un-guided magic. An aura so strong, so expansive there was no definition to it. He said it didn't feel like threads or ribbons but a sheet.

And Mavyn's aura had looked like that during the ceremony – which I still can't believe I saw because people cannot *see* aura's – but to have a magic that strong you'd have to at least be some sort of celestial. People cannot just create blue flames.

I nod anyway. She was the first person to leave the ceremony so she would have had time to go to Stone House and somehow start the fire. "Yes, they'll want to question you. But Varian will be questioning you, and he has empathic magic."

Something flashes through her eyes as she looks once more at me. "You think I did it?"

"No!" I step towards her and raise my hands but stop right before I touch her. Even though there's a layer between our skin I don't want to risk hurting her in anyway. She's already been through enough pain. "I'm just warning you. Varian's magic is strong and demanding. Even when you don't hide the truth it can still be painful."

She slightly shakes her head and then looks past me. "Can we just get this over with then? I'm starving."

The night of the party flashes through my mind and my true devil rumbles at it, but I silence it and ask, "Do you need food or blood? I can get someone to bring you something."

She shakes her head again. "I drank all my blood bags when I woke up this morning, I'll just wait till lunch."

I stretch out my mind to call for Varian so they can come back as I mentally scold her because she will not be waiting several more hours. I'll be getting her something to eat the second we're finished with all this bullshit.

The crowd comes back, all of them standing in a group to the side instead of where they all had been before. Mavyn glances at my and Thorne's fathers and her upper lip twitches. I don't blame her for hating them. They're part of the reason she's here and not with her family. Not that I can be entirely angry at the situation, it led her straight to me, and she is *mine*.

"Are you finished. . . *conversing*, Callahan?"

I have always seen Edmond Arcturus as like an uncle. Growing up and schooling with my own father – and Darian's – the three of them were best friends. But right now all I want is to pummel is distasteful expression into the ground.

Varian steps between us and gestures towards the office I had just been in. A mediator between us because I could feel Uncle Edmond's magic gathering around him to challenge me. "Let's just begin this so we can figure out what happened."

Guards fall in line behind Mavyn but I grab her hand and tug her away from them. I place her ahead of me and lead her into the room with everyone else behind me. All the damn guards is overkill.

The Dean is the last one to enter and flicks his fingers to close the door. Varian approaches us and his red eyes pierce into me. The rest of the men stay behind him and wait. I know how these things go.

Turning my back to them, I face Mavyn and her pink eyes look even paler right now. Her under eyes are more pronounced and her skin is drained of most of its color. But she looks at me openly, trustingly, waiting for me to explain.

"Varian is going to be asking you some questions. In order for his abilities to properly take affect he needs to place his hand over your heart. He won't enter your mind, but it will feel like it because he's tapping into your emotions and spirit."

Nothing about her changes when I say that. She just looks exhausted, but she dips her head. That's when I take a step to the side and Varian approaches.

"Can you pull your shirt down?" he actually asks. I can count on one hand how many times his questions have sounded like actual questions and not demands. But I can see why now because panic flashes in Mavyn's face.

Her hands tremble as she lifts them to her neckline and a shot of fiery rages fills my veins. Not only will she have to expose her scars to all these people – all these *men* – but Varian will have to touch her bare skin. He'll be touching her scars as he pulls the truth from her.

Dejection slowly transforms her face and numbness dulls her eyes. I step to intervene but her deadened voice stops me.

"It's fine." She sounds like she's preparing for her death. "It won't hurt."

Which I know she's lying about but I'm stuck with needing to help and protect her and heeding to her words.

She pulls her collar down and silence fractures the room. The bitemark under her collarbone gets exposed, along with more scars, but it's what's right over her chest that stills the room. I hadn't seen it before. Didn't notice it among all her other scars when she had changed in front of me.

My vision goes in and out of focus but I reign it in for her. Because she had told me to get ahold of my true devil and so I will. But it peaks right on the surface of my conscious.

Peering through my eyes even though I know his have not consumed my own eyes.

Right over her heart, in a perfect circle, are black scarred bitemarks. So many fang imprints he must have bit her from multiple angles to form the circle. So many black *claiming* bite-fucking-marks. And right over her heart.

Her expression doesn't waver even though mine does. Varian's does too. I can't look back to see everyone else's, but I can feel them. For the first time in my life I can hear Thorne's thoughts. So potent with strong enough emotions that his mental shields are unable to hide it.

She's claimed.

SHE'S CLAIMED!

SHE'S –

"Not," she whispers. Dull pink eyes on me with a resigned expression. "He's dead. We were not fated, so after death it becomes void. The only reason I'm left with the mark is because of the poison."

That doesn't diminish the fact that she was. That the devil who tortured her claimed her. Had his fangs in her flesh and marked her. She was a *fucking. Child.*

Breathing deeply in through my nose, I suck her scent into my lungs and it calms me. I focus on her words instead of my emotions. I focus on her and what she said I need to do instead of the all-consuming that wants to take place.

She said the claiming is void because he's dead and they weren't fated. That means something. Despite us already being fated there have been stories of someone having more than one. But he was not one.

"You're right," I console. "It means nothing."

And that resignation, the dejected expression on her face flinches as she gives me grateful eyes. That's why she had always said bitemarks and claiming's and blood sharing never mattered. And despite all those things being very important to any being, especially those with fangs, I won't let it define all that connects us.

Varian swallows thickly as he takes another step closer to her and makes to place his hand over the marking. There's a tremor in his hand right before he makes contact. As if he doesn't want to touch it. . . or rather he wants to kill the one who made it.

Even the feathering whispers of his thoughts I can hear.

When his hand makes contact with Mavyn's chest her eyes immediately glaze over. Varian flinches back at it but Mavyn clenches her jaw, grabs his wrist, and pulls his hand back to her chest. Holding him in place as her nails dig into his wrist.

"Don't bother stopping now."

Barely a breath and then it's like a light that goes out. As if a film goes over her physical body, she looks like a walking corpse. She hadn't been able to even speak when I grabbed her arm, the pain was too great. It consumed her and I had only felt a flicker of it through her mind when she had to tell me to let go non-verbally.

"What is happening to her?" Varian rumbles. Furious eyes point to me but he must have enacted his empathic magic because Mavyn answers him with truth filling her words.

"Burning," she whispers. Monotone and lifeless. "He said he'd make sure I burn for all eternity."

"Who?" Varian growls. Fiery eyes roving over her exposed skin.

But Mavyn keeps her mouth shut. It might be called

truth pulling, but the one answering does have an option not to speak. Once they open their mouth they have no choice but to speak words of truth, but they can always choose not to open their mouth to begin with.

Another growl rumbles in Varian's chest but he doesn't push it. He can't *force* her to open her mouth and speak. It doesn't matter much anyway though, because we already know the answer. There's only one being who could have caused her to burn. *Caused her curse.*

But there had been so much pain before. She had crumbled, crippled by it, unable to speak, unable to move. Yet now she stands perfectly still, whispering her answers but still speaking them. You wouldn't know how much pain she's in. Not until you look in her eyes and see nothing.

No expression, no emotion, no life. *No soul.*

It's grating on my own soul.

"Where did you go two nights ago after the Willow of Lore ceremony?"

The force that is Varian's voice when he's truth pulling is so great even I can feel it without him touching me. Heeding me to answer even though the question is not directed at me. I can't image how it feels for Mavyn.

Not that she shows it at all.

"Running."

Even with my advanced hearing I have to strain to hear her. *It won't hurt* my fucking ass. She may not show she's in pain but you can fucking tell. She's barely breathing and her voice and words reflect that.

Varian rumbles, "Running where?"

Something slashes through her eyes. A flash of light or

an emotion that was too quick for me to process. "Away."

"Why?"

"Because it's not fair."

A tremor shakes her entire body and a rainstorm scent bursts through the room as Mavyn's nails puncture through Varian's skin. He doesn't flinch at it but liquid builds on Mavyn's waterline.

"Music is mine," she barely breathes. "And he hates me because of it. Thinks I'm too worthless for it."

Confusion vibrates through Varian as he asks, "Who?"

"Blood demon." And I think I might just kill who I've always seen as a brother. "Not even the sun devil took my song away."

I'm going to kill him.

I glance at Varian with questions. The first being why he also wants to murder Thorne.

"Is that why you destroyed Thorne's rooms?"

The room goes exceptionally quiet as we all wait for her to answer. I already know she didn't do it – couldn't have done it – but for some reason the rest of them think she did.

"I did not," she states.

You wouldn't be able to notice it unless you were right next to him as I am, but Varian expels a soft sigh. If I didn't know any better I would have thought he was relieved by her answer.

"Then where did you end the night? Where were you between the events of the Willow of Lore ceremony two nights ago and your dorm room this morning?"

That flash in her eyes happens again. “Burning.” My true devil claws at my soul. “In the sun death realm.” I think my eyes go black for a second as my true devil takes control before it’s reminded that he can’t come out. Mavyn’s voice in our head telling me I need to keep it in check for her.

Varian’s aura deepens with a destruction that could cripple this entire school. His voice darkens into something that isn’t entirely his. His magic growing to a new level I’ve never seen.

“Did you burn Thorne’s rooms?”

A final question, a blunt question. Nothing but truth pulling, this time giving Mavyn no choice but to answer.

“No.”

And the second the word leaves her lips Varian rips his hand away from her. He turns away and disperses his magic so we’re no longer all suffocating.

“She was telling the truth,” he states to those still in the room. Thorne, his and my father, and the Dean. “She didn’t do it.”

I step towards Mavyn ready to grab her because she doesn’t look any different. Varian let her go and yet her eyes are still glossed over and lifeless. Her right hand is still holding her collar down and her left is in its same position when she had been grabbing Varian’s wrist.

“Then we need to question the staff and groundskeepers again. We might also need to ask one of the stone witches from Corr to come extract the sights from the gargoyles around the university.”

“Of course, Mr. Arcturus, I’ll have a letter sent to Moiraio Academy.”

"Mavyn?" I whisper, ignoring the conversation happening behind me. I can't hear her breath anymore. "Mavyn, can you look at me?"

Her skin has gotten paler and the circles under her eyes have gotten darker. Her color is draining away and my aura begins thrumming tightly around me.

"Mavyn?" I try again. "Firecracker?"

My eyes dip down to the claiming mark on her chest and there's a tremor through the ground. The conversation behind me dies but nothing can take my focus away from my fated. I can't even try running invisible fingers over her mental shields because I don't want her thinking I'm trying to read her thoughts.

It feels like when she first disappeared and all that remained were ashes.

Helpless.

Worthless.

I can't do *anything*.

"Mavyn?"

Desperation hangs on each syllable. Someone says my name but it's background noise. Something inside cracks and I know I need to keep it together. I can't let my true devil out. I can't let him gain control.

But I am not as strong as Varian. I am not as controlled as Darian.

I don't have the calculated mind of Thorne or even the knowledge of Castiel. I am not powerful like my father or practiced like Uncle Edmond Arcturus or even tempered like Uncle Jerusil Kyros.

I am nothing.

I am nothing.

I. Am. Nothing.

How am I fated to *her*? How could I possibly be worthy of her?

It's simple. I'm not.

Twenty-Six

Mavyn – Septmust 3

Callahan is out because he would never do it. And I would rather slit my own throat then ask Thorne. I can't subject Jullia and Asher to that, so maybe Hanna? I also don't need to be owing the professors any favors so they're a definite no. And Darian is. . . he would be the absolute last resort.

Something flickers somewhere further in me and I remind myself I still need to pay attention. But the burning has stopped. Did I answer all of his questions? The last one I remember hearing from the devil was if I burned Thorne's rooms.

I had to smirk at myself for that. Because technically I did not. Technically my magic did – my flames. He did not ask if I used magic to burn Thorne's rooms down. If he had then I would have said yes. But he only asked if I had done it, and to create blue fire only magic itself can do that.

I'll have to thank Elsa for that. A high fae noblewoman who loves frequenting the club every so often. She's not from this side of Miy but the opposite where the Mage Board has less control and monarchy's are of more influence.

High fae cannot lie, however omissions are not lies. I had known that speaking less words can be more powerful, but she taught me the art of speaking only select words. The art of truth telling and the art of bending – twisting and knotting – truth telling. And just because you answer a question does not mean you answered the whole question.

Truth pulling empathic magic requires you to tell the truth when you speak. However, you can always choose to simply keep your mouth shut. So I only answered the parts of questions I wanted to, leaving them to all think I simply answered all questions with only one answer.

But the devil has not asked any more questions and it has been a while. The burning has also stopped, so did he remove his hand from my body?

The second he did that I did what I have only done once before. I locked myself within my mind. My body becomes detached from myself, even though I can faintly hear and see and speak.

It doesn't last long, and the downside is if I stay in this state for too long my body will shut down. I'll become trapped in my mind unable to do anything. First my breathing will stop, then my heartbeat slows until it stops.

I had been dead for twenty-four minutes before the

shocks of a defibrillator flickered in my mind and I realized I needed to unlock my mind. It's almost like when someone goes brain dead and their body is unable to function.

Not only is that a downside and why I never did it while the devil beat me, but it is also incredibly hard to unlock myself from my mind. So many thoughts, so much thinking, so much, too much, going, going, going.

Thoughts will pass and I won't realize it's been several minutes. And it's so safe here. There's no pain, though my thoughts can consume me in a different way.

I force myself through the barriers of my mind to peak out my own eyes. The red devil is no longer in front of me and instead it's the golden devil. The one who is causing something further in me to tug. His eyes are distant as they watch me and there's something in them.

Something I only see when I look in the mirror.

I need to leave this place. I realize now I stopped breathing a couple minutes ago. I need to unlock my mind.

The black ring around the edge of his iris is starting to slowly consume the gold.

I told him to keep a lock on his devil. Why is he not freaking listening.

His eyes flash and the black retreats. Mavyn. His lips moving and that reminds me I need to unlock myself. I need to come back to my physical body.

I huff within my mind. I do not really want to. I am so tired of feeling pain.

Mavyn. His lips moving again. Can you hear me firecracker? Can you breathe for me? I need you to wake up.

Oh yes, I forgot about that. I'm technically killing

myself like this.

I really wish I didn't want to live.

Pushing further past the barriers of my mind, I see more than just pinpoints through my eyes. The edges of the golden devil come into focus, and then his body, and then the room we're in. I can feel myself blink, and then I suck in a deep breath after not doing so for nearly eight minutes.

And then it's just as I suspected.

Pain.

. . .

Why can I not feel my legs?

It's my first thought when my conscious wakes up. The last thing I felt before – I assume – I passed out from the pain. I had locked myself in my mind, I remember, because I was being questioned about Thorne's rooms burning.

My lips curl at that and my stellar truth telling. I technically did not lie.

"Why are you smiling like a fool?"

I frown and loll my head to the side. The rest of my body feels kind of numb as well, and my head feels light. I feel. . .

Panic shoots through my veins and adrenaline rushes as my heart pounds.

I'm drugged.

I'm drugged and I can't regulate my heartbeat or my blood flow.

"Yes." The deep voice speaking again. Gold ringed red eyes watching me like I'm a lunatic about to go off. Rude. "Drugged, but with pain relievers and healing tonics. You were also a bit dehydrated and malnourished so there's a feeding bag and fluids entering your system."

I roll my eyes up to all the bags connected to tubes attached to needles pricking the tops of my hand. That doesn't explain why I feel drunk, all floaty and flighting and light. And I still can't feel my legs.

"Your feet were incredibly burned so there's a salve on them with a powerful numbing agent that helps alleviate the pain. So you won't be feeling them for a while."

I try to snap my eyes from the bags to him but they lag and it feels like a glitch. Still, once I do I slit my eyes and glare at him. Can he read my thoughts?

He rolls my eyes. "Your mental shields are still up but yes, I can hear most of your thoughts."

Oops.

I giggle but it sounds gurgled in my chest.

LMAO.

He sighs and shakes his head. "Aside from that, are you feeling better?"

Now it's my turn to roll my eyes. I try to open my mouth but my body does not cooperate. It makes me wonder just what kind of drugs they used.

"*Healing* drugs," he grits. "You were in a lot of pain and then afterward you weren't breathing for a while and then passed out. You want to tell me about that?"

I look away to think. All of him is just too much. Where's Callahan? He was the last thing I saw before I went unconscious. But I didn't go into a nightmare for some reason.

"Why do you say that?"

Shit.

So like this he can hear my thoughts?

"*Yes*. Now answer me."

Answer me.

Of course. . .

"Of course, what?"

His voice is strained as he leans into me. Slowly consciousness eases out of the sluggish, drunken-feeling state. I return his gaze and glare.

Nice fucking try, devil.

I solidify my mental shields and my thoughts. Containing everything so he can no longer hear. He straightens and neutralizes his expression to closed off but irritated.

"Nice fucking try, what?" We both turn to golden eyes narrowed at Professor Asier before softening at me. "What was being tried?"

I look up to the professor and smirk, but I won't be saying anything. Cleaver fucking devil. Thinking that I'll have loose lips because I'm drugged. Simple pain relievers and healing tonics do not feel like this. Even the stronger stuff they use. I know when I've been drugged.

"How many times have you gone into your nightmare realm?"

He asks it to me, but I don't feel like answering it. It's not his business. It's not any of their business.

It's barely been two months at this fucking school and already so much bullshit has happened. This was supposed to be easy. I go to my classes, I graduate, I go home. It was never supposed to be this complicated.

Why the fuck did I not notice that damned vampire in the ally?

I grit my teeth and curl my nails into my palms. "I had asked if you would stay out of my business, Professor. You said yes." Like a good boy.

When I look up to him his glare is infused with more than just annoyance and anger. There's a frustration in his eyes that goes beyond irritation. It's a pointed, fiery rage at me. Borderline hatred.

Well get in line.

"This is my business," I state. Calm and clear and deadly.

A muscle in his jaw twitches. "And you don't want to inform your *fated* about such things?"

I glance at Callahan who's watching our exchange with inquisitiveness. There's no negativities or possessiveness coming from him. Which is at odds with how he was before when Professor Asier placed his hand on my shoulder before we begun truth pulling.

"Being fated means nothing until our souls become bound, there's a claiming mark, and the proper documentation has been filed. The only person who needs to know my business is me. And unless the Mage Board or the Dean of Syngenia University explicitly asks for the inner thoughts of some nineteen-year-old, I don't need to tell anyone jack shit."

There's a sharp tug now, but I ignore it. Callahan doesn't say anything as he takes the seat to the left of the bed and Professor Asier – who's on my right side – brings a wall up. A mask slips over his expression until I can't read anything from his face.

But his body. . . that is thrumming with damnation.

"I see," he says, cool and neutral. "In that case, I will be seeing you Friday. There will be a written-only test on the first millennium of Syngenia that will be a quarter of your final grade. I will also not be accepting anymore late work for the rest of the semester so you better ace the test or else you'll be dropped out of Magic History. It will be the same for Intro to Power Compulsion about late work."

Then he leaves and that bomb hits like I'm sure he intended.

The Mage Board is going to kill me.

Callahan scoots his chair closer to the bed and grabs my hand. "It'll be fine. We can study tonight and tomorrow after – "

"I have work."

Or I did. I don't know what time it is or how long I've been out. At least mentally I'm no longer feeling the effects of whatever drug Asier gave me. I'm probably fired.

Callahan's hand squeezes mine. "You'll probably say no but. . . could I just pay – "

I rip my hand away and turn in the opposite direction as him. He doesn't finish what he was saying. Good. It would probably just make me mad anyway.

"You could always pay me back if you wanted to later," he tries. When I don't answer he sighs and doesn't reach for my hand again. "You were only out for about thirty minutes, but the healers want you to stay for the rest of the day to make sure you're alright. They said you should also stay the night but they can't force you."

Only thirty. . . ? That means it's around seven thirty – maybe. I could technically just show up late to Magic History and then go to the rest of my classes. That way today wouldn't be counted as an absence.

Throwing the sheet off me, I push myself up and will myself to make my feet move. Callahan jerks back and out of the corner of my eye I see him glare at me.

"Don't even think about it, Mavyn. You're still practically paralyzed."

Except I won't be.

Taking my wrist, I pull up my sleep shirt and bite myself. I'll have to run back to my room to change and then run to class. How freakin nice would it be to shadow twist right now. That or fold.

The pricks of pain don't register, but my venom does.

Because of how hungry I was during that party I had attended, I wasn't able to control my venom when I bit the demigod. However, normally, I have excellent control of it. Both the aphrodisiac aspect as well as the defensive aspect.

Like with other creatures who inject venom into their prey, it's usually something that either neutralizes or strictly kills them. If I injected enough of my venom into someone I could eventually kill them, but right now I measure the dosage for a paralysis effect.

On anyone else it would do just that – paralyze them. But because it's me and with the help of the blue belladon in my blood, it becomes a counter antidote to both poisons and venoms. Meaning it will neutralize the effects of whatever drugs I was given.

Needles of pain begin stabbing my legs as it begins working. My blood drips from my tongue to the side of my mouth. I let it waste. My poison infused blood that tastes like the best thing you could ever taste. Then I remove my wrist from my mouth and wipe the rest of my blood on my face onto the sheets.

Berries with a hint of floral clog my nose and I even scrape the sheet against my tongue to try and get the taste out of my mouth. But it worked. I can now move my toes and while pain slices along my feet and legs, I let it.

At least I'm alive.

Throwing my legs over the bed, I stand and turn towards the door. Callahan is standing in front of the pathway with his back straight, shoulders wide, and arms crossed. As if he could stop me.

"You need rest."

"I need to get to class."

He glares at me. "Your body was put through extreme trauma the last couple days. Class can wait. Varian won't fail you."

This is going to be fucking annoying.

"Move, Callahan." I take a step towards him but he doesn't budge. I contemplate comparing him to the sun devil with controlling my life, but that would be a step too far. There is too much self-loathing and hatred within him, I don't want to break him.

I do, however, do the next best thing.

I roll my sleeves up and hike my shirt up and barrel straight for him. Immediately he moves out of the way, his arms going in the air so as not to touch my bare skin. Since he's only wearing a short sleeve shirt and not his uniform he isn't as covered.

"Mavyn what the fuck!"

As soon as I pass him I bolt for the exit. Pulling my shirt down and not bothering about my sleeves because I can't have him catch me and I'm also on a time crunch. Students walk here and there, most of them turning towards me as I run and Callahan bellowing my name behind me.

Regulating my heartrate and blood flood, I up my pace and focus on my breathing instead of the pain shooting up and down my legs.

Rounding one of the corners I see Jullia with her arm linked with Asher. Her face lights up when she sees me and opens her mouth to speak but I'm already past her.

"I'M COMING TO CLASS," I shout back with Callahan yelling after, "NOT A FUCKING CHANCE!"

Ignoring him, I make a beeline straight through the courtyards until I get to the west side of the building and I can see the dorm rooms. I don't have the longest legs, but when all else fails, run. After the sun devil I made sure I was able to run faster and longer than anyone if I needed to.

Sometimes that's the only thing you can do. And I don't mean it just because of the devil or the shitty foster houses. You could be the strongest, most powerful being known, but even then there are times when all you can do is run.

It's not weak. People associate running with fleeing and cowardness and self-preservation in a negative aspect. It can be – to a certain point. But facing the monsters, bravery, selflessness. . . children shouldn't have to do that. People as a whole shouldn't have to only endure.

I ram through the door of my dorm and take the stairs

two at a time to my floor. When I get to my door I barely slip through before slamming it shut and invoking a barrier. Asher had created a spell so me and Jullia don't have to use our keys to keep locking and unlocking the door, but if someone has our key they can come and go. Which, Callahan does.

So I create my own barrier to keep him out and hopefully he just assumes it was another protection Asher made for us when he put the spell and sound barrier up.

A second after I solidify it there's a crash into my door. It actually shakes the entire wall.

"Mavyn! This is bullshit, you need rest!" There's a click from the key unlocking the door but when the knob twists the door doesn't budge. "MAVYN!"

I huff a laugh as I quickly turn to my wardrobe and begin stripping. It takes me a moment to actually process that I did just run all the way over here. And I ran without my umbrella. Meaning I was. . .

No. The storm clouds. That's why I hadn't burned. I had been so caught up I didn't realize I nearly killed myself by going head first outside. No wonder Callahan kept screaming at me to stop before I went outside.

There's another bang on the door as I start getting dressed. I wish I could shower, but there's nothing I can do about that.

"Mavyn! Even if you get ready I'm not letting you leave this room. This is a hard no for me, you need to rest. You've locked yourself in!"

I roll my eyes at him. True, true. . . but there's still the window. And since there's enough cloud cover I can walk outside without my umbrella, I'm just taking that exit.

Callahan keeps knocking on the door but I ignore him

and roll on my thigh highs. Then I slip on my flats and pull my desk a couple inches away from the wall before standing my chair on top. My bed still looks like a mess, most of it ashes, but I'll deal with that after everything else.

Stepping onto my desk, I rip the blackout sheet away and flip the latch for the lock. There's a loud-ish snap as the frame snaps up and there's a crunch from the ivy covering it. I have never been more grateful for that sound barrier Asher made. Callahan can't hear a single thing.

Stepping onto my chair, I push the window all the way up and heft myself over the edge. There's a sharp bite in the air as a rain scented breeze blows. It makes me smile as I get to my feet and crouch down.

Pushing the window shut, I close my eyes and let another key within me, sitting in another lock to another door within me, twist. This door only cracking the barest bit open and allowing me to curl those vines that had covered the window before back over the glass.

Since I can't lock the door from the outside like this, this is the next best option.

Satisfied, I close and lock that door within back up and softly hum to myself as I walk along the roof. I take my tablet out from the inside pocket of my blazer and check the time. Seven twenty-eight. It almost feels like a miracle. Even though I can't run to the opposite side of the school in only two minutes. . .

I check my surroundings. There's nothing but the forest curving around the back of the dorm and the only creatures with blood I'd be worried about are ones still inside the dorm or further away.

There's a chance I could be seen, but it's not unheard of for vampires to have certain types of magic. Elemental portaling is common, afterall.

Strengthening the storm, I wait for just the right moment. Reaching into the ether and then I blink. Like always, it feels like my feet didn't even leave the ground. And thankfully, there's not a single body out that could have seen me.

I blink again at the courtyard I landed in. This one technically on the outer side of the main building with no roof. And all I have to do is go through the entrance that leads into the building and Professor Asier's class is right down the hall.

I make a run for it. Straight down the hall I can see the open door and Professor Asier's desk. The bell rings and he turns towards the door. Normally he keeps it open and I'm r*ight there*. But his gold ringed red eyes latch on me, make eye contact, and at just the last second his door slams shut.

I'm too close to stop my momentum and I slam into the thick wooden door.

Pain vibrates through my bones and shocks the rest of the pain I had been trying to ignore. It also doesn't help that my legs, which are still prickling with the last remnants of numbness, shoot shocks of lightning up from my feet. The blisters are only just barely healed.

I slam my fists into the door and the force actually shakes it.

That rage I had felt two days ago flickers. Like embers sparking once more after the fire should have been doused. The bell hadn't even finished ringing when he shut the door. I wouldn't have been late. I would have been right there, on fucking time.

I get it. They hate vampires. I have my secrets. I've challenged someone who is very clearly at the top of the food chain. But this kind of pettiness. . .

There's no physical lock on the door, but there is some sort of spell or barrier. I run my fingers over the wood and once more twist that secondary key in its lock. The door not even opening, but it's enough for me to *feel.*

Some sort of lock made of shadows and. . . golden flames. A chain wrapping the door that also extends over the entire room.

Closing my eyes, I twist a third key within and let that magic slip through the links of the chain. Roving over golden aura until I find the actual lock.

In my head I envision it like a vintage metal lock you use one of those skeleton keys to open. Then I curl claws into it and crush it.

It splinters to pieces as the door swings in. I step through the doorway to a class that goes silent and a professor that is staring at me with pure shock. It would be amusing, but I don't waste time and take the stairs closest to me to the third row.

Pulling the chair next to Jullia out, I set my tablet down and sit. My friend is also staring at me with wide eyes, but she says nothing and whips her head to the front as the professor roars my name.

Softer, giving everyone whiplash, in a voice I should be wary at, he demands, "Who the fuck do you think you are interrupting my class?"

My skin is bruised, my feet are on fire, lightning strikes of pain are shooting up my legs and spine, my bones ache, my head is pounding, I am still starving. . . but it all disappears when I meet the devil's eyes.

Vivid, pure red iris's ringed within stark gold.

So much power. So much demanding aura. He doesn't have to expel any magic because you can see it in his eyes. The amount of control he has, and the force that's shown just by looking at him. It had rivaled Callahan's father by leagues. I'd bet the only thing he would *have* to bow to was the primordials.

Could I get him to somehow bow to me?

His fangs flash at me as he snarls, but I don't apologize for that thought – or for letting him hear it.

"I am a student," I state calmly, answering his demand. "One who wants to learn."

The tension in the room could be cut with a dull knife with how taunt it is. Everyone barely breathing as they watch us. Waiting to see what the Professor will do. I'm a bit curious myself. Wondering if he's going to retaliate against me, or be a good boy and teach his lesson.

Something flickers between us and he drops a mask over himself. In a blink, doing what he had done in the infirmary, he neutralizes his face and back is the stoic blank-faced professor.

"That spell on the door was a *Devil's Lock*, Ms. Tsuki," he rumbles through the room.

Leaning back in my chair, I cross my arms and hold in my smirk. "I know."

A muscle in his jaw feathers right before he turns around to face the chalkboard. Almost. . . *almost*, I say the devil who claimed me thought they were fun games. But then I'd have to explain *how* they were games and *how* a *human* learned how to break the locks that are known to be nearly impossible to crack.

I bet it's just killing him. The curiosity and frustration. Too bad he won't be getting the answers from me.

Twenty-Seven

Varian – Septmust 3

I'm going to beat her fucking ass.

Another presence is made down the hall right where she had been running from. I glance away from the chalkboard to see Callahan with furious eyes making his way here. He looks like he ran around the whole damn school.

And he's not in his uniform.

Gritting my jaw, I open my mouth the second he steps foot into my classroom but he beats me to it.

"Mavyn, so help me God of Fire, get your *ass* out of

this classroom right now!"

His words echo in the room as I shut my mouth and turn to face the problematic bloodsucker. Her eyes are round and her plush lips hang open as she stares at Callahan. Her friend and roommate next to her has the same expression, but neither of them move.

Callahan begins climbing the stairs to their row.

"Mr. Armani," I warn, but he dismisses my words with a shake of his head.

"Get your – "

"Do not tell me what I can and cannot fucking do," she snaps, but Callahan pulses a wave of his magic to try and silence her.

Stupid.

She stands up so fast out of her chair it hits the step and desks behind her with a force that mirrors how it felt when she slammed on the door. It *shakes* the ground. I'm surprised it doesn't splinter the chair itself.

"If you *ever* – " And I can feel her aura. The same blackened rage I had felt for a fraction of a second when she threatened me. Now a simple flame but with the power to consume us all in fire. " – try to silence me again, Callahan Rusilan Armani, I will reduce you to dust."

Her aura disappears again like it was never there but the energy remains. *Fire.* Like the remnants that had remained burning in Thorne's rooms even after he should have been able to douse them.

Blue flame is a lost magic. There is no one alive still who has the art – let alone the type of powerful aura needed to contain it. The last person in recorded history was from five thousand years ago. A blood witch who was an expert in runic magic and a vampyr with an exceptional blood art who were able – together – to harness the magic of blue flame.

They were the tipping point in the War of Gods and both of them were consumed in the end by their flames as they ended a war that had lasted a millennium.

And before that I only know of one other person. Syngenia the first Vampyr. Daughter to Syngenia the Blood Witch, first witch created at the dawn of beginning.

But she had answered my questions. She said she did not burn down Thorne's rooms. She answered the question bluntly and without hesitation. Not to mention she doesn't have the magic or aura to do it. Though, that fraction of a feeling of her aura I did feel. . . it makes me think she does have some sort of a power. Something strong and having to do with flame – which would align with her pink eyes coming from a vampyr line of red eyes.

But that is not what makes my own eyes go wide, along with Callahan's. No one, and I mean *no-fucking-one*, knows our full names. It's a type of tradition with devils – and usually angels – to keep second names secret because they're the names of our true forms. The *things* we harbor within us.

Fire and wood snake through the room with a toasted quality. There's a warmth with Callahan's scent as his name continues to echo in the room. His expression of shock morphing into complete awe and admiration. Making his aura go soft and gentle like a warm campfire in a fairy glen.

"Say it again," he whispers. Gentle in only a way a devil can be because of his fated. They may have not bonded their souls, but being fated goes above all minor traditions. They either finish cementing their bond, or one of their souls dies.

The bloodsucker twitches back at Callahan's display.

Does she know the power of saying a devil's full name? Does she know what it means to say it to them?

More importantly, how the fuck does she know his? Not even I knew it. Not that I would ever say it. For anyone other than their fated – or occasionally their parents – to use a devils or angels second name is practically a death sentence.

Her pale pink eyes glance at me but immediately look away. I doubt she'd find anything helpful, considering I'm still reeling about the fact that she still has secrets that she won't tell me, she challenges me at every incident, *and* the fact that she broke a *Devil's Lock*.

It's not hard for a celestial to break the lock, but even Castiel and Edmond have trouble with mine. There's a reason I'm responsible for keeping the old books secure in the catacombs of the library. No mere student, let alone a nineteen-year-old vampire who was just barely turned, should be able to break it. Even if she does have power from the blood of the vampyr who caused her to turn.

Because she didn't just pick and unlock the damn thing, she full on crushed it.

"Why?"

Her voice snaps me out of my thoughts. It reminds me the interruption that is happening in my classroom during my class.

"Because." My voice demanding and full of annoyance. "Second names, or what you would call a middle name, is the name given for a devil or angel's True Form. To say it would be equivalent to accepting both the being and their beast."

She jerks back and panic rises up. A flash of hurt crosses Callahan's face as she starts shaking her head and gets lost in thought but he covers it. An interesting reaction from someone towards their fated. She had a similar emotional state when I asked if she was keeping secrets from her fated as well.

Callahan gently raises his hands like you would so you don't scare a meek creature. "It's alright, Mavyn. You didn't know, it's okay. It doesn't have to mean anything."

There's an off-ness about his tone. Knowing Callahan his whole life from partially growing up with him and how he's viewed romantic notions and beliefs about fated's and claiming's and blood sharing. . . this does not sound like the Callahan I know. He has only ever been surrounded by true, unfiltered, pure love and that's all he would talk about for a year when he was ten – wondering when he'd find his fated. It's a thought that has always been at the back of his mind.

He did the same thing when we were in the Dean's office too when we all learned she had been claimed already. And while it's true that it becomes void if one of them dies and they aren't fated, her marking from him will never disappear. And it being right over her heart. . . I'd rather skin myself than have a forced claiming mark on me like that. It's a disgrace.

Mavyn straightens and grabs her chair. "I'm fine, Callahan."

But her voice is cold and speaking to Callahan like that grates on my nerves. She has no right to use that tone with him. My mood is shifting from wanting to spank her ass as a punishment to actually wanting to punish her. Callahan above all of us does not deserve any hardship.

"I don't need rest, I need to not fail this school." Her frigid eyes point at me. "And if I don't pass this class then I automatically fail, and if I fail I'm dead. Your father said so."

Guilt pricks in the back of my conscious but I ignore it. I didn't know she was on a death sentence if she didn't graduate. I had assumed – actually I hadn't assumed anything. I hadn't thought about it and what would happen. All my focus was if she was a spy for the Mage Board, but after finding out she wasn't I didn't look further about why she was here.

It should have been obvious. Illegally turned vampires are immediately sentenced to death. Usually on the spot by the enforcer who found them. With their newly gained strength, human mentality, and bloodlust they're a danger not only to us but also to humans – most of who know nothing of their non-mortal world.

Still. . . I shouldn't care. Afterall, she said I needed to stay out of her business. Meaning she, and whatever happens to her, is not my concern.

"If you both don't sit in your fucking chairs right now," I rumble, letting my magic influence my tone, "I'm automatically failing you both right here, right now."

I can't, nor would I, do that to Callahan, but the bloodsucker doesn't have to know that.

She immediately sits, focusing her eyes on her tablet. Callahan glances at me with an emotional exhaustion before looking away and taking his seat. These two will be the death of me.

After a moment, Callahan finally takes his seat next to her and I turn back towards the board. So many minute thoughts are running through my mind. About the bloodsucker, her past, her herself. I have questions about what her magic is, why the Mage Board let her enroll, does she have anything to do with what happened?

Or. . .

Maybe it's not the Mage Board she's a spy for. It could be the rebels.

They've been more active lately. More bold with their

attacks and standoff's and energy. Something has shifted with their underworking's and everyone is getting antsy about what they plan to do next.

In the beginning their goal had been to overthrow the Mage Board. There may be eight seats each with a different race, but favor tends to point towards the mages themselves despite not being a celestial. They have the closest relation to witches and while it isn't common, mages do have the ability to adapt and learn how to wield other elements they weren't born with.

Especially after the fall of witches, the mages were smart with conducting their power. They have only grown stronger in recent years as well.

The rebels wanted to disrupt that unbalance. They also believe that because there is not a seat for each subrace opinions are mute. Fliers and waterways are both shifters, but they have been enemies of each other since they were first created. The rebels do have a point in each race and subrace should have a seat, but the Mage Board does not want to change.

At least the mages don't.

But it would be obvious if she was a rebel, and they wouldn't send a fucking vampire.

My questions need to stop. I shake my head slightly at myself and right my thoughts. She is not my business, she is not my concern. She said she only wants to make it these five years and then leave. There was truth spoken when she said those words.

Finishing writing my lesson for today, I turn back towards the class. I consciously make sure I do not look towards her, and for good measure I don't look at Callahan either. I'm about to open my mouth when a hand shoots up.

"Mr. Rothwhile." I nod my head to the tiger shifter who looks like he'd be better suited to some sort of thin, long-legged creature. Normally he's silent in class and turns every assignment in long before it's due.

He shifts in his chair and for a millisecond glances at a certain bloodsucker. "Well. . . " He swallows thickly and faces me but avoids eye contact. "I know today's lesson is on thirteen goddesses, but. . . well, I wanted to ask if there was ever a record before of the spirits of the Willow of Lore changing their aura color?"

Several bodies sit forward at that and curiosity about the event that happened Monday night emerges in the air. I should have anticipated this question being asked. We're not allowed to explicitly teach about the Willow of Lore unless directly asked, but most know all there is to know about it.

Stories being passed down through the generations of the first sign of life birthed after the destruction of the War of Gods. Where each race and subrace that were left after the war came together. A symbol of renewal, growth, friendship, family, and home after tragedy.

Each year the spirits of the willow waking and reminding us with their song and dance about the costs that were paid to ensure we all lived. A song with words that have not been sung since the blood witch who first created them did so. A lullaby that had been passed down from daughter to daughter from Syngenia the first Vampyr.

Not only did she know the words, but the spirits accompanied and harmonized with her. They changed their blue and fluttering purple aura – which is the only aura anyone is able to actually see because of the potency of their magic – to red. To a color that could only be meant for a bloodsucker.

Of course, they have questions.

The only problem is I have no idea about the answers. Not even the Dean knew what to make of it, and Edmond and Aslan had no words. The blood demon and devil chairholders of the Mage Board's only comment had been that the force of the magic was felt all the way past this world and onto Earth. That Esmirra of Ebony confirmed she felt it – the only bone witch who resides on Earth and somehow is familiar with Edmond.

Which, a bone witch and a blood demon being familiar is unheard of and peculiar on a whole different level. Though it could explain Thorne's progressive mental shields and control. Since he grew up with the witch.

But the power of the Willow of Lore passing *universes* is. . .

"There is not," I finally answer. "However, the spirits of the Willow of Lore are a species unto themselves. They are as mystic as the gods and goddesses and have a will undefined by the fates. There are many things we do not know, and many things we will never know about them."

He shoots his hand back up into the air and I nod for him to ask whatever question he will. The sooner I can get through this curiosity the sooner I can be done with it.

"But isn't there a Prophecy of Old about a fortune teller and a red sun? It goes. . . when aura's bright with blue wisteria light, roaming through under a glowing new moon, a fate with knot and lore of old, shall turn the burning sun into bloodred gold. A god forgotten, killer of all, fallen and bound by her blue flame and blue belladon, will rise with wrath and sanivin of roi, devouring this world in cursed blood moons and noise."

A chill goes through the room that raises the temperature after he finishes reciting the prophecy. It happens every time someone mentions the damned thing.

"For the first time ever," he continues, "not only did the Willow of Lore's ceremony happen two and a half months ahead of its set time, but it happened on a new moon."

I shake my head and the action catches pale pink eyes that are nearly red with a face devoid of color. I glance at Mavyn who has that glazed look over her eyes, but instead of them being dull they turned several shades darker. It almost looks like all the blood in her face moved to color her eyes.

I shake my head again and look back at Mr. Rothwhile. "That prophecy has been spoken long before the Willow of Lore was created and before even the War of Gods. Prophecies of Old have never transpired more than a millennium after being told. It's what's called a deadened prophecy. Spoken and holding power, but lacking in magic influenced by fate and destiny."

It's an old grandmother's tale told to keep children's minds open and seeking. A helping hand for expanding their mind and creative play, while also serving as a threat when children are bad.

What is a cursed blood moon? Which sun burning now could be turned into gold? How can a fate be knotted?

Or, as a threat, parents would say eat your vegetables or the god forgotten will snatch you up at night and make you forgotten with him.

Either way. . . "It's as powerful as any human fairytale is. And there has been records of the Willow of Lore ceremony happing in advance of the winter solstice, as well as even after it. As I said, the spirits are their own entities and perform their ceremonies as they like. Uninfluenced by our organized time system and fate."

Eyes are burning into my head and I know I shouldn't, but I can't help it.

Damning, wrathful, *burning*. Red eyes like the blood moon that occurs every year the day before the spring equinox hold mine in a vise. I couldn't look away even if I wanted to.

She blinks. Then I have to blink because my mind studders as I am now staring at pale pink eyes. They had just been red. They were glowing like. . .

I shake my head and rub my eyes with my thumb and fingers. I couldn't have imagined it, but it happened within a fracture of a second. Yet, it felt like an eternity had passed as I observed those red eyes.

Too many thoughts now of prophecies and red suns and blood moons and curses. Damn Rothwhile, having me think of things that should have no connection.

I shake my head again. "Now, moving on. . . "

I turn towards the chalkboard and gesture to the lesson name.

"Do you know why, Mavyn?" *Unholy gods.* "Why the spirits changed their aura for you? Or if it has to do with the prophecy? Also how did you know the words?"

I'm about to punch the board but I take a deep breath instead and turn to face the bloodsucker. If she won't answer me maybe she'll answer with an audience.

Rothwhile is turned facing her but her pink eyes are on the ceiling. Leaned back in her chair with her arms crossed. She looks like she's relaxed, peering at something none of us can see.

"Well. . . " she hums. A soft smile curls onto her face as she thinks. "Did you know that it was actually a vampire who created the University?"

I create a sound barrier faster than I ever have before

around the room right as I feel Callahan's magic doing the same.

"He was a descendant of Syngenia the Vampyr and fought alongside Aora and Genifer the Twin Flames during the War of Gods. They say it was the mages who made the university, them that hate the vampires, but it was a mage who killed the last vampire still standing on this world."

I do not know how she knows this knowledge, what memories she has from whichever vampyr blood flows through her veins or who could have told her, but that information and those names had been locked up and sealed. There were blood oaths taken to keep those alive who still know those things quiet.

I didn't even know their names or the truth. I knew there were secrets, and I knew it was not a mage who built up the university, but a vampire. . .

"Telling falsehoods like that, Ms. Tsuki, will get you expelled," I warn. Wariness for the bloodsucker is drawn on Callahan's face as he stares at her. He knows there are secrets too. . . ones that people have died for to keep unknown.

She looks down at me with confusion and a tilted head.

"Falsehoods," she murmurs. It sounds like she doesn't understand why I said that. What I would give to be in her head right now. "It was a vampire who wrote the song. Syngenia the Vampyr's daughter, born without a drop of magic and with a mortal lifespan and wellbeing, died at nineteen from the consumption of blue belladon. So Syngenia, who was an expert in runic magic and curses, etched onto her daughter a symbol Syngenia herself created. A mark that should have held no power, but because of the magic within Syngenia and her grief at her lost daughter, she *created* a rune."

Power that belongs to no one swirls in the space. Raw magic and the things that created it are listening.

"Then," Mavyn whispers, as if she's telling a story from an age ago and the words carry more weight than just fairytales, "she fed her blood to her daughter, and bit her to inject every drop possible of her venom, and thus, the first vampire was created. But the universes require balance. So an act of trapping a soul within a body with a runic curse tipped the scales, and to right the equilibrium fate tied a knot around vampyr and vampires. Only humans can be turned and only a vampyr can turn them."

Our meeting from a little over a month ago filters through my head. Her coming to ask about runic magic and curses. Saying she herself was cursed – that being cursed as a vampire was made through runic magic. Castiel had said being turned into a vampire was not a runic curse, and she made that face she does when she disagrees and knows the truth.

How the *fuck* does she know these truths?

"It didn't help either," she continues, "that Syngenia the Vampyr was associated with the Sun God Ruu and instead of seeking his help she called to a different god. A goddess over a moon and in retaliation Ruu scorned the vampires from his day and cursed them to the night. Which is why vampires cannot be exposed to sunlight."

She hums to herself as she looks around at the darker corners of the room. That power, whoever's spirit it is, hums along with her.

"Vampires are a cursed product of a mothers love. Hated by all for a valid reason no one can name." She turns towards Rothwhile. "In truth, all vampires once turned hear the hum of Sanivin's song. That's what Syngenia the Vampyr had named her daughter come back from death. It's why vampires have a bloodlust. Sure, because they initially need it since they were just killed and everything, but because her song aligns with blood and soul. We are all cursed together and therefore all connected."

The shifter who is normally a scrawny, silent spectator, who has jumped from someone standing right in front of him and asking a question, has words galore now. He's also watching Mavyn like she's something he would worship.

"So all vampires know the words. And all the vampires could sing the song."

She blinks and snaps out of whatever slight trance she was in. Turning towards the shifter she contemplates what he said – even though he didn't ask it as a question.

"Not exactly. All vampires technically do know the words but for the most part it's knowing the feeling they can induce verses the actual words themselves. I'm sure some of them know the actual words, but I can't say they all do." She shrugs a shoulder and makes a face like she's thinking. "I also don't know why the spirits let me sing it. Or why they changed their aura color. It shouldn't be possible for a being to change their aura – the shape or color – however the spirits of the willow are spirits taken in from all sorts of races. The likelihood of what really happened is a spirit of the willow had aura colored red and they influenced the change."

She turns towards me and there's a soft expression on her face. She looks serene. . . just like she did when she was singing. But recognition passes as she processes who she's looking at and a cold mask falls over her features.

"I doubt it really matters though." Her tone reflects her expression now. "Despite all that vampires are still nothing. They don't matter, I should be lucky they didn't eviscerate me when I started singing."

Callahan frowns at her and Rothwhile looks away but says, "It was beautiful though. Your voice, singing, even the spirits harmonized with you. I've never felt a truer form of an embodiment of soul."

She flinches at that. Just barely, but I and Callahan notice it. She doesn't say anything more and turns away. Finally, an ending to the conversation.

"Are there any more questions?" If my tone is any hint there shouldn't be. And thankfully no one else raises their hand or speaks. "Good. Now, today's lesson – "

A ringing echoes in the back of my mind cutting me off. I snap my gaze up to Callahan who is hearing the same thing. Dropping the sound barrier the blaring of warning bells goes off and I reinforce my Devil's Locks sealing off the room.

"Callahan," I bark, who's already down the stairs. "The rest of you stay here. There is an infiltration in the school by rebels using deadly force."

Despite me trying not to, I glance at the bloodsucker. There's a spark that lights in her eyes as she stands up and takes a step to the side as if she was wanting to come with.

"*Stay*," I growl. Stilling her and everyone else in the room. "Only four and fifth year trained students are permitted to help, everyone else is required to stay secured in your rooms. *Do. Not. Come. Out.*"

I doubt there will be anything close to a battle, but it's custom. The rebels have numbers and races with magic that far surpasses most first, second, and third years. Unholy gods, some of them surpass even my own and we cannot have any more casualties.

Callahan disappears out the door with shadows and feathers of pure light drifting around him. His casual clothing disappearing and being replaced by tactile gear as I follow him out. Closing the door behind me, I finish sealing the lock and add another one on for good measure. If the bloodsucker was able to break my first one with her limited magic, I do not need someone more powerful than her breezing through.

Once it's sent I pull my own shadows to form and solidify into my weapons. I roll the sleeves of my white button up over my forearms as holsters become strapped to my body and blades fill them. The weight of a long sword appears on my back and two tactile handguns are strapped at my thighs.

Callahan's own holsters and sheaths wrap around him. At his back are two long blades crisscrossed with a golden chain between their handles. On Earth the closest weapon similar to it would be called a kyoketsu-shoge. Darian has a similar one, though his chain between them is longer and he uses his more similar to a whip dart.

A bang rocks part of the school. Callahan and I glance at each other before we take off towards the noise. We meet Thorne and his father – both strapped in their signature weapons – coming around the corner.

"*Fucking rebels*," Edmond sneers. "You would have thought the stint at the capitol would have taught them something."

The rest of us don't get a chance to respond as we exit into one of the courtyards that extend out to a wide field. It's expansive and eventually leads to a cliff that overlooks the sea. But off to the left is a battalion of soldiers.

Darian and his father are already on the field holding out with a shield to prevent their magic from striking the school, but apparently a blow already landed. Half of the training arena is already in cinders. What a fucking pain.

Jerusil Kyros – who is the most gentle and kindhearted devil I have ever met – turns back and shouts for us all to get our asses out here. Darian smiles at his father before he takes a step back, drops his shield for a moment, extends his arms out wide, and then forces them together with a clap.

The shock from the sound shatters every window on this side of the university and forms a crater around Darian.

A fucking warning would have been nice, I wince through my mind into his. Forming links between the number of us. Castiel and Aslan are further out throwing offensive blows at the rebel group still holding.

You're late to the party, Darian chuckles. *I warned my father and the rest of us who have been holding for the past ten minutes.*

Thorne shadow twists from where he was next to me to the field with Castiel. Each of us work in tandem as we instinctively coordinate with one another. With how small this group from the rebels are we won't even need the other trainees.

Very sloppy.

The battle was over the second we stepped onto the field.

Twenty-Eight

Mavyn – Septmust 3

Is this what it's like having a hard lock down in America? I would assume so, since half the kids are freaking out and hitting the floor to cover their heads while others are lounging in their chairs and chatting like nothing is happening.

Another bang shakes the eastern wall of the classroom and Jullia hums to herself as her fingers fly over her tablet. Since Asher is a third year he doesn't have to help fight, but he was supposed to be in his additional external controlling class that takes place in the morning. And their classes are always on the eastern field.

Her voice is barely above a whisper as she breathes out, "He says most of the training arena is gone. Some sort of being with strong fire magic. It can slip through an angel and devil's shields."

I look over the rest of the class. I, myself, am lounging back in my chair with my arms crossed. I had wanted to follow them. The professor and Callahan. Mostly because I wanted to see these so-called rebels. Jullia had mentioned it once my first week here when I was delirious with starvation and sleep.

Asher also mentioned them once and how they've been around for a couple centuries. He said that's why despite Syngenia not wanting to solely produce warriors and soldiers, they can't not offer the classes and training because of it. Asher himself coming from a long line of warriors proficient in earth element magic.

But they apparently haven't attacked the school for a century and mainly focus on disrupting things strictly for the Mage Board.

Ms. Elaycia had mentioned them before. She said she's glad they haven't taken their fight to Earth and have remained on Miy. Though she can agree with some of their ways of thinking, their deliverance is too deadly.

I hadn't cared about looking into it further. Jullia cares more about reading the news and articles and staying up to date. I was more focused on trying to get through each day. And with how this year has already gone, I couldn't care any less than I do about the rebels.

Even now I have mild curiosity about them, but I will not be deep diving into them or their reasons or what they have done. Any information I want I just ask Jullia for. She says it hasn't gotten to a point where there is an all-out war, but battles have waged with neither side winning, only retreating.

The power – and destruction – of magic. And the rebels are made up of all kinds of races. Including, if rumors are to be believed – according to Jullia – the last remaining witches alive.

Another force shakes the wall. This one more powerful and silences the room. Anxiety builds up through my stomach as I shift in my chair. My body and muscles tensing with a want to do something. I need action.

"Does he know how many rebels are there?" I ask Jullia. Her nails tap against her screen and trepidation fills with the anxiety. She's been glued to it, messaging back and forth with Asher and Hanna.

"He said at least a couple hundred," she breathes. Her eyes not leaving the screen.

"And how many people does this school hold?"

"There are about a hundred professors, most of them proficient in either defensive or offensive magic. About fifty bodies for staff and school council, three thousand students all together – four hundred of them making up the fourth and fifth years. But of that there are only a hundred or so officiated for battle."

So about two hundred. Only two hundred people – most of which are still students – to fight if there is ever an attack.

"But," she whispers, "we have Thorne, Darian, and Callahan's fathers here. Two devils and a blood demon all with years of experience with all their guards. So we should be fine. We should be fine. We should be fine."

She keeps repeating that as if she's trying to convince herself. Of the celestials, minimum, that means we have four devils, a demigod, two blood demons, and an angel. They'd be able to eviscerate at least a hundred beings of moral by themselves. That with the councilmen's guards and the other professors should be enough.

I relax into my chair and the anxiety only barely flickers. I'd be more worried if there were *several* hundred rebels and they had an active witch with them.

Jullia's nails tap in vicious succession. Her screen sliding from message thread to message thread.

"At least this is happening now and not at the end of the week," she breathes out. Her body frozen but for her fingers moving. "None of our families are here for family weekend."

Right. I forgot. Family weekend begins Friday. There's no class that day as well because –

There's no class Friday.

There's no-*fucking*-class this Friday.

Motherfucker.

There is no class this Friday meaning Professor Asier lied about whatever bullshit test that was going to be worth most of my grade.

I roll my eyes at that and glare at the door. He had also placed another *Devil's Lock* around the class. Several, this time. Not only preventing anyone from coming in, but also preventing any of us from getting out. I'd say that's a fire hazard, but honestly undoing those locks would be light work.

Whatever.

Jullia is right though, at least it's happening now. The families of the students are permitted to come and stay at the school for the weekend as a mark for the first two months of school passing. Since there is no Thanksgiving or Christmas breaks this will be the last time anyone sees their family until the end of the school year. Which also coincides with the end of the year. Our last day of school is the last day of the year, the day before the spring equinox.

Not that, technically, a student couldn't just pop over during a weekend, but if they're caught, they'll be expelled. We have to stay on Syngenia grounds. Which extend into the town a few miles away and Syngenia City which is a metropolitan, but most students come from all over the world.

I wish I could see Ms. Elaycia. Her and Nana and Rosemary and Cordellia and Caleb. There's only limited space so only immediate family is allowed, and three non-family members in place of your immediate family if they can't come.

I wonder if there will be a way I could get a letter or something to them. Ms. Elaycia attended school here so maybe she could somehow get a pass.

Another boom shakes the wall and makes everyone else jump.

"Asher says they're retreating," Jullia murmurs. "No casualties, but some of the guys are hurt. Nothing fatal, just mild wounds and exertion."

That's good at least. I wonder if classes for today will be cancelled because of the attack.

But. . . while the whole ordeal sucks, maybe I won't be fired because I can help clean up with the rest of staff. I'm contemplating that idea when our door gets thrown. As in, it's ripped off the hinges and crashes into the opposite wall.

Colossal damnation fractures the air with an aura tainted a color darker than black. An aura so influenced by the soul of this being that it *feels* like evil incarnate. Magic should not be influenced by morals, and yet this magic is teeming with imbalance.

Jullia shrieks and most of the students scream as a force walks through the door. A tall figure in a black cloak. A hood covers his head and when he looks up a mask of gold covers his face. Feline in its features and there are two slits where his eyes should be but I can't see anything through it.

Another figure – another man – walks behind him with a controlled calculation. Raging eyes the color of a stormy sky roving over us.

Most of the students had huddled near the back rows and the rest of us closer to the door vault over desks to get as far away as possible. Even Jullia hits the floor and starts scooting away. Her lavender eyes full of pure terror and panic as they plead at me.

Despite the damnation aura feeling like it could seize my soul, I'm still sitting back in my chair with my arms crossed. There's a sharp, pointed tug within me that fills with horror, but it is not my emotion. I don't feel in the least bit afraid.

Stormy eyes point at me and his head tilts. Icicles freeze throughout the air as his gray eyes dip like waves to a pale blue and back to gray again. Inhaling it feels like shards of glass are slicing down my throat and into my lungs.

Excluding Jullia, I fucking *hate* water magic and all its forms.

Standing, I block out Jullia's whimpered pleas for me to get down and face the intruders. "Rebels, I presume?"

The water mage quirks a brow and rights his tilted head.

"So much confidence," he whispers, but his words thunder through the room. I can feel the vibrations in the ground. The frequency shifting in the air. Water *and* sound. A mage with *two* elements. "So much, for someone who has no aura. What a downfall of Syngenia, allowing a *vampire* onto their grounds."

I smirk, and then glance at the one full of damnation.

His hood covers his features but I can *feel* his eyes on me. The weight, they're even more powerful than Professor Asier. But his aura only comes close.

Devil.

I have the perfect song I could play right now for what is about to happen. The second the mage said vampire their energies changed. Death is the only course for me to them. I can see it in their aura. Coiling tightly like a snake ready to strike.

How quickly they shifted their energy just because of what they think I am. Promising me my death.

But devil. . . that won't be me.

Death strikes and time seems to slow when it gets within a foot from my heart. I watch as a bolt of straight *death* is about to hit me. No way to regenerate or heal from a blow like that. I'd be gone in an instant.

I twist that third key within and rip that door open right as the devil's death strike is about to hit me. Bloodred aura explodes into the room as that death strike hits a shield stronger than any type of beings. And then, just as fast, I slam that third door shut and lock it right back up.

My aura had dominated the devil's for a split second. Now it feels as I was before. Magicless with no aura.

Both of the intruders step back. The mage widening his eyes as he coils his magic around himself. Pulsing with a power that sharpens the very air.

I roll out my neck as I begin making my way down the row. No one even twitches as I move, taking the stairs down until I'm facing off with a devil who has control over the death element and a mage who can control two separate elements.

A measly vampire would have been dead the second

they stepped into the room.

Shrugging off my blazer, I place it on the desk behind me and twist the keys of that first and second door. I don't open them yet, but just unlocking them builds my aura past the confinements of my body. It hovers like a sheet of smoke around me and they can feel it.

"Pink eyes," the devil reverberates. "Which red-eyed bloodsucker turned you to give you power as you have?"

The depth of his tone almost sounds familiar, but I can't quite place it. Not that it matters. He'll be dead soon anyway.

Taking my hands, I dig my nails into opposite palms and rip them open. My blood flows in a steady stream onto the floor as my scent billows around me. Building up my aura even more, and when they both realize what my blood smells like they both take another step back.

"A dead one." His magic flinches and I think I've perfected my threatening deadened tone. "Just like you will be."

And his magic explodes but I'm already waiting for it.

I still the blood falling from my hands and then solidify it. Rearranging the molecular structure and turning my blood fallen into my own weapons. Pulling up the two whip-like strands, the devil's death strike hits it instead of me.

Connecting the ends, I sharpen the other side and twist, using my materialized weapon of blood like the precious whip dart it is. Letting it circle around me in twining strands as I show them part of my blood art.

And then I fracture the air with them.

Long threads of my solidified blood slice through the air before me. Cutting into the icicles from the water mage and towards the rebels. There's a hum vibrating through my blood as it cuts. An age old song vibrating I know the mage can hear.

Power.

The devil blocks. A visible shield of transparent gold with runic markings, but my blood does chip the edges. He twists the runes and then shoves his shield towards me. Turning it into a force that hits me like a goddamn tank.

Runic-fucking-magic.

I go flying back into the wall and crash onto the desks below. The students huddled, most in states of shock and panic, don't even breathe with a movement to help me. It jars my brain because they have magic. They have something to defend themselves, and most of them something to attack with. I mean there are giant shifters in here.

I'd say it's pathetic because I've seen humans – who have no magic at all with no weapons – stand up against threats they know they can't beat. But I can't say they're pathetic. I can't, because they're kids. We're all still basically kids and we shouldn't have to fight.

People as a whole shouldn't have to only endure.

But all I've ever done my whole life is endure. So I cough up the blood stuck in my throat, grit my teeth, and force my body to stand. Right now I am the only thing between them and the students, and they may hate me but I will not let Jullia become a victim.

That hit was hard. I can feel a lot of my ribs broken and my head throbbing. I bet they thought it would keep me down. I grin bloody teeth at them as I straighten. The mage is fuming as I roll my shoulders out and crack my neck.

Pain.

In a twisted way it feels like home. It's been a long time

since I've felt pain from a beating.

Another golden shield comes from the devil but this time I cross my arms up in front of my head. My blood forms an X with them and the shield splits. Shattering against the edge of red.

It feels good. To have those doors within unlocked. To let my blood flow free in my veins without the control.

So much control, so much calculation, all the damn time.

Twisting my blood back around myself, I sharpen them to thin razored edges and pulse with aura from that third door still unlocked but not open. I can feel color from my blood rushing back into my eyes. Another tightly controlled moderation, keeping my aura from my eyes so they appear their rosy pastel pink instead of the bloodred they actually are.

Coiling my blood whips in the air until they're teeming with barely restrained control. The magic vibrating with a need for release.

"This is impossible," the mage whispers, and yet it thunders back through the room. "You are nothing."

Slowly, I curl my fingers into my palms from where they're raised in front of me. My left hand horizontal before my stomach with my right at an angle before my chest and face. I let my blood flow from my still open wounds on my palms, but instead of falling I wrap my blood around my hands. I let it cover my wrists and stain my shirt.

"How do you smell like that poison?" the devil reverberates. His voice, it's irritating that I can't figure out where I've heard it from. His death damnation aura thickening in the room and for a moment his effect touches me.

The panic, the terror, freezing.

But I shake it off and curl my blood stronger around myself. He is nothing like the sun devil, and I am not six-years-old anymore. I just need my blood to touch them. Just like my blood touched *them* when I was ten.

I let that third door crack open. I let my aura expand. I let that fury I felt two nights ago free.

I can see it in the mage's eyes. In the posture and body language of the devil. I wonder if they can see it, if it's visible in my eyes now.

The devil raises up his own death magic around himself in preparation. Picking up on the influence and strength. Within, I twist a fourth key to unlock a fourth door but not open it. It expands my magic further. Past this room and further out. Past the aura of the devil with his death damnation.

The hum in my blood hitches and then I release.

Relaxing my fingers and hands as I let the blood covering them finally fall. Droplets like rain that are about to hit the floor and then it almost feels like nothing. My magic explodes towards the intruders and it will kill them. I know that to be truth. This expulsion, this release, it's not something you can survive.

Too strong, too powerful, too *raw*. I've kept it locked up for too long.

An exhale and time moves at a pace that shouldn't be real. My droplets of blood are about to hit the floor and the devil and mage are about to be dead, except time moving at a pace that shouldn't be real flinches back.

My blood does not hit the floor and when I look down I see it hovering an inch above the hardwood. Something, someone, outside of this fight is controlling my blood. Stopping it from hitting the ground and by extension stopping my force that was supposed to kill the devil and mage.

My magic ripples and the force is lost and instead of killing the devil and mage as it was going to, it hits another golden shield.

The impact shakes time from its slow movement and everything resumes at its right pace. At the doorway another type of force enters. Fuming rage and an aura that consumes the space steps through. Red wrapped in gold lock on me and I make it all disappear. I shut every door and turn every key to lock it all back up.

The devil and mage rebel don't even glance at Professor Asier, they simply disappear. Leaving only a wisp of shadows and a faint scent of copper and ozone.

What. The. Fuck.

Callahan comes bursting through the door next, his golden eyes wide and fearful. When they find me and the destruction around he hesitates. I hadn't noticed the room before. Chairs and desks crumpled between me and the professor. The power of me and the rebel devil destroying the room. There are even cracks through the walls that extend onto the ceiling.

Rolling out my shoulders, I wince at the pain fluttering around my body. Callahan jerks towards me at it, and then slowly, carefully approaches me.

"Mavyn. . . "

I turn to the students behind me all huddled together. Most of them in states of shock. Jullia stands from where she had been crouched in front of everyone. Twin transparent blades are strangled in her hands as her wide lavender eyes blink rapidly.

My shoulders drop seeing her. She's okay, and even

scared she had been ready to defend.

Another body pumping blood in a rush bursts through the door with a single name roaring from their mouth. Jullia drops her blades that turn to water and splash onto the ground as Asher flies up the stairs and wraps his arms around her.

Lovesick fools.

But I smile at them because they are both alright. Probably terrified, but alive and seemingly unhurt.

A presence draws behind me and my name is whispered on their lips. Callahan's shadow falls over me and I can feel the warmth from his body caressing my back. "Can I please touch you?"

He sounds. . . strangled?

"I need to know you're real. That you are alright."

I am, even though I feel like my skin is just a sack holding crumpled bones. I know he needs the confirmation, but my blood is still rushing. My magic is locked up and my aura once again feels nonexistent, but I can't quite get the grasp of control to slow my heartbeat and blood flow.

It's still vibrating with that hum.

I should have been able to kill them.

Stepping to the side, I turn to face the professor. He's surveying the damage and behind him is Darian and the two councilmen from before. I can feel other blood-filled bodies large enough to be people near, but they don't enter the room.

"This is. . . " The devil chairholder turns up to us. His burnt gold eyes looking at me and his son. "Who was it to face against *Kolasi* and the second lead of the rebels?"

Burnt gold faces against pale pink. The force of red

circled within gold burns too, but I don't look at the professor. I keep my attention on the devil chairholder of the Mage Board. If only they had listened to me before. I already told them.

I am not a vampire.

But they did not want to listen. They did not care about the blatant facts right in front of their fucking faces. And with their hatred towards the vampires. . . well, now I'm just going to make sure they rethink their entire opinion of the race. Because they wanted a vampire, so I'm going to give them a fucking vampire.

"A worthless," I begin, gaining every eye in the room, "powerless, weak, auraless, piece of *nothing*."

Because that's what they think vampires are. That's what they think I am. And they are correct – about me. Vampires as a race are just as complex as any other, with their faults and difficulties, but they are not scum. They are not nothing.

I am.

But I will make them regret ever talking down about the vampires.

Twenty-Nine

Jullia – Septmust 3

"A worthless, powerless, weak, auraless, piece of nothing."

Mavyn's words echo in the room still teeming with Professor Asier's aura and magic. I shift in Asher's hold to watch. To look and actually process all the destruction. That devil. . . my soul had trembled. I had frozen because of the force, and I hadn't been able to do anything until Mavyn's aura became known.

And her aura. . .

Her power extended further than that devil's. Her magic exceeded his by leagues.

Weak. . . ? Auraless. . . ?

I mean, technically right now she does feel auraless, but not before. Most definitely not before.

The men still standing below, all their eyes on Mavyn, lower their brows as they survey the space again. I don't blame their confusion. A vampire against a devil? There's no comparison, no doubt about who would win and who would lose.

No, it's not possible. No matter who the vampyr was. Mavyn *can't* be a vampire.

So what is she?

"Ms. Tsuki. . . " Chairholder Arcturus steps further into the room. His red eyes slightly glowing as he peers at Mavyn. "We were led to believe you have no aura and barely any magic."

Her back is to me so I can't see her expression, but I do see her head cock. "I don't remember ever telling anyone I had no magic."

Her tone chills my spine and has me tensing in Asher's hold. She went from zero to infinite and back to zero again. I didn't know it was possible to conceal your aura to the point where others can't feel it at all.

"So what *exactly* is your magic that could go against *Kolasi*? He is a devil who has no leash on his *true form*."

I can't move. Asher is rubbing my back – I think – but I can't feel it. Mr. Arcturus had asked who was able to go against Kolasi before but it didn't process. My brain didn't register that the *Death Devil* had been in my presence. Who was going to kill us all.

His stories proceed him and they're drenched in blood

and broken bodies. For a devil or angel not to have a lock on their true form. . . those *things* can decimate worlds. They say he's gone insane because of how all-consuming his true form is over him.

He's a lunatic.

A psychopath.

A *monster*.

And Mavyn's magic surpassed him. Both in power and emotion.

Her head twists and I catch a glimpse of pale pink. Her eyes lock on mine with a blank expression, and then they shutter as she looks at the ground. Her shoulders drop and she looks back over the room. Looking at the mess, the ruined room.

She could have annihilated us.

I push Asher's arms off and stumble over debris before righting my footing and stepping over to Mavyn. Steeling my spine, I level a glare I know my mother would be proud of to the blood demon. His red eyes that look exactly like Thorne's widen at me.

"You sound like you're accusing someone of something malicious when she is the reason we're all alive and unhurt." He blinks at me and his sneer drops. "I would think the wellbeing of the students of this prestigious university would come first when faced with an attack from an enemy the Mage Board should have been able to handle decades ago."

I step in front of Mavyn and shield half of her body with my own. My aura of water and ice and frost dropping the temperature in the air. It's no match for the celestials – not even close to a match against Mavyn – but even the weakest, at times, can be more powerful than the gods.

"When all of us shrunk to the furthest corners of the room, helpless despite all of us having magic that is anything but, Mavyn stood before two beings with magic and aura that surpasses most celestials. When she has only ever been discriminated against, hated, faulted, berated, tormented, Mavyn was the only thing standing between us and death. She *saved* all of us. She, who you sentenced to this school because it was either this or death, protected us without any of us offering even a promise of help."

I point my finger at them. The celestials who do have hatred for her. Fury fueling my blood because of the unfairness to my friend who has been tortured but never asks for anything.

I didn't help her before, but I will now. She didn't hesitate before. Starting now neither will I.

"So watch your fucking tone."

Warmth seeps into my shoulder as a hand grips it. I twist my head and am greeted by shining rosy pink. And then warmth consumes me in total as I'm pulled into Mavyn's arms.

My frost melts from where it had been spreading onto my skin, and while most people can't stand to touch me when it covers me, Mavyn does not stop. Not even Asher can hold me when my frost freezes. But this girl who I've only known for two months, who was resigned for me to already hate her before I met her, she doesn't care.

"Thank you," she whispers beside my ear. It takes me a second to knock myself out of my trance and I throw my arms around her too. Pulling her tighter to me as I hug her like I hug Hanna. Tears building within my shut eyes because she did save me. I would literally be dead right now without her.

Someone clears their throat and she pulls away. Turning back to face the celestials and now the Dean. For once he isn't scowling.

"Ms. Tsuki," he greets. He nods to her too. "Thank you. For protecting our students when the rebels slipped through our defenses. It takes a truly courageous being to stand against the Kolasi."

"The Gods punishment," she says – not directly at the Dean. "No wonder his true form was that of damnation. To wield the death element is a magic I've never seen before."

The Dean nods again. "With that, would you mind telling us how it was possible you were able to face the devil?"

Her eyes snap from point to point. Looking at all of them below who are all probably wondering what she is. She's insinuated she is a vampire. She's delivered proof she has the makings of one. But. . . as I think about it now, Mavyn has never said herself that she *is* a vampire.

I am a vampire, has never left her mouth. Though when Asher said weeks ago that she wasn't one, she did say he was wrong. But even that deliverance with her answer could be twisted if you look at the situation long enough.

This is where many would say not to overthink. Sometimes the simplest answers are the correct ones. But that response doesn't work with the high fae or oracle's and fortune tellers. It doesn't work for all magics.

It does not work for Mavyn.

She is complexity at its definition. A paradox and contradiction.

"Magic," she answers simply. "The only way you would be able to face a being who uses magic as powerful as his is with magic."

I'd laugh at the answer because of how obvious it is. Of course only magic would be able to defend – let alone go up against – a being like the Kolasi. But I'm learning that *that* is

Mavyn's specialty. She simply answers the question front face. She never gives context unless she wants to.

How did she face the devil?

With magic.

Obviously. But the celestials didn't specify what or how she used the magic. She's a freakin genius.

I notice Professor Asier fisting his hands as he glares at Mavyn. Clearly he didn't find her answer amusing.

The Dean clears his throat and straightens. He doesn't scowl, but his facial muscles do twitch as if he wants to.

"My apologies, I should have been more clear." I'm sure that took a lot out of him to say. "What kind of magic could have been used to be powerful enough to go against the Kolasi? And how did you wield it?"

I glance at Mavyn and the corner of her lip twitches. Like she wants to grin but forces herself not to.

She looks around the room again, rosy eyes following the cracks lining the walls that cover the ceiling too. They almost look like lightning bolts.

"The kind of magic that goes against death," she answers simply. As if it is a simple answer. "And I wielded it like how everyone else is able to wield their magic."

Answering the question without giving an actual answer. I catch Callahan grinning now but bowing his head to try and hide it.

The Dean clears his throat again but I get the feeling he really wants to growl. Frustration is so easily written on him as well as the professor and the councilmen. Darian off to the side looks like he's calculating while being intrigued. Seeing him makes me wonder where his father, Thorne, and Professor

D'etre are. Asher had said they were all working together to stop this battle.

Before the Dean can ask another question, Mavyn shrugs a shoulder and shifts away from them. "I didn't think it mattered. Afterall, this is a school catered to beings with magic with classes they're able to take throughout their five years that can help them control and further their manipulation of abilities. I am not human, so therefore I have magic. It's not required to have listed individual abilities. We are supposed to request the classes we believe will help further us ourselves."

The Dean takes a step towards the destruction between us but Mavyn doesn't spare him another look as he asks, "And what classes will you be requesting for next years?"

She's still looking up at the cracks along the ceiling. This time the corners of her mouth lift all the way into a smile.

"I'll let you know when we're all able to reenroll. We'll have to see if I'm even still alive then." She glances at Professor Asier. "Apparently I have a test on Friday I need to take that will be the defining factor if I pass a class I need in order to not be expelled. And therefore, killed."

I glance at Callahan, the professor, and then Asher. He has the same confused expression that's marring Callahan's face because we don't have classes on Friday, and teachers aren't allowed to assign any work for this weekend.

The Dean side-eyes Professor Asier but doesn't say anything to him. "Well, classes will be cancelled for the rest of today and tomorrow. . . along with Friday. Classwork will also be put on hold until next week. And everyone is required to visit the infirmary before returning to their dorms. The rest of the university has been secured."

He nods to Mavyn and then turns towards the councilmen. Both of them watch Mavyn for a bit longer before they turn with the Dean and head out. She's still staring at the cracks with a light smile on her face.

I take a step towards her. "Mavyn? Do you want to go to the infirmary now?"

She hums but doesn't say anything. I know she's probably in an enormous amount of pain. When the devil hit her with his shield she had slammed into the wall and crashed with so much force I was sure her spine was shattered. At the very least she has to have a few ribs broken.

Callahan comes up behind her but doesn't touch her. "Firecracker?" he murmurs. He doesn't look too good himself either.

She closes her eyes for a second, tilts her head down, turns, and then snaps them open. A wisp of her aura flutters around her and her sweet poisonous scent wafts around us.

Her expression hardens as she stares at Professor Asier. His own glare falters for a second as he takes half a step back.

"They should have been dead," she murmurs. Some of the people in the corner had started to stand and move towards the stairs to leave, but we all freeze at her voice. She sounds *almost* like how the mage did. Whispered words that ricochet in the air. "My magic was about to kill them when something stopped it. Almost like time tripped and within that empty space someone lessened my blow. And then they shadow twisted."

It was peculiar. The way they had been so ready to fight and then Mavyn's magic. I had felt it. It seemed like she hesitated but. . . no. *She* didn't hesitate, her magic did. A blood art magic I've never seen before.

A *blood* art.

And the sc –

I think it would be best, Ms. Waterstone, if this was something you did not overthink.

I jump and then freeze. Asher comes to my side but I feel stuck in my head as those words from a voice that is not my own echo in my mind.

You are a bright student and an excellent water mage. I think your future at Syngenia could be bright. I wouldn't want anything bad happening to you.

I keep my eyes locked on the blood staining Mavyn's shirt. It's what I had been looking at when I thought –

I don't even finish that thought. I try not to think about it. I can't look at him either because I don't want a chance of anything happening. I'm already shit at keeping secrets and Asher can read me like a damned –

Then you better start working on your mental shields, Ms. Waterstone.

Why?

It feels like I whisper that word even in my mind. Professor Asier is quiet for a moment. I hadn't been asking why I should work on my mental shields because that is very much obvious right now, but why did he –

Because, he faintly growls. *It is not what you are thinking and I do not have the patients right now to explain it. In addition, I do not want you making accusations that are wrong without knowing everything. And you do not know anything.*

"I thought," the professor says – out loud, "that the magic I was feeling was Kolasi aiming at you. I created the shield between the magic and who was being attacked. I did not know you were the one creating a death blow."

I still can't look away from Mavyn's bloody cuffs, but I'm sure she does something along the lines of rolling her eyes. She's good at that. She gives bratty energy perfectly. She'd be the perfect main female character in a dark romance.

"We had felt your aura," he continues with a deep, dark tone, "all the way on the other side of the school. For a fraction of a second a magic flashed and then there was nothing. And then moments later we felt it again. A gradual build that seemed to strength more and more with no signs of stopping."

Mavyn crosses her arms and more blood is smeared on her shirt. It's already stained from dust and debris and blood on her back from when she hit the wall. That won't be washing out. Not that she seems to care. I'm sure she forgot that there was even blood on herself.

"What is your point, Professor?"

A low growl sounds. I'm glad she's standing up to them.

"My *point*," he hisses, "is how in unholy gods do you have magic like that as *nothing*."

Mavyn flinches right as I snap my eyes to the professor with a steeling glare. He almost looks unhinged. Covered in dirt and grime with weapons strapped all over his body and a glare that could freeze over hell.

No.

Actually, it's the opposite. His glare holds only fire, but a heat from Mavyn overwhelms him. She had felt like she was almost burning when she hugged me and melted my frost. She's said before she's always burning. Normally it's always around when she's about to or just coming out of a nightmare. Or like when Thorne pushed her in the sun our first day of classes.

She said she'd burn for all eternity.

I can actually feel the heat coming off of her. Glancing at her I expect to see steam floating off her, but instead I find eyes several shades darker than her usual pink. While she was fighting the rebels they had been a deep red. Like blood.

Something happens in her head, I know something has to happen, because she goes primordially still. And then she becomes nothing. As in there's not an energy, a scent, a *feeling* from her. I'm staring directly at her but I can't feel her, can't comprehend that she's actually in front of me. I can't even touch the water within her. An organic material *every*one has.

It makes everyone, all of our instincts sharpen. Because somehow, however she did it, Mavyn just became the deadliest thing in here.

"This," she murmurs, but the shadows in the corners of the room flinch at her voice, "is the third time you are questioning my business, Professor. You may not have the spiritual moralities of blood demons, but devils are known for their word keeping. *Especially*, a truth-pulling empath."

He flinches and steps back. His head lowering an inch before his face twists into a snarl and he bares his fangs at her.

"Will I be needing to remind you again?"

She sounds. . . she sounds like something unreal. Like when fates are spoken and Prophecies of Old are whispered for the first time. Both eternally old and charmingly terrifying.

Professor Asier holds her stare that is bordering on red instead of pink as his magic and aura flares through the room but Mavyn remains like nothingness. A war between two dominants. Two predators who are facing off and there will only be one top alpha.

There wouldn't be a world where I would bet on anyone other than her.

And cha-ching. Professor Asier snaps his back straight and consorts his face into controlled fury. "No." His voice barely distinguished from a graveled growl. "You will not."

He doesn't wait for Mavyn to say anything else and stalks out of the room. Only leaving us, the people behind us, and Darian on the ground level. He's still watching Mavyn with intrigued curiosity. But Mavyn doesn't look at him as she turns to me. Her eyes once again pale pink.

"Want to go to the infirmary now?"

She asks it as if I'm the one with multiple broken bones and who just fought Kolasi and a mage who can control two elemental magics.

A bubble of laughter works up her throat as she stares at me. Probably because I'm looking at her like the crazy person she is.

"You all worry too much," she chuckles. "Let's go."

Ha. As if she had a choice.

Thirty

Varian – Septmust 4

The corridors are quiet with only a few scones lit as I walk back towards my office. There were no casualties and only a few minor injuries. Everyone had been seen during the duration of yesterday after the attack and I hadn't seen anyone out and about during my rounds around the school.

Edmond and Aslan thought it would be best for us to patrol just in case. The rebels on the field had started to retreat not long after the rest of us got on the battle scene. But it was a distraction tactic because multiple beings came around the back to sneak into the school.

That was when we felt a wave of power indescribable.

The magnitude. . . it was colossal. Far greater than Kolasi and even the leader of the rebels.

I make my way down the hall to my office. Castiel had turned in for the night directly after his patrol – right before mine. Despite only being about two to three hundred bodies from the rebels and not even too powerful of races, it had taken a toll. We were all in sync with each other, but we're all out of practice with actual battle.

I'll have to up the training next week. Not only Castiel and I, but Thorne, Callahan, Darian, and the rest of the trainee's. The rebels are becoming more bold. An attack on Syngenia could be an act of actual war. The rebels have the numbers for it.

I enter my office and shut my door directly behind me. The second I do I grab the wrist that was lifted and aimed with a knife towards me and slam it into the wall.

He uses his other hand to punch my side, but his force is relaxed as I grab his neck and slam the rest of his body to the wall. A breathy chuckles puffs in my face as I tighten my hold on him. Irritation flickering throughout my body. I already had to deal with one problematic bloodsucker yesterday, I did not intend to deal with another one tonight.

"I could drag you to Aslan and have them behead you right here right now," I grit. My jaw aching with the force of clenching it.

He takes his free hand and pulls his hood back to reveal his face. Golden tanned skin that looks darker in the low lighting and twin red eyes encased in gold. "How much you want to bet you won't though. . . twin brother."

I shove off him and step back to properly look at him. "I bet the Mage Board would let me leave this damn school if I turned you in. A hundred fucking years as a professor because of your bastard ass."

The left corner of his mouth curls up in a grin revealing his lone dimple. It's the only difference in our appearance, otherwise we are identically identical.

"How much you want to bet you'd never leave now?"

A knowing in his eyes has me glaring harder at him. Technically, he is older by four minutes, but I have always acted like the eldest. Percius – or as everyone alive calls him, Kolasi the Death Devil – never fully matured. Even to this day.

"Stop acting like a drama-seeking child. It's unbecoming."

"So is denial." I scoff at him but he uses his shoulders to push off the wall and becomes serious. "Speaking of – "

I wave my hand to silence him as I turn around and head towards my desk. I can feel him following and his own glare burning a hole straight through the back of my head.

"You can be in denial about *that*," he roughs, "but not the rest. She is not a vampire, Varian."

I shake my head and rest my hands on my desk to *not* think. "She burns in the sun and needs blood to survive."

"She used a fractured blood art," he says as he comes up behind me. Lowering his body so his head becomes level with where mine is bent down. "Her blood didn't dissipate after using. A blood art user isn't able to reuse their blood once it's been spent. They shouldn't be able to expand it to the extent that she did."

My chest rumbles with unreleased frustration. "I can't, Percius."

He snarls at me. "She *dominated* you. She got you to sub – "

"NO!"

My face becomes before his with my aura pulsing in the room. Despite us being twins and his true form resting on his surface obediently, my aura is still more powerful than his. I am more dominant than he. I became more dominant than our father right before Percius ripped his heart out.

But he does not submit before me. Just as he never has. A lack of self-preservation instead of because his instincts are telling him to challenge me.

"Why haven't you learned anything?"

He tilts his head up a fraction but steps back first when I don't immediately answer. Blowing out a breath while rolling his eyes. He's also never cared about primitive hierarchies and never had that possessive and dominate nature to be on top. He simply exists, which is probably why he has the control over his true form that no other devil or angel does. They are aligned, going against every base instinct we have, and simply exist.

"I said I would stay out of her business." Frustration scalding within. Percius's eyes flicker with understanding as he turns away and hums. The bloodsucker had been correct in her presumption that devils are known for their promise and word keeping. Not that we always follow it, but in the situation I was in with Mavyn outside of my office, it would grate on my conscious if I didn't keep my word. Even though it's currently grating on my conscious right now *not* knowing her business and secrets.

"A clever one," he chuckles. Even though there is nothing funny about this situation. "And Thorne said she was Callahan's fated?" He blows out a breath and shakes his head. Looking up to me there's amusement in his eyes. "Is she Darian, Thorne, and Castiel's as well?"

I narrow my eyes at his smirk and shake my head. "I

don't think so. Definitely not Castiel's. She had bit and drank from him several weeks ago and while her mark stayed for longer than normal, he said there was no tie or knot or bond between them. He thinks he only craves her because there's blue belladon in her blood."

I look off to the side to think about the other two.

"I doubt there will be anything between her and Thorne either. He would have realized in the same moment as Callahan did a couple days ago. Darian hasn't had enough contact with her so I can't be sure, but it's unlikely they'll be fated."

Percius hums and bores his eyes into me. "But you are. You and her."

His words hang in the air between us as I look back at my twin. The reason I was punished and have been forced to teach the same four classes for the same nearly hundred years since he killed our father and joined the rebellion.

A fucking idiot.

"Have you seen her soul, yet?" he asks on a breath.

His body stills as I answer. Even his true devil within freezes and shrinks back.

"She doesn't have one."

Which is impossible. All living things have souls. Only some primordials and select monsters are without souls. And she has aura so she *has* to have a soul, but when I was truth-pulling I looked into her eyes, *past* her eyes, and had seen nothing.

"Or if she does," I continue, "it's pitch black. Because all I saw was an abyss. Nothingness behind her eyes."

His exhale of breath shutters as he looks down and away. A flicker of remembrance and fear in his eyes as he replays a memory. Then he nods and clenches and un-clenches his hands.

"I'll have to profusely thank Thorne," he whispers. "If he didn't halt her blood and given you a chance to create your shield Rovan and I would be dead. I could feel it. Even my death element was resigned because it knew. We were supposed to die. And there should have been nothing that stopped it."

I release a breath through my nose and hang my head. I'll have to thank Thorne as well. I have never felt the type of terror as I did when I realized my twin, my brother, was going to die. *About* to die. Because he's standing right here in front of me. Safe – for the moment – and alive.

He sighs and shakes off the negative energy as he always does. He is a terrifying force nearly everyone runs from in battle but in truth he has a similar personality to Castiel with their charming, nonchalant, party-boy energy.

It reminds me of when the three of us were in school. Back before all the bullshit.

"Well," he shrugs, "good luck with your fated and all. I hope the next time we see each other, brother, it's not on a battlefield."

He turns towards the door and I return my glare to his back. "What *is* Alexandros's next move? He hasn't attacked the school in a century and he was supposed to keep his war away from it."

I only catch the edges of his smirk as Percius turns only his head back. His fucking dimple appearing before he faces the door and cracks it open.

"Don't die out there, brother."

Then he slips through and is gone.

I let out a groan as I rub my face with a hand. Frustration now coursing because of both problematic bloodsuckers in my life. Why couldn't they be like Thorne, or even Callahan, without any secrets and major problems.

Turning to my desk, I go and basically fall into my chair. It groans as I lean back in it and shut my eyes. It doesn't help though as I see two circles of pale pink. Her eyes bordered with long, dark lashes and narrowed into an almost glare.

They flicker to a red so deep it looks like the blood that had been staining her hands. As dark as the blood moon that appears on the last day of the year. A final ending to the year before the first day of spring and a symbol of beginning and life.

She had so much control over her magic. It appearing with a crash like the crest of a tsunami before disappearing like a switch being flipped. So much power shouldn't be able to be contained that quickly. And then when she had actually felt like *nothing*.

She had looked more like a thing than an actual being. If I didn't know better I would have said a true form replaced her conscious in that moment.

Pulling both of my hands over my face, I check in with Callahan. He's been ignoring and blocking me out since I had truth-pulled. But he lets me in this time, though it's only to bare invisible teeth at me.

What do you want?

I don't think he knows. . . neither of them could know. An unsealed bond between fated is finicky. She probably thinks the tugging pulling within her is only for Callahan.

I wanted to make sure you are alright.

Fine.

Exhaustion is starting to weigh. I haven't slept in this last week.

Is Mavyn alright?

His growl vibrates in my mind. *She's exhausted. Not only did she not get any sleep after the ceremony, but she was starved and then forced to perform your truth-pulling and then threatened to be expelled if she didn't go to class so while she was hanging on by a thread she attended your fucking class because my father and fucking uncle will kill her if she fails. And then*, he seethes, *she faced your fucking true formed twin brother.*

His fury claws in my mind and I let it. She hasn't been given a single break. And I don't count the Mage Board letting her enroll into the university instead of killing her a break.

And then you, his voice is barely understandable, *confronted her with power stronger than your unhinged brother and demanded she tell you how it was possible for her, who you called nothing, to do it.*

A pain deeper than just my body, my mind, my emotions stings. I had still been terrified for my brother when I said that to her. Terrified that I hadn't made it and she really did kill them. I wasn't thinking, and it was made worse when she challenged me.

The succubus, he murmurs in a dark tone, *is Elaycia Sorenli of Havebeth.*

You're fucking kidding me.

And the bone witch is Esmirra of Ebony.

No.

I can feel his sneer. *Thorne confirmed that was the blood she threatened him with during the party. And it aligns with her always saying she grew up in a brothel because Elaycia has a strip club in New York races of all kinds frequent. Darian ended up confirming all the information and with someone going over there to connect with the succubus herself.*

I rub at my face again.

I'm having them both be welcomed so Mavyn's family can be with her tomorrow.

Are you kidding me?

I blow out a breath as I try to process one of the most powerful bone witches of our era coming back to this school when she hasn't been back to Syngenia since she first saw the university open. And Elaycia. . . she's royalty from an entirely different world and universe unaffected by the powers of the Mage Board. A royal expat that has full immunity from anything.

Mavyn misses them, he rumbles. *And they're alumni. The Dean can't say no.*

True, but hissy-fits will be thrown. A witch hasn't stepped foot on Syngenia grounds in over a thousand years.

I'm going to sleep now, he grouches and then kicks me out of his mind.

I blow out a breath as I try not to think about all that is about to happen tomorrow. So many beings and races and dominating aura's in one place? It's bound to be a bloodbath. Like it usually is every year.

I sigh for what feels like a millionth time. How did one little girl get wrapped up with so many powerful beings? What kind of fate was twisted to draw her into all of our lives?

Thirty-One

Mavyn – Septmust 5

I'm back, almost, where I was nearly exactly two months ago. The front courtyard on the north-east side of the grounds where all the tables to get your schedule and tablet is below us.

We're all currently on a terrace above it that half overlooks the eastern field. The other half of the balcony is over the front doors of the main building off to the right, though I stand in a further corner staring up at the gargoyles on the third level watching below.

There are gargoyle shifters. I wonder if any of them on the third level are shifters too.

Hopefully not. If so then my 'no proof of burning Thorne's rooms down' goes out the window. There are gargoyle's on every corner and ledge of the main building. They would have easily seen me walking right into Stone House.

Past them I stare at the heavy-clouded sky. So dark and thick it blocks the sun completely and allows for me to walk freely without my umbrella. Not that it matters since the only thing that would be exposed is my face and hands since I'm in my uniform. We may not have classes today, but we're all supposed to be in uniform to represent the school.

People mill about around me, the whole ordeal starting earlier in the morning. Everyone woke up earlier than we all did yesterday because of everyone's families and loved ones arriving. Jullia had been up and out of there before I even woke up. Callahan had slept on the floor beside my bed. A bed that had been replaced with a brand new frame, mattress, sheets, pillows, comforter, and blankets.

My argument with Callahan held no fight because I had already been exhausted past my normal point. Wednesday night I had stayed in the infirmary and let them re-hook all the feeding and liquid bags. They added more healing salves I catalogued in my head. Thankfully I was not drugged this time.

But yesterday afternoon I told Callahan I was sleeping in my own room, showering in my own dorm, or I was going to claw my freaking skin off. That was when I came face to face with my new bedding and my so-called argument was me glaring at Callahan.

He hadn't asked what happened to my bed or why there was a pile of ashes underneath it. I was worried for half a second that he would connect it to burning Thorne's rooms, but he's said nothing. I've also not been carted off by guards or enforcers to be killed.

Exhaling a breath, I turn and catch sight of Jullia with

Hanna and their family. She had told me yesterday she wanted me to meet them. She also said they would not act like Hanna did when she first met me.

But, I've been staying in my little area near one of the doors that lead inside and directly to some stairs exiting onto the path that leads to either the eastern field or the north-east courtyard. It's my getaway in case I don't want to be around anymore family reunions.

I glance over the heads and faces looking for dirty blond hair. He said he was going to get me and him a drink, but it's been several minutes already. I was planning on staying in my room with my earbuds ignoring everything about today. I'm also still exhausted from this past week and I could probably sleep all weekend.

I'm only here now because I did promise Jullia I'd meet her family and Callahan slightly begged me. I know his father is roaming around somewhere. Callahan also said his mother, two younger sisters, and uncles would be here.

I wish I didn't have to meet them. I also wished everyone wasn't whispering about me and Callahan being fated. Gossip spreads like you would think at this prestigious goddamn school. Jullia even said there's a whole thing on their social media app. I still haven't looked at it once since Jullia showed me the video that was taken of me calling Darian a winged bitch.

That makes me smile and a smooth voice asks, "Are you expecting anyone?"

I turn and am met with burnt gold eyes and simple curiosity. I could tell him off because he is part of the reason I'm here and I was never given a chance to contact my family, but all that rage from earlier this week is ash. I don't want to care anymore, I only want to get through these few years and then go home.

I start to shake my head because words feel like too much but I stop when my name is called from across the yard.

Every conversation stops as people look around and a sort of path is cleared through. Needles prick my nose as tears build along my waterline as I stare at the person ahead. The *people.* Four people to be exact and I don't even know when it happened but I started running.

Ignoring the looks and the whispers as I collide into a perfume of orchids and blackberry. Ribbons of deep purple flaring around her as they always are and there is nothing but warmth. Her long sleeved covered arms and gloved hands wrap tightly around me as lips purse on the top of my head.

"My love," Ms. Elaycia murmurs and those tears spill over because I missed her. I missed her so much and the rest of the girls and home and my own room. I missed Ana in the attic with her sweets and Nana in the kitchen and Cordellia always talking about her books. I missed Rosemary scolding me about making the girls late for work and Caleb with his harmless flirting.

I missed *home.*

Someone behind her tisks and a fucking sob leaves my throat but I don't even care. Pulling away from Ms. Elaycia, she turns to reveal Nana with her coiled white hair twisted on the top of her head and her dingy brown frock.

She's shorter than me and much curvier and I crash into her next. A disbelieving scoff leaves her mouth but she doesn't push me away.

"You are embarrassing us, Mavyllora Sanivin Tsukkenai," she barks.

I pull back and her face is blurry from my tears but I can't stop them. I can't stop them because this has to be some sort of nightmare. I have to be dreaming right now and at any moment it'll twist.

Nana's features soften as she now pulls me into a real hug. "Oh my poison girl."

Another sob hiccups and we squeeze each other tightly. She knows more than anyone about my nightmares and frequent trips to the sun death realm. Then I let go and turn towards Rosemary. Her mossy green eyes are shining as well as she grabs my arms and pulls me into her. She's taller than Jullia and even Ms. Elaycia who's tall at six foot two.

I'm cocooned in her soothing aura and warmth. My warrior princess goblin who has always treated me like a little sister. Who wraps her strength as well as her arms around me.

Then I'm allowed to hug Caleb and the stupid light mage has a cocky smirk as he looks down at my watery smile.

"And you say I have no effect on the ladies," he jokes.

I crash into him like I did Ms. Elaycia and he huffs out a laugh as he wraps his arms around me. Warmth warmer than just body heat seeps into my skin and I never want to let go.

Except I do when a throat is cleared and I look over and up at golden eyes darkened and fixed on Caleb. Fucking shit.

I twist in Caleb's arms, though he immediately lets me go, and I stand between the two males. I can feel Caleb backing away and I sharpen my stare to point at Callahan until he looks down at me. I do not need any alpha-male fucking bullshit. Not today, not when my family here.

Golden eyes soften even though I'm still glaring. Then he smirks as he looks at the other three surrounding me. "You can't be mad at me today, Firecracker."

I can sense Ms. Elaycia stepping closer to me. "He's

right Mavyllora. Where are your manners? I thought I raised you to be polite. You better thank Mr. Armani for pulling some strings and allowing us to be here today."

I whip my head back and up to her, then back at Callahan. "You. . . you brought them here?"

He smiles softly at me and slides his hands into his pockets. "Can't have family day without your family."

My nose begins needling again and I crash into Callahan. It surprises him and he's frozen still for a moment before he wraps his arms around me too.

"Thank you," I whisper into his chest. "Thank you so much."

His hand rubs up and down my back a couple times before he pulls back and turns me to face my family again. "So are you going to introduce me?"

His tone is light and smooth, but when I glance up he has a sharp stare pointed at Caleb. I roll my eyes but smile big because they're here.

Stepping away from Callahan, I approach Ms. Elaycia. Her dark olive skin smooth and glistening where it's exposed at her neck and shoulders. Aside from that area and usually her cleavage, she is almost always covered. Including her hands, which have a habit of stroking my cheek when she passes me.

She never wore gloves before I came to the club.

"Ms. Elaycia," I greet, and her smile shines in her deep purple eyes. "This is Callahan Armani, a. . . classmate."

"You mean fated," Nana interrupts. I glare at her but she's smiling big at Callahan. "Last time I saw you, you were still crawling around on all fours."

Excuse me?

Callahan's cheeks turn pink and my brain glitches because that is the first time I've ever seen him blush. I didn't even know he could blush.

Nana tisks at me. "I told you about my own family here. The little boy I helped train and said you would get along with wonderfully. His father and Callahan's father are best friends. They grew up and went to school together."

Her smile grows as she see's someone behind Callahan and when he steps to the side my own smile that's been stuck on my face immediately drops.

"My boy!" Nana greets with more joy than I've ever seen her give another person. She actually claps her hands as she meets Thorne – the blood-fucking-demon who *hates* me – Arcturus and pulls him into a hug. His father is behind him and smiles in greeting at Nana as she pulls back from Thorne and fusses over little things.

She turns back to me with a wide grin and pulls Thorne over to us. His face stays neutral as he approaches and doesn't make eye contact with me at all.

"Mavyllora, this is Thorne. Since you're fated to Callahan I'm assuming you've already met, but he was the boy I watched grow up when I still primarily lived here. He was my first student."

She's so happy when she says it. A *bone* witch linking arms with a *blood* demon. No wonder I thought his instincts were shit. He wasn't afraid of Nana's blood because he *grew up* with her.

Nana scowls at me. "Why are you making that face at Thorne, Mavyllora? I know fucking well Ms. Elaycia taught you better manners than that. Introduce yourself properly."

My mind is glitching.

Did he not try to kill me the first day we had met?

Dumbly, because I don't know what else to do in this moment, I do as Nana says.

I hold my hand out ready for him to shake it as I say, "Hello." I sound almost robotic. "My name is Mavyn."

He still hasn't looked at me but I can see the wheels of his mind working. When he does finally look at me I can't read anything from his red eyes. He shakes my hand but I'm numb to it.

"I didn't know your full name was Mavyllora," is all he says.

Of course he didn't. It's a very unique name and one I never use myself. I'm sure he would have had a very different opinion of me if he had. Nana always talked about her '*boy*' when she would come back from visiting. How big and strong and powerful he was getting. How his training was coming along.

She had told me once that she would bring me with her on one of her trips eventually so we could meet. She said he liked my name, but she had never mentioned his name. She had never mentioned his race either.

Nana tisks again. "You probably had no idea who she was because of that too. She always introduces herself as the shortened version even though that was the name given to her at birth."

Ms. Elaycia steps up behind me. "And she has her reasons for not wanting to use her full name, Esmirra."

Nana huffs but nods. "But that does not mean you should condone it for the actions of someone else."

I lower my brows at her but she refuses to look at me.

Actions of someone else. As if the sun devil simply used my name out of turn.

I shake my head at her and turn away because I don't want to think about that. I don't want to think about the past. My family, which I have not seen in nearly four months is here and this is real and I am so happy.

I am.

Truly.

Until I realize it was all a lie. This is a nightmare. And the sun devil is staring directly at me.

I actually freeze this time instead of bracing. Because it had felt more real this time. Normally it's the pain that is the only thing that feels real. Normally the foreplay doesn't last that long before he comes into the picture and burns me.

Icy blue eyes blink at me and then pitch black brows lower in confusion.

What kind of game is he playing?

My name is said but I don't know who said it. His lips hadn't moved and it would have sounded like him if they did.

Slowly, he makes his way over. My name is said again but I can't move. I can't do anything as he and others approach our circle. I had felt so peacefully warm a second ago and now all the peace has eviscerated.

"Hello," he greets as he stops a few feet from me. My heart palpitates because it *is* his voice. "Are you alright, my dear?"

Mine.

In every lifetime.

I'm going to make sure you burn for eternity.

"Sun devil."

He jerks back and I don't even know how I was able to form those two words. I'm waiting. I'm waiting for the pain and torture and burning. Unless he's waiting as a type of torment. He doesn't look right. There isn't a malicious aura around him or that twisted look in his eyes.

"How – " His voice slightly cracks. He clears his throat and it shocks my brain because he never hesitated. I now notice a woman beside him with silky straight silvery white hair and hazel eyes. Fractures of gold and brown and green sparkling. Not wavy black hair and solid chocolate brown eyes.

"You're not a water mage," I whisper, and she glances between me and the sun devil. He looks shocked and also saddened.

He clears his throat again. "How did you know my twin brother?"

My world tilts and everything goes tumbling.

Twin.

Brother.

I blink but I still can't move. On his other side I finally notice the other person who had walked up with him. Darian with his constant curiosity and has the wheels in his mind turning. That was why he looked so much like the sun devil. That was why I always braced when confronted with him.

Everyone is watching us and for a moment I wish Ms. Elaycia wasn't here so I could just go to my room and sleep. I wouldn't have to meet any family members and I didn't have to learn this.

"Darian." He stands up a bit straighter. "Kyros. That's

your surname. . . Kyros."

I had never heard anyone say his last name before. It would have clicked instantly if they had.

"Lyalthil Kyros was your uncle," I breathe.

The devil – the twin brother to the sun devil – shifts drawing my attention back to him.

"You knew my brother and his fated? His wife, she had been a water mage."

I slowly turn away from them because my heart is still thundering and I can't get it under control. My blood is rushing and there's no stopping it.

"He was the devil who tortured you when you were a child," Darian finally answers. Not loudly, but enough that everyone within our little circle can hear. There's still chattering happening outside of our group so I don't think anyone is paying us much attention anymore. "He had adopted her when she was a toddler and then he tortured, fed, marked, and *claimed* her."

I snap my head towards him. His icy blue eyes – the exact same almond shaped eyes as his father, as the sun devil – are on the ground. His back straight and head held high, but he won't look up.

His father chokes along with multiple other people. Someone gasps and then a warm, peaceful presence comes towards my back. Orchids and blackberries – I suck her scent deep into my lungs to help ground me. To remind me this isn't a nightmare, I am not before the sun devil, I am okay, I am safe.

"Mavyn," she gently calls, not saying my full name now. "Will you take some deep breaths with me? Your blood is rushing too fast in your veins."

Yes.

Yes, she's right. It is rushing too fast. Too out of control and that's never good. That's always a disaster.

She breathes in and I copy her. She holds it and I begin counting in my head. Forcing my mind to say each number. To focus on that.

After sixty-two seconds she slowly releases and I do the same. Then she sucks in another deep breath and I copy. Counting to eighty-eight this time before releasing. We do it four more times before my heart begins to slow.

I suck in another deep breath for good measure but I don't hold it. I'm finally able to gain complete control back over my heart and blood. Then I turn to face my audience and even though I hesitate for a moment when I look at him, that panic does not come back.

"I didn't know Darian's last name was Kyros," I start. He's still not looking at me, but his father does nothing but stare.

I can see it now, the differences. Their aura, his body language, the emotion in his eyes.

His eyes widen a bit as I push my shoulders back and straighten my back. My energy shifting because the sun devil and his bitch of a mage are dead. I made sure of that. And even though I am still tormented by him within my mind, he doesn't exist in the real world.

I am not weak.

And they see it now.

"It's nice to meet you, Mr. Kyros. And I apologize to *you* about any videos you may see or already have of me calling your son a winged bitch."

The tension that had stretched taunt between all of us after Darian had said how I knew the sun devil shatters as his mother chokes on a laugh. She covers her mouth with her hand but her eyes are sparkling as they stare at me.

Mr. Kyros also has a grin slowly curling onto his face with his eyes lightening with amusement.

"Trust me," he gently rumbles, "that video had made my entire *month* and I had been counting down the days until I was able to meet the young woman who put my son in his place."

I smile and glance at Darian to see his eyes still glued to the floor. Thorne is beside him with his parents behind him. Callahan next to them with his own parents and sisters huddled in. So many eyes has me shifting in place.

"Well," I drawl, "at least all the awkwardness is out of the way." A few people chuckle. I shrug a shoulder and then relax my body. Comfortable with my family behind me. "It's not like it could – "

BANG.

Did I ever say the universe was against me?

I can imagine perfectly Cordellia leaning in close to me and whispering with a straight face, "You jinxed it, Mavie." And then she'd burst into laughter because it was always something stupid I jinxed. That explosion that just occurred was not something stupid.

Alarm bells start going off and a ripple of power I've felt before hits us. Pushing through our circle and past the crowd, I stand against the stone wall sealing the terrace to keep anyone from falling. The stones were laid mimicking the guards wall of a castle, but it goes with the rest of the architecture of the university.

Looking out over the eastern field though, a line of black mars the edge of the forest. And that wave of power hits with a second ripple.

Devil.

The alarms continue to blare as someone yells, "*REBELS!*"

It causes a panic for most. There are thousands of people filling this terrace and within the school. Though when I look back I see the celestials with their parents calm and most of them with twisting shadows around. When they clear they leave behind harnesses and sheaths full of weapons.

My fingers twitch with a need to draw my own weapons. I had been told to stay put the last time. Even though the enemy came to me, we didn't actually fight. That was little more than an altercation between magic.

I glance at Nana who's just as calm though not drawing any weapons. Ms. Elaycia watches the warriors turn from polite partygoers and councilmen into war-ready. Including Rosemary, who has somehow changed from her oversized sweater and skinny jeans to leather looking pants and a breastplate. Weapons strapped to her and a dark silver colored metal mask that fits the top half of her face.

She holds it in her hand as she walks up to me and observes the scene. Her muscles properly displayed and rippling as she rolls out her shoulders and stretches out her neck. Never straying her gaze from them. The rebels marching over the field on their way here. Their numbers looking a lot more than just a couple hundred.

She smiles down at me and her glamour flickers in and out giving me a glance of her real form.

Warrior goddess.

"Will you be joining us?" she challenges.

"Absolutely not," a voice answers for me. I slowly draw my gaze up to golden eyes. "You've barely recovered from the last time."

"Last time?" Rosemary echoes. I roll my eyes.

"The rebels attacked two days ago with Kolasi faced against me."

Out of the corner of my eye I see both Nana and Ms. Elaycia pale. And Mr. Kyros raises his brows high as all the rest of them finish readying themselves and approach.

"You went up against the *Death Devil*?" Mr. Kyros asks, almost sounding like he approves. I decide right now that I like him. Even though I'm sure I will be having nightmares for the rest of the week because of his face.

"I think you mean," I correct, "*he* went up against *me*."

He chuckles and there is no condescension or hesitation or disbelief. His eyes light and like his son, his expression morphs into acute curiosity. Despite what is happening right now with rebels attacking.

"I mean no offense, Ms. Tsukkenai, but may I ask how you who I feel no aura from challenged a devil who is one with his true form?"

I smirk as three more bodies approach us. Professors Asier and D'etre are both already ready with the Dean behind them also strapped with twin long swords across his back.

"They have more numbers," he says by way of greeting. His signature scowl hesitating when he sees me but nodding to the councilmen and Mr. Kyros. "I see you're all ready. Let's hope this will be as short as the one before was."

They all nod and then most of the men disappear leaving only a wisp of shadows and distinct scents. I turn and spot those that shadow twisted already on the field. Darian, the demigod, Thorne, Mr. Arcturus, Mr. Armani, and the Dean spread out around and all of them pulling up shields.

Rosemary folds to behind their defensive stance with multiple people, including Caleb, standing watch at the wall. Their magics coiling around them and most of them feel like mages with offensive magics. A defense in case the rebels make it past the celestials.

Callahan places a hand on my back and when I look up at him his eyes are narrowed at me.

"I am serious, Mavyn. You are still recovering, so just rest."

I know he means well, so I don't snap at him for that, but I do step out of his touch. Another wave ripples and makes me grin. Callahan's face slightly falls.

I give him an almost pitied look. "You don't get it." I place my hand over his chest. Over his heart. "My blood is singing."

I step back and let him leave. Not moving to change my clothes or grab for weapons. Then he disappears. All that are left are Mr. Kyros and Professor Asier. The former still watches me with intrigue while the latter doesn't make eye contact.

I turn to Mr. Kyros and wink. "Just signal if you need my help."

He grins, and then he disappears too. Professor Asier follows him and I watch them appear on the field. Ms. Elaycia and Nana come up behind me to watch. Both of them curling their magic around themselves.

"Are you going to listen?"

I playfully side-eye Ms. Elaycia but she doesn't

chuckle.

"You haven't properly trained in months," Nana adds. "I can see it in your muscle definition."

I continue watching the rebels approach. Select ones in the front lines moving further ahead. They feel. . . different.

Thunder rumbles above and in my peripheral I catch Asher standing close to Caleb with his earthy element ready. Jullia is standing tall with frost covering her clothes and skin behind him.

I focus on those beings coming first. There's something familiar about them.

Within, I turn the fourth key in its lock but keep the door shut. It still flushes my aura out and both Ms. Elaycia and Nana jerk at it. I can feel other bodies jerking to, their heads swiveling to me. But they're not the bodies full of blood I am seeking.

I open my eyes that I hadn't realized I closed. I can feel my aura flooding my eyes, deepening them to a rich red as I expand the reach of my magic. Roving over the bodies full of blood on the field and past them. To those bodies that had been drawing closer to us faster than the rest.

My blood hums with a powerful vibration and I can almost taste the cloying scent of *earth.*

I rip my nails into my palms which overloads my sweet scent in preparation as the largest wave of all damning magic rips through the shields below. It caresses over me like a soft breeze but that doesn't last long as balls of fire rain down.

Our battle begins.

Thirty-Two

Callahan – Septmust 5

I whip my head toward the terrace as a wave of power I had felt a couple days ago once again hits us. A group of mages line the edge of the terrace all readied with their magics, but this wave. . .

Mavyn stands near the edge where she had been before. I had told her to not interfere, which I know was a mistake, but she is still recovering. Not all of her ribs are fully healed and the healers said she'd need at least a week of having a good sleep schedule before they could even be okay with saying she's alright.

That doesn't even include whatever other pain she was induced to because of her nightmares or the sun death realm before the Willow of Lore ceremony.

Her dark hair lays in waves down her back. The ends freshly colored sapphire blue and rosy pink. But even from here I can see her eyes are dark red.

I face the oncoming rebels and allow Varian into my mind to link us together. His brother had shattered Darian and Uncle Jerusil's shields and some sort of being rains fire on us. Select shields are placed back up as Thorne draws from the already brewing storm and cracks a dozen bolts of lightning throughout the field.

There had been select beings running faster past their first line of rebels, but now they hang back as that front line comes to greet us.

They're planning something, the Dean shouts through our mind as thunder nearly makes us go deaf. *For the love of gods and goddesses, Kyros, keep the sound actually facing the rebels.*

Darian chuckles and a migraine is starting to form as all the minds within me conjoin together. He doesn't say anything but thoughts that are not mine keep fluttering. Blocking them out as best I can, I focus on what is happening ahead.

Castiel and Thorne are the furthest out in the very front greeting the first line of rebels. Their weapons drawn and slicing as the rebels meet them. Varian stays towards the western side as the front line of rebels spreads sideways. Their numbers seeming to come out of nowhere. Much more than there had been two days ago.

My father and Thorne's handle those that past Thorne and Castiel, with Darian and his father keeping hold of shields and Darian occasionally blasting them with his sound element.

Rosenbail of Maril steps up with me watching the fight begin. Both of us at the very back.

On Earth she had gone by Rosemary, but on Miy she is known as that. Attending Syngenia with Ms. Elaycia and was one of the first goblin war leaders with an intellect and charm that made her the best. Rumor was she became one of the first spies for the Mage Board before disappearing off the face of the world. Literally – since she left this world.

I know she has a glamour on hiding her true body, but this one looks like it would be just a force. As tall as me with a silver breastplate and mask I'd be wary of if I saw against me. Not that they're entirely scary looking, but her aura pulses with a controlled violence.

"You know Mavyn will not sit by and watch." Her voice light and almost twinkling. "You would have had a better luck knocking her out and locking her in a room. She was trained by all three of us."

I glance at her but only for a moment to keep my eyes on the battle. All of them out there are so formattable, most of them with experience. But there are still rebels who slip through. In the back of my mind I hear Varian rumbling orders and checking in with all of them. Spread out through the field.

"She's back up there on the terrace, isn't she?"

She hadn't made a move to change or get ahold of weapons. Though with just the bit that I have felt from her aura I wouldn't think she necessarily needs weapons. She *is* a weapon.

Rosenbail hums. "You do not know yet, but I think you will. You are fated but there is not a sealed bond between you two. You have not seen her soul."

I take my eyes off the battle to snap them at her. How

could she have known that?

"When she first came to us I thought she was human with how she felt. No aura, barely any sparks of magic, eyes the lightest shade of pink I have ever seen. Not even Esmirra could tell. And then she told us what she did to that devil and mage who hurt her."

I process what she said and shake my head. "What are you talking about? Mavyn was human."

I can feel Varian at the back of my mind listening. Thorne too, even though they're both preoccupied with the many people they're currently fighting.

There's another boom from where magic was able to get past Darian's shields but I can't even look at it. Rosenbail is shaking her head at me with furrowed brows.

"Mavyn was human," I repeat. I'm realizing now I never told Elaycia and Esmirra what happened. None of them know Mavyn was turned. "She said she had been attacked by a vampire on her birthday who shoved vampyr blood and venom into her and turned her into a vampire. That's why she's here. The Mage Board gave her a choice of graduating the school or death because she didn't have bloodlust."

There's another blast that shakes the ground and then a rumble of that death damnation aura.

Rosenbail actually laughs at me as aura responds back to Varian's twins. An aura scented with berries and florals. Scented in god killing poison.

She throws her arm out and points at where Mavyn is still standing. "That girl is the furthest thing from human. She was *never* human." Another blast explodes and it rocks more than just the ground. "Mavyn is *not* a vampire."

How?

I can't even silence Varian, or Thorne who's attentions are both on me even as they continue to fight. More rebels are seeming to appear out of nowhere and I'm still stuck behind waiting. A last defense if everyone else fails.

Rosenbail laughs mockingly again as she shakes her head and faces the field. "You don't know, but you will," she repeats.

Damnation rolls and I cross my arms forming an X in front of me to add another shield behind Darian and his father's. Except there's something different with this wave. A feeling threaded through Percius's damnation.

Faintly, I see something shimmering. A line curving up and towards us looking almost red. One of those beings from before who had held back from the front line has their hands up. And then a voice I've grown too obsessed with screams one word that has my blood turning cold.

"WITCHES!" Mavyn's voice echoing down here and onto the field. "THEY HAVE WITCHES!"

Which is impossible.

We would have known if the rebels had witches.

That line of red whips down towards us as all the rebels who had been fighting disappear from the field. They all reappear behind those select beings who had run first and then hung back.

Behind the witches.

. . . nine, ten, eleven. Behind *eleven* witches.

There aren't even that many witches left alive.

Time seems to slow for a moment as that line of red splits into a web and crashes down right where my family is. Where those that I had seen as brothers and uncles are. Where my own father is.

They're all going to die.

And there's nothing I can do to stop it.

Thirty-Three

Mavyn – Septmust 5

A few minutes prior. . .

They're perfectly synchronized. Fighting in patterns and forms all together even though none of them are working together. Thorne, his father, the demigod, Professor Asier, Callahan's father all spread out on the field wielding weapons I'd love to have in my hands.

Even the Dean is practiced and in time with them. Darian and his father hanging back constructing the shields and keeping everyone up here safe from the flying attacks. The fourth and fifth years taking over to organize people with the help of the council of the school before taking places around the terrace and helping with shields and their own offensive magic flying.

My aura is still roaming as my eyes are drawn to Asher. Jullia glances at me with a worried expression, but when she sees me she straightens and nods her head. Not backing down or hiding. But Asher still draws my attention with his different earth aura.

His is not cloying.

But his is also faded with crackling and soothing and guarding.

Leaving Ms. Elaycia and Nana, I go towards him and wipe my thumb through my bloody palm. My blood wrapping around my wrists since I had rolled my sleeves up and holding as I wait.

His nostrils flare as he looks at me and startles when I wipe my thumb across his forehead. His green eyes widen with alarm and he opens his mouth but I have no time for questions.

"Make a runic shield," I demand. Which gains many eyes and Caleb who's next to us looks at me and then to the blood smeared on Asher's forehead with understanding.

Asher shakes his head. "Mine won't do any – "

I let that fourth door crack open and it makes Asher choke as his green eyes begin glowing. My aura floods the entirety of the terrace as recognition pricks in the back of my mind. People around begin murmuring as I slowly turn my head back to the battle.

A whip of blood is soaring through the air and that cloying earth dips into copper.

A golden light begins glowing to the side of me as I

suck in a deep breath and scream for them on the field. Stepping onto the stone between the two teeth of the saw-tooth looking wall I thunder my voice through. For some reason I look directly at Professor Asier when I say it.

"THEY HAVE WITCHES!"

And then that line of blood spreads to a web of death sailing straight for the celestials. The rebels they had been fighting winking out of existence and reappearing behind the witches. They had been the ones to run past first, but they had stopped at some point and let the rest of the first line of rebels pass.

A distraction to keep the celestials in place until they were able to use that web of blood like a blade.

I catch movement and icy blue eyes glance at me with resignation.

In a fraction of a moment I twist those first two keys within me to crack those doors open and release my control of my blood while a bolt of red lightning comes for me.

I keep my head up and don't blink this time so I know exactly when. . .

It almost feels like a glitch and then time hesitates right as that web of blood is only a couple feet above my head.

Clever, clever devil. Hiding the witches aura within your own.

He should have tried harder to kill me when he first faced me. I bet he could have too after the Professor halted my magic. But not this time.

A golden shield drawn from runes appears over the school solidly protecting them from the rebel attacks. I can feel the energy being used from my blood that I had marked Asher with. The third magic vampyr can have.

We did not technically blood bond, but there is a blood oath connecting us and that is as good as it'll get. Though I do not give him my magic, I give him the strength of my aura. Allowing him to create the expansive shield that he just did.

And I create my own.

The blood covering my hands and forearms moving to their own whips and curving around me and this space. Faster than the normal eye could ever see, they expand and blood webs that should have killed us shatter against my shield.

Turning, I see the celestials. Professor Asier's face faulters when he processes it's me out here. Standing further past Thorne and the demigod who also have their eyes on me and their mouths open.

The rest of the celestials. . . I think most of them had expressions of acceptance. Mr. Kyros did when he glanced back at me. This was a death blow they knew there was no way to block. The blood too close and too powerful – it would have sliced through any of their shields.

That's what fate is.

I face the witches again and take a step forward as I throw my arms out and around. Pulling my blood and wrapping their whip-like shape around in a circular form around me. The ends of the whips dancing as I take another step, and then I spin – collecting all my whips in my hand – and throw them out in an arc towards those witches.

My weapons soar through the air faster than that witch's blood had. There's no stopping or blocking that. And they slice straight through the blood witch who had tried to kill the celestials.

Their head rolls and I let more of my blood spill to

gather again around myself as I pull those whips I had thrown back. I let my aura flood behind me as I check each of the celestials. Letting my presence be known as I run invisible finger-like sheets over them.

Only a few light injuries. Most of them seem fine enough and still with plenty of stamina.

That death damnation roars through us as I widen my stance and physically grab onto my whips. A black cloak with a metallic mask comes straight for me. His form imposing and in his hands are twin blades flickering with black flames.

So much power.

But my blood hums as he gets closer and I attack first with a solid strike from my whip. He blocks the blow easily and then he's on me.

Magic soars past us from the remaining witches and rebels against the celestials. Trading metal for magic while I go against *Kolasi*. The *Death Devil* himself.

I am very much smaller than him, but my whips make up for it. His shadow blades coming down with such a force that the blow creates a crater below us. The cracks lining the earth look like lightning and that second door *sings*.

Nana was right. I've lost some strength from the months I hadn't been training before. But I flood my blood still in my veins with more power. That and my magic will be enough.

His movements are swift as I block and trade my own blows with him. Gliding through the air like he isn't a six foot five muscle packing devil. Trails of black and red being left behind with how fast we move. My whips of blood circling us like our own sort of boarder blocking us from the rest of the fight.

But that is only these whips of blood circling. The ones

I had first created are extended further. Slithering through the battles of magic and now metal helping the celestials against the rebels. Blocking when needed and killing when I can. Lightening the load because there are still witches with powerful magic working.

His shadow blades that look like they're flickering like black flames come down and around and up at me. He's already nicked me a couple times, and I know if they had cut anyone else they'd already be dead. I can feel it in his body language. The frustration after every time he cuts me and I stay standing. He should have figure it out though, when he scented my blood.

Blue belladon counters shadow flame no matter the dosage.

And vise verses. Which is why when I land a deep cut through his upper arm and he barely flinches, I know his shadows creating his weapons were not just an element.

I twist away from a blow that creates another crater in the earth and whip my blood out like spider legs around me. His black cloak billows behind him revealing black pants tucked into black boots but nothing else.

"You fight," he reverberates, "like you've had this new strength for longer than just the few months you've been turned."

The shock strikes like ice up my spine but I don't let my guard down because of it. I twitch my hand and release my coiled aura within my whips of blood to permeate the air.

Raw power thickening and I let it expand past us and remind everyone around I'm still here. I'm still a threat.

There's a jolt in his stance and then his aura pulses.

"If not, then what are you?" *What?* "Why do you still burn in the sun if you're not a vampire?"

This time I can't hide the shock. And he takes his advantage, which isn't really an advantage because I meet his shadow with my blood. But I can feel my body will start lagging soon. I don't have the fury from before fueling me. I don't have the emotion behind my magic.

Before, there wasn't anything but mild curiosity that served my purpose for why I intervened. I wasn't panicked or angry or scared. Slight discomfort, maybe, because I did not want Mr. Kyros to die after just meeting him. And. . .

I had looked at Professor Asier first. The fucking red devil who –

"What did you just say?"

His aura pulses again and he comes at me with his blades like he has before. Sharp blades that don't have any poisonous effect on me but have still cut me several times. I am so lucky the clouds haven't cleared because the cuts around my legs are more exposed with the fabric of my thigh highs pulling open more. And my shirt is drenched in blood both from my magic usage and from more cuts.

I'd be so exposed right now, but there is coverage and now my sole purpose is to rip that fucking hood off his head.

Panting between breaths and avoiding death blows, I heave, "Say it again."

He adds more force to his blows even though we've been going at this for a while. Even with my magic adding strength, Nana was right, I haven't been properly training.

But now a bubbling of emotion trickles with that song in my blood.

Because why *the fuck* does his voice – which I couldn't place before, couldn't figure out where I've heard it before, couldn't remember – sound *exactly* like Varian Asier's.

I twist and wrap my whips around us and pull. It drags us closer together, but I'm never able to properly slice him because of glowing runes that appear on his cloak every time my blood touches him.

Runic magic.

And the movement surprises him which gives me the second I need to land a punch that brings him to his knees and tug the back of his hood.

Red tinged hair is shorter than the professor's but still curled and landing just above his ears. The same red tinged hair that could look black in lower lighting.

Pain obliterates my middle as I'm flown backward and land hard on my back. A second later another hit comes for my face but I block at the last second. His fist lands against my blood covered forearms and sends me several feet into the ground creating the largest crater he has so far.

Disbelief wafts through my system but another emotions drowns it.

I finally twist that third lock and before I even open the door power splinters the air. The devil pummeling me freezes and I draw more of my blood before me to expel. Striking out, I send Kolasi flying and simply lay for a moment to process.

First it was the sun devil and his twin. But now this. . . Professor Asier's – what? Father? Brother? Son? The man is over two hundred years old. He could have a child.

I take a deep breath and let that third door crack open as the other three already are. My heart beats and it feels like the space glitches with it. Getting up, I survey the scene. The rebels are still going against the celestials. Kolasi is just now getting up from where my blast landed him. The golden shield from Asher is still holding even as explosions of fire hit against it.

The devil slashes his arms through the air and roars.

"WHAT ARE YOU?"

He wouldn't have asked why I can still burn if I wasn't a vampire if he didn't know. I will not be delusional enough in thinking I can dissuade him from that.

He comes for me again and I repeat his question.

What are you?

I let that first door swing wide. And that other emotion, that one that drowns the disbelief and everything else, it's like gasoline on a flame.

What are you?

Well, the answer is simple.

Burning.

I am burning.

I am always burning.

His shadow blades extend past the points and become shadow whips now that he slashes through the air. So I consume them.

God, I am so fucking tired.

I am so exhausted. The golden devil had been right when he said I was not fully recovered. In truth, I never even recovered from thirteen years ago. Or would it be sixteen years. . . ? When that devil and mage took me in. Maybe it was even before them. When I was born and my parents left me on the side discarded. Cast aside like trash.

A current of ash begins to fall from where those shadow whips had been ready to strike me. The devil is left struck frozen as I finally stand.

Blazing. . . burning.

Blue flame covers the blood that is covering my hand. And when I look into what I know are gold ringed red eyes, all I feel is rage.

I slowly turn towards the rebels still fighting. Hundreds. Possibly thousands. The hum in my blood becomes a low tenor as I watch them all cast their magics.

For a moment I contemplate unlocking that fifth door within. A key I've never even touched before because even locked I can feel true uncontainability.

But instead I slowly nudge that third and fourth door open and power consumes. A red sheet of aura so palpable I wouldn't be surprised if they could see it now. Expanding across the entirety of the field. Past even the furthest reaches that I have tested before.

That deep tenor hum erupts in my blood and I begin the movement to circle my blood whips around myself. Feathers of blue flame flutter after them as they create an almost shape like an ophanim with me within. Rings within rings that for some reason remind me of a supernova. Red from my blood, blue from my flame.

I can feel threads from green and purple representing my other magics.

I am too tired.

Pure, damning wrath vibrates with every molecule and spark within me. I am ending this now.

The remaining witches had been inching closer and I can feel their auras. I can feel the ground responding from the wood witches who smell like that cloying earth scent. But there's another that is almost familiar.

Bones burning on a pyre.

I lock eyes with milky glazed ones and pain eviscerates my body. Hairline fractures split through every bone in my body with the *need* to move. To bow, to kneel, to obey.

I had thought the last bone witch alive was Nana. Was Esmirra of Ebony who wanted to leave that title five thousand years ago.

"What a child," I breathe, but my words thunder through the field. It stills the witches for a moment and I can feel eyes on me. That voice did not entirely sound like my own.

Cracks riverbeat loudly inside my head.

Pain, pain, pain.

"It's not the same." And I'd laugh if I was able to feel anything. I step my foot back without a waver of difficulty and twist my arms around and up. "You think this is pain?" The song in my blood whispers in the space with a melody. "You don't know burning."

There's a sort of click as I keep the witches and that death devil in my sights. Like in the classroom before. An inherent knowing. Fate.

"But I'll show you."

They're dead. They just don't know it yet.

That hum hitches right before I release.

It knows now. Uncontrolled and raw. There will be no stopping it this time. No way to prevent it. No way to block.

Fate.

I release.

Thirty-Four

Varian – Septmust 5

A few minutes prior. . .

It was always there, right in front of our faces. She is not a spy for either side, but she also isn't a vampire. She was *never* human. *Never* turned. And the goblin didn't even hesitate with Callahan. She spoke as if it was obvious we had always known.

It should have been so blatantly obvious.

I slash my longsword through the body in front of me a second too late. Pain cripples my left leg and while their body hits the ground mine does as well.

Luckly, when I look around there are no more near me. Neither are they around Castiel and Thorne who are closest to me, but I doubt they would have noticed since they're both locked on the battle happening before us.

We were all dead. When we realized it had all been a distraction it was too late. A blood witch had sentenced our deaths and once made, there's no way for survival. So I had turned back. I had allowed myself to have one more look at her.

Except she hadn't been there. And then magic erupted and that web of blood that was our death sentence shattered. The little bloodsucker had somehow appeared in the middle of the field past me, Thorne, and Castiel.

Ropes of blood were curved and hovering over us. Blood that smelled like something I couldn't live without while being the only thing that would always kill me. And when she turned back I met eyes that were the same color. Full, vivid, and teeming with magic I've never seen before.

She feels like Sanivin, Edmond had whispered in the back of my mind. The oldest of all of us. Old enough to have actually met the first created vampire right before her immortal life came to an end when he was a boy. We may say we're immortal, but we are not gods. All things eventually die.

Then she had looked back towards the blood witch – *a fucking blood witch* – without an ounce of any emotion and killed her. Killed four of the eleven witches and at least a hundred people in those front lines.

I couldn't feel anything when my brother, my twin, came at her and they began their battle. They moved like choreographed dancers, landing blows at speeds I almost couldn't follow. Percius with his shadows and Mavyn with her blood.

Blood – because she has a fractured blood art and isn't

a vampire and was never a human or turned and has blue flame.

I don't know how she lied to me while I was truth-pulling, but after she blew Percius away and he came for her again with his whips made of shadow it was fire that decimated them. Blue flame that accompanied her blood art and then raw magic, uncontrollable, froze us all in petrification.

It's why I was able to kill the skilled bone witch I had just been fighting. Even though she shattered part of my leg, she now lays lifeless before me. Such a fucking waste.

But there's something different about Mavyn now. She feels the same as she had when she told me to stay out of her business. The type of primordial stillness from her while magic pours from her and a sheet of bloodred aura is cast out over the grounds.

Red aura, the same color the spirits had changed to when she sung their song for them. Red aura – *her* aura.

I am seeing her aura as she faces my brother and the rest of those witches who have been gaining the upper hand above us. There was a reason it was being discussed so long ago about aligning the witches with celestials.

It also feels like when she had been about to kill Percius and Rovan. Thorne had been able to halt her blood in some twist of fortune, but I can hear his minute thoughts. He won't be able to do it again. He won't be able to stop what is about to happen again.

My brother is about to die.

Run.

I break my promise to him and force myself into his mind instead of asking for permission. I had asked for permission a second ago when I told him she was not a vampire. But I do not ask now.

Run, Percius, or you will die now. Tell them all to run because she is about to kill you all.

His terror floods my mind and I can see Thorne and Castiel flinching at it.

“What a child,” we all hear her voice thunder. Ricocheted through the air with a force that has me wanting to slam my knees into the ground.

The unfiltered dominance in her voice. It’s greater than even my fathers.

“It’s not the same. You think you know pain? You don’t know burning.” Her voice pauses for a note and I scream into Percius’s mind. “But I’ll show you.”

Time stills and we’re all helpless watching as she releases her hold on whatever last control she had. More rebels keep appearing from within the forest but there’s no use. I know there is no use. Especially as she says eight words that will make it impossible for me to ever hate her for killing my brother.

“You hurt them, my fated. Now you’re dead.”

That is the first time she’s admitted it.

Then my mind goes blank.

She said them.

And then a star implodes.

Thirty-Five

Mavyn – Novam 11

Death feels. . . weird.

That's what happens with a supernova. An implosion. It's the death of a star.

I wouldn't consider myself a star by any means, but it was the last thing I felt. That hitch in my song right before release. I eviscerated everything – including myself. The sun devil was right. I burned for an eternity, and now I'm dead.

Stop being so dramatic, Mavyllora. It's unbecoming and you have already looked bad as my student these past two months. I had told Thorne you were as good as him, do not make me a liar.

Do not make me a liar.

She would say that whenever I was underperforming.

Do not make me a liar, Mavyllora. I know your potential and I have told people of it so you better become what I know you can be.

I've been hearing that phrase since I was fourteen. It was one of the first things Nana –

Nana.

But I'm dead.

There is nothing here and –

I know, I know. I've been saying that every day but I just. . . for the goddesses, Mavyllora, please just wake up. You can't be gone, child, I know you are not gone. Not if your mental shields are still up and most definitely not if your devils cannot get in. So just. . . wake up already.

Wake up.

I need you to wake up.

Ohh, but I do not want to.

There had been so much pain before. I am tired of always feeling pain. I want sleep. I want a solid black abyss of darkness. Nothingness where existence and enduring are not real.

Please.

That was not Nana.

Please, Firecracker.

There's a tug somewhere further in me. A place I would have to travel to get to. I would have to leave this place of nothing. I would have to *feel*.

It didn't work, Esmirra. We do not have a cemented bond. It's more likely she wouldn't wake up because of me. She told me once to never enter her mind.

I do not like devils in my mind.

Silence.

Then. . .

Mavyn?

What?

I think someone chokes. Pinpricks of emotions stab through my nothingness and I wish they would stop. I do not want to leave.

Mavyn?

I huff and roll my eyes. *I already said what?*

You can hear me, Firecracker? Can you wake up for me?

Mavyllora, Nana snaps through. *Why can I not feel you? Why is there nothing here? It's like darkness. Where are you and how are you hiding within your mind?*

I curl tighter into myself and glare. *I do not like the light.*

Yes you do.

No –

Yes, she hisses. *You miss the warmth without the burning.*

That's not fair. All I ever do is burn. How can I miss something I don't remember feeling? I wish I was just dead. That would have been easier. Why am I not dead? I died. I had to have died. I made sure on that field there was nothing left.

Wake. Up. Now.

I feel like when I was fourteen and being scolded about getting up for my lessons. I would stay up too late reading textbooks and grimoires and trying to learn any and everything. I wanted to absorb all the knowledge I could. I wanted to remember.

I wanted to make sure I never forgot.

I always thought it would help so one day I could figure out how not to be forgotten. We say we're immortal, but I always viewed life through a very human gaze. Wanting to remember and be remembered. They say a person dies twice – once when their soul leaves their body, and a second when their name is said for the last time.

Still haven't figured it out. I'm not a writer or someone famous or anyone of special importance, but I had been accepting of my death.

And they want me to wake up as if this is just a dream.

I do not want to wake up.

You owe me.

A new voice – and yet not. Lazy and drawling. I bare my teeth at the sound.

I do not, demon.

You do. It was my blood you drank on that field that prevented you from dying. Nearly sucked me dry, so you now owe me.

I curl tighter within myself and wrap dagger-like claws into my blood. Sensing my aura and power and rhythm from my heart. Scenting the poison and. . . thunder. Ozone and blood but it is not mine.

I'm calling in my favor now. Wake up.

I want to scream. Clever fucking *demon.* I want to rip his neck out. This is not fair.

You will regret this.

And I can feel his amusement. *Wake up and make me then.*

I will.

I can *almost* feel him smile. *Stupid* fucking demon. He doesn't realize how much of a promise I mean that as.

Playlist

Fate ~ Kaia Jette
Bite Marks ~ League of Legends Music & TEYA
Trouble ~ Valerie Broussard
Little Girl Gone ~ CHINCHILLA
Thing of Beauty ~ Danger Twins
Fool ~ margo
Playing with Fire ~ CRMNL
Aimed to Kill ~ Jade LeMac
Legendary ~ Welshly Arms
Which Witch ~ Florence + the Machine
Nod-Krai ~HOYO-MiX & AURORA
Breath of Life ~ Florence + the Machine
In This Shirt ~ The Irrepressibles
Origin ~ Besomorph & Neoni
Power ~ Kanye West
Legends Are Made ~ Sam Tinnesz
Here I Am (feat. Brooke) ~ Tommee Profitt
Devil Devil ~ MILCK
Seven Nation Army ~ Ely Eira
Darkness ~ X V I

Acknowledgments

I firstly want to acknowledge my parents. Without them I literally wouldn't be here and none of this would exist. So, thank you mom and dad. You guys have always supported me and encouraged me to keep writing and to actually publish my writing. And well, here we are. I wouldn't be where I am without you and I couldn't be more grateful to you two.

Next, well, honorary mention to my Dr Pepper right here cause these are my acknowledgments, and I can acknowledge whoever (or whatever) I want.

On a serious note, though, I have to acknowledge my brothers. They didn't really do anything, but they are always happy for me when I give them little updates now and again. They do also give me honest feedback about my covers and summaries when I send them over, so thank you Keaton and Jason. I love you two.

My two best friends. I know you two are always happy for me about my writing and excited when I finally get around to finishing and publishing said writing. Even though I know I can go off, detailing the plot and characters and certain plot twists or foreshadowing, and I know it can be a lot, but thank you for listening to me.

I want to acknowledge everyone who has read the bits and pieces I've let them. Even though half the time there's no context, just you reading what you will means a lot. And thank you for all the feedback from it. Making sure the spelling is right in those scenes and offering advice or asking all of your questions. Making your guesses for things is always my favorite.

Lastly, a very special thanks to all of you. To everyone who had seen the videos from TikTok or Instagram and supported me as I finished writing and editing. To you guys who were so excited for this book and couldn't wait to get it in your hands. Thank you so much for the eagerness about this new story of mine and I hope you love it as much as I have.

About the Author

A believer in fate, wishing stars, pinky promises, and the red string theory, K.R. Simons is an Aries, an INTP personality type, and her favorite color is blue because it reminds her of magic. She's the oldest of four, with two brothers and a sister. Born and raised in Las Vegas, she's the exact opposite of a desert rat. Lover of rain and lightning storms, the ocean, and deep forests, as well as matcha, coffee, and tea – equally – Dr Pepper, and casual games of chess. And if she isn't reading or writing you'll find her either drawing her next tattoo or scrolling through TikTok – vicariously living through the people she watches.

www.ingramcontent.com/pod-product-compliance
Lightning Source LLC
LaVergne TN
LVHW020518100826
845148LV00010B/1274